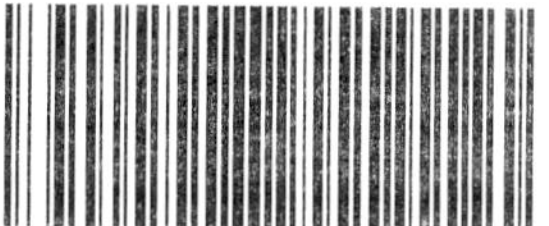

Part I

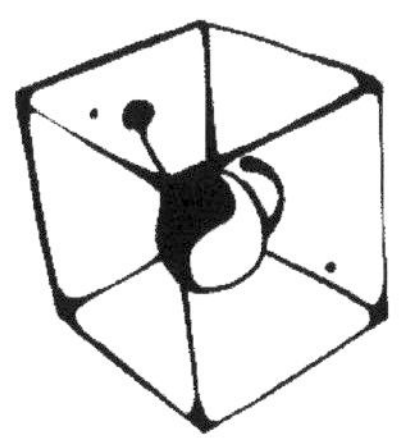

The Quad

1

BROM

Brom's life was about to change forever. Today he was going to take his first step toward doing something that mattered, something to be proud of. Lightning crackled in his belly—a new sensation that had started this past week. The lightning came upon him when he was inspired, which was every day now that he'd found his vocation.

The beautiful spring sun beat down on the five boys who sweated in the practice yard. The smell of springtime flowers and budding trees punctuated Brom's soaring spirits, but even better was the lingering scent of dust, which hung in the air from the final bout between himself and Thol. Thol was bigger, stronger, and looked more like what a guardsman should look like, but Brom had put him in the dirt. Now Thol stood stone-faced and breathing hard in the line of five boys, ignoring the trickle of blood leaking from his nose. Brom stood next to him, also breathing hard.

Guardsman Roland walked slowly across the front of the line, got to the end, reversed direction and walked slowly back.

"Impressive," he said.

This spring the guardsmen of Kyn had put out the call to every able-bodied young man who wanted to carry a sword and protect the village, who wanted to become a village guard. Hero's work.

Every boy sixteen and older had rushed to try out.

Now it was down to five, and Roland was going to choose the two who would train to become village guards. Two. And one of them was going to be Brom.

There had been thirty in this line at the beginning of the week. Now there were only five, and Brom had bested them all.

He'd outfought them. He'd outridden them. He'd shown an aptitude for tracking through the woods. When put to the test of diplomatically convincing a group of villagers to stay away from the dangerous springtime mud pits and head back toward town, Brom had excelled. He liked people, and they responded to him. This was what he was made to do. The lightning surge of inspiration crackled inside him when he put his mind to this work. It carried him with an enthusiasm he'd never felt for Father's work.

Father was going to be livid when he found out Brom had been accepted into the village guard. He'd thought Brom, because of his size, would wash out in a day. Of course, Father also wanted Brom to follow in his own footsteps as a builder.

Brom's father was stocky, wide-shouldered, and big-muscled. A perfect physique for hauling and cutting stone. He was also even-tempered, except when it came to Brom, and patient. Repetitive, mind-numbing work didn't bother Father at all.

But Brom wasn't stocky. He had a slight build and average height. He had quickness, but not brute strength. Hauling stones in the hot sun was torture for him. He had no sense for it and no desire to gain one. Brom longed for greater things: adventure and the opportunity to make a real difference. Spending monotonous, sweat-dribbling, muscle-aching hours cutting stones...well, it sounded like the worst life imaginable. Except, of course, for the drab existence of being a farmer, which was the only other livelihood available in the village of Kyn.

So when they'd put out the call for guardsman trainees, it was like Brom had received a stay of execution. He had one chance—

just this one slim chance—to take hold of his destiny, and he was determined to grasp it with both hands.

Guardsmen had a life akin to the legendary Quadrons, the mystic warriors who came from the Champions Academy and rode across the kingdom righting wrongs and dispensing justice. Of course, Kyn guardsmen only patrolled the perimeter of Kyn. And they didn't have magic. But it was the closest thing to becoming a Quadron Brom was ever going to have.

After all, just like the Quadrons, guardsmen rode horses. They trained with weapons. They stood as the shield against brigands who might harm the people of Kyn. In short, they did something that mattered.

That was the life for Brom.

Guardsman Roland stopped in front of the line, exactly in the middle, and looked at each of the boys in turn.

"Brom Builder," he called out, and it was like a jar of butterflies had been opened in Brom's stomach. "Please step forward and face your fellow applicants."

Brom stepped forward. He'd seized this opportunity, and he was about to rush through a door to a new world.

"To the rest of you," Roland said. "I would like you to look upon young Brom as an example for you all. In every area, from feats of arms, to tracking his quarry, to crowd pacification, to the administrative needs of the guard, he has excelled."

Brom was surprised to see that two of the remaining four applicants actually looked happy for him. Garn and Thol didn't, of course. Thol glared daggers at Brom, and Garn looked just as resentful. The twins had excelled at the tests, more so than any of the other hopefuls aside from Brom, and he knew they'd wanted to take the two spots together. Now only one of them would.

"Brom has all the qualities we prize highly here in the Kyn village guard," Roland continued. "All save one." Roland turned to look at Brom, and Brom felt a sudden jolt to his euphoria. "Brom Builder, you are expelled from these barracks forthwith. And should we ever have another opening, you needn't bother applying."

Two gasps burst from the line of boys.

Brom felt like someone had scooped his insides out and thrown them on the ground. He couldn't breathe.

"W-What?" he whispered.

"What makes the guard strong, young Brom, is each guardsman's ability to follow the rules. A solemn bond to work together. An unbreakable fellowship. Without this, there is no trust. Without trust, there is no fellowship. I have no room in this guard for a rule breaker."

Brom's dream turned to mist in front of his eyes, but still he tried to grasp it.

"W-What rule, Master Roland? What rule did I break?" he asked, though he could feel the heat in his cheeks as his face grew red. He knew exactly what rule he'd broken. And somehow, so did Roland.

During this last week, the guardsman applicants were required to live in the barracks. During the day, they were given tasks about the town, or in the nearby forest, but at night, they were to unfurl their bedrolls in the practice yard under the stars and sleep there while the real guardsmen slept in their bunks.

They had been strictly prohibited from leaving the barracks at night. But Brom had sneaked out last night, stolen away to the graveyard to meet Myan the miller's daughter.

Myan was as cute as the day was long. She had a round face and a button nose with freckles that just drove Brom crazy. Her lustrous brown hair curled down to her chin, cut shorter than most girls in town, and it exposed her pale, slender neck.

All the boys had become intriguing to the village girls the moment they'd applied to become guardsmen. But it was Brom who Myan had approached. She'd stopped him yesterday after he'd successfully helped Guardsman Lothu relocate the half-dozen villagers who'd gotten too close to the springtime mud pits. As Lothu had been talking with Myan's father, the miller, she'd sidled up next to him and whispered in his ear.

"Meet me tonight?"

Brom's eyes had widened.

"At the graveyard," she had whispered, her breath tickling his ear. "At midnight."

Gods, she'd smelled so good, like fresh flour. Brom had told her she was intoxicating, and her smile had come out like the sun rising through mist.

She'd touched his arm and repeated, "Midnight." Then she'd run away to rejoin her father.

Was he supposed to miss that chance? Myan wanted to meet him! It was going to be just the two of them, alone, and who knew what would happen? He'd been longing to kiss her—every boy in the village had—since early spring when her dresses suddenly got tighter in certain areas.

He'd thought about how he was breaking the rules, but the thought only lasted a moment. What was the point of that rule, anyway? There wasn't one. Was he supposed to simply let the opportunity pass him by, let some other village boy take his spot while he was confined to the barracks? It wasn't as if getting a kiss from Myan was going to make Brom a worse guardsman.

So he'd put all of his skills into solving the problem of how to escape without detection. He'd envisioned it as a personal test for the village guard. He was going to pit his wits and skills against actual guardsmen.

He'd waited until everyone was asleep in the barracks and practice yard, save the night watchman, whose rounds Brom had memorized on the third day. Brom had evaded him with ease, climbed over the guardhouse wall and run into the night. And he'd met Myan. Gods, he'd met Myan, and it was everything he'd dreamed it would be. They'd kissed until his lips hurt. After, he'd taken her safely home. Only once she'd slipped through her window, turned, and blew silent kisses at him, did Brom finally return to the practice yard.

He'd successfully sneaked back in, evading the guard and not rousing his sleeping fellow applicants. After crawling safely into his bedroll, he must have lain awake for another hour, staring up at the stars and feeling as though the gods had conspired to give him everything he'd ever wanted.

He'd been so sure no one had seen him. But obviously, one of the other applicants had awoken during his absence, had somehow noticed he was gone.

Brom turned to glare at the four boys still lined up. Two of them looked bewildered. Garn and Thol, however, had begun to grin. The truth became as obvious to Brom as the nose on his own face. They were the ones who'd told on him. Now they'd both be in the guard.

And Brom wouldn't.

He quivered with anger and frustration. He wanted to invite Garn or Thol, or even both of them, to the practice ground again. He wanted—

Roland put a hand on his shoulder. "Don't blame another," Roland interrupted him, "for your own wrongdoing."

"I didn't do anything wrong," Brom said. "It was just... It has nothing to do with being a guard!"

"It has everything to do with being a guard. You left these barracks last night, flaunting the rules to go to the town graveyard to consort with a girl."

Brom was dumbstruck. How... How did he know that? If Garn or Thol had seen Brom leave the barracks, that was one thing. They'd know he'd gone missing. But how could they know *where* he'd gone...?

A wash of guilt swept over Brom. Myan! Gods... If they knew where Brom had been, then they knew who he'd been with. Myan had said her father would kill her if he knew she was out of the house at midnight. Now punishment would come swift and hard upon her. Of any crimes Brom might have committed last night, that was the worst.

I'm so sorry, Myan, he thought, even as he forced himself to look up, to clench his teeth and look into Roland's disapproving eyes.

"You have great skills for a young man of sixteen," Roland was saying. "But did you think no one in the guard had greater?" Roland shook his head, then looked at the other boys. "The rest of you look upon Brom as an example. This is what happens to someone—even someone so talented—who breaks the rules. Ask yourself: do you want to be a rule breaker? Such arrogance can only lead to a fall."

Brom swallowed, and tears burned his eyes. He looked at Garn and Thol with their slitted, backstabbing gazes.

"I understand the impulses of a young man," Roland said. "By gods, I do. But they do not stand above our rules. They do not stand above our fellowship." He pointed to the gates that led out of the practice yard. "Go now, Brom. Don't come back."

Dazed, Brom turned. A moment ago, he felt like he could fly. Now, it felt as if his legs could barely hold him up. Roland and the other guardsmen had praised him every day, day after day. And now, suddenly, he was nothing? And for what? He went to the wooden barracks wall and numbly retrieved his bedroll. When he reached the gate, he turned.

"You talk about fellowship?" Brom said, his voice shaking. He looked at the smugly satisfied Garn and Thol. "Then good. Take them as your fellows and take your pointless rules. Let the twins guard your backs like they did mine."

Roland's face reddened.

Brom left the barracks and he didn't look back.

2

BROM

Brom took another swallow from the bottle, letting the whiskey burn down his throat. It was Father's good whiskey, saved specially for highborn visitors like Lord Deremon. Father was building the lord's new manor up on the hill overlooking the lake. And the bottle was almost empty. Of course, it had only been half-full when Brom stole it from the house, but Father was going to rage about that regardless. A bottle like this probably cost as much as Father made in a month.

He thunked his head back against the wooden wall of Kyn's only tavern, *The Ox and Cart*. He hadn't even gone inside, though if this had been any other day, he would have. There was a huge russet-colored stallion that Brom didn't recognize tethered out front, which meant someone new was in town, probably someone interesting. Strangers could sometimes mean stories from beyond Kyn. But today, Brom simply wasn't in the mood. He had just come around back and hidden from the world, trying not to think of what he'd given up today. Trying to understand why it had to happen that way.

He had ruined his life, his one chance at a better life. But he still wasn't convinced he was in the wrong.

Bala, the bar maid from *The Ox and Cart*, peeked around the corner of the building and spotted him.

"Thought I saw you come 'round here." She came to stand in front of him, hands on her hips, and her gaze fell on the bottle. She cocked her head, obviously trying to read it around where his fist gripped it, and her eyes widened. "A bottle o' Kelto's Cairn." She shook her head. "Ah. So you've come for serious drinkin'. I see. And you've gone and drained most of it already."

With a wry smile, she squatted down next to him while deftly managing her skirts. "How much was in it?"

He raised the bottle in salute. The dregs sloshed around. She took the bottle out of his hands. "Then that's quite enough, I think. Gonna make yourself sick."

"I lost my chance, Bala. S'gone." He made a fluttering gesture with his hands, like birds flying away.

"Lots o' chances in life, luv."

"Not anymore."

"You were training to be a guard, yes?" she asked.

Thoughts of Myan rose in his mind. The freckles across her nose. That eager look in her eyes before she leaned in to kiss him. Her soft lips pressing against his. How was he expected to resist that? He shouldn't be punished for doing something so...right.

"I kissed a girl," he said.

"Ah," Bala said, and she smiled as though she suddenly understood everything. "Which girl?"

Brom shook his head.

She ruffled his hair affectionately. "Well aren't you the sweet one, protecting your lady."

He didn't say anything.

"It's a hard knock, luv," Bala said, like she'd heard this story a dozen times before. "But don't kick yourself too much. Smarter men than you done stupider things where women is concerned. And smarter women done stupider for men, to be sure." She winked. "Just you remember, a kiss is as good a reason as any for doing something. And better'n most."

She was trying to make him feel better, but he just wished she'd go away.

As though she'd heard his thoughts, she stood up in a swirl of skirts, taking the bottle with her. He thought about making a grab for it, but he didn't.

"Sure I can't tempt you to come inside?" She cocked her head. "There's a storyteller, spinning tales 'bout Quadrons and The Four. He come into town just today."

Brom thought of the giant reddish horse in front of *The Ox and Cart.* He'd been right. A traveler. A storyteller. Usually, stories about Quadrons would bring him like a pig to slops. And stories about The Four were even better. Arsinoe, Olivaard, Wulfric and Linza were known by every man, woman, and child in the two kingdoms. They were the only reason the Fendiran-Keltovari war had stayed confined to the Hallowed Woods, not become all-out war. The Four, seen as benevolent demigods who watched over the two kingdoms, only stepped in with a guiding hand when it was most needed. They were the leaders of all the Quadrons.

Usually, Brom loved hearing anything about Quadrons, but today such stories would only remind him how close he'd come to being part of the village guard.

"No," he said. "Thank you, though. It's nice of you to come looking for me."

"You really are something, aren't you, sweet boy?" She leaned over, touched his cheek, then stood straight again. "He'll be disappointed, though. He was asking for you."

Lightning crackled in Brom's belly, like it had done on the barracks practice yard. "He *asked* for me?"

"Knows your parents or somewhat."

"Oh." The lightning died. Brom definitely didn't want to talk to anyone who knew his parents. "Never mind."

"Suit yourself." She bustled around the corner of the building and was gone.

He slumped back against the wall and looked up at the skies. The swath of fields stretched out before him, green with early spring. As he breathed and enjoyed the hazy euphoria of the whiskey, he realized he was breathing through his mouth. He closed it and forced himself to breathe through his nose. Then he realized his eyes seemed to want to slide shut. He forced them open wide. Once he got them where he thought they ought to be, he realized that he'd begun breathing through his mouth again.

That made him laugh. Maybe being drunk wasn't so bad.

Every time he'd come to the tavern to listen to a storyteller, there were always the same seven people sitting at the bar, drinking. And they always looked so beaten-down.

Up until now, he'd thought being drunk *made* them unhappy, but he realized today that it was actually the opposite. They'd come into *The Ox and Cart* disappointed. They got drunk to make the unhappiness fuzzy, along with everything else.

"Ah, drowning in one's sorrows," came a voice to Brom's left. "The classic fix to a disappointing day."

Brom craned his neck around to behold a man dressed all in red, standing where Bala had been only minutes ago. He wore a wide-brimmed red hat, a red doublet like a nobleman, red breeches, and burgundy leather boots. He had a long black mustache that curled at the ends and thick black eyebrows that Brom could barely see beneath the shadow of his hat. He was thin, about Brom's height, and his clothes fit him very well.

The stranger whipped off the hat with a flourish and bowed. The silver stein in his other hand—brimming with ale—remained perfectly level, and neither the doffing of his hat nor the depth of his bow spilled even a drop of it.

Without the hat, Brom suddenly saw that the man was older. His long ponytail was gray, and the wrinkles on his face put him at fifty at the least.

But the twinkle in his lavender eyes was impish.

Lavender eyes... Bala hadn't said the storyteller was highborn!

Brom scrambled to his feet and gave a bow so hasty he almost fell over. He stumbled, got his balance, and bowed again. This time, he managed to do it right.

"I'm sorry, my lord," he said. Only Keltovari nobles had irises in shades of purple. The darker the shade, the purer the blood, it was said.

The man waved a dismissive hand, smiling. "I'm no lord, son.

Though I do appreciate the bow. It's more civilized than grappling with a man's hand, don't you think?"

"I..." Brom was now very aware that his tongue was numb and his words slurred. He tried to make them coherent. "I wouldn't know, my lord."

"I told you, I'm not a lord. I'm a Quadron. You may call me Cy'kett."

Brom spluttered, gaping. He had to have heard wrong. The man did speak rather fast, and Brom wasn't at his best right now. "Did you say Quadron?" he slurred.

"I did, young Brom." The man tilted his head forward and fixed the hat back in place. Brom's heart beat faster. The euphoric haze of the whiskey was suddenly a burden. He wanted to think faster, react faster. But a gloom of suspicion descended upon him. Had Bala sent this stranger to cheer him up, to spin tales of being a Quadron?

"I don't believe you," Brom said. Quadrons were legend. They didn't just show up to talk to builders' sons in a tiny town like Kyn.

"I was waiting for you in *The Ox and Cart*," Cy'kett continued. "But I misjudged where you would land. After your crushing disappointment at the practice yard, I assumed you'd go one of two places, a lad such as you. You'd either head straight for a tavern, or you'd return to your alluring young miller's daughter."

Brom's excitement turned cold. The man knew about Myan. Had Garn and Thol spread the word so fast? "How do you know about her?" Brom said.

The stranger continued talking as though Brom hadn't said anything. "I'm not often wrong about matters of the heart. That's for certain, but here you've surprised me. You sought solitude. To lick your wounds in private. A manly response." Cy'kett nodded in approval. "I like it."

"How do you know about Myan?" Brom repeated, and he felt heat in his cheeks as his anger rose.

"Because I've been watching you, young Brom. For a week now, you've caught my full attention. Your potential is...remarkable, and I like you more the more I discover. So I took the necessary steps to guide you."

"Guide me? I've never even met you."

"No, but I have been nearby, nevertheless. A whisper here. A nudge there. Did you really think it was one of the dullard twins who informed Roland the Rigid of your lovey paramour?"

The man's words hit Brom like a gut punch. "*You* told Roland?" A roar filled Brom's ears, and he clenched his fists.

"Of course."

"You told him Myan's name?"

"For shame, Brom. A gentleman doesn't take a lady's kiss and tell her secrets, and he certainly doesn't tell another's secrets. Your lovely Myan remains unknown. I told Roland only enough to serve my purpose."

"Your purpose?" Brom stepped toward the man. "You ruined my chances at becoming a guard on purpose?"

The man tipped his head, and the ridiculously wide hat bobbed down and up. "It worked perfectly. And you're welcome."

Brom stepped in and swung at the man, but somehow Cy'kett sidestepped. Brom's fist whooshed through empty air and he stumbled past. With a chuckle, Cy'kett gave Brom a little shove with his foot. With the momentum of his wild haymaker, Brom stumbled forward, off balance, and thudded into the wall. He fell to the ground.

He leapt to his feet and tried to shake off the ringing in his ears. Brom was going to unleash all of his frustrations on this preening, meddling imposter.

"I think that's quite enough of the whiskey." Cy'kett raised a hand, then brought it down like he was chopping an invisible log in half.

Brom's emotions vanished.

His rage and his desire to hit Cy'kett were simply...gone. He felt like a giant cauldron that had been dumped out, leaving nothing but a deafening, empty silence.

He sucked in a breath, and it stuck in his throat. In his belly, lightning crackled.

That hollow, crackling moment seemed to last forever, then fear and awe rushed in to fill the cauldron. Brom gasped.

"What did you do?" he whispered.

"I need you to pay attention, Brom," Cy'kett said, and his jaunty expression became serious. "I need you to look beyond today. Beyond packed dirt practice yards and miller's daughters. You don't want to be part of the village guard much more than you wanted to be a builder's apprentice. You've always wanted something more. So let's talk about what really matters."

Brom's head rang with the reality of what had just happened. This man had used magic on him! He really was a Quadron!

"You want..." Brom whispered again. He couldn't seem to get enough air. It was as though Cy'kett had reached inside Brom and taken his emotions, just...drained him. "You want... What do you want from me?" he finally managed.

"I find it important to know my recruits. So yes, I followed you. Yes, I ruined your chance to become a village guard. And yes, I know the name of your paramour. Believe me when I tell you that she's in no danger from me. But she, and all those like her, are obviously going to be a problem for you if you accept what I'm about to offer. So let me say this and say it once: I understand why you left the barracks. In your place, I'd have done the same. But where you're going, you can't just flaunt the rules. You'll soon find fetching temptations around every corner, women who will make you forget you ever knew a girl named Myan. The academy brings recruits from all over the two kingdoms. Ladies of the Keltovari court in their satin gowns. Priestesses from Fendir with their exotic braided hair. Women so beautiful they light up a room. Put them from your mind. Or at least, resolve to do so for the next four years. At the academy, there will be no midnight trips to lock lips. Break the rules and you'll feel more than just a heartbreak and a whiskey hangover."

Brom was stunned. Cy'kett had said the academy. And if he really was a Quadron, he could only mean The Champions Academy! That was the cradle of the Quadrons. Young hopefuls went in. Quadrons came out. It was like the village guard all over again, except this time, Brom would emerge as an actual Quadron.

Suddenly, the stupid village guard seemed drab and dull. This was all Brom had ever wanted—a dream that was literally coming true.

"You want *me* to go to the Champions Academy?" he said. His heart raced like mad.

"You're one of us, Brom," Cy'kett said.

"How do you know?"

The old man chuckled, then he said, "Motus, Mentis, Impetu, Anima." With each word, the ball of lightning in Brom's belly spun, crackled, and spat. It was almost painful.

"Gods!" Brom gasped.

"That is how I know," Cy'kett said.

"What did you just say?"

"The four paths to magic: Emotional, Mental, Physical and Spiritual."

"And yours is emotional," Brom said. That's how Cy'kett had stripped his rage and sadness away. "You use Motus?"

Cy'kett leaned his head back, regarding Brom thoughtfully, obviously impressed by the response. "Yes," he said after a moment. "Yes, that's right. Except I don't *use* Motus. I *am* a Motus."

"And what am I?" Brom asked.

"That remains to be seen. It depends on your Quad. You will..." Cy'kett faltered. He cleared his throat. "All you have to do is tell me..." He trailed off.

"Tell you what?"

Cy'kett cleared his throat. "You have to tell me you want to be a Quadron."

"I do," Brom said.

Cy'kett hesitated. "Then you have to say it. Say the actual words."

"I want to be a Quadron," Brom exclaimed.

As though from a far distance, he heard a deep ringing, like someone had struck a huge piece of iron with a log. It sounded, then faded so quickly he wasn't sure if he'd actually heard it.

"What was that?" he asked.

"That..." Cy'kett said, "means The Collector is coming." He turned, breaking eye contact with Brom for the first time, and Brom thought he looked suddenly stooped, older somehow, than he had a second ago.

"The Collector? When? Is he taking me to the Champions Academy?" Brom's heart soared, and he wondered at the change in the man's posture.

"Yes..." Cy'kett said. He leaned his head forward, and his wide brim covered his face in shadow. "Yes, he is."

"Not you?"

"No." Cy'kett turned away. "I won't be taking you to the academy. I've done my part. I've done...quite enough."

Brom watched the old man go. The tone of his words was confusing. He'd gone from jaunty to serious to...sad? It was strange, and the opposite of the giddiness that raced through Brom. He felt like he should offer an arm to the old man, to help him into the tavern as he suddenly looked so frail, but Brom somehow knew the old man would take offense.

Once the old man disappeared around the corner of the tavern, Brom's excited thoughts got the better of him. The Collector was coming for him. Brom was going to the Champions Academy. His life was about to change forever. He was going to become a Quadron.

He raced off to tell someone about his exciting news.

3

OLIVAARD

The dreadful clang grated on Olivaard's nerves and rang in his ears as he stepped into the Hallowed Woods. The shining portal—which had brought him here from the Champion's Academy—vibrated in the air. The pulsing border of light grew wider, then narrower, then wider again, crackling like lightning. The portal made no sound. Well, nothing except for that dreadful clang as it opened.

Olivaard turned his keen eyes on the scaly trunks of the Lyantrees all about him, their purple-silver leaves blocking the waning daylight, and he calculated. No one was within view, but whether they were within earshot, he couldn't say. Different people had different abilities. And the ones his Quad hunted, according to Linza, had broken the key barrier between *normals* and Quadrons. They'd split their souls into Soulblocks. They weren't allowed to do that without coming to the academy first.

Wulfric's hulking form stepped next through the doorway. He lifted his helmeted head, sniffing, then raised his bulging, muscled arm and pointed northeast. Wulfric could catch a person's scent from more than a mile away, depending on the breeze.

Linza came next, deftly managing her black robes as she stepped through the oval portal onto the loamy floor of the forest. Her black-slippered feet made no sound. Her face was lost in the shadows of her cloak, as it had been for half a century, but he could hear her take a deep breath of the rich outdoor air. She raised her thin arm, draped in a hanging black sleeve, and pointed in the same direction as Wulfric.

Arsinoe came next, his cocky, youthful face smiling as he hopped through the portal. He looked around the forest with pursed lips and eager eyes, like he was searching for one of his nightly bed companions.

The moment he stepped through, the magic within Olivaard's body rose like the tide of the Coral Sea, but tenfold. When he and his Quad mates separated, Olivaard's magic was cut in half, and even the short jaunt through the portal—where he was separated from his Quad for only a few moments—was like having both his legs amputated and then reattached.

It was a tragedy he needed to be near these three to be at his best, but Olivaard had long since come to terms with that.

"Isn't there a way to stop that clanging when the doorway opens?" Arsinoe asked, as though reading Olivaard's thoughts. "Can't we do something about that? I'm stunned all the armies of Fendir and Keltovar couldn't hear."

"Whoever hears it won't know what it means until it's too late," Wulfric growled.

Arsinoe rolled his eyes. "Succinct, Wulfric. As always, you've grasped the superficial and lost the meaning."

Olivaard pressed his lips together, forcing himself to stay silent. The truth was, he agreed with Arsinoe. And agreeing with Arsinoe was something Olivaard strenuously avoided. He wasn't about to start doing it this late in the day. That would simply make him ill.

"Leave it," Olivaard said. "The war front has been focused on the west side of the forest for months. That's why these little rats were able to do what they've done here."

"I thought the war was supposed to stop the soul rich from gathering in the forest," Wulfric growled.

"I thought they were here because Linza didn't spot them when she should have," Arsinoe drawled.

Linza's cowled head turned toward Arsinoe. He smiled winningly at the dark cavern of her face.

"Arsinoe," Olivaard warned.

"Come now." Arsinoe spread his hands helplessly. "Am I wrong?"

"Still your tongue or sleep in pain tonight," Linza hissed.

Again, Arsinoe rolled his eyes. Olivaard was never sure whether Arsinoe was as reckless as he seemed, or if he knew exactly how far he could push Linza.

"You should have sent The Collector months ago. Am I wrong?" Arsinoe appealed to Olivaard and Wulfric, but they both ignored him.

Linza glided over the purplish, leaf-strewn ground.

The damnable thing was that Arsinoe wasn't wrong. Again. That would make twice today. How distasteful. It made Olivaard feel like he had swallowed a rotten fish head.

They followed Linza to a little glade no more than twenty feet across. Olivaard picked his way forward carefully. He could never be as silent as Wulfric or Linza, but at least he could minimize his noise somewhat.

As he viewed the scene, he wondered why he'd even bothered. The little miscreants lay in a puppy pile, naked as animals: three young women and one young man. They slept like there was nothing in these woods that could threaten them, with nothing more than a thin blanket draped across them in some small concession to modesty, he supposed.

No doubt they had spent last night, and every night over their short stint as illicit Quadrons, in rituals of debauchery. The bonding required to form a Quad, combined with the powerful rush of new magic, created a powerful sexual urge. Being physically intimate could spark an even more powerful bond, making a Quad more potent. This was why sex between two or more people within a Quad was forbidden at the academy. It was grounds for expulsion because it could create a bond that made the Quad more powerful than The Four themselves. Olivaard, Wulfric, Arsinoe and Linza didn't want full Quads at all, let alone a powerful Quad loose in the lands.

Olivaard studied the pile of young people. The swarthy girl stirred first, identifying her as their Anima. No doubt she was having a nightmare, her subconscious connected to the Soul of the World. She had sensed that The Four were near. The young man, with his leonine mane, his cat-like muscles and wide shoulders was obviously their Impetu. The other two girls, well, Olivaard would guess the small slender one was the Mentis and the voluptuous one with the long black hair was the Motus. Arsinoe was probably licking his chops at the sight of them both.

The Anima girl opened her eyes. She saw them, and she screamed.

"Don't let them get away," Olivaard murmured dramatically, though he didn't think for a second the little rats could escape. Linza had already vanished from view, lying in wait in the shadows of the trees for the first of the Quad to flee.

But none fled. Not yet. Olivaard made a bet with himself that it would be the Anima who broke first. Animas were twitchy and prone to disloyalty.

The young Impetu leapt to his feet first, of course. He was the fastest, the one driven with the need to protect. He whipped the blanket off his companions and wrapped one end around his fist, creating a makeshift whip. The young man gave no thought to his own nakedness or that of his companions, and he faced the intruders with determination and an absolute lack of fear. His gaze flicked to Wulfric, then Arsinoe—who leaned against a tree, regarding his fingernails—then settled on Olivaard. The young man stepped forward, putting himself in front of his companions.

It was worse than Olivaard had thought. These four had already bonded deeply. Deep in the woods, by themselves, this little Quad had unraveled the secret that The Four would kill to protect: that burgeoning magic users didn't need the academy to become Quadrons.

This little nest of rats represented what the Champion's Academy had been built to prevent.

"Who are you?" the young Impetu demanded.

"Tarvic," the small slender girl gasped. She touched his shoulder. "That's The Four!"

So the small one *was* their Mentis, as Olivaard had thought. Everyone knew the names of The Four, of course, but Olivaard had worked hard over the last forty years to ensure that no one knew their faces. The girl had read one of their minds without Olivaard realizing she was doing it. Impressive.

"Do you know why we are here?" Olivaard asked.

The younglings looked confused. Their Impetu, Tarvic, shook his head. But the Anima girl spoke up. "You've come to take us to the academy," she said hopefully. The young Quad's collective bewilderment transformed into excitement.

Oh, the optimism of the Anima, Olivaard thought.

"In a manner of speaking," Olivaard said. "You see, my colleagues and I have taken great pains to convince the two kingdoms that the only safe way to learn magic is to come to the academy. What you've done here..." He waved a hand at them. "Proves that we've been lying for a century."

"Lying?" Tarvic asked, still not understanding.

Arsinoe gave a loud stage whisper. "He means you could tell the other students they don't need us." Arsinoe held his hands up. "And then they wouldn't come to the academy and put their necks into the collars we've prepared for them."

A long silence fell over the glade.

"They're here to kill us," their little Mentis whispered, her voice shaking as she realized the truth. She held up her hands to The Four, as though that would stop the inevitable from happening. Her slender arms shook.

"No," the Anima gasped, stepping back.

"What?" the voluptuous Motus said, still not understanding what was happening, though surely understanding the fear that flowed through the glade.

Their little naked forms, so brazen before, suddenly seemed pitiful and vulnerable. Olivaard's pulse began to quicken.

"You have bonded quite deeply," he acknowledged. "I salute you for that, and I don't give praise lightly."

"He really doesn't," Arsinoe interjected.

"In fact," Olivaard continued, "your power is so impressive you might one day become something that could rival the power of The Four." He offered them a brief smile. "Our power. And I'm sure you can understand, we simply cannot allow that."

Tarvic's mouth dropped open, stunned. The little Mentis whimpered, looking from one face to the other.

Olivaard glanced at Arsinoe. "I assume you would like the voluptuous one?"

"You know me so well." Arsinoe leaned forward like a cat ready to pounce. There was drool on his chin. Actual drool. Olivaard checked his sigh. The man was disgusting.

The voluptuous girl screamed and fell to her knees, clawing at the air, feeling all the terror Arsinoe could shove into her.

Tarvic roared, swinging his pathetic whip at Wulfric, perhaps hoping to pull him off balance. The sheet wrapped masterfully around Wulfric's forearm. The boy really did have talent, and that much of his plan worked perfectly. But he didn't have any idea what he was up against.

Wulfric yanked the sheet with such force the boy flew off his feet and into Wulfric's enormous arms. Wulfric flexed. Bones crunched. Tarvic screamed as he died.

Their Anima screamed with him, and she bolted into the woods.

Animas always break first, Olivaard thought. *What was it about young Animas that made them so ready to be the first to abandon their Quad? They were supposed to be the spiritual center. It was ironic, really.*

Olivaard let her go. Linza was back there somewhere, and after her mistake in allowing this Quad to grow in the first place, she'd make sure the girl wouldn't get fifty paces.

Olivaard turned his attention to the frightened little Mentis, the only one remaining who wasn't screaming, fleeing, or dying. He walked toward her slowly and deliberately. As good a Mentis as the girl was, she'd have calculated all the aspects of her dire situation. She couldn't run, obviously. The path of the Mentis didn't lend itself to feats of athleticism. She'd try another way. Perhaps she would appeal to his humanity.

"We didn't know," she said, tears brimming in her eyes. "Please!

We didn't know! We wanted to come to the academy. We still would. Please let us. Don't do this."

"It is too late for that now," Olivaard said. "You know the secret that no one else can know."

With a pitiful squeak, she made a mind stab at him. It was strong, but not nearly strong enough. He shielded himself and struck back. She screamed.

He whispered inside her head, spoke to her as he cracked her mind like a walnut. Her sanity collapsed in on itself. Blood leaked from her ears as he destroyed her, whispering into her mind the last words she'd ever hear.

Now you know, little rat. There can be no four except The Four.

4

BROM

Brom ran from *The Ox and Cart* with the intention of telling his parents that he'd been invited to the Champions Academy...

...and he pulled up short in the middle of the dusty street. A one-donkey wagon trundled by, hauling hay. Its driver, a man named Malden who worked on the Eigan's Farm, gave Brom a disapproving look for standing in the middle of the road. Brom ignored him.

No. He couldn't tell his parents. First of all, they'd never believe it. So far as Brom knew, magic had never visited Kyn. Ever. If he told a story about how Cy'kett had performed magic on him, they'd think he was telling stories. In fact, they'd scoff at the idea of a Quadron in Kyn at all, just as Brom had done to start.

And if they did believe him, that would actually be worse. Father would hate the idea of Brom leaving Kyn for four years. And maybe forever. He'd do everything he could to make sure it didn't happen. Would The Collector refuse to take Brom if Father balked? That was a sobering thought.

No, he wasn't going to tell his parents. Not today.

Instead, he set off in the direction of the mill, which stood alongside the river and a bit out of town. It was actually close to Brom's house.

The other night, Brom had found a way to sneak up to the mill, and he used it again. His hidden path on the north side of the river wasn't quite as invisible in broad daylight, but it worked to get him within fifty yards of the slowly revolving water wheel attached to the mill, a large stone building that Brom's father had built. The entirety of Kyn's flour was ground here, and the building had a thatched roof and four windows on the upstairs, as well as a door and an external stone stairway that descended to the ground. Myan, her two sisters, and her parents lived above the mill, and the work was done below.

Still giddy at his meeting with Cy'kett, Brom lay down in the tall grass near the big ash tree with the clothesline. Based on what Myan had told Brom, this was about the time of day when she'd come do the washing. She'd said she usually did it sometime in the afternoon, and somewhere close to this tree, which had a post set firmly in the ground about a dozen feet away and two lines pulled taut between the trunk and the post.

The sun had begun to sink into the western sky, and Brom laid back to wait. Brom's father would be at the quarry until dark, and Mother didn't expect Brom home tonight at all. He was supposed to be sleeping at the barracks.

Brom had time, so he just lay in the grass, feeling the sunshine on his face, looking up at the blue sky and dreaming of the things he'd do when he became a Quadron.

The sun settled along the tree line to the west, and Brom began to think maybe he'd missed wash time, when Myan emerged onto the landing on the second floor of the mill. She had a wicker basket full of clothing under one arm, and she shouted back through the open doorway.

"—not enough daylight left!" she yelled at someone inside.

"Then by Kelto, girl, you'll do it in the dark!"

"I hate you!" Myan yelled, slammed the door, and took the stairs dangerously fast, thumping down them like she was stepping on the person inside—Brom assumed it was her mother—who had offended her. A long stocking fell onto the steps without Myan noticing, and she flounced away from the mill toward the river, toward Brom's hiding place.

She stopped about a dozen paces downstream and threw the basket to the ground. It creaked, toppled, and dumped the laundry onto the bank. Myan stared at it, her face red and her mouth drawn up in a pout, and then she burst into tears.

She dropped to her knees, still crying, and dragged the laundry close to a wide, flat stone angled up from the water. She grabbed a soap cake from the basket, dunked one of her father's big shirts in the river and slapped it on the stone, then began pushing the soap up and down upon it, creating a lather.

Brom was about to sneak out and surprise her, but her tears stopped him. Slowly, his spirits sank. He began to think about what he was doing here, and how selfish it was. He'd come to tell her his excitement about going off to the Champions Academy, that he was off to become a Quadron.

But he hadn't stopped to think about what it meant to Myan. He was coming to tell her that he was leaving her, and he'd be gone for four years.

He'd would be the first to admit he didn't know much about girls, but he had a sneaking suspicion she wouldn't receive the news well.

Once he was a Quadron, he'd be off to adventure. He'd go where The Four pointed him. It suddenly occurred to him that he might not ever come back here.

He watched Myan again. She sniffled, scrubbing at the shirt, and raised her shoulder every now and then to push strands of her hair from her eyes. She dunked the shirt, rinsed it and wrung it out. Rising gracefully to her feet, she walked the few paces to the clothing line and hung up the shirt. He watched the sway of her walk, the way her summer dress swung back and forth. If he left his hiding place to say goodbye...certainly there would be more kisses.

But what was the kind thing to do? Reveal himself, have his kisses, then tell her he was leaving? Or simply let their lovely night stand alone, a single dot of light in a night's sky that would never have any more, and not risk any further hurt to her?

The sun sank below the horizon, leaving only twilight behind. He watched her and wrestled with his dilemma. Eventually, Myan stopped sniffling and set about her work methodically. Scrub, rinse, hang. Scrub, rinse, hang.

Brom scooted quietly backward until he was far enough that she wouldn't see him when he stood up. He paused one moment, just watching her. She was so lovely. But he couldn't do that to her. He wasn't going to stay, so what really was there to say?

He turned and jogged up the hill, back toward town.

His spirits were still high, but he realized he didn't know where to go now. All of his friends worked the fields, so they'd just be returning home to supper. He wasn't going to bother them. And his parents didn't expect him home until tomorrow. There was absolutely nobody he could tell, so he went back to *The Ox and Cart*.

The tavern had filled up in the few hours he'd been gone. The men who didn't have wives at home—and weren't young enough to live at their parents' homes—had come here after the day's work in the fields. Quiet conversations created a rumbling in the dim room. It smelled of pipe smoke, and tendrils of it crept through the air like pale, translucent snakes.

"Back again?" Bala greeted him.

"I took a walk," he said.

She raised an eyebrow at his lucid speech, and she laughed. "Looks like maybe you can hold your liquor. You don't seem nearly as deep in cups as you did when you left." She cocked her head. "Not going home tonight, are you?"

He shrugged.

She turned, expertly tucked a mug underneath the keg against the back wall, and twisted the tap. When the foam started to peek above the rim, she twisted the tap off, then plunked the mug on the bar in front of him. "Here you go. A little softer than what you're used to." She winked. "But I think it'll do you right."

He held out his hands. "No, I—"

"It's on me, luv. A drink for the boy who takes a risk for a kiss. And who protects his lady."

"Thank you." He took the beer and took a sip. It was warm and earthy, with a generous froth.

"Your family's friend is in the corner, if that's who you're wanting. He picked up where you left off."

"My family's friend?"

"Sir Red Breeches."

Brom turned and spotted Cy'kett against the back wall. He sat in the darkest corner by the fireplace. In the winter, that was the warmest spot in the tavern, but with no fire burning, Brom had completely overlooked the man upon first glance.

"Uh, thank you," he said, and took the beer with him.

The old man was leaning over that same silver stein he'd held behind the tavern. Seven empty shot glasses were scattered about the small round table, next to a mostly empty bottle of whiskey that looked even more expensive than Father's.

Brom had seen men drink like this before. This wasn't drinking to forget a bad day. This was how a man drank when he wanted to forget he was alive.

What had happened?

"Cy'kett?" Brom said.

The wide brim came up, and Cy'kett's shadowed lavender eyes met Brom's.

"Ah," Cy'kett said. "You're back. Wonderful." But he said the word like it was anything but wonderful.

"I... Why are you drinking so much?"

"Because I'm a horrible man with a horrible purpose." Cy'kett's words slurred. "But I'm changing my mind, changing my legacy. I'd rather protect your innocence than throw you to the wolves."

"Wolves?"

"I think you should leave, good fool." Cy'kett blurted, flecks of spittle hitting the table. "Go now while the roses still bloom in your young heart. Spend them elsewhere. Go now before the snows fall. Winter comes so early... So early to us all..."

Brom slid out the chair opposite Cy'kett and sat down. "Are you okay?"

Cy'kett chuckled darkly. "I'm trying to tell you that I'm not. I'm trying to tell you that you are not. But you don't care because you're young. Because you're the rule breaker. You'll set your sights and not let anything stand in your way. If I tell you what's best for you, you'll do the opposite. As sure as the sun will rise."

"Are you talking about the Champions Academy?"

"Yes. I filled your head with dreams, good fool. But I didn't tell you all." His head dipped, and the wide brim of his hat swung down. "I've doomed you. I didn't tell you that you've one chance in a hundred of becoming a Quadron. And no chance of..." He trailed off. "I've hung an anchor around your neck while I smiled at you."

"What are you talking about?" Brom asked.

Cy'kett's fist clenched. "I should put the fear into you," he whispered. "I should make you run."

Brom's elation from earlier curdled. What was going on here?

"Is this about the academy?" he asked, his heart sinking. Had this man lied to him? Was there no Collector at all?

Cy'kett laughed, low and dry. "Of course that's all you're thinking about. Your place in the academy. Your chance to become a Quadron like me. Listen. Don't hear what you wish to hear. Listen to my words. I'm trying to save you, boy. With the last pure part of my blackened soul."

"Save me from what?"

Cy'kett opened his mouth like he had an answer for that, but he paused, mouth open, then clacked his teeth shut.

"You know what a Quadron is, boy. Do you know what a Quad is?"

Brom blinked.

"There are four paths to magic," Cy'kett continued. "I spoke their names to you. You'll be tasked with learning one of them, but in order to do that you must bond with three other students, each of you learning a separate path. It's the only way. It takes four."

"But—"

"You'll show them pieces of your soul you never dreamed of showing to anyone, pieces you didn't know you had. These four will become yours, and you theirs. Stronger than family. More intimate than a lover."

"This is what I'll learn at the academy—?"

"Shut up," Cy'kett snarled, and Brom flinched. The man was so fierce it took Brom's breath away. "You didn't listen before. Listen."

"I'm listening."

"It's a trap."

"What's a trap?"

"Listen!" Cy'kett hissed. "It's not a school, boy. The Collector is coming for you. But he's not coming to help you. He's coming to kill you."

"What?"

Cy'kett slammed his palms on the tabletop. Shot glasses spun. One fell on the wooden floor. "He'll stuff you behind those walls, and you'll never make it out."

Brom gripped the sides of his chair so hard he thought his knuckles would crack. He'd never felt fear like this before.

"Run," Cy'kett whispered. "You have four days. He always takes four days to arrive. Run away, and don't ever come back."

"Run away from Kyn?" Brom asked incredulously.

"If you stay, he'll find you. The Collector—"

That deep gong Brom had heard earlier sounded again, far away. Behind the walls of the tavern, past the horizon, all the way to the sea.

Cy'kett stood up so suddenly it was as though he'd been stuck in the butt with a knife. The table tipped. The mug, the shot glasses, the bottle of whiskey, everything fell to the floor, and the whiskey bottle shattered.

Everyone in the tavern turned to stare. From the bar, Bala raised her head, a worried look on her face.

Cy'kett clenched his teeth. He was even more stooped than before, suddenly seeming ancient. His legs trembled, and his arms shook.

Brom leapt to the old man's side. "Let me help you upstairs—"

Before he could even touch the man, terror hit Brom like an icy wind. He gasped and Cy'kett's bony hand caught him by the tunic, hauled him close.

"Listen," Cy'kett snarled. His breath was a whiskey fume. "I'm trying to do right by you. Gods damn me, I'm trying to do right for the first time in my life. Flee. Run as fast as your young legs can carry you. Take that miller's girl if you must, but go. Do it tonight. If you run, it might just be enough. Maybe you'll run far enough and fast enough that they'll never find you." He clenched his teeth, his lavender eyes flicking back and forth, searching Brom's own.

He seemed to find something there, and then his lip curled. He released Brom, who staggered back and sat down hard on the chair.

"But you won't, will you?" Cy'kett said.

"I want to be a Quadron like you," Brom said, his body shivering with fear, his voice quavering.

Cy'kett clenched his teeth and turned away. "Fool," he said. "Drink your poisoned hope, then. Pay your price. You've rung the bell, and The Collector is coming."

Brom was so scared he could barely form a coherent thought. He desperately wanted to ask Cy'kett why this sudden change of heart. Just a few hours ago he'd seemed jovial at the prospect of Brom going to the academy. But Cy'kett had paralyzed him with fear.

He seemed to have paralyzed everyone else in the tavern, too. That, or they were all too stunned to do anything.

The old man shuffled to the door and paused. He looked like he was considering leaving, and he shook as if from a palsy.

Then he turned slowly and went to the stairs like a man walking to the gallows. One step at a time, he climbed. He seemed so frail, but he made it to the top, then into the hallway that led to his room. Only once he was out of sight did Brom's fear vanish as though someone had snapped their fingers.

The tavern went as silent as a grave for long minutes, and Brom just sat there, trying to puzzle through the warning Cy'kett had given him.

Finally, Bala arrived, began picking up glasses and the stein. Brom knelt down to help her.

"If I've seen it once, I've seen it a hundred times," Bala said philosophically. "You never know who's going to be a bad drunk. Shame, really. The man was quite charming this afternoon, with all the stories. I was of a mind to ask him to stay a fortnight."

Brom didn't say anything. He didn't tell her about his

conversation with Cy'kett, the indecipherable speech and the dire warnings. He hoped she was right. That it was simply the whiskey talking—

The lightning in Brom's belly struck, and he felt a thump on his chest like there'd been a thunderclap right inside the tavern. He jumped, dropped a glass, and Bala looked at him in alarm.

"What is it, luv?"

Brom looked up at the ceiling.

"His room. Where is his room?"

"Leave him be, luv. He'll be all right in the morning. Just let him sleep it off."

"Which room? Tell me which room!"

"All right then." Bala picked up on his urgency and she bustled to the stairs. He followed her up and she opened the door to Cy'kett's room.

They found the old man dead in his bed. His hands had curled into claws, elbows bent and forearms pointing toward the ceiling. Bala turned away, hands over her mouth, but Brom stared. He thought he saw a green glow inside Cy'kett's mouth. He rushed to the bed, but the glow was gone. The old man's mouth was open and not breathing, but there was no green light.

"Kelto's mercy," Bala murmured.

Brom continued to stare at the old man's wasted body. Without the light in Cy'kett's lavender eyes, he looked like he'd been dead a hundred years. His body was desiccated, as though his vitality earlier today had been a lie, as though only his powerful will had given this shriveled husk any life at all. And once that will had gone...the truth was stark and horrible.

Brom stayed with Bala while the town undertaker came, wrapped Cy'kett in black and took him away. After, Brom looked through Cy'kett's rooms for anything that might offer a clue, but it was as though the man hadn't traveled with any possessions at all. On a whim, Brom went looking for the giant reddish horse Cy'kett had ridden into town.

It was gone.

Spooked, with too many conflicting thoughts to know what to do, Brom went home. He told his parents he'd failed to get into the village guard. Mother offered sympathy, gave him a hug. Father gave Brom a commiserating chuck on the shoulder, doing a fairly good job of hiding his smile.

But Brom didn't tell them about the Champions Academy, didn't tell them about Cy'kett. Of course, news of the old man's death would race through the town tomorrow. But that was tomorrow's problem. By then, Brom hoped to know what to say.

He never got that chance to craft his believable lie, though.

That night, The Collector came.

5

BROM

Thoom! Thoom! Thoom!

Brom jumped, and lightning crackled in his belly.

"Kelto!" Father sat bolt upright in his chair at the loud knock. He shot a scathing glance at Mother, as though it were somehow her fault. Mother dropped the soup spoon into the pot. She cursed and glared at Father as though it were somehow his fault.

The knock boomed again. The last time someone had knocked on the Builders' door after sundown was when Corman Green's wagon had slid into the mud pits and landed on top of his son.

"Who would be coming 'round now?" Father flung at Mother as he stood up and went to the door.

"By Kelto, how should I know?" she shot back.

Brom's heart beat so fast he could barely breathe, and fear crept over his scalp like an icy trickle of water. He knew who had to be on the other side of that door. He knew it in the pit of his belly.

He drifted into the archway between the kitchen and the family room, watching as father went to the door, his steps loud and irritated. He flung the door open like he was ready to spit vitriol...then he froze. In the doorway stood a tall, black-robed, black-hooded figure. The only part of him that could be seen beneath that cowl was a pointed black beard and a wide mouth.

Mystery and power wafted off the man like a fog, and the lightning in Brom's belly crackled like crazy.

"Yes?" Father finally managed to blurt, and now he sounded like a guilty child.

The cowled stranger murmured something too low for Brom to hear.

"No..." Father said. "I don't think that..."

Again, the stranger murmured. Brom strained to catch even one word, but he couldn't.

Father cleared his throat, and his face turned pink. "Well...no. You've caught us during the dinner hour." He tried to make his voice sound commanding, but it didn't. Father sounded like that guilty child again, trying to convince his parent to extend his bedtime.

More murmuring.

Father glanced over his shoulder, trying to seem in control, but he looked confused and scared. Mother watched him, spooked to see Father so hesitant.

Then, astonishingly, Mother motioned that Father should let the stranger in. "Let him in, Brochan," she said.

"Well," Father said. "I suppose we can spare a moment. Please come in." Father invited the forbidding man inside, bid him sit down in his own chair. As soon as the stranger sat, still not removing his cowl, Father shook his head, as though he was surprised at what he'd done.

"Thank you. You are very kind," the stranger said.

"Well..." Father began, still looking bemused. "What can we do for you?"

"I am here to offer admission to your son to attend the Champion's Academy," the stranger said.

Dead silence descended on the room. Mother's ingratiating face turned ill, like she'd swallowed a piece of rancid chicken. She stumbled with the words, and she left the kitchen to come into the sitting room. "Excuse me. But who are you?"

Father had gone beet red, caught between rage, surprise, and a dawning fear that he'd unwittingly let a predator into the house. His anger seemed to give him some of his spine back. "Yes," he said. "Yes, that's right. You tell us who you are first. You tell us who you are before you start making...such statements. Champions Academy? That's ridiculous!"

"You may call me The Collector," the stranger said.

"And you want to what?"

"Your son is coming with me to the Champions Academy to learn how to become a Quadron."

Father's face became so red Brom thought he might have a fit. "Over my dead body!"

"That won't be necessary," The Collector said. "Why don't you ask the boy what he wants?"

"What he wants?" Father blurted loudly. "He's a boy. He's not going to be a village guard and he's not going to some mythical academy. He's going to stay right here in Kyn and he's going to be a builder."

The Collector spoke in calm, quiet tones, like he was coaxing a horse to cross a stream. "Any invitee to the Champion's Academy must be allowed to attend if he wishes. None may bar his way, not even his parents. This is by decree of King Leventius." The Collector turned his hooded head toward Brom, then said, "You called me. Did you mean what you said?"

Cy'kett's death and bizarre warnings rose in Brom's mind. In his drunk ravings, Cy'kett had called the school a trap. Did he mean that Brom wasn't up to the rigors of the school?

Lost in thought, Brom suddenly realized Father was speaking.

"...is of common blood. Only royalty can become Quadrons," Father said.

"Royalty," The Collector said.

"Yes," Father said. "I'm sorry you wasted a trip. Now I must ask you to leave, sir..."

A low, bubbling sound came from The Collector's hood, and Brom realized that it was laughter. The Collector brought his hand up and threw back his cowl. His face was thin, with a pointed chin and pointed goatee. He had high cheekbones, but his shoulder-length oiled hair was thick and black, combed back from his face and down to his shoulders. His eyebrows were also thick and black, like Brom's own, like his father's. Nearly every one of the common folk of Keltovar had black hair, black eyebrows and black eyes.

"Do I look like nobility to you?" The Collector asked, not waiting for an answer. "The academy does not recognize high station nor low birth. It would no more deny entry to a priestess druid from Fendir than it would to King Leventius himself. It does not care about the war in the Hallowed Woods. It does not care if you are short or tall, male or female. Such distinctions are meaningless within the academy's walls. It recognizes only the aptitude for magic, and your son has it."

"He has an aptitude for magic?" Mother said. "How would you know such a thing?"

The Collector steepled his fingers beneath his chin and waited, deigning not to answer.

"I say he is not going!" Father said.

"It is not up to you," The Collector replied calmly.

"I'll be damned if it's not!" Father shouted, looking around wildly. He stomped to the mantle and lifted grandfather's sword from the iron studs. He yanked the sheath off and bared the dull, steel blade. The steel looked awkward in his hand, and the tip wavered about in the air. Father was no swordsman. "This is *my* house!"

The Collector carefully put his cowl back into place and turned toward Brom. "It is time to make your decision. Do you wish to be a builder? Or a Quadron?"

A moment ago, Father seemed ready to attack, but now he was rooted to the spot, sword shaking in his hand. Neither he nor Mother moved, and they both stared at Brom.

Lightning crackled throughout Brom's body now, and with it a feeling of utter rightness, of invincibility. He knew what his answer would be. He'd always known. What Father wanted didn't matter. Cy'kett's warnings didn't matter. Brom had a chance to be one of the heroes he'd always read about, and he wasn't about to pass it up.

"I want to be a Quadron," Brom said.

"I won't have it!" Father shouted at Brom, then turned to The Collector. "He doesn't mean it. Brom, tell him you don't mean it. You are staying here. You're *my* apprentice. Tell this...man to leave!" He held the sword high, but still only stood there, shaking.

"Pack whatever you wish," The Collector said to Brom. "I will wait with your parents."

In a daze, Brom found himself walking to his room. Father's anger coursed through him, but he saw his own future. He saw the only path that seemed right to take. He was going to become a Quadron.

After stuffing his belongings into his pack and attaching his bedroll, he shouldered it, returned to the kitchen and gave Mother a hug. She cried.

Father snarled and cursed, but he still hadn't moved from where he stood, sword in the air. It was as though his feet had been nailed to the floor. He watched, anger turning to despair as Brom moved to the door.

Magic...

Somewhere deep down, Brom felt he should have been horrified that The Collector was using magic on his father, but the Collector hadn't hurt him. He'd just stopped him from stopping Brom. In fact, if Brom thought of it that way, The Collector had stopped Father from breaking the king's law.

And as it had been with Myan, wasn't this the kindest way? Father wasn't going to let Brom go without a fight. Best to do it quickly. Best to do it now.

"Please understand, Father," Brom said, hesitant to come any closer lest Father grab hold of him. "I will return. And I'll be a Quadron when I do."

"You will stay right here, Brom!" Father demanded.

"A Quadron, Father. Imagine it. *Me.*"

"Drop the pack. I'm warning you!" Father thundered, spasmodically clutching the hilt of the sword, but he didn't lower it. And he didn't leave the dais of the hearth.

Brom turned away. The Collector stood by the thick oak door, holding it open. Brom left without a backward glance.

He heard his father shouting until they reached the edge of

Kyn, it seemed.

6

BROM

It took four days to reach the Champion's Academy, and each day traveling with The Collector was a strain. At first, Brom had visions that The Collector would immediately begin imparting secrets that only a student of the academy was allowed to know. Like the words Motus, Mentis, Impetu and Anima. But most of the time The Collector acted like Brom didn't exist. And when the forbidding man did speak, it was in terse, one-word answers.

A chill came off the man like a breeze from a winter lake. It was as if, underneath those robes, he was actually made of ice and not flesh and blood at all.

For the first day of travel, Brom questioned if he'd made the right decision to go in the first place. He wanted to be a Quadron more than anything, but Cy'kett's dire warnings hung in his mind. Brom almost changed his mind and rode going back to Kyn on that first day.

But every time he got close, he envisioned what that would look like, and his heart sank. To return to Kyn was to condemn himself to being a builder for the rest of his life. And for what? Because a drunk old man had spooked him with indecipherable warnings? Brom wasn't even sure what Cy'kett had meant. Should Brom just run away in fear?

In every Quadron story he'd ever read, there were dangers. There was danger in anything interesting. After all, Brom hadn't signed up for the village guard because he'd wanted safety.

After that first day of uncertainty, as they drew further away from his home, Brom's decision galvanized into certainty. No. This was his path and none other, and he'd see it through to the end. He was going to become a Quadron if it killed him.

He stopped thinking about the frosty Collector or the drunken Cy'kett, and Brom set his mind to thinking about everything he would do once he became a Quadron.

On the fourth day, he and The Collector crested a hill, and the Champion's Academy rose into view.

Brom reined in his horse, fearful he'd fall off through sheer surprise. His mouth hung open.

The Champions Academy was enormous, a keep so large it beggared the imagination. The white walls were higher than the tallest trees Brom had ever seen, twice as tall as the castles Brom had seen depicted in books. From his vantage on the hill, he could see the buildings inside. Square dots of small houses, buildings larger than Kyn's entire main street, a huge domed building in the center and towers at each corner.

A river ran underneath the northeastern wall, creating a meandering blue line that flowed diagonally through the center of the keep and past the southwest wall into a many-forked estuary, finally emptying to the Coral Sea. One pennant snapped in the breeze at the top of each tower of the giant keep: blue, white, red and black. The largest tower was so tall it beggared the imagination, looming over the walls like a stern parent over its children. The tower's pointed top seemed so high it touched the clouds.

And the entirety of the academy was white marble. The buildings, the towers and the walls themselves were pure white, dazzling in the sun. The entire keep was like a bright beacon of hope and civilization.

Just looking at it made Brom dizzy.

"Tuck that wonder back behind your slack lips, boy," The Collector said. "Or you'll only last a week here." He kicked his heels into his mount and started down the hill.

Brom hurried to catch up. The giant portcullis, made of interlaced riveted bands of iron, began to rise. The metallic thunking of enormous chains reverberated as the two of them rode beneath thousands of tons of stone wall.

Brom drew in a breath. As they passed beneath, he felt a tingle over his scalp and then over his entire body. The lightning in his belly danced about. It was as though something in this place identified the lightning inside him and touched it.

It was as though Brom had been living in a dark prison cell and hadn't known it until he'd stepped into the light. Every part of him felt alive.

Cy'kett had been mistaken. In fact, Brom couldn't even remember the specifics of the old man's warnings. The fear Brom had felt, the foreboding he'd had, all of it fluttered away.

By the time Brom came through to the other side, he could barely recall the old man's name, let alone his warnings, and he didn't care to do so. All possibilities opened up before Brom, and he knew he could do anything.

He looked from one vast, pillared, white-marbled building to another. Were there no normal houses in this place? His father was a talented builder, sought after by lords and commoners alike for his skill, but Father had never built anything like this.

Of course, the only villages Brom had seen outside of illustrations in books were his own hometown of Kyn and once in nearby Seldyn. Both towns could easily fit inside the walls of the Champion's Academy, with room enough for three more towns just like them. Most of the houses and shops in Brom's town were made of granite or wood, but here, everything was marble, and most of the buildings were two stories tall or more. The academy grounds were exactly square, and the northwest, southeast and southwest corners each had a white marble towers that reached to the sky. But none were even half as tall as the giant tower to the southwest. Everything was made of marble, and it made the city seem filled with light, that this was where divinity had come to live.

It felt eternal, like these marble structures had stood for centuries and would continue to stand long after the kingdoms of Keltovar and Fendir crumbled into the sea.

The Collector led Brom down a crushed gravel path between manicured lawns and toward an enormous four-story building. Brom followed him up wide steps and through columned archways that had to be three stories tall themselves, and into an open room that was as long as Kyn's main street. Brom caught The Collector's supercilious smile, and he suddenly realized the man *wanted* Brom to be awed. His gruff dismissals and haughty stares were all meant to make Brom feel small.

Brom paused inside that grand hallway, struggling not only with the grandeur, but also with a ringing realization: The Collector was trying to scare him. Suddenly, it all seemed staged, from the scene at Brom's house all the way to this moment, designed to make Brom feel smaller.

But would such a powerful person try to intimidate a fresh student?

The only answer was that The Collector was simply cruel. But why would The Four, the benevolent demigods who looked after the two kingdoms employ someone cruel to bring new students to the school?

The second and only other reason Brom could imagine was: Brom was somehow a threat. It was ludicrous, but it was the only other reason one person might try to intimidate another. Could Brom somehow be a threat to The Collector?

He couldn't answer that question, but just knowing it, sensing deep in his belly that The Collector was intimidating Brom on purpose completely changed Brom's view of the man.

He decided he would take The Collector's advice—the only real words the man had spoken on their long journey. Brom clenched his jaw and put his wonder away.

The Collector paused, as though looking for that awe on Brom's face. When he didn't find it, he turned away and opened a door just off the main hall.

They both entered a noisy room with dozens of boys and girls who looked roughly the same age as Brom. There must have been more than a hundred, but the enormous room still didn't seem even half full.

The din of conversation died as The Collector entered, deposited Brom at the threshold, and left, closing the door behind him.

The young people in the room were as varied as they could be. The Collector had said neither a person's birth nor their allegiance, Keltovari or Fendiran, had significance in this place. Brom saw some young people dressed in little better than rags, and some in expensive gowns and doublets.

One tall girl, who stood apart from the throng like a disapproving older sister, had the indigo eyes of high Keltovari royalty. Cy'kett's eyes had been a faded lavender, but this girl's eyes were deep and dark. She was exquisite, with flawless pale skin and meticulously braided silver and gold hair. She was the kind of woman artists would paint portraits of. Her finely embroidered, cream-colored gown had actual pearls as buttons, stacked up to her throat, stopping at a stylized rose created from clever folds of stiff fabric just below her chin. She wore an elaborate bracelet on her right wrist and a golden headdress, each studded with rubies and purple gemstones. Each of those stones had to be worth more than Brom's father made in a year. The display of wealth was staggering.

But it wasn't her wealth or even her beauty that held Brom's attention. He found after his initial survey that his gaze went to the girl's hands. They were...large, out of proportion with the well-displayed symmetrical perfection of the rest of her. He found himself staring at those pale, long-fingered hands, and he realized that the girl was making no effort to hide them, and that suddenly struck him as unusual. Other boys and girls his age often went out of their way to conceal their oddities. This girl did not. For a moment, he dared to imagine that she found her unusually long-fingered hands beautiful.

His heart warmed, and he fell in love with the haughty girl just a little bit.

The girl turned an icy glare upon him, as though she'd known he was staring, thinking about her, looking at her, and that she'd waited quite long enough—out of sheer tolerance—to allow him his fill. The glare struck him like a blow, promising a headsman's axe if he didn't find another place for his roving eyes. Brom jerked his gaze away.

His nervous eyes immediately latched onto the next-most-obvious person in the room, the way eyes were drawn to a mountain in the distance. Gods! The boy had to be seven feet tall, and his shoulders were twice as wide as those of any other boy in the room, and he was obviously a Fendiran.

He towered over the rest of them like a giant. Brom would have thought him an adult, some guard left behind to keep an eye on them, except the young man had no whiskers on his chiseled face. His muscles were already big, but they promised to swell ridiculously as he aged. He wore a woodsman's garb, soft leather breeches and quality black boots, and a green tunic belted at the waist. On his belt was a sheath that had once held a dagger, but the dagger was missing. The Collector had told Brom no weapons were allowed in the academy until students had been divided into their Quads, but obviously this boy was used to carrying one.

He had the swarthy complexion most Fendirans had, the light brown hair that *all* Fendirans had, and he bore a thick Fendiran face tattoo that looked like two lines, one thick and one thin, that swept up the left side of his face. The tattoo looked like a stylized tree trunk with one branch angling out from the trunk then pointing straight up. Both trunk and branch crossed his left eye and forehead before vanishing beneath his hairline.

Everything about the giant boy was pure Fendiran except his dark blue eyes. Like the lowborn Keltovari, all Fendirans had brown or black eyes. Brom had never even heard of a Fendiran with blue eyes. He wondered if it signified noble birth, like purple eyes did in the Keltovari.

The giant Fendiran glowered at the Keltovari girl in the stunning dress. She studiously ignored him. Keltovari and Fendiran nobility were immediate mortal enemies. If these two had stood this close to each other on the street of any town outside the academy, they'd have attacked one another. Obviously, this was the reason no weapons were allowed here.

The Collector had said the Keltovar/Fendir war wasn't

supposed to matter in the academy, but quite clearly it did.

Brom's gaze went next to a cluster of three boys who had become particularly loud. One of them pitched an insult at a girl standing against the wall, teasing her for her ragged clothes. The other boys laughed.

The girl was obviously poor—some urchin The Collector had snatched off the streets. She was wrapped in clothing one could expect to find in a dirty alley or rubbish bin. Or perhaps stolen from someone's laundry line. She had short black hair, cropped with sheep shears, apparently, and her eyebrows were thick and black like Brom's. She was so much smaller than the rest of the group that at first Brom thought she was a child. But as he looked closer, he realized his mistake. She wasn't younger; she was just small. And those fierce, angry eyes held suffering Brom could barely imagine. In her own way, the girl was probably older than everyone in this room.

She wore a skirt that might once have been white, but was now dingy with dirt and dark smears, worn threadbare in some places and torn in others. A nicked, lopsided belt had been wrapped twice around her hips, obviously far too large for her, and three mismatched pouches dangled from it. She wore a leather bodice with puffy half-sleeves that revealed her dingy peasant shirt through the slits. The bodice looked like it might have been a garment of quality once upon a time, had probably been worn by a woman of standing when new, but it had been so scarred and used since then that it looked comical on the girl. Several rips in the leather had been stitched together with different colors of thread. Bright yellow laces pulled the hardened leather together in the front. Brom guessed the laces had been a find for the girl, a splash of color to add to her dingy garment. She was probably proud of those laces.

It was the laces the boys were mocking.

The tallest of the three had just finished his disparaging comment and was laughing with the stockiest of the three.

"I thought girls were supposed to know about clothes," Tall said.

"That's a *girl?*" Stocky said with an exaggerated disbelief.

The third kid, a skinny boy nearly as small as the girl, laughed nervously.

The urchin's hateful gaze burned, fixed on Tall, like she was about to leap on him and bite his neck.

He took an involuntary step back, then realized he had lost face in front of his little gang. He flicked a glance at them, embarrassed, then turned a deadly look on her.

"No..." Brom whispered, guessing what was about to happen. He'd watched bullies before. A challenge to authority couldn't be borne. Tall had flinched, and he needed to make up for that; he needed to show his bully friends who was really in charge. He'd need to cow the girl, by whatever means necessary.

"What are you looking at, trash?" Tall demanded, clenching his fists and stepping toward her.

Brom started toward them, knowing he was already too late, too far away. The tall boy would strike the girl down before Brom could ever get there.

But the bully pulled up short as the giant Fendiran stepped between him and the tiny girl. The bully was nearly six feet tall, much larger than Brom, but he wasn't anywhere close to the size of the giant Fendiran.

"I don't like your jokes," the Fendiran said. His deep voice cracked in the middle, jumping into a high-pitched boy's voice, then dropping back down to that deep baritone.

The bully looked up, open-mouthed, then shut his mouth with a clack. His face reddened. He glanced back at his friends, Stocky and Skinny, perhaps hoping for help. But Skinny was already backing away, pretending he hadn't been part of the trio. Stocky seemed stuck in indecision. He looked at the Fendiran, glanced at the bully, then back at the Fendiran. Stocky gave a sickly smile to his friend and shrugged, then backed away.

The bully swallowed, looked up into the unforgiving blue eyes of the Fendiran.

"I wasn't...talking to you," he managed to say, as though that would make the Fendiran go away.

"You're talking to me now," the Fendiran rumbled, and this time his voice stayed a baritone. He looked deadly.

The room had fallen silent, and all eyes were on the two, except the highborn Keltovari girl, who still focused on some unspecified spot in space as though everyone in the room didn't matter.

The bully opened his mouth, perhaps to say something snide, but he obviously thought better of it. Instead, he took a step back.

"Fine," he said lamely, trying to recover some scrap of dignity. He backed away like a wounded animal.

Fast as a squirrel, the urchin girl darted forward and drove a tiny dagger into the giant Fendiran's calf.

The Fendiran roared in pain and collapsed to one knee. He twisted, looking incredulously at the girl, who darted back, out of reach.

"Why did you stab *me*?" the Fendiran roared. Rage flashed over his face, and confusion.

She crouched, bloody dagger held tight, as though she was ready to attack again. She ignored the Fendiran's plaintive cry and pointed the red blade at the bully, who stared at her, open-mouthed.

"If you *ever* touch me," she whispered lethally, "I'll put this in your neck."

"You're crazy..." the bully said in a hushed voice, backing away.

The giant Fendiran stood up, his face rigid. Bright red blood leaked onto the back of his boot. "I was *saving* you!" he roared.

"*Saving* me?" The urchin spat, a snarl on her face. "Try to *save* me again, and I'll take your balls next time." She did a slow turn, showing the red blade to the rest of the room.

The big Fendiran looked even more confused. He didn't seem to know whether to crush the girl with his giant fists or back away. After a moment, he retreated. Brom was impressed to see that the huge Fendiran didn't limp, not even a little. The boy wasn't just enormous, he was tough.

Still staring defiantly at the room, the urchin raised her stiletto and licked the blood on one side. She let that image sink in for everyone who continued to sneak glances at her, then she licked the other side.

She *was* crazy...

Or...

She's doing this on purpose.

The tiniest person in the room had just backed down the largest, showing everyone she was deadly, unpredictable, and probably crazy.

That little street urchin had just made herself safe in a room full of hostile strangers. Who would threaten her now that she'd sent the giant of the group shuffling into a corner? She was ruthless and brilliant, a survivor.

Brom fell in love with her then, just a little bit.

The door opened suddenly, and The Collector entered. He looked around, perhaps feeling the tension, then he said, "Some of you may know that you've been gathered here until the masters have chosen your Quads. For those of you who don't know, your Quad is your life here at the academy. You will live by them, you will die by them. The three other people in your Quad will determine whether you learn your path to magic or whether you will eventually be pushed outside these walls."

The Collector surveyed the room, perhaps waiting for any questions, perhaps looking for any dissent.

There were none of either.

"After I leave, other masters will come with lists of who is to be grouped with whom. We will match you with those who fit your specific talents, who will merge with you most easily. Your Quad mates will be hand picked according to who will best encourage you to grow, and with whom will be easiest for your to bond. Understand we will do our best for you, but in the end, the bond you make will be up to you and your Quad mates. This bond will be one of the most difficult things you will achieve here at the academy."

The young people in the room looked around at each other, each no doubt wondering, as Brom did himself, who was going to be part of their Quad.

"Now..." The Collector said after a long pause to let his information sink in. "Most of you will fail. Get that through your hopeful little heads right now and you'll save yourself pain later on. Exactly half of you in this room will be sent home as one of the Forgotten. You'll leave here as a *normal* and you'll never practice magic again." He paused. "For the half of you who will remain, I wish you luck."

Murmurs broke out across the frightened young people in the room. Brom watched The Collector, realizing that Brom hadn't been the only one the man was trying to intimidate. He'd just tried to do it to the whole room.

More and more, Brom was finding a strong dislike for The Collector.

"The first Quad has already been chosen. By me. When I speak your names, follow me. I will show you to your respective dorm rooms, then I will show you the practice room where you will spend most of your time this first year." He gave a wolf's glare to the room. "Whether that time will be useful or wasted, we'll yet see."

Brom glanced around the room, wondering who would be first.

"Vale of Torlioch," The Collector said. "Brom Builder of Kyn, Royal Peronne of Gille..."

With each name, he felt a crackle of lightning in his belly, like when Cy'kett had first spoken the words: Motus, Impetu, Mentis and Anima.

"...and Princess Oriana Siffeyn Keltodanta of Keltan, come with me," The Collector finished.

Princess! Brom watched, stunned, as the daughter of King Leventius turned her indigo gaze on The Collector and glided across the floor as though she wasn't even touching the ground. Brom had known she must have been highborn, but he'd assumed a duke or baron's daughter, not the crown princess of Keltovar!

The giant Fendiran frowned when he saw the princess move, and he resolutely stumped toward The Collector. Brom hesitantly went to join them and looked over his shoulder at the remaining group. He didn't search for the fourth, because he knew who it had to be. Somehow he knew that the first three people his gaze had been drawn to would be his Quad mates.

Sure enough, the little urchin with the hidden knife flashed a hateful gaze at The Collector, then started forward.

Brom's heart sank as he contemplated those who would be in his Quad. What was The Collector thinking? He'd said he would form Quads based on how easily it would be for them to bond. But this group would never bond. A Fendiran rebel and the Keltovari princess? They'd kill each other on the first day! And the urchin looked like she'd knife them all in the night. He couldn't see even one possible path that led this group to bonding.

When the Fendiran realized who their fourth was, he pointed at the urchin. "No. Not her. She stabbed me."

"Yes," The Collector said. "We know."

Without another word, The Collector swept through the door. The princess was the first to follow, head high like she couldn't abide the stench of this room any longer. Vale hissed at Royal—actually hissed at him—then followed. The big man narrowed his blue eyes, then he followed, blood still trickling down the back of his calf.

Brom hesitated so long that the door began to close. Setting his mouth in a firm line, he rushed forward slipped through just in time.

7
BROM

Master Saewyne's high, smooth voice dipped and rose animatedly as she neared the end of her lecture in Magic Mechanics. Class time had been a wonder to Brom in the first half of the year. He'd absorbed the information rapidly, readying himself for the day when the magic would begin to come to him, the day when his Quad would bond and they'd begin progressing down their individual paths.

But after the first six months, there had been nothing. No breakthroughs. Winter had set in. Snows covered the flat fields and bare forests, and Brom felt as bleak as the landscape. Quad after Quad had bonded before them, and each delighted as their group discovered which paths they fit and began using their magic, but Brom's Quad did not.

Brom's Quad, such that it was, excelled at the theory of magic. They'd learned how to see and divide their Soulblocks into four parts faster than the other students. But unlock them? Use the magic within? No.

Early on, Brom had taken heart from that one victory.

Soulblocks were the foundation of magic use. They were what gave a Quadron the ability to work magic. Every living person had a soul, and magic could be cultivated from that soul like water diverted from a lake. The problem was that diverting magic from it could cause a leak that would drain you down to nothing. And without a soul, you died.

But because of The Four's discoveries a hundred years ago and their subsequent founding of the Champion's Academy, the soul could be divided. Instead of one reservoir for the entire soul, the soul could be compartmentalized into four Soulblocks, three of which could be emptied and used to make magic. The fourth, of course, must be kept closed and never touched. Like an undivided soul, to open the fourth Soulblock was certain death.

There were stories about those who attempted magic without the training of the Champion's Academy, without first splitting their soul into Soulblocks. The endings of those stories were alway grisly.

Of course, first-year students were restricted to using only the first of their Soulblocks, and the thick tomes they studied taught that Quadrons rarely ever used more than the first two. The more of their soul a Quadron used, the greater the toll it took upon them. Using the first Soulblock required an hour's rest to recover. Using the second Soulblock required an entire night's rest after. But to use the third Soulblock, well, it put a person down for a week or more.

Though Brom's Quad created their Soulblocks faster than anyone else, the victory had turned sour when their progress creaked to a stop shortly afterward.

His Quad had not progressed at all since then, and Brom himself had progressed only a little.

Now Springdawn had come and gone. Springmarch had marched past, and they were at the beginning of Springwatch, staring down the road to the end of the year. Barely three months from now, they'd all be expelled. It was practically a certainty. The Collector had promised that only half of them would continue on to become second students. The rest would become the Forgotten, sent home as "*normals,*" unable to ever use magic again.

When the first day of Summermarch arrived three months from now and the Tests of Passage—where Quads showed what they had learned in head-to-head competition against other Quads—were taken, only the top half would be given their writs of passage. Only sixteen Quads out of thirty-two would continue on to become second-year students.

Master Saewyne tapped on the slate board with her chalk. She had written the names of the four paths of magic, and below them the four aspects of each: internal, external, constructive, and destructive.

First-years were tasked with mastering the internal first. Second- and third-years were expected to master the external and sometimes bits of the constructive aspect. Only fourth-year students were allowed to delve into the destructive aspects of magic.

Brom watched Master Saewyne for a moment and found himself smiling without meaning to. She was like that: a collection of mysteries wrapped up in a soft grin, and you always found yourself grinning with her, even if you didn't actually want to. She wore a stylish dress, only slightly more sedate than the gem-studded courtly dresses Oriana wore. All of Master Saewyne's dresses were, of course, in shades of red, the color of a Motus. They were always long and proper...and yet they hugged her form as though she was trying to catch young eyes. She was by far the nicest of the masters at the academy, but Brom had an uneasy feeling about her, like her wide smile, her spellbinding voice and her "this-tempting-dress-isn't-supposed-to-tempt-you" attire were tools she used to pull you in just to see if she could do it. He always left her classes feeling emotionally confused.

Master Saewyne tapped the chalk on the board three times in emphasis. This always crushed the tip against the slate, sending little shards tinkling to the ground like snow. She did it every lesson, and always near the end. Brom imagined that she liked the feeling of chalk cracking beneath her fingers. Again, he felt confused, like it was a bit of violence pent up within her, a small flash of her true personality. And the only way a student could ever know to be wary of her was by noting the cruel death of the chalk stick.

"Remember that there are many levels to each aspect of each path," Master Saewyne said. "Some Quadrons strive to utilize all aspects. Some Quadrons delve deeply into only one, specializing. It can take a lifetime to truly master an aspect. And if you make it to your fourth year, you will get to choose for yourself which suits you best."

An excited murmur went through the class.

Master Saewyne gave a beatific smile, and the whole class smiled back at her. Brom found himself smiling, too, though he didn't really want to.

"Dismissed," she said, and the students all stood up, feet shuffling, desks squeaking against the floor.

Brom gave a quick look over his shoulder for his so-called Quad mates. Oriana, as usual, sat in the first row all the way to the left. Royal was always in the second or third row in the very middle, like some mountain anchoring the center of the class. And Vale always skulked in the back. His Quad mates stayed as far away from each other as they could get.

Brom sighed, got up, and left the class with the mass of other students, not waiting for the three that were supposed to be his "best friends."

He tried to put down his disappointment, but he just couldn't. Not anymore. It was a weight that hung around his neck from the moment he woke to the moment he went to sleep. His dreams had become hopeless nightmares where he chased his Quad mates down long, dark hallways but could never catch them.

Brom had come to the Champion's Academy with a dream, and it lay in ruins around him. He'd wanted to be a Quadron more than anything. He'd left his parents behind, left Myan behind, left the only home he'd ever known before coming to join this colossal disappointment. He'd come prepared to do anything he could. He had intended to work hard, study hard, to do more than anyone else in the entire school. But fate was cruel, because it had ensured his destiny was failure. Brom's future lay in the hands of three angry idiots who refused to bond. Oriana, Royal, and Vale were barely capable of being civil to one another. How were they going to lean on each other long enough to work magic?

After a year of gut-clenching training, the result for Brom's Quad was a disaster. They were so far behind every other Quad at this point that, even if they could bond today, this very day, they'd never catch up.

Brom walked solemnly up the wide hallway of Westfall Dormitory toward the door of the practice room reserved for their Quad. The vaulted ceilings rose three stories over his head, ringing by balconies on the second and third floors that overlooked the foyer. The first-year practice rooms filled the ground floor, in addition to some first-year classrooms and the eating hall, called the Floating Room. The second and third stories above were all dormitory rooms.

He could practically feel the leaden footsteps of his three Quad mates a hundred feet behind him. The entire northern hall on the ground floor of the dormitory held practice rooms for all the first-years. Brom had often seen other Quads exiting their practice room at the end of the day clapping each other on the back and laughing after some new accomplishment. That never happened for Brom's Quad.

They'd done this every day and only met with failure. He had no hope that today was going to be different.

Royal, with his long strides, passed Brom up before he reached the door. Royal had continued to bulk out as the months had passed, and he put his huge mitt on the door and opened it. He went through, left it wide open for the others. That was about as much courtesy as any of them showed each other.

Brom entered the room for another disappointing day of attempting skills they could not master.

The practice room was a marble square with high ceilings and four stations to help a student hone their Quadron skills. Near one wall sat a giant pyramid of steel with a ring welded to it. Near another, four people sat unmoving. Draped in gray robes and wearing masks that shielded even their eyes, they were called The Invisible Ones, and their sole purpose was to be living practice puppets for Motus and Mentis students.

An elaborate mechanism of gears, spars, blades, and suspended buckets of poison loomed against the third wall. The last wall, across from the door and the Invisible Ones, had eight pedestals with objects whose purpose Brom didn't understand: A cask spilling over with jewels. An empty glass pitcher. A large clay pot with a small tree growing out of it. A small pool of water. A lump of mud that never seemed to dry out. A dagger carved from Lyanwood. A live goat in a pen. And a beautifully made, but unadorned, steel sword.

Oriana's aloof gaze passed over the room and her Quad mates, no doubt trying to decide at what she'd like to fail today. In the beginning, she had flung out orders out at them, suggestions about how they might bond. At first, they'd ignored her. Then, as Brom had become desperate, he'd tried some of her suggestions. Even Vale had joined in for a time, though Royal refused to take orders from the princess of Keltovar. But when Oriana's mandates hadn't worked, Brom had gone back to ignoring her. And when Oriana had realized they were all studiously ignoring her, she'd stopped telling them what to do. She had stopped speaking to them entirely about two months ago.

Royal was the same, though he didn't benefit from Oriana's inscrutable mask. His frustration and anger glowed around him like a nimbus of fire.

He grunted a desultory greeting to Brom every morning as if he were checking it off a list of required politeness. Brom gave a half-nod and a little wave. Royal gave a greeting to Vale, though she never answered him back, only stared at him like she was going to put another dagger in him. For his part, Royal never let her get too close—none of them did. They all treated her like a rabid dog that might bite at any moment.

Royal never gave a *good morning* to Oriana, only glared at her. He did that every chance he got, which was essentially a thousand times a day. On that first day, they'd all learned that Oriana was none other than King Leventius's daughter and the heir to the Keltovari throne. From that moment forward, Royal had embarked on a mission to exude as much hate toward her as he could. And as time slipped painfully forward day by day, their failures as a Quad only seemed to affirm for Royal that Oriana was the cause of everything wrong in his life, at the academy, and in the two kingdoms at large.

Vale hated everyone equally, it seemed. Her eyes constantly flicked from person to person, keeping track of who was within striking distance, he supposed.

Brom was heartsick. This was supposed to be his new family. The more time Brom spent at the academy, the more he felt his soul dying. His dreams were right in front of him, held close enough that he could touch them with his fingertips, but never fully grasp them.

In the beginning, he had made a few attempts to bring the Quad together. Now he just stayed away from them as much as he could. The terrible irony was that, when it came to the study of magic theory, every one of Brom's Quad excelled. In the classroom, even Vale thrived, and he suspected she hadn't even known how to read when she'd arrived. They all understood the basic principles of magic, but none of them could put it to use in the practice room.

None except Brom. During these past few months, he'd had some limited success with his own magic, without any help from the Quad. It was a pitiful wisp of the great power he could feel within him, but better than nothing. Somehow, he'd been able to access some of his first Soulblock, a mere trickle, he was sure, compared to what he might gain with a fully functioning Quad.

A few weeks ago, Brom had actually discovered his path to magic. He was the Anima. While practicing on his own, far away from the pall of hate in the practice room, he'd suddenly picked up the wisps of a person's soul.

It hadn't come in words. It had flowed to him in pictures, like memories in his mind that weren't his own, memories of pivotal moments. Sometimes it came as colors, or even rarely as scents. Mostly, though, it was just an...understanding, like feeling the wind on his face, feeling its desire to push, to blow. It enabled Brom to instinctively know what a person wanted, which direction they were inclined to go and, in two rare cases so far, what a person might do in the next few moments.

Strangely, Brom couldn't use this power on his Quad mates.

He'd tried. While he could read the souls of other students he had passed on the paths or the lawns—or sometimes even the masters—Vale, Royal, and Oriana remained locked to him.

He hadn't told his Quad mates about his breakthrough. He thought maybe he should, but then he'd see how horrible they were to each other. He didn't want to share this fledgling power with them. Just looking at them made him clench his teeth.

So he didn't practice here. He practiced anywhere except with these people in this room of failure.

Brom watched his Quad mates as they flailed at the various stations in the practice room. He watched Vale move over to The Invisible Ones to try her hand at manipulating their emotions.

Royal moved to the pyramid of steel and put his huge hands around the ring, obviously attempting to lift it again. It was pretty obvious that, of all of them, Royal was likely their Impetu. And based on what Brom had read this year, Royal should have been able to lift that pyramid six months ago. But he was going to fail. Again. This Quad wasn't going anywhere. Brom was on his own.

He felt the power of his Soulblocks, crackling like lightning in a box, longing to be used.

He got up and left the room. He wasn't supposed to do that. The masters had told him that the Quad was to attend classes together and practice together until they made their bond.

Ha.

Not one of them looked up when he left, though he was sure all of them saw. He'd been doing it every day for a week. Nobody called out. Nobody tried to stop him. Nobody cared.

He emerged into the hallway, exited Westfall Dormitory and headed for Quadron Garden, where students not actively practicing went to gather, mostly second-, third- and fourth-years who weren't required to spend their afternoons in the practice rooms. Brom was pretty sure some students, like him, used their powers on unsuspecting others. It was against the rules, of course, but Brom's Quad was already on the path to expulsion. The masters didn't care about his success, so he didn't care about their rules.

He opened his first Soulblock and let the magic crackle through him.

Quadron Garden was full of a couple dozen students. Most were just relaxing, lying on the grass looking at the sky, or sitting against trees. A few were playing the sports introduced to keep students fit. Some sat at the tables, reading from or writing in their journals. Library books weren't allowed out of doors, of course, but students could jot down notes from any and all things they read. Everyone carried a personal journal of class notes, experiences and snippets from textbooks.

Brom cleared his mind and began to push the lightning in his body into a tunnel of focus. He closed his eyes and let his body take over the task of walking as he neared the group of students. Slowly, little glowing impressions appeared in his mind. Brom couldn't see the trees, rocks, benches or tables with his eyes closed, but every single person in the garden became a multicolored, glowing figure, like embers in a fire. He didn't quite *see* them, but the impressions of their souls translated to light, and each had its own combination of colors.

He caught a brief image of a female student having a fantasy about a boy she liked. Her desires were fierce and red with edges of pink. Brom smiled. The next student was a blast of purple, his soul large because he was running, and he loved athletics. The next was blue and green, mixing together like multicolored flames in a fire and...

Brom stopped walking as he saw an image of himself within the soul of the girl right in front of him. She was thinking about him! And she was...looking at his soul...

He felt her intentions, similar to his own. She liked people, was curious what they looked like on the inside. And she loved the rush of breaking rules, doing what the masters had forbidden, wondering if she would get caught.

Suddenly, he felt her delight. She'd caught Brom doing exactly what she was doing. They stayed like that for a moment, viewing each others' desires and intentions in that wispy realm of magic.

Brom blinked, opened his eyes, and looked to his right. Sitting against a tree was a lanky Keltovari girl with honey-colored hair. Only Keltovari nobility had light-colored hair, which hinted at her parentage. But her eyes were black, which meant she was likely bastard born. She blinked against the sunlight and smiled at him. She was about twenty feet away and she spoke softly.

"Come over here," her lips said, though he didn't hear her words. Over the distance, the noise of the Garden, and the slight breeze that ruffled his hair, he didn't hear the words at all, but he still knew what she wanted, as though her soul had communicated to him her desires without words at all.

He went to her. She squinted up at him. He moved to the block the sun and cast a courteous shadow over her.

"Thank you," she said.

"You're..."

"Doing what you're doing," she finished for him. "So... You're a fellow Anima."

"I don't... I haven't chosen yet, so I don't know."

She laughed. "How can you use Anima magic if you don't know?"

"I'm not..." He trailed off, embarrassed to tell her that his Quad was failing and that none of them had been able to choose a path yet. "I can't really do much at all. I'm..."

"Oh!" she said, as though something had just occurred to her. "You're with Quad Princess, aren't you? The one that hasn't formed yet."

Great. They had a reputation.

Brom glanced at his boots, but the girl didn't mock him. She sat up straight, seemingly interested. "So let me sort this out. You haven't bonded with your Quad, but you're using Anima magic? Really? That's...wow. It's not supposed to be possible. How did you even do that?"

"I just...do it."

"You not supposed to be able to do that, though. You know that, right?"

He shrugged. "I'm not much for rules. Since my Quad is floundering, I thought I'd try doing something without them. They're just..." he trailed off.

She chuckled. "You misunderstood me. I didn't mean it was against the *rules*; I meant it's impossible," she said. "No one can work magic without bonding to a Quad. It's impossible. The Quad gives everyone a boost that enables them to work magic for the first time. But you do it once, and you can do it on your own after."

"Boost?"

"It's so cute that you don't know what that is. First-year babies..." She rolled her eyes in mock exasperation, then smiled again. "You know that bonding with your Quad doubles your power, right? It was that boost that flipped open my first Soulblock. It was the only way I could even start doing what you're doing."

"I read that. But nothing is doubling with my Quad. We're all just...stuck."

"And yet you're doing magic all alone. I just... Wow."

Brom thought the girl might be teasing him to get a rise from one of the failures of Quad Princess. But her soul seemed calm and open. Her basic nature indicated she was curious, straightforward, and...lusty.

"I'm Caila." She stood up, dusted off her breeches, and stuck out her hand.

He shook it. "Brom." A little jolt passed between them at the touch. They grinned together.

"So you're a rule-breaker?" she said, like it was a naughty secret. "Using magic on people you're not supposed to be using magic on?" She nodded her head at the other students in Quadron Garden."

Her attraction for him swelled inside her soul like a warm red light. His heart began beating faster.

Caila was a flirt. He thought of Myan back in Kyn, and he was suddenly intensely curious what it would be like to kiss Caila.

He cleared his throat. "Some rules don't serve a purpose," he said.

She smiled, and her teeth were white and straight. "I couldn't have said it better myself. Did you know that students are not supposed to...you know...fraternize with each other?" She raised an eyebrow.

He felt a flush creep into his face.

She laughed, and his gaze strayed to her body. She was long and lean, and just a little taller than him. She was obviously Keltovari, but he could easily picture her spending her days running through the thick southern forests and jungles like a Fendiran warrior druid. She crossed her arms beneath her breasts and grinned at him. "Best thing about being an Anima," she said. "You can't hide your nature from me."

"And?"

"And we're two of a kind."

"Two?"

"Maybe one, if we work at it." She winked. "Would you like to break some rules?"

The unabashed desire and mischief in her soul made him laugh, and he fell in love with her a little just then. After the confidence-shriveling failures of being with his Quad, the idea of spending time with this lively, flirty Caila seemed heavenly. "I would," he said.

"Let's." She took his arm and began running across the grass. He stumbled along behind, laughing.

8

BROM

Brom snuck across the campus, keeping close to the river and out of sight. The sloped banks were over six feet tall in most places, and it was thick with willows and oak trees, the perfect place to travel from one side of the school to the other without being seen. Caila had showed him this trick.

They'd been lovers for several heady weeks, but Caila had soon moved on. She was more interested in finding new students to corrupt than staying with one person. Brom had moped about her for two days before he realized he was being silly. Caila had never promised him fidelity. She'd promised him rule-breaking and adventure. And she had delivered, introducing him to an entire campus of beautiful mischief.

Caila had opened doors to a way of thinking Brom couldn't have imagined before. She scoffed at duty, laughed at guilt. She loved what was in front of her and she didn't seem to care what anyone else thought about it. She was like a rock skipping across water, somehow defying what seemed to drag so many others down. He'd always love her just a little for that, for her wild nature, and for stopping long enough to take him under her wing.

There was a banquet of pleasures all around, in every moment, and these had blessedly taken Brom's attention away from his Quad's dismal failures. He only spent time with his angry Quad when he had to, and only for long enough to allay suspicion if the masters happened to look his way.

So, since Caila had flitted on from her relationship with Brom, he'd decided to wreak a bit of corruption himself, and he found he was rather good at it. He'd been breaking the rules of "fraternization" for almost a month. Gods! It fed his soul. It was the only thing he looked forward to. His passion for his morning classes remained, and he tried to match up what he learned with his personal magical practice.

But his afternoon sessions in the official practice room, well... He dutifully spent the required hours with his miserable Quad, but he barely cared about them anymore. Brom lived for the nights when he could break free and use his meager Anima skills to find other interesting souls and play with them.

He jumped a log and continued jogging quietly along the rushing river. He was close enough to the water that the ground was spongey with moss and river grass, but not so close that he made squishy sounds.

"Let your feet be silent," Caila had told him when she pointed out her secret silent thoroughfare across the campus.

An odd, muffled sound up ahead caused Brom to stop in his tracks. He shrank against the trunk of a tree, blending with its silhouette.

Who would be out here? Anyone spending time by the river at this time of night was breaking curfew, and Brom wondered if he was about to stumble across Caila with one of her new lovers.

The notion dissolved as he recognized the sound. That was sobbing. A woman was crying. The fronds of a giant willow tree obscured her, but it would only take another couple of steps to part the veil and find out who it was.

He considered clambering up the slope to the Quadron Garden. His giant marble dormitory was just a quick jog away. He could vanish without the crier ever knowing he'd been here. He almost did. He really ought to leave the poor person to their private distress. They had obviously come out here to hide, to be away from people.

But...

Brom had never seen into a person's soul when they were crying, and he suddenly had to know what it looked like. The woman, whoever she was, would never know Brom had been here. He could 'touch' her without ever seeing her. He opened his first Soulblock, and the magic crackled into him. With his mind, he reached out and...

There was no one there. No one and nothing.

He shook his head, closed his eyes and reached out again more carefully, but no... Nothing. To Brom's ears, some girl was crying just a few scant feet beyond that veil of willow branches. But to Brom's Anima vision, the little hollow beneath the trees was empty.

A chill thrilled up his spine as he suddenly realized what that meant.

The unseen crier had to be one of his Quad. Only Royal, Oriana, and Vale were blocked to his newfound sight.

The crying was unquestionably female, which meant it had to be the emotionally volatile Vale. Oriana wouldn't cry. He'd bet she'd never cried even when she was a child. He'd bet the ice princess didn't even *have* tears.

Brom had maintained a cautious curiosity about Vale since he'd first met her. Suddenly, he felt a swift sympathy for the street urchin. She was vicious and hateful, but her life couldn't have been easy before the academy. This lucky break, the chance to become a Quadron, must be the greatest opportunity she'd ever known, a singular chance to change her life. And she was failing because their Quad was failing. They all knew they were just marking time until their inevitable expulsion at the end of the year.

Brom had been so wrapped up in his own disappointment, it never occurred to him that it must be twice as difficult for Vale. If Brom was ejected from the academy, he had a place to go. He had a home, a family. So did Royal and Oriana. Royal would go back to Fendir and no doubt continue their war. Oriana would return to her palace. But if Vale failed, there was nothing waiting for her except poverty and an early death.

Brom swallowed and pushed aside the long branches of the enormous willow tree—

—and stood in stunned silence.

Princess Oriana sat next to the river, hugging her shins, forehead against her knees...

And she was crying.

Her expensive slippers pressed into the mud at the river's edge as water rushed over her toes. The hem of her ridiculously ornate dress flowed downstream, rippling and twisting in the current. Her slender back shuddered with sobs.

He couldn't breathe. Seeing the ice princess of Keltovar crying was like seeing a fish climbing a tree. He didn't know how to react. To cry she'd have to feel pain. To feel pain she'd have to *feel*, to have warm blood pumping through her veins.

Brom hadn't made any sound, but Oriana caught the movement of the willow fronds. She raised her head elegantly, like she did everything, and her tear-stained eyes focused on him.

He couldn't glimpse the colors of her soul, but her face told her anguish plainly for one raw moment. Then she stopped crying. Her face went stony and she looked as haughty as ever.

"Have you come to watch, then?" she asked, her voice rough. "It's fine entertainment. The princess in shambles." She flicked a tear from her eyes with the edge of her finger.

"I didn't...come here for you," he said.

"I see." She glanced up the river from where he'd come, then turned her gaze back to the water rushing over her feet. "How was your latest conquest?"

He swallowed. She knew. She knew he'd been sneaking out of the dormitory, breaking rules.

"You...knew?" he asked.

"Please."

"Why didn't you...tell someone?" One word from her to the masters, and it was an immediate punishment. They might have even yanked him from the Quad. "You could have...replaced me," he said. "It might have increased your chances of becoming a Quadron."

"You are my Quad mate," she said firmly.

"But you hate me."

"Do I?" she replied.

But she did. Of course she did. She had said so with every withering glance, every frosty silence. If she'd had the chance to hurt him—or any of her Quad mates—he'd have assumed she'd take it.

But clearly she hadn't. And the way she'd said he was her Quad mate, so protectively...

Seeing her now, he questioned everything he thought he knew about Princess Oriana.

He stepped through the willow fronds and let them fall behind him. The river's rushing noise filled the sheltered little cove, as did the smell of moving water. He sat down next to her, put his boots in the mud by her slippered feet and mirrored her pose, wrapping his arms around his shins.

"Well, thank you for that," he said softly. "For not telling anyone."

"I only postpone the inevitable," she said. "They shall rid themselves of our disastrous little Quad soon enough."

They sat for a time. With every moment that passed, the silence felt more strained. Brom sought desperately for something to say, but nothing came.

Finally, he cleared his throat to ask the only question he could think of.

"Why were you crying?" he asked.

At first, he thought she wasn't going to answer, then she said, "My mother died yesterday."

For a second, he couldn't breathe. "Oriana, I'm... I'm sorry."

She gave him a sidelong glance. After a long moment, she looked back at the water. "Thank you."

"I... How did it...?" he began, then stopped. Silence was better than an invasive question. Wasn't it? He suddenly thought of his own mother. A swift pang of homesickness hit him.

"The loss of a queen. A stab at the heart of the monarchy," she said. A self-mocking little smile twisted her lips. "You could sell the information to Royal no doubt. He would pay to know it." She looked up, lips tight, indigo eyes flaring as she watched for his reaction.

Brom was still for a moment, then he cleared his throat.

"As if Fendirans have money," he said.

Her fierceness softened into puzzlement, and then she laughed. It was a little laugh, there and gone, but he'd never heard her laugh before. He'd never even seen her smile before. "I didn't know you were funny," she murmured.

"I didn't know you...cried."

"I don't," she said, flicking away another tear.

He wasn't sure if she was joking, too. He thought about replying, but then too much time had passed, and he simply listened to the rushing of the river. It was so loud he could barely hear the riot of crickets beyond the slope.

"You know..." She broke the silence. "You're the only one of us who doesn't hate the others. Though you should. We have ruined your chances of becoming a Quadron."

"Eh," he said, as though he didn't care. "Fuck it."

"You are irreverent in all things," she said under her breath, an edge to her tone. "Perhaps failure is okay for you. But I have never failed so utterly at anything in my life."

Her words stung, and suddenly the Oriana he knew had returned. The tears had vanished. Her face had become a stony mask, and her true colors were on display. Judgment. Arrogance. Saying that it was okay for Brom to fail. He must be used to it, after all. But not for her.

"Perhaps it's time you get used to it," he shot back.

"Perhaps," she said, as though she didn't even notice the sting, as though his opinion couldn't matter any less.

"You think I'm giving up?" he blurted. "Is that what you think?" He wanted to rage at her, to tell her that he'd been working magic for weeks without her or any of the rest of them. And what had she been doing? Nothing. So high and mighty and impotent.

She looked over at him, and her indigo eyes seemed so large. He thought she might fling some lashing retort, but she didn't. Instead, she awkwardly scooted closer in the moss and mud and leaned into him. He froze like a rabbit.

He couldn't recall Oriana ever touching anyone. Not another student or an instructor. She didn't even seem to touch the floor when she walked.

Reflexively, he thought about saying something snide like, "Am I supposed to kiss you now?"

Instead, hesitantly, he reached out and put his arm around her. He expected her to violently shrug him off. Or even claw at his eyes.

Instead, she rested her head on his shoulder.

"Perhaps we've been doing this all wrong," she said. Her slender arms wrapped around his waist, and she hugged him like she needed him, like she was so desperate to hold someone that even one of her horrible Quad mates would do. She nuzzled her face into his neck.

It was like a violent Fendiran jungle cat had docilely crawled into his lap. He froze. She didn't smell like danger, though, but instead of new fabric and rain and flowers. Her body was warm. This was bizarre, like he'd stepped into a dream. He'd never seen Oriana falter, never seen her weak. For the first time since he'd met her in the initial gathering room and she'd lashed him with a glare, he felt compassion for her. The ice princess wasn't made of ice after all. He didn't know what to do.

But yes. Yes, he did. Of course he did.

"It's all right," he said. He tightened his arms around her, and then spontaneously kissed the top of her head. Not like a lover. Not like he'd kissed other women at the academy. But like a friend.

Suddenly, like a rising sun, the colors of her soul flared in his Anima sight. She was a cool blue, tinged in pink and yellow, and she was every inch as controlled as she seemed, driven by a need for strength.

The goals of her life opened to him.

Oriana's life belonged to her kingdom, not to her. That was how she saw herself, at least. Any attempt to take what she wanted for herself was beneath her. She was heir to the Keltovari throne, and she had an obligation to lead her people, no matter what came. She was here at the academy for that purpose and that purpose alone.

The futures she saw for herself rolled out before him. She must marry. She must produce heirs. She was betrothed to a powerful Keltovari duke's son, and the marriage was set for the moment she graduated from the Champion's Academy. He felt her distaste for the betrothal and, at the same time, her iron determination to follow through.

Unexpectedly, Brom dove even further inside her. He hadn't thought there was further to go, but he fell into Oriana like a bottomless well. He felt the power of his magic expand. He not only saw her intentions but her hopes. And he saw a secret so personal that no one else in the world knew it.

Oriana's heart had already been captured, and not by her betrothed. She had a lover. A woman with dark brown hair, freckles, and mischievous eyes. A woman surrounded by horses.

Brom couldn't see the woman's name. Anima magic didn't seem to work that way, with words and names and concrete things that language could define. There were only impressions, images of what the person would do or hoped to do.

Brom saw the woman as Oriana saw her. He saw the woman as she turned, her dark hair flinging out in a halo, her profile outlined by the setting sun. He saw the woman crying. The woman laughing. He felt the future that Oriana wished to have with this woman, and he felt Oriana's certainty that it could never be.

He drew a shuddering breath and pulled his Anima sight out of Oriana. He felt like a voyeur seeing her hidden dreams. But when he tried to sever his connection to her like he'd done with so many people these past weeks, it didn't work. He surfaced from her deep places, but he couldn't pull away. It was like he'd hugged her, but when he tried to release her, his hand couldn't let her go.

Exultation burst within him as he realized what this meant. This wasn't just some person on Quadron Garden. This was a Quad mate. His increase in power, the dive into her hopes and dreams. He had broken through their barrier.

Brom had just bonded with Oriana.

9
ORIANA

Oriana sat in the mud at the edge of the river. Grief raked through her like claws. Mother's bloody cough had begun the night Oriana had accepted The Collector's offer to attend the Champions Academy. She'd known it would kill Mother, probably within the year, but nevertheless the horror of it had slammed into her hard when she'd received the message tonight.

She hadn't been fast enough. She'd come to this academy to cure the Bloodbane—the disease ripping through the highborns of Keltovar—, and her only hope was magic. And Oriana wasn't any closer to becoming a Quadron. She could feel the magic in this place, could feel it locked within herself, but she couldn't get her hands on it.

Her grief had driven her from her dormitory tonight. She'd run blindly until the river had stopped her. Here, she'd fallen to her knees, then curled up to sob by the water.

She had never felt so helpless as she did now. She thought she'd come here to gain power, but instead this place had stripped her power from her. She wasn't really even a princess here. She was just a girl trying to do the impossible—

The willow fronds moved to her left, and Oriana jolted upright.

Her Quad mate, Brom, materialized from the darkness like a wraith.

She froze. With effort, she gulped down her tears. Anger bloomed in her, giving her the strength to lock her grief behind an iron door reinforced with years of training. She wasn't supposed to appear this way, not in front of people.

And aside from the brawny Fendiran, Brom was the last person in the world she wanted to see her weakness. Brom cared for nothing. He'd abandoned his studies. He'd fled his own Quad. He recklessly dared expulsion to bed equally reckless girls.

Father had told her of men like him, arrogant men who believed they were invincible. They pushed their luck until it ran out. And then they always looked bewildered when the axe fell, never admitting they themselves had called the headsman. Oriana almost stood up and left.

But then she heard Father's voice in her head.

What others see as disaster, a leader must see as opportunity.

She held herself still. This might be such a moment. A tiny voice in the back of her mind said that somewhere in this horrible mess lay the key to bonding with Brom. She couldn't see it, not yet. But if she could just find it and take control of it, perhaps this was the opportunity she needed.

The end of the year was only weeks away, and if Oriana didn't do something, her entire Quad would be expelled. She wouldn't bring magic back to Keltan, and the Bloodbane would prevail.

If any of them had a chance to become a Quadron, her Quad mates had to bond, and they had given up on trying. If they had only listened to her, she could have knit them together.

Except that her Quad mates detested her. Her very existence was offensive to them. Royal hated her because she was Keltovari. Vale hated her because of her station.

And they hated each other only slightly less. In the end, they'd walled themselves off. Brom didn't seem to care about becoming a Quadron anymore, only about how many skirts he could raise.

The Fendiran had wrapped himself in his righteousness,

refusing to bow to Oriana's suggestions, no doubt swearing to himself that he would rather die than help her, even if it meant failing to become a Quadron himself.

And Vale... Well, Vale just wanted to kill them all, it seemed. The more their Quad spun toward certain expulsion, the more worried Oriana became about Vale's undisguised malevolence. Oriana had actually begun locking her door at night, not knowing if Vale would come calling with a knife, intent on exacting some bloody revenge for her ruined chances.

And Oriana... Well... She had tried everything she could to bond with her Quad. And she had tried everything she could to learn magic on her own. She had started with her natural strength: research. She'd absorbed all of the first-year texts, the second-year texts, and even some of the third-year texts. But there was only so much she could understand without actually practicing magic.

And for that, she needed the others.

She had tried commanding the Quad to work together, but that had been a disaster. Royal, eternally suspicious of her, had ignored her. Vale had hissed at her.

Oriana had been stunned to learn that the skills she'd been taught didn't work in every situation. They were predicated upon power and authority, and she had no authority here. The academy brought all students to the same level, whether they were street urchins or princesses.

She'd finally abandoned trying to connect with them and tried to discover which path was hers on her own, starting with Mentis, which seemed the most likely. She'd tried every mental exercise on the Invisible Ones. Nothing worked.

Frustrated, she'd turned to Motus, projecting her emotions. That had been just as useless. She'd tried to dive into their souls, as an Anima would. She got nowhere.

She'd even tried to focus her strength and lift Royal's stupid steel pyramid. But there was simply no way around the necessity of the bond. She'd circled the dilemma for months. It was a question of breaking down the barriers between herself and her Quad mates.

She couldn't fathom breaking down Royal's barrier, and Vale's was just as hopeless.

But Brom, on the other hand...

He had no deep-seated hatred for her. His dislike was situational, based only upon their interaction of her trying to lead him and him refusing. Despite his uncaring attitude, he might be the one Quad mate with which she might form a bond.

The only question was: how to achieve it? What command could she give him that would break him open, make him vulnerable, make him...

No. Wait. Maybe that was backward. She'd tried all that, after all. Perhaps it wasn't about breaking down *his* barriers, but about breaking down her own?

The realization was excruciating. What if, rather than making them cooperate, she must make herself vulnerable? What if she must open herself up and hope they chose to bond with her?

It sent a shiver up her spine.

Hope...

Hope was a horrible idea. She'd have no way to control the outcome. Not only that, but making herself vulnerable left her open to attack. She could hear Father speaking.

A ruler who relies on hope is lost. You must have a plan.

But she'd followed her plan. She'd followed all the plans, and each of them had led to a dead end.

This, however, was new. Perhaps this was what the masters had intended all along. She must step outside of herself, choose to become like those to which she desired a bond. To become, in Brom's case, like a commoner.

What did residents of Kyn do? She imagined it. They thumped each others' backs, hugged and laughed and talked about their problems. Oriana had never done that. Moreover, Father had told her she could not respond as others did. Her subjects expected her to be more, to project perfection.

So when Brom came near, sat down next to her, she tried to joke with him. It felt awkward, and she was horrible at it. But surprisingly, he responded, joking back.

Her spirits lifted. They were connecting. It was the closest she'd come to making a bond.

Then he downplayed the importance of becoming Quadron. He

said "Fuck it," and she rebuked him.

If he didn't care about becoming a Quadron, why was he even here? Why would he put himself through this torture? It cast her own dedication—her need—in the mud, as though it didn't matter. Becoming a Quadron, for her, mattered more than anything.

Failure reared its head again as Brom closed off, tossing a verbal stab at her. He shrunk away from her, readying to stand up, and she realized she had made a misstep. In this, as with her previous attempts to bond, it didn't seem to matter that she was right. It only mattered if they…somehow drew closer.

As long as this rule-breaking boy saw her as trying to command him, he'd never bond with her.

Desperately, she leaned into him.

He went stiff. She thought he might stand up anyway, but instead he relaxed.

Slowly, his arm encircled her. He was tentative at first, but then more sure, pulling her tight. He leaned down and kissed the top of her head. She went stiff...then caught herself and tried to relax.

There. She was snuggling with a boy who cared for nothing and no one. Surely that was enough to crack open her first Soulblock.

She waited for it to open, to reveal her path to magic. But it didn't. No magic came spilling forth. No bond formed.

Her heart beat faster. This insidious magic demanded more. She shrugged off the notion that she was failing again. Did she think it was going to be easy? No. She could control this outcome; she simply had to give more. She couldn't just hug Brom and expect lightning to fill her. She must deliver something he wouldn't expect, something powerful.

Something private.

"I want to tell you something," she said hesitantly, and she found it was suddenly hard to breathe. She swallowed, and her scalp itched. "A…secret. Something no one else knows about me."

"Oh?" he said, and he got quiet.

In that torturous calm, she hesitated again. This admission would betray the one person she loved the most. Then she thought of the oath she'd made when she'd left Keltan with The Collector.

My life does not belong to me, she had sworn to herself. *My life belongs to my people.*

She must protect them no matter what. Even if it cost her what she held most dear.

"I'm...in love..." she said. Her throat constricted, choking off the words. "I have a lover. No one knows about her. No one knows that I... That she..."

It felt like her heart was a piece of paper and she was slowly tearing it in half. Ayvra was full of life and passion. She was glorious and innocent. She and Oriana had discovered each other, held hands, shared secrets. They had even kissed a number of times. It had been a stolen season of happiness.

But the truth was, it could never be. Such a thing was utterly forbidden for a princess betrothed to another. She had duties of marriage and childbearing. If Father found out, he'd put Ayvra to death. In Father's eyes, she could only ever be a threat to the throne.

Oriana was so tense it felt like her own fist was clenched around her entire body, and if she could just clench hard enough, she'd hold herself together. She'd find the right path and steer this awkward pairing to the required bond.

But she couldn't speak, couldn't breathe. She had given her most personal secret to this reckless builder's boy who had no allegiance to anything, least of all Oriana. Even if he didn't decide to intentionally hurt her, he would surely hurt her through his negligence, letting this secret slip while bragging to another boy or exchanging pillow talk with one of his lovers.

Surely, this vulnerability, so raw and reckless, would fulfill the needs of the magic. Surely this would precipitate the bond.

But Brom just sat there, silent for a long while. "Okay," he finally said, without any surprise. He evinced no reaction, neither interest nor condemnation. It was like he'd already known.

And still, her Soulblock didn't open. No magic came.

Despair welled up within her. She'd just told him what she'd never told anyone, something that could kill Ayvra...

And it hadn't worked.

"Gods…" The exclamation escaped her lips, unbidden. She had done everything, and yet still no magic. Perhaps The Collector had been wrong. Perhaps Oriana wasn't meant to be here.

She saw Uncle's black lacquered coffin in her mind's eye, draped in purple. She saw Mother lifting her chin, eyes flashing in denial as she pocketed the white handkerchief with the blood on it.

And then, unbidden, the specter she'd feared the most rose in her mind: an image of Father sitting upon his throne, blood in his beard as he tried to lead a kingdom.

Her grip on herself faltered. She couldn't see any way to control this, to make this bond happen. Despair swelled within her like water crashing toward the top of a dam. Uncle's death. Mother's death. The specter of the Bloodbane.

It was too much. Kelto, she fought to hold onto it, but she couldn't. Her emotion spilled over.

Her control shattered.

"We're dying," she blurted helplessly, and the horrible truth spilled out. "It's killing us. All of us, and I'm not strong enough to stop it."

"You mean your mother?" Brom said, his body shifting.

"My mother. My father. All the highborns of Keltovar," she whispered. Her mind screamed at her to stop speaking. This was the secret no one could know. This wouldn't just destroy Oriana's heart, not just one beloved person.

This secret could take down her entire kingdom.

The words stopped coming as Oriana fought to breathe. Finally, she sucked in a deep breath, and she sobbed, openly and shamefully right in front of Brom.

"It's why I'm here," she said through her sobs. "It's is the only reason. I came to find magic…to find a cure."

She sobbed so hard it hurt, held him so tightly that something broke inside her. It felt like a rib cracking, a swift pain. A hot, wet guilt flooded through her.

She was lost. All she wanted to do was die. There was no coming back from this. Whatever she had been before—princess, daughter, ruler—she was nothing now. She'd told this lowborn boy how to destroy Keltovar. She had given up everything. For nothing.

She pulled away from him, curled into a ball on the mud of the bank. She couldn't stand to touch him anymore, couldn't stand to even be inside her own skin. Every tear this builder's boy saw was a new stripe of humiliation, a new mark of failure.

I've failed. And in my desperation, I've lost everything. I betrayed my people. I've done everything I swore not to do.

Brom broke the silence.

"...trying to bond with me?" he asked. *"The tears and the confessions. Wow."*

Her guilt turned then, twisting and rising up like a horrible snake, transforming into rage. Brom's irreverent musings made her hate him. She turned a venomous glare on him, ready to unleash a torrent of vituperation, ready to destroy him as she had just destroyed herself.

But her indrawn breath hung there, and her anger withered.

Brom's lips weren't moving.

"When she told me about her lover, it was like she was forcing herself to stand still while someone slapped her. But... Not the Bloodbane. I don't think she meant to say that at all. She's letting loose...everything. She's doing everything she can to make a bond with me. Gods...the strength of her! The courage. I never knew..."

Those weren't his words. Those were his *thoughts*!

Elation flooded through her. His thoughts continued to tumble into her.

"I have to help somehow, but I feel like if I even move, she's going to claw my eyes out."

That warm, wet feeling inside Oriana wasn't guilt, it was magic! The 'crack' hadn't been a rib. It had been her first Soulblock opening!

She focused her attention on it, and the wet feeling transformed into lightning, sparking and crackling. This was the same thrill she'd felt when The Collector had appeared in Keltan in that rainstorm a year ago, except a hundred times stronger.

"I did it," she said breathlessly. "I'm reading your thoughts."

"What?" he asked, surprised. *"She's the Mentis..."* His thoughts tumbled into her. *"Gods, she's the Mentis!"*

"Yes," she tried to think back to him. "*I am our—"*

"I broke my barrier," his thoughts trammeled over hers,

unresponsive to her attempt to communicate. *"Then she broke her barrier. We just bonded! Both of us!"*

"Yes," she thought to him again. *"We—"*

"I should have known *she was the Mentis,"* His thoughts stampeded over hers again. *"Of course she is. She's trapped in her head all the time, so cold and distant. It makes perfect sense."*

He couldn't hear her. She couldn't speak back to him mind-to-mind. But she didn't care about that right now. The barrier was broken. It had worked!

She took a deep breath. By Kelto and all that was sacred, she had a chance now, the one slim chance she had needed. What she'd come for—impossible only a moment ago—was now within her grasp. She was a student of the Champion's Academy, the member of a Quad. Her tears of despair turned to tears of joy.

"Do you feel the magic?" she asked. She'd heard his thought about bonding with her. "Did you open your first Soulblock?"

"Weeks ago," he said. "But not like tonight. With you, my magic power doubled. Tripled. I tumbled into your soul without any effort. I saw your betrothal. I saw your lover."

"You saw her *before* I told you?" she asked.

"Not her name, but I know what she looks like. I know...how you see your future, and that you long for her to be a part of it."

"You're our Anima." She swallowed. That's why he hadn't been surprised when she'd told him. "You're using it on me right now. Looking into my...soul."

It was suddenly hard for her to breathe, thinking about all that he could see within her, but she forced herself to remain calm. This was the bond. This was what it would be like. Brom, Vale, Royal…this moment of naked vulnerability would never be over. She might keep secrets from her future husband, from Father, from her people, but there would be no secrets from her Quad mates. They'd be inside her forever.

And she would be inside them. She couldn't simply achieve the magic of a Quadron, pocket it, and walk away. This was her new life.

Kelto's mercy...

The same choice came again, to shut him out or let him in, and she realized this wouldn't be the last time. She would be making this choice over and over for as long as the Quad existed. Would she be the invulnerable princess? Or the vulnerable Quad mate? Someone who shared herself. Someone who...trusted....

"Her name is Ayvra," Oriana said, and somehow the sharing was easier this time. She didn't feel the squeezing, like there was a hand around her middle.

"Who?" Brom said, not understanding.

"You said you couldn't see my lover's name. That is her name. Ayvra."

"Your lover?"

"And you should know that I can never be with her for a number of reasons. Not the least of which is that I am betrothed to Duke Dronokot's son."

"Duke Drown-a-cat?"

She favored him with a small smile for his attempt at humor. "My betrothed, Edmure."

"And that's a man?"

"Yes," she said laconically.

"But you..." He seemed genuinely concerned and confused. "How is that going to work?"

"It will work because it must work. Becoming a Quadron doesn't change my duty. I have an imperative to continue the House of Keltodanta. The kingdom needs it to survive. For that, I will need heirs. And for that, I will need Edmure. I must bury my feelings for Ayvra."

"That's...the saddest thing I've ever heard..." His thoughts came to her. "Because your life isn't your own," he said. "Because it belongs to your kingdom."

He spoke the words of her soul aloud, and lightning crackled inside her. He could see her, her intentions, her dreams. She swallowed.

"This is going to take some getting used to," she whispered. She'd feel less exposed if she stripped her clothes off and stood naked on the bank.

"I know. The fact that you can look straight into my mind—"

"Try having someone look into your soul," she said flatly.

He laughed. "Fair enough."

They fell silent for a moment, listening to the rushing of the river and the chirping of the crickets.

"If you're reading my thoughts..." He said inside his own mind, but it was obvious he was talking to her because his words came slow and plodding, like he was speaking to a child. *"Then hear this: I won't ever tell anyone. About the Bloodbane. About Ayvra. It stays between you and me."*

Her surprise must have registered on her face, because he smiled at her, realizing she'd received his message.

"You understand why, don't you?" she said. "The Bloodbane must be kept a secret because—"

"It doesn't matter why," he interrupted. "You are my Quad mate." He said it firmly, with the exact same inflection she'd used earlier.

She began to think that maybe she'd misjudged Brom. His thoughts about her were honest, and in that honesty, she saw…admiration. Suddenly, he didn't seem reckless so much as…daring. She began to suspect he actually liked these women he dallied with.

"There's more to you than meets the eye," she said.

"Don't tell anyone." He winked.

That annoyed her. "You'd rather the world perceive you as reckless and faithless?"

"They can perceive me however they want."

His own thoughts didn't contradict him. He really seemed to feel that way. What must it be like, she wondered, to simply do whatever he wished in whatever moment? What would happen if everyone acted that way? It would be chaos. But in Brom, it… He saw things, accepted things, that she had never even considered.

Perhaps there was something to be admired here, in his perspective. She strained to see it. Brom had accessed his magic before even bonding with a Quad member. That was an impossible feat. She'd never even heard of that, and it was perhaps as powerful a secret as the Bloodbane, in its own way. What if his extraordinary ability stemmed from this…ability to be reckless and yet to care at the same time? Brom had been exceedingly resilient tonight. He'd stayed with Oriana when he could have spurned her. He'd been…open to something new.

As she considered this, she took his hand. This time it felt natural, even needed. A warm, safe feeling grew in her belly, a feeling she hadn't had since she was a little girl.

She kept reading his thoughts through the sheer excitement of using magic. His mind jumped all over the place. He thought of how Royal was going to react to this, and Vale. He thought of the swirl of Oriana's dress as it turned in the current. He thought of some girl named Myan back in his little town. Of a fellow student named Caila. He thought about his father, who'd been angry with him when he left. He thought of how beautiful Oriana was.

It was like Brom was a little boy in a world of wonder, and she found herself charmed by his thoughts despite herself.

Finally, though, she decided it was time to go. She stood up and pulled him to his feet. Without a word, they walked back to the dormitory together.

When they were halfway across the moonlit Quadron Garden, Kelto's light casting an indigo glow over lawns and trees, Brom spoke again.

"Do you want to hear a secret?" he asked.

She gave him a sidelong glance, and his thoughts tumbled to her. Fragments of thoughts, all about kissing. All the girls he'd kissed.

By Kelto, she could scarcely believe there were girls who would risk their place at the academy for a taste of his lips and...whatever else. She didn't want to hear about one of his gleeful gropings. But she realized this was a good opportunity to strengthen their bond, so she said, "Of course."

"When you put your arms around me," he said. "I absolutely thought you were going to kiss me."

"Did you?"

"But you weren't, were you?" he asked. He glanced up at her. He was about average height for a Keltovari, which made him a couple inches shorter than her.

"I'd have cut off my left hand to create the bond," she said.

"So you *would* have kissed me."

"Unless I could have cut off my left hand."

"Was that a joke?" he asked. "Some grisly kind of princess joke?"

"Grisly jokes are the only kind we have," she said with a straight face.

He laughed.

They entered Westfall Dormitory, went to her dorm room and stopped outside the door. Brom grasped her forearm in a firm, meaningful grip. She turned to face him, and for the first time, his roguish smile faded.

"Oriana… I wanted to let you know that..." He began solemnly, but seemed at a loss for words.

"I have to tell her. She has to know. We're in this together now." His thoughts tumbled to her.

"That even though I joke a lot..." Again he trailed off, and his thoughts became loud in the silence.

It's not like I'm an idiot. I know this is serious. She has to know that I take this seriously.

"I just wanted you to know that I can't imagine how difficult this was for you," he said. "Your courage to be willing to..."

"To kiss you?" she interjected drily. She had never had the compulsion to set others at ease before, and she found it curious. It was as though his pain was now her pain. His awkwardness was her awkwardness.

"Or cut off your hand." He grinned. *"Gods, the ice princess has a sense of humor. Who would have guessed that? I think I'm falling in love with her a little bit."*

His capricious thoughts quieted, and Brom's face turned serious again. "My point is that you were willing to do anything—*anything*—for the Quad. You were willing to step into dangerous waters. I haven't been."

"Your liaisons are dangerous, Brom. They could kick you out for what you're doing."

He shook his head. "But I didn't do that for the Quad. I did it to run away from the Quad. But you've shown me what a coward I've been. Right here, now, I want to make a promise to you: I'll do what needs to be done. I won't ever run away again. I'm with you.

I'll wade into the dangerous waters. I'm with you, whatever it takes."

"We're going to be the best Quad this school has ever seen," his determined thoughts came to her, like an excited little boy.

Her perspective on Brom finally settled into place firmly. She saw him in a new and final light. He was not the ne'er-do-well she'd thought, depending on luck, ignorant and arrogant. He was a seeker, a lover of…everything, in its own way. His women weren't entirely an escape, and they weren't just disposable pleasures. Brom was simply…open to all possibilities. He wasn't afraid, as he put it, to wade into dangerous waters.

She reached out, surprising even herself, and put a gentle hand on his cheek. She found herself wanting to stay connected to him. It was such an odd and exhilarating thing.

"I think perhaps I've fallen in love with you a little bit, too, Brom Builder," Oriana said softly.

His eyes went wide, realizing she'd read his mind when he'd thought that exact thing. He laughed. "I'll hold you to that friendship."

"And I," she said, smiling, "shall hold you to your word."

"For the Quad," he said.

"For the Quad," she echoed.

10

ORIANA

That night, Oriana slept like the dead. When the sun rose the next day, she awoke groggy, with a hangover like she'd had too many glasses of brandy.

The pain baffled her until she remembered what she'd read about Soulblocks. An opened Soulblock, unused, went to work on the body like a night of heavy drinking. She made a mental note that when she opened one of her Soulblocks again, she'd use it all before she fell asleep.

She was late to her first class that morning, but it hardly mattered. After the first month at the academy, she had barely paid attention in class anymore. She already knew all this information, and next year's information. She never received anything but the highest marks for her classwork.

The only thing that intrigued her now was practicing. She wanted to meet with her Quad in the practice room.

Once classes and lunch were finished, Oriana held back, waiting until all of her Quad mates had left the Floating Room where they all ate lunch. She stalled for another five minutes, then followed them to the practice room.

Royal was still trying to move the steel pyramid with sheer brute force when she entered. Huge muscles stood out in his neck, shoulders, and arms, and his face turned purple with the effort. He really was a paragon of physical strength, but no *normal* would ever move that weight. Only an Impetu could.

Vale stood before the Invisible Ones, trying to affect them, but they just sat there, impassive in their gray robes and gray masks.

Brom was already there. He sat on the windowsill with a grin like he had a mouthful of sweetmeats. He had obviously been waiting for her to arrive. He knew today was going to be a day of wonder, a day of bonding. Today they would found their Quad.

She was mildly surprised that he'd waited for her, instead of bursting forth with the news, perhaps even trying to bond with each of them. But just as holding his hand had seemed natural, so too did this. Brom had waited for her because they must do this together, and that was the way things were going to be from now on.

Oriana had been thinking about this all morning. Her heart beat faster, and she heard Father's voice, angry and berating her in the back of her mind.

The perception of others creates the truth of rule. Your every action weighs upon our family name. Never lose face in front of an enemy.

Once, that voice had been her absolute authority, but to fulfill her duty, she'd left the princess behind. The shards of her lay by the riverside. She would be a Quadron, or nothing at all.

She strode toward Royal.

He saw her coming, let go of the pyramid's ring and stood up, huffing. His thick eyebrows crouched over his blue eyes, and his lips pressed together tightly. His fists clenched as she approached.

Father's voice screamed at her to sneer back, to raise her chin and give him an imperious glare.

But she didn't do any of those things. She held Royal's gaze and looked at him with hope. Her heart hammered, and she let go of her control like she'd done with Brom. She imagined his resilience flowing through her. Open to all possibilities…

She descended to one knee and knelt before Royal. She bowed

her head in submission and opened her hands, palms up.

Vale gasped. Royal took an incredulous step back.

Oriana waited, feeling horribly vulnerable. Unable to see anything but Royal's shins, she didn't know what expression was on his face, and she refrained from reading his mind. She couldn't have that power over him, that unfair advantage, in this moment.

They were mortal enemies—had been decreed mortal enemies since before they were even born—and their animosity was the greatest chasm dividing this Quad. The two of them needed to cross this bridge together, and the only way it would work is if they were equals.

She could walk all the way to the middle of that bridge. She could kneel before him, supplicate him to accept her, but Royal would have to cross the remaining distance. She couldn't make him.

She waited for his snort of derision, for a wad of spit to land on her neck.

Instead, his thick ham-hand came into view, palm open, and she looked up.

His thick muscles trembled. He was like a mountain lion poised to flee. He looked at her with a riot of emotions in his blue eyes. Surprise, distrust, anger...

But beneath it all, there was a battered hope. Like her, he wanted this. He, too, wanted to find a way to form the Quad. And like her, he was willing to do whatever it took.

Relief flooded through her. That battered hope, twin to her own, was all she needed. She took his hand, and he gently lifted her to her feet.

"What the fuck?" Vale said.

Royal's barrier broke. Oriana felt his Soulblock open like it was opening inside her. The crackle of lightning within him awoke the lightning within her.

He drew a sharp breath and looked at her in astonishment.

He turned to the steel pyramid that had so recently stymied him and grabbed it. With one hand, he lifted it like it was made of paper.

"Fendra! What did you do to me?" he roared in unbridled joy.

"Will you consent to take a walk with me, Royal?" Oriana said, unable to hold back her smile.

"I...will," he said. "...Your Highness." She saw the struggle on his face as he tried to get her honorific past his lips, words he no doubt thought he'd never say.

She knew Royal was breaking his own barriers. His old self was cracking and falling away just as hers had. She had compassion for him, having so recently experienced it. It was disorienting and hard to know what to choose next.

"That isn't necessary," she said softly. "Call me Mentis, if it please you."

"Mentis..." he said, tasting the word.

"And I will call you Impetu, as if there was ever any doubt."

Royal's thunderstruck expression softened into a grin.

"And what the fuck am I?" Vale spat. She stood, fists clenched as she watched the spectacle, obviously feeling left out of the sudden power shift.

Oriana glanced at Brom, who was sitting at the edge of the deep windowsill, kicking his feet against the marble wall like a boy waiting to play. Oriana turned her attention to Vale.

"If it please you, Vale," Oriana said. "Would you walk with us as well? I will explain."

Vale narrowed her eyes, suspicious. She flicked a thin glance at Brom. "What about him?"

"Him, too," Oriana said.

"All of us?" Vale asked skeptically.

"All of us," Oriana said.

11

VALE

Vale's instincts bid her follow these beautiful people, the ones Mother called the "white horses" of the lands, and that was the only reason she did.

She didn't want to go with them, didn't want to be anywhere near them. She couldn't attach her hopes to them. They were absolutely the wrong people in every way.

Hope led to vulnerability, and if she let herself be vulnerable to these people, she was asking to be trampled beneath their uncaring white hooves. White horses lied. They betrayed. They didn't see her as an equal; they didn't even see her as a person.

Vale had been promised a chance to become a Quadron here, to rise above the streets of Torlioch, but like so many promises given by the white horses, it was a lie. The masters didn't want her in this Quad. They'd sabotaged her on purpose, putting her with these people. The masters of this school had never intended to let a street urchin walk away with the powers of a demigod. Like everything else, the Champions Academy was rigged against the dark horses, against Vale and those like her.

The pretty white horses that pranced in front of her had bonded. They'd found their power and now they'd have no further need of her. They'd leave her behind as the white horses always did. Vale had read about replacement students being brought in to bolster a Quad that had one failing member. A white horse would fit nicely here. But not Vale. Vale was never intended to be the fourth.

So, only because her instincts nudged her to follow them did she do so. She trusted her instincts. They were the reason she was still alive when so many others were dead. She didn't know what she would find, but she would follow her instincts until they told her to bolt. Or attack.

Of course, it was a farce that she had to bond with others—especially these others—in the first place. From the first moment, she loathed the idea of helping the pretty white horses achieve their dreams.

If Vale was going to help *anyone*, it should be the people in the mud, the people that the perfect princess, the righteous giant, and the reckless boy walked all over while they were twisted up in their own problems. Vale wanted to help the dark horses—not the white ones. She wanted to live by Mother's final words.

Make them brilliant...

Mother had told Vale all about the white and dark horses. Even now, Mother's words burned in Vale's mind as she trailed after her Quad mates, wondering how she could get from them what she needed without helping them. Perhaps a student could become a Quadron without a Quad somehow. Just because the masters said it couldn't be done didn't mean it couldn't. The masters were white horses, too. And the white horses lied all the time.

Make them brilliant...

Vale's last memory of her mother was of her corpse bobbing to the surface of the Lioch, the lake near Torlioch that gave the town half its name. Whenever those final words returned, Vale could see Mother's filmy eyes swiveling to look at her, Mother's pale, dead lips forming the words.

Make them brilliant...

Vale had discovered that words were meant for lying, mostly.

They were made to say what someone wanted to hear in order to get what you needed, but not Mother's final words. They had meant something that went deep into Vale's bones. They had become her sole purpose. They rose in her mind whenever Vale reached a crossroads, like now: where her Quad would leave her behind and she must strike out on her own again.

That was why becoming a Quadron was so important. As a Quadron, she would never have to beg again. No one would ever cast her aside again. She'd never have to steal, never have to flee in fear.

She left the marble dormitory a dozen paces behind the white horses. The morning sunlight struck them first as they stepped onto the lawn of Quadron Garden.

Each of her so-called Quad mates was destined for renown. It was written on their faces and in their privileged upbringings. Each considered greatness their right. They had been pampered and petted and well-fed their whole lives. They had never spent a night shivering in the cold, their stomachs twisted into knots with fear and hunger. They didn't know what it was like to be despised by everyone, to be kicked aside like a rat.

But oh, the white horses tossed their heads when something didn't fall their way. They stamped their pretty hooves at supposed slights, all the while never once having tasted real injustice.

Oriana was the worst. The perfect princess had been given everything she'd ever wanted from the moment she was born. She wore as many fine dresses as Vale had fingers, each garment made of deftly woven cottons and silks, sewn with fancy patterns and sometimes even jewels. Any one of those jewels could have fed a dozen of Torlioch's urchins for a week. To see them so brazenly worn for decoration made bile rise into Vale's mouth.

Oriana had never worn a pair of sack pants or a patched tunic, had never piled garbage on herself at night to keep from freezing. And outside of the Champion's Academy, the princess wouldn't have noticed Vale except to raise her nose and sniff. To Oriana, Vale was just a dirty stocking lying by the side of the road, and the stocking had somehow been tossed into the princess's Quad.

Royal, for his part, had tried to pity Vale, had used his picture of Vale's life as a brick in his fortress of ideals. *See how good I am? See how I stoop to give help to this wretch...*

The righteous Fendiran tromped around, trying to intimidate everyone with his giant, well-fed body and his condescending ideals. A man like that saw himself as oppressed when he knew nothing about it. A man like that thought hunger was the growling in his belly after he'd missed a meal.

He didn't know hunger. He'd never felt the dangerous, insidious listlessness of starving to death. He'd never felt the bones coming closer to the surface of his skin because there wasn't enough meat in between.

His righteousness made her want to stab him in the eye.

And Brom...

She didn't want to stab him. No, she wanted to...do other things with him, and that made him the most dangerous by far.

She watched him as he walked ahead of her, the lean cut of him, the relaxed way his hands swung at his sides. Her gaze lingered on the nape of his neck beneath his short, wavy black hair.

Often, when Brom looked at her, it was with a mixture of wariness and interest. And whenever his glance had passed over her, she'd wanted to look back. She was drawn to his dark eyes, to the errant curls of hair that fell over his forehead. She was spellbound by his wide mouth, often found herself waiting for him to speak. She wanted to touch those cheekbones, run her finger along his square jaw.

At first, she'd been ready to knife him just as she'd knifed Royal, but Brom had kept his distance, as if he knew what she was thinking. He'd never approached her except to offer a pleasantry or to occasionally, carefully, relay a snide comment about Oriana or Royal. It was almost as though he...respected Vale.

No, Brom was something of a mystery, and she'd spent most of the year trying to determine his agenda.

Then, not long ago, she'd realized he was actually trying to see her, that he didn't have an agenda. He didn't seem to want anything from her except to understand her. That's when the floor had dropped out from under her. Since then, every time he'd looked her way, she'd felt a strange lightning bolt of pleasure.

After that, she had found herself wishing he would come closer. She dreamed of receiving a compliment from him, a casual touch of the hand. When she was alone in her room, she dreamed of him lying next to her, his naked skin against her naked skin...

And that was exactly what made him the most dangerous of her three Quad mates. She had violently stuffed her feelings down inside herself. It was a weakness, and weakness killed.

If she'd met Brom on the streets of Torlioch...if he had been one of the urchins she'd known, she would have quietly knifed him in the night. That was how one dealt with weakness. Cut it off. Cut it away. Make sure it couldn't ever hurt you.

But she wasn't in Torlioch. The rules were different here. Knifing Brom would get her expelled from the academy, and she might as well die if that happened. She was never going back to the streets. Not in Torlioch nor any other place. Not ever.

Her education grew here every day, revealing more of what existed beyond the life she'd known, beyond stealing food and clothes. She'd learned to read. She'd learned more about the two kingdoms than she had ever dreamed existed. Already, she had elevated herself, and she wanted to continue rising. She wanted Oriana's life, Royal's life, even Brom's life.

She needed to succeed at the Test of Passage at the end of the year, needed to be given permission to study here a second year. Even one more year could make a huge difference in her life. Becoming a Quadron... Well, that would solve every problem she'd ever had.

And then she could truly fulfill Mother's dying request. She'd have the power to help the dark horses. All of them.

Make them brilliant...

Vale had been seven years old when her mother died. In her last moments, Mother had lain in the little alley outside The Wayward Inn, wracked with the mud fever and hacking up bloody chunks of her lungs. Vale had held Mother's cool hand while, just a thin wall away, travelers and locals laughed and drank by a warm fire.

"Why won't they help us?" Vale had asked her, scared of the mud fever, scared of being alone. The wealthy of Torlioch looked at Vale and her mother like rats. They weren't seen as people, just something vile to avoid. Make a face and kick it away.

Vale had already gone into The Wayward Inn, tried to get someone to come help her, but a man had kicked her in the side so hard something had cracked, and now it hurt every time she moved. "Why do they hate us?" she had asked.

"We are the dark horses," Mother had told her, her face as pale as a noble and as gaunt as a skull wrapped in skin. Vale's instincts had glowed hot. She'd known, in that fated moment, that her life was about to change forever. She was going to lose Mother. Mother was going to die and Vale was going to be alone.

"No one..." Mother had begun, then coughed. The cough had turned into three coughs, then into a wracking fit. For a breathless moment, Vale had thought those would be Mother's last words, that she would die before finishing. But the spell had subsided, and Mother had continued in a thin whispery voice.

"They are the pretty white horses. They feed and brush each other, but not us, not the...dark horses. But...the dark horses...are special."

"Special?"

"When they catch the sunlight... When they catch the sunlight just right...they flash more brilliantly than the whitest horse ever could. That is you, my little Vale. It is you and all the other dark horses. You must...catch the sunlight. You must make yourself brilliant. And when you do, you must do the same for all of us...all of the dark horses. Because *they* never will. *They* never will..." Her voice had begun to fade. "You could be the sunlight, Vale. Shining upon the dark horses. Make them brilliant..." And then Mother had stopped talking. Her hand had gone cold, and that was the end.

Vale hadn't had a shovel, and she hadn't known how to dig a grave, so she had dragged Mother's corpse to the Lioch. She considered giving Mother their only weapon—a metal spoon that had been sharpened on the thin end—to fight the Ragged Man during her trip to the afterlife, but Vale had guiltily kept it. Instead, she'd given Mother a pointed piece of hardwood, put it in her curled, cold fingers, then slid her body into the water. At first, it had seemed a simple and elegant burial, but the body hadn't stayed down. Mother had floated to the surface and caught in a thatch of brambles just off the shore. Vale had stood transfixed, horrified by the corpse.

She'd heard Mother's last words again as though she'd awoken to speak them one more time.

Make them brilliant.

Vale had fled and had never gone back to the Lioch. Not until the Quadron had come to town, of course, had changed Vale's life by leading her here.

Make them brilliant, Vale. Vale... Vale...

"Vale."

Vale's head snapped up. Oriana and Royal had stopped on the lawn and turned back to look at her. Beyond them, other students played athletic games in the sun or sat in the shade of trees.

Brom had come back for her.

Vale stood in the dormitory's shadow, right at that line between darkness and light. The beautiful white horses, of course, stood in the sunshine.

Jealousy raged inside her. She shoved it down.

"You've all opened your Soulblocks," she said tightly to Brom. They were the laughing, drinking, callous patrons of The Wayward Inn all over again. They were kicking her to the side like a rat. "You've used magic. All of you."

"Yes," Brom said. He extended his hand, and it crossed from light into shadow.

She twitched, but she didn't take it. Her belly got fluttery at the very thought of touching him. Instead she gripped her dagger, hidden beneath the folds of her first-year uniform. She almost drew it, almost stabbed his hand, but she didn't. Her heart raced as if she were fleeing Jondry and his malevolent street gang back in Torlioch.

"Vale," Brom said softly, as though reading her mind. "We have to trust each other. That's the key. Trust us. Just this once, and you'll see."

The truth twisted inside her. She'd seen the change in Oriana and Brom, in the way they looked at each other. They'd found that trust. And then Oriana had done the same with Royal, striking a spark that Royal had made into a flame.

"You're going to replace me," she said, waiting for Brom to lie to her, to sling soft words of comfort and ask her to calm down.

"No," Oriana interrupted with authority before Brom could answer. She strode forward, joining Brom at the line between darkness and light.

Vale flicked a glance from one to the other as Royal came up, his hulking form looming behind Oriana.

"Is that so?" Vale sneered. "You think I don't see how you look at me? You'd happily cut me from this Quad like a bad limb."

"No. You are my Quad mate," Oriana said firmly. "And I will not give you up."

"Nor will I," Royal echoed in his deep voice.

A pleasant warmth spread through her, and she hated herself for it. Oriana's arrogant words, Royal's thundering declaration—they should have made her sneer. But both of their gazes were earnest. Those gazes promised protection, promised to stand between Vale and those who would hurt her.

But it couldn't be real. They were white horses, so they had to be lying. The white horses didn't care about the dark horses. They weren't like her.

"They made a mistake, Vale, throwing us together," Brom said softly. She looked up into his dark eyes. "They thought they'd make the worst Quad in the school. But they made the strongest instead. And not in *spite* of you. *Because* of you." He gave a little wiggle to his extended hand, which she hadn't taken yet, and he invited her again.

She didn't know what to do.

Trust them? Kill them? They were everything she hated, what she'd sworn to always hate. White horses like these had let her mother die.

And now, of all times, her instincts had gone quiet. They didn't tell her to flee. They didn't tell her to attack. It was as though this was right where she was meant to be. As though, miraculously, this one spot was safe.

She had never felt so lost or afraid. She desperately wanted to become a Quadron. But to bond herself to these, the worst of the white horses? They would betray her. As sure as the sun rose, they would cast her aside. It was inevitable.

"I-I don't know..." she said.

"I do," Brom said. "Take my hand." She'd have to step to grab it, step into the light.

His words from a moment ago floated in her mind, refusing to go away, like they were important somehow.

They made a mistake, throwing us together. They thought they'd make the worst Quad in the school. But they made the strongest instead.

The princess, the Fendiran, the builder's boy, all enemies...

The Collector *had* done this on purpose. He'd thrown them all together, never thinking they'd succeed, never *wanting* them to succeed. He had sabotaged this Quad, taking the powerful and turning them into misfits...

Taking the white horses and turning them dark.

Her view of her Quad mates pivoted so abruptly she gasped, and she saw them with new eyes. Not a perfect princess, but a broken one. Not a righteous giant, but an impotent one. Not a reckless boy, but a frustrated one.

They were the dark horses. All of them were.

Make them brilliant...

She stepped into the sunlight and grasped Brom's hand.

Her Soulblock burst open inside her, spilling magic into her body. With a cry of joy, she flung her magic out at them like a whip. She felt Royal's honest conviction. She felt Oriana's adamant determination and Brom's giddy excitement. Their emotions flooded through her, and for the first time in her life, she felt that flash of sunlight that her mother had spoken of, that flash that made her brighter than all the others.

"Brilliant," she gasped, and tears slid down her cheeks.

"Brilliant!" Brom laughed.

"Brilliant!" Royal roared, putting his giant fist over Vale's and Brom's clasped hands.

Oriana gave a tiny smile, the first smile Vale had ever seen on the princess's face, and she put her long slender fingers over the mass of hands. "Absolutely brilliant," she said.

The Quad had formed, and Vale hadn't been cast aside after all. She was part of it. They were bonded.

Their training could begin at last.

Now the only question was: Could this fledgling Quad learn fast enough to keep from getting expelled in three weeks?

Vale didn't know the future, but she knew she wouldn't sleep or eat for those three weeks if that's what it took. She felt the same determination radiating from each of her Quad mates like heat from a fire.

They were all going to be Quadrons. They were going to do it together.

Or they were going to die trying.

Part II

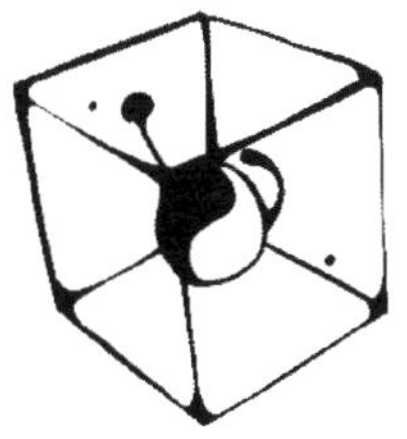

The Tower

1

BROM

Brom, Oriana, Vale and Royal—the newly formed Quad Brilliant—watched as the dead emerged from The Dome. The three coffins came on carts, each drawn by a stoic wagoner who looked only at the road, not at the two hundred stunned students lining it.

"Three out of four," Vale murmured. "Dead."

"A heavy toll," Royal said. "But the survivor will become a Quadron."

For the first ten months, Brom's Quad had barely spoken to each other. In the last five days, they'd talked non-stop. They had helped each other with new discoveries and blazed past threshold after threshold. They had crammed to learn all they could, and the change to Quad Brilliant was astonishing. Since they'd broken their barriers and bonded, their collective magical abilities had surged.

"So we're happy with that?" Vale asked. "Three dead. Don't worry. Let's get back to studying?"

"Happy?" Oriana raised an eyebrow.

"You know what I mean. We just accept that?" Vale clarified.

"You are always free to leave," Oriana said, seemingly barely interested in Vale's outburst. "We all are."

"That's not what I'm saying," Vale said darkly.

"It is the Test of Separation," Royal interrupted, as though that settled the matter.

This morning, the Test of Separation—the final test that transformed students into Quadrons—had been given to Quad Moonlight. No one knew exactly what happened in the Test of Separation save those who survived it, but everyone knew failure meant death. All four members of Quad Moonlight had entered The Dome. Only one had emerged. It put a sobering pall over Quad Brilliant's recent successes.

"It is the most rigorous test in the two kingdoms," Royal continued. "No Quad save The Four has emerged with all four Quad members still alive."

"That's exactly what I'm saying."

"Except you are not saying anything exactly," Oriana stated pointedly.

"One of us is going to die. And if we're like Quad Moonlight, three of us."

"Not this year," Oriana said.

Only fourth-year students were invited to take the Test of Separation. For those fourth-year Quads who were ready, the Test of Separation was always announced without warning. The announcements usually came near the end of a Quad's fourth year, but particularly talented fourth-year Quads were sometimes tested near the beginning. In the hundred years the academy had stood, only two Quads had been called at the end of their third years: Quad Soulforge and Quad Adamant. Quad Soulforge had only lost only one of their members during that Test, while Quad Adamant had lost three. Brom had been shocked to discover that the old Quadron Cy'kett was that fourth member from Adamant—its Motus, its sole survivor. Cy'kett was famous among the older masters and librarians.

The three wagons rolled closer. Red velvet embroidered with a fierce dragon—the sign of the Motus—draped the first coffin.

White velvet embroidered with a haughty owl—that of the Mentis—draped the next, and the last bore black velvet with a moth flying before a moon, the sign of the Anima. Only one member of Quad Moonlight, their Impetu Dwinn, had survived. Today, Dwinn would become a Quadron. He would go through the ceremony in a room with The Four themselves, and they would strengthen Dwinn's Soulblocks so that he could work magic outside the walls of the academy.

One of the first lessons the masters had taught all of them was that Soulblocks were fragile. The only place they could be built and stay built was within the academy walls, where The Four had wrought powerful spells to preserve them. It made the academy a safe haven, a place where fledgling magic users could learn their craft. But only a full Quadron who'd passed the deadly Test of Separation—and then underwent Soulblock reinforcement from The Four—could work magic outside these walls.

Any student was free to leave the academy at any time but leaving without the rigorous spell of reinforcement destroyed their chances of using magic forever. Soulblocks crumbled outside the academy. Brom didn't fully understand it, but he understood enough. He wasn't going to leave until he was a full Quadron, and that meant facing the Test of Separation.

The wagons reached Brom, Oriana, Vale, and Royal, then trundled slowly past, heading up the crushed gravel path toward the giant portcullis leading out of the academy.

"Quad Seabreak got called for their Test," Vale said, obviously still frustrated by Oriana's dismissive answers.

"Mmmm." Royal nodded.

"The invitation came just after Quad Moonlight...passed," she said. "They'll test tomorrow."

"No they won't." Oriana didn't take her gaze from the coffins. "They've taken the path of The Forgotten."

The Forgotten were those who left the academy voluntarily, who came to the school but lacked the courage to finish. Most often this happened during the rigors of the first, second, or third years. But occasionally, a Quad would decide not to take the deadly Test of Separation. It didn't happen often, but sometimes a fourth-year Quad packed up their belongings and left the academy without having taken the Test, forfeiting their magic and letting all of their training be for naught.

"Seabreak lost their spines. They'll leave school as *normals*." She used the word that the students used to describe everyone outside the academy. "They're choosing safety over a chance at magic." Oriana gave a sidelong glance at Vale, who narrowed her eyes.

"Are they really?" Royal exclaimed in a hush. To a student from the academy, there were only three types of people in the two kingdoms: students of magic, Quadrons, and *normals*.

Of course Royal wouldn't back away from the threat of death. Brom felt the same, and it seemed as though Oriana and Vale also felt that way. But Vale had come dangerously close to indicating that the threat of death wasn't worth the prize.

Brom tried to imagine himself in Quad Seabreak's boots, watching Quad Moonlight get torn apart. Moonlight's carnage could crack even the most hardened confidence.

"Four years, and they've chosen to become *normals*," Brom murmured to himself.

"What about the other two Quads?" Vale asked. The student body of the academy dropped by half every year, leaving only four Quads—sixteen students—during the fourth year. "Were they invited to test?"

"There are nineteen days left before the end of this year," Oriana said. "Plenty of time for an invitation."

Silence fell among Quad Brilliant, and all they could hear was the creaking of the wagons and the trundling of the wheels, slowly fading. Somewhere down the line, someone started crying. Brom looked, trying to spot the student, some bereaved friend of the dead.

"Three dead," Vale repeated. "Maybe there's something wrong with the Test."

"Three of them were not strong enough," Royal said. "That is all."

"Why make it so hard that people die?" Vale persisted. "It's almost like they don't want people to become Quadrons."

"They say the Test of Separation is created by the student

taking it, that they face their own fears and weaknesses," Royal said. "Who knows what Quad Moonlight conjured?"

"Bullshit," Vale said. "The masters make the Test."

Royal winced at Vale's profanity, and Brom hid his smile. Royal didn't like it when she cursed.

"Not everyone can be a Quadron," Oriana said coldly. "Those who can't—yet try anyway—die. Quad Seabreak chose wisely. If they don't think they are up to the challenge of the Test, then they aren't."

"What if it's more than just hard?" Vale asked.

"What are you talking about?" Royal returned.

"The masters are cruel," she said. "What if they set Quad Moonlight up to fail?"

"Cruel?" Royal said. "Learning magic is difficult, the most difficult thing there is. The masters don't make it difficult. They're here to teach us. Harsh methods are required."

"Death isn't a harsh method. It's death."

"You know what I mean," Royal rumbled.

"You're just saying what they want you to say." She shook her head, agitated. "What if the Test is horrifically unfair, but no one wants to speak out because they're afraid they'll get banished from the academy?"

"What are you talking about?" Royal growled.

"What if we were supposed to fail this year?"

"If we weren't strong enough, then we were supposed to fail. But we were—"

"Oh, stop acting so righteous!" Vale snapped. "If Oriana hadn't popped your cork by bowing to you, you'd still be wrestling with that stupid pyramid. I'm saying: What if The Collector set us up to fail, except we didn't?"

"We may yet," Oriana said quietly. "We are still far behind the other Quads. We may yet become one of the thirty-two sent home."

"Just answer the question," Vale said. "Why would they have put us all together? This group, who didn't have a chance of bonding?"

"Perhaps it just seemed that way," Royal rumbled. "We're not the only Quad who had problems bonding."

"It took us until the end of the second semester. Every other first-year Quad bonded in the first!"

"Well... We had additional issues," he said haltingly. "They didn't intentionally set us up to fail."

"We were the first Quad chosen out of a hundred and twenty-eight students," Vale said. "How could it *not* be intentional?"

"You see danger in every shadow." Royal's voice rose to match his growing anger.

"Because there *is* danger in every shadow. And what if it's not just the masters? What if it's The Four?"

"Don't say that," Royal swept his hand down like a sword. "It's bad enough to speak lies about the masters. But The Four are... It's..."

"Sacrilege?" Vale offered.

"Yes."

"They're not gods."

"Shut your mouth!" Royal barked.

"You don't find it suspicious that *no* full Quads ever pass?" she asked. "None. Never. Except The Four themselves."

"None are as great as The Four," Oriana intoned. "None ever have been. They're above our comprehension."

"Maybe they're just above the rules."

"What is that supposed to mean?" Oriana glared at Vale.

"Vale, I'm warning you." Royal's face darkened.

"I'm just—"

"Without The Four, there would be no Champions Academy," Oriana stated coldly. "Without The Four, there would be no Quadrons. They *invented* Soulblocks. Without The Four, there would be no students of magic, just ignorant novices draining their souls and dying. They made this place where even the *ungrateful...*" She put special emphasis on the word. "...might have a chance to learn. Simply because the Test of Separation is beyond most *normals'* abilities doesn't give you the right to speak ill of The Four."

A frosty silence fell between them.

"I'm sorry," Vale said softly, backing down. "I didn't mean it."

"You're damned right you didn't mean it," Royal said, looking larger than ever. He crossed his arms over his great chest.

Vale looked troubled and upset. "I don't know what I'm saying," she said contritely. "It's just...sad. Three out of the four didn't make it."

"Don't focus on your emotions," Oriana said coldly. "Put them away and, when the time comes for *your* Test, be prepared."

"I'm *supposed* to focus on my emotions," Vale said. "I'm a Motus."

"I'm prepared," Brom offered, wanting to break the tension.

"You're cocky," Royal rumbled, still red in the face and glaring at the ground.

"He's brilliant," Vale said in as cocky a tone as she could manage, obviously trying to needle Royal. She seemed far more inclined to push the line with him than with Oriana. "We're *all* brilliant."

Royal shook his head gravely. "Oriana, tell her to take this seriously."

But Oriana didn't answer. Her indigo eyes might have been little purple flames for how hot they burned as she looked at the now-distant coffins, as though if she stared at them long enough, she'd discover what those poor dead souls had done wrong.

But Brom couldn't stop thinking about Vale's sudden criticism of the masters, the very people who taught them magic. Brom had a hard time trusting them himself, always had. None of them were nice, except for the seemingly beatific Master Saewyne. Except she might be the worst, with her chalk violence, tight dresses, and manipulative smiles. Brom was half certain she was working Motus magic on them all the time, though he couldn't tell how.

He'd been leery of the masters ever since he'd discovered The Collector was intentionally intimidating him on that first day. What if it wasn't just The Collector? Could it be that all the masters secretly wanted the Quads to fail? That seemed ludicrous. Why even have a school, then? Why teach anyone if you only wanted them to fail?

What if the stern faces of the instructors weren't simply a challenge to make the students tougher, self-reliant? What if the masters were, as Vale said, simply cruel? The Collector certainly seemed so.

Vale had walked it back, but she'd watered a seed that had already taken root in Brom's mind.

The wagons passed underneath the giant portcullis and into the world. As a *normal* or as one of the dead, those were the only two ways to leave the Champion's Academy.

Unless you became a Quadron.

I'm going to be a Quadron, he thought. *I'm going to walk under that portcullis with my magic intact.*

The portcullis descended, and the students began walking the path toward The Dome where, after Dwinn met with The Four in private and they strengthened his Soulblocks, he would receive his amulet and become a Quadron.

That's going to be me, Brom thought.

2

BROM

In the remaining nineteen days between Quad Moonlight's Test of Separation and the end of the year, Quad Brilliant rarely slept, barely ate, and flew through all the lessons they had missed during the months they'd languished. Brom felt like he was racing down a hill, barely able to keep up with his own legs.

Vale's burgeoning Motus abilities helped the Quad the most at first. She gave each of her Quad mates a jolt of excitement to start the day, making two hours of beleaguered sleep suddenly seem like a full night's rest. Royal followed her lead, delving into the "external" application of the Impetu and instilling his Quad mates with physical strength and health.

With her new Mentis abilities, Oriana found she could not only keep vast quantities of knowledge at the forefront of her mind, but she could also transfer it to her Quad mates. She researched at night, and during the day she fed the Quad a constant stream of knowledge mind-to-mind even as they practiced in the practice room. It was much faster than sitting in a chair and listening to an instructor lecture or demonstrate. Once they learned that little secret, they didn't attend classes anymore. Instead, they went straight to the practice room and targeted a new magical threshold each day, sometimes two. Brom was worried the masters would come looking for their truant students, but they never did.

"Why aren't they checking up on us?" Vale put a voice to Brom's thoughts that morning as they gathered in the practice room.

"She's right," Royal rumbled in his deep voice. "I've not seen the masters in days, save in the grand foyer."

"Perhaps this is their way of being kind." Oriana gave a thin smile. "Giving us one last week with the magic before expelling us."

"Kind?" Brom said, wondering how anyone could attribute that quality to the masters.

"You think they've given up on us?" Royal said.

Oriana shrugged. "What else?"

"Let's shove it down their throats," Vale said.

"Vale," Royal growled. "Respect them. They are here to teach us."

"Respect this." She stuck her behind in his direction, then smacked it with one hand.

Royal clenched his fist and started forward. Vale spun and crouched with one hand in her tunic, no doubt on the hilt of her hidden dagger.

"Enough," Oriana said in her commanding voice. "We stay together. We stay united. We pass. That is our goal."

Royal, red in the face, stopped moving toward the impudent Vale.

"Are we agreed?" Oriana asked coldly.

After a moment, Royal spoke through his teeth. "Yes."

Vale's deadly scowl flipped to a grin. "That's all I want," she said. Her hand slipped out of her tunic as she straightened. She crossed her arms.

"Brom?" Oriana turned to him.

"I don't know." He held his palms up like they were a scale and he was weighing a decision. "Gain our writs of passage or watch Vale and Royal kill one another. It's so hard.... Can I think about it and tell you tomorrow?"

Oriana rolled her eyes and turned away from him.

That next week, they doubled down on their studies. Instead of sleeping just a few hours a night, they slept only one hour. Instead of simply catching up with the other first-year Quads, who studied only the internal aspect of their paths to magic, Quad Brilliant studied the first three aspects of each path: internal, external, and constructive. Beyond the paths, they studied their Soulblocks, and discovered each member's four Soulblocks doubled to eight when the four of them were together, giving them twice as much magic to use. Also, and this astonished them, they found they could actually loan most of their Soulblocks to another Quad mate. If they made a concerted effort, three of them could effectively make one of them a "super-Quadron" by giving them twenty-eight Soulblocks of magic!

This was the true power of a Quad and, based on Oriana's research, not something students learned until their third year at the academy.

The final day of the year arrived. The entire academy gathered on Quadron Garden, the first-years standing at attention by Quads in two lines of thirty-two students facing each other. Between the two lines, four Invisible Ones sat in chairs, and three pyramid weights—one the same size as the pyramid in the practice room, and two even larger—rested on the grass. Tables waited at a distance, filled with browned chicken legs, cooked vegetables, ale, water, and a sugary drink called Fendiran wine.

The second- and third-years also gathered to watch, giving this end-of-the-year passage a carnival atmosphere. Ale flowed before the masters even began their inspections, and raucous comments were lobbed at the first-years as the masters asked them to perform all the basics required to gain their writs of passage.

Brom wondered what exactly was the point of throwing shame and ridicule upon the students by having the older students mock them? Of course, many of the older students were respectfully quiet, but those who chose to heckle were loud. Brom spotted Caila, embarrassed and tight-lipped as others laughed at a first-year bungling a recitation. But the masters simply smiled thinly, seeming not to notice.

It was another reason to hate them, Brom thought.

Quad Brilliant waited its turn as students earnestly showed their skills and responded to the questions leveled at them. Some failed. Some succeeded. And some buckled under the stone-faced scrutiny of the masters, fumbling to exhibit skills they had long since mastered.

The Quads had been arranged first to last according to how they had performed at the half-year assessment, and the masters tested them in this order. This, of course, put Quad Brilliant at the end of the line. By the time the masters moved on to them, there were several first-year students crying behind them, having failed, knowing they would be expelled when the exam finished.

The laughter and catcalls rose to a crescendo as The Collector, a smiling Master Saewyn, the short and stocky Master Jhaleen, and the dour, long-faced Master Tohn Gelu formed up in front of Quad Brilliant. Everyone knew the "Princess Quad" was going to fail, and the most vicious hecklers seemed to draw in a breath, readying to sink their teeth in.

The Collector cleared his throat. "You have chosen a name?"

"Yes, Master," Oriana said. They'd all decided she would speak for them.

The Collector raised an eyebrow when Brom, Vale, and Royal remained silent. Master Saewyne gave Master Tohn Gelu a sidelong glance. No doubt they'd expected a display of discord among the four of them, arguments about who was in charge.

"You realize," The Collector said in a condescending tone, "that a Quad must bond first before choosing a name."

"Yes, we understand," Oriana spoke to The Collector's mind, including Brom, Vale, and Royal in the reply, just as they'd practiced.

The Collector's eyebrows shot up. Master Saewyne's eyes grew wide, Master Jhaleen's muscular bare arms twitched, and Master Tohn Gelu frowned.

After their moment of collective stupefaction, The Collector cleared his throat angrily. "You are not to use your magic in this exam until you are asked to do so, do you understand?"

The jeers quieted at The Collector's tone. The hecklers suddenly realized something different was happening. A few jibes rose from the back of the group, but the rest of the students were suddenly attentive.

"Our name is Quad Brilliant," Oriana said aloud, ignoring The Collector's admonition. The hecklers laughed raucously at the name. "Please tell us what we must do to gain our writs of passage. We wish to show you what we have learned. And then we wish to return to our studies."

The Collector showed teeth this time, seemingly about to spit some epithet at her, but he managed to contain his anger. "How clever you think you are," he said in a deadly whisper.

She held his gaze, her face impassive, seemingly unaware of his barely concealed rage. It was all Brom could do not to laugh.

"Let's begin," Master Saewyne said, her unnerving smile back in place.

They started with Oriana first, intent on humiliating her. They asked her about the five components of mind control, which was part of the destructive aspect of Mentis. A ripple of murmurs went through the line of first-years. One of the third-year hecklers in the back squawked.

"Of course," Master Tohn Gelu said. "This is fourth-year magic. We completely understand if you cannot conjure the answer."

"The stunning, the infiltration, the quelling, the grip, and the command," Oriana said without hesitating, as though reading it from a book.

Master Tohn Gelu's eyes widened. His frown dissolved into confusion. It was clear he'd expected Oriana to stumble over words or complain that this was fourth-year magic she'd never been taught. He glanced over his shoulder at The Collector as if looking for guidance.

Oriana looked down her nose at Tohn Gelu, waiting.

"You speak so confidently." The Collector stepped forward. "As though you've mastered this spell."

"No, Master," Oriana said. "I only took it upon myself to read ahead."

"Did you?"

"I did."

The Collector seemed ready to lash out at her, perhaps to ask something outrageous of her. But they'd already done that, and she'd pushed the correct answer back in their faces.

"Let's move on," Master Saewyne said with her stiff smile.

They asked Royal to lift the three weights—a three-hundred-pound pyramid of steel, a five-hundred-pound pyramid, and finally a thousand-pound pyramid. When he did these with ease, they demanded he uproot one of the trees in Quadron Garden. He tore it out of the ground and laid it respectfully at their feet. Even the most diehard hecklers had gone silent by then. Everyone was in rapt attention.

They moved on to Vale. They pushed hardest on her, Brom thought. Perhaps in their stunned realization that Quad Brilliant had bonded and continued their studies on their own, they thought the weak link must be the once-illiterate street urchin, but they had no luck in humiliating her. They asked her questions about the internal and external paths of Motus. She answered them all. They requested she perform a glamour on one of the Invisible Ones. In less than a minute, she had him following her around, hanging on her every word. It was such a powerful glamour that Brom felt it working on him, too. He began to have scandalous thoughts about Vale. Several of the nearby first-years had barely concealed looks of lust on their faces.

In frustration, the masters told her to fill the four different Invisible Ones with four different emotions. This was second-year magic. They hadn't taught the practice of it yet, though they had taught the textual learning. Vale set to work.

By the time one Invisible One was howling with rage, one sobbing on the grass, one laughing hysterically, and one gibbering in fear, The Collector brought things to an end.

"Enough!" he said through his teeth. He threw back his cowl and his glittering black eyes found Oriana's. "You have earned your writs of passage."

"What?" Brom spoke up. They hadn't even tested him!

Oriana reached out and put her hand on his shoulder.

"Stay silent," she said in his head. *"It is over. We have passed. That is all that matters."*

"But they didn't even test me!" he thought back to her.

"Let it be."

Reluctantly, Brom held his tongue.

In the graveyard quiet that followed, the masters silently handed out writs of passage to half the Quads, including Quad Brilliant, along with the little golden pins to be worn on their academy tunics. The moment they put the fanciful scrolls and the accompanying pins into the hands of each Quad mate, the masters turned and left Quadron Garden.

The gathering was silent until the masters were gone, then one of the first-year students let out a great *whoop*! Cheering rose now from the second- and third-year students. And while those first-years who hadn't passed slunk off to Westfall Dormitory, those who had emerged with their writs began the celebration. Flagons of ale were passed around.

Oriana looked at the sudden revelers, then turned back to the Quad. "Well done," she said, and her mouth quirked in the barest of smiles. "Brilliant, some might say."

"Though with Oriana doing all the talking, we're the Princess Quad forever," Brom said.

"They'll remember the name Brilliant," Royal said.

"I was kidding, Royal."

"Oh."

"I've never felt this way before," Vale said, her eyes alight with victory. "We were better than any of the other Quads. Far better."

"We have proven ourselves worthy," Royal agreed.

"My part was particularly hard," Brom said.

"Well," Oriana said, glancing over at the food tables surrounded by excited students. "I've never tried Fendiran wine," she said. "I think I shall avail myself of a glass."

"Avail?" Brom said.

"It's delicious," Royal said. "I'll get you one."

"I'll go with you," Oriana said. Together, they moved toward the crowded tables.

Vale and Brom watched them go.

"You were amazing." Brom turned to Vale. "They were stunned. Even I could scarcely believe it, though I've been with you these past weeks. It was..." The carnal thoughts he'd had when Vale had thrown her glamour at the crowd flashed through his mind. "It was impressive."

She glanced up at him. "They were certain we'd fail. Did you see that? We shoved it down their throats, sure enough."

"You three did," he said, feeling glum that he hadn't had a chance to stand with his Quad, to show his prowess as they'd shown theirs.

She laughed. "I'd rather be in your shoes."

"What? Why? You were brilliant."

"Sure, but by the time they were done with us, they were afraid of you. I'd love to have seen that look in their eyes. Afraid to test me because they knew I'd fly by their expectations."

Brom hadn't thought of it that way.

"So..." Vale smiled up at him. "Fendiran wine?"

"Yes." He nodded. "That sounds—"

"That was brilliant!" Caila interrupted exuberantly as she bounded up to them. She stopped, out of breath. "I've never seen a first year exam like that. Never. The masters seemed... Well, they seemed..."

"Embarrassed?" Vale asked. Her smile was gone.

"I couldn't believe it." Caila sidled up to Brom with a sly look and took his arm. "You were particularly amazing. You know, the part where you stood there and did absolutely nothing."

"Ouch!" he said. "Hey, I was ready to—"

"Come on." She tugged on his elbow. "To the victor go the spoils. Let's drink." Laughing, she pulled him toward the crowded food tables. He laughed, shrugging as he glanced back apologetically at Vale.

She kept the smile on her face, but she narrowed her eyes, then she turned away.

3
BROM

"You may go," Oriana told the Invisible Ones as Quad Brilliant finished their afternoon practice. The Invisible Ones stood up and filed out the door.

Brom lingered by the wall of the practice room while his Quad mates headed toward the door as well. They were three months into the new school year, and for the first time since their resounding successes, Brom was feeling stuck. His Quad mates had excelled, but Brom hadn't progressed much since the first month of the year.

"I think I'll see if the stewards need a hand," Royal said.

The man simply couldn't stop working. It was all he ever wanted to do. The sun was going down already, and the stewards who managed the livestock and the fields that fed the Champions Academy would have buttoned up their activities for the day, but Royal was going to go find out anyway.

"Well, I am taking a bath," Oriana stated.

"You had a bath yesterday," Royal said.

"And?" She raised an eyebrow.

"You didn't even break a sweat today."

"I must be slathered in sweat to warrant a bath?" she said disdainfully.

"You have to be dirty first, yes."

Oriana rolled her eyes and moved to the door. "Go wallow with the pigs, Royal. May it bring you joy."

He shook his head, but there was a smile there. It had been six months since they'd astonished the masters last year and gained their writs of passage, and as a whole, Quad Brilliant was thriving. Their successes drove them to further successes, and the glow of victory hung about his Quad mates. Other second-year Quads had already begun to look up to them.

"I'm going to eat," Vale announced.

Royal chuckled. "Will it be a bean this time? Or a leaf?"

Vale socked him in the arm, and he smiled fondly down at her. It was true that Vale didn't eat much when she did have a meal, but she never seemed far away from food. She almost always carried dried jerky in a pocket of her academy tunic, almost always had a half loaf of bread and a chunk of cheese wrapped in an oil cloth in her room. It was as though having food nearby made her feel safe, but the idea of gorging herself was somehow dangerous.

They headed toward the door, and Oriana—who always seemed to know where each of her Quad mates were—stopped and turned. "Are you coming, Brom?"

Vale and Royal turned back to look, and his three Quad mates regarded him from the doorway.

"I'm going to stay here, work on a few things."

"Not the Gauntlet," Oriana said sternly. Brom glanced at the huge killing apparatus with its blades, spikes, and poison darts in the southeast corner of the room. "The first time you try that, I want Royal standing by." More than a few Anima students had been killed attempting the Gauntlet before they were ready.

"No, I'm just...pensive. I'm going to sort through a few things, then go to bed."

"You're always pensive," Royal said. "Come help me assist at the stables."

"No thank you," Brom said immediately.

The summer before their second year had been the closest thing to being home at Kyn that Brom had experienced at the academy. The students took an official break from their studies, but as none of them could leave the academy without destroying their Soulblocks, they stayed inside the walls. And the masters made good use of them. They were required to help the academy stewards with the harvest of crops, slaughter of animals, preservation of meat, and the cleaning of all the various buildings. Impetus had been especially coveted by academy stewards during those months, and Royal was the most popular worker by far. He'd done the work of ten men, harvesting, hauling, and stacking with endless endurance. Brom suspected Royal would have done the work of five regular men even without his magic. He just never stopped.

But Brom had suffered through those months. His magic—seeing into the soul, understanding the nature of people—was little help to him while wielding a scythe or feeding chickens. He'd left Kyn because of this kind of work. It was everything he'd never wanted to do.

The one bright spot had been that Caila had started up with him again right after Quad Brilliant achieved their writs of passage. During the summer, the masters didn't seem to care where the students went or what they did, as long as the stewards of the chickens, cows, wheat fields, or barley fields got the help they needed. It made it much easier for Brom to find moments to slip away for the most wonderful form of rule-breaking with Caila.

"It will get your blood moving." Royal broke Brom's reverie. "Work is good for the soul."

"Your soul," Brom said.

"Dinner then?" Vale saved Brom just as Royal took a deep breath, no doubt ready to press his point further.

"Not hungry, thanks."

"Well, I'm not offering you a spot in my bath," Oriana said drily. "Good night, Brom." She left the room.

Vale shrugged, then dramatically sniffed the air as though she could smell dinner from here. "Food," she said, waving over her shoulder as she left.

Royal looked disgruntled, like he wanted to try again to convince Brom to spend his evening mucking out horse stalls. Then he shrugged. "Good night, Brom." And he also left the practice room.

Usually, seeing them all so invigorated at the thought of their evening activities would have invigorated Brom, too, but an unaccountable malaise had fallen over him these past weeks. He'd tried to shake it but couldn't. He was failing, and his Quad mates were doing so well that no one had noticed.

He'd stopped seeing Caila months back because he wanted all of his attention focused on the Quad. Breaking the rules could put his Quad at risk, and that was the last thing he wanted. He hadn't cared about hurting the Quad when they were abjectly failing in their first year, but now the masters took a great interest in Quad Brilliant. Everywhere Brom went, he felt the masters' eyes on him, watching, waiting.

So as the summer wound down and lessons began, he saw Caila less and less, and then not at all. She didn't seem to mind. To Caila, life was like a flower garden where she plucked whatever flower caught her interest. It had taken her a total of three days to find someone else to play with. And then someone else. Today he'd seen her smiling, sitting next to a muscle-bound third-year Impetu on Quadron Garden. Caila would be just fine.

But Brom's cessation of all sexual activities and his rededication to the purpose of his Quad didn't have the effect he'd wanted. Instead of filling him with a fiery drive to succeed, he'd languished.

He strolled over to the Gauntlet. The contraption had been designed to test an Anima's proficiency in connecting not just to one's own soul or to the soul of another, but to the Soul of the World. It was third-year magic, and Brom didn't know how to do it yet. He fingered one of the pine spars that held the Gauntlet together, then lightly touched one of the blades settled into its catch.

"Her Royal Highness told you not to touch that," Vale said from the doorway.

Brom turned to see Vale leaning against the doorjamb. She'd changed clothes. Instead of the academy tunic and leggings—red for a Motus, with silver piping to denote a second-year student—she wore the skirt instead. Men at the academy only had the one uniform, but the women could choose leggings or a skirt. Or, if you were Oriana, the gown-like dresses that had been specially made and sent to her from the Keltan palace.

Brom had never seen Vale wear a skirt before.

"I thought you were hungry," he said.

"I am hungry." She went to bench where the Invisible Ones usually were and sat down, crossed her legs. The orange evening sunlight slanted through the windows, turning dust into sparkles and illuminating Vale like she was posing for a painting.

He desperately wanted to look at her soul, but he didn't. They'd made a rule in the Quad that they wouldn't use their magic on each other unless they asked first.

"What's going on here?" he asked.

"You're faltering," she said.

"I'm what?"

"You're working on second-year spells," she said.

"I'm a second-year student," he said defensively. He'd thought no one had noticed he was having trouble.

"Oriana is working on third-year spells."

"Well, she's Oriana. She's—"

"So am I. And Royal is nearly there."

"Well..."

"Cut the shit, Brom," she said. "You're the most talented among us, but you're falling behind."

"That's not true—"

"It is true."

"Will you let me finish a sentence?" he asked.

"If you stop saying stupid things."

Self-loathing rose inside him. She was right, and he knew it. He'd been stuck on the external aspect of the Anima, reading other people, seeing their souls, but he hadn't been able to move past it. And if that wasn't bad enough, the internal aspect that he'd learned last year was starting to slip away: his clarity, his confidence. He'd hoped something would come along to break him out of his stagnation, but nothing he'd tried had worked.

"I...don't know what happened," he said. "I'm more dedicated to the Quad than ever. I've been following the rules. I've even..." He trailed off, about to say something about Caila, but he decided against it. "I'm doing everything I can, but it's having the opposite effect. I'm not getting better. I'm getting worse."

"You stopped seeing Caila," she said.

He looked at her sharply. "You know about her?"

Vale laughed. "We all know about her."

"Gods..."

"Okay, Royal doesn't know," she corrected. "But that's because Royal thinks everyone is just like him. But Oriana's not stupid. She's the opposite of stupid, in fact. And I read emotions. Of course we know about Caila."

"You read my emotions about Caila?"

"In general, Brom. Come on. We practice magic on each other. You think your emotions don't spill over from one moment to the next?"

"Well, it's not a problem—"

"It *is* a problem," she countered.

"No," he said. "I stopped months ago. I didn't want to endanger the Quad. I wanted all of my focus here, with all of you."

"I know," she said. "It's sweet. For a man who sleeps around all over the academy, you're actually really sweet."

"I don't sleep around all over the academy."

"Maybe you should."

"I don't— What?" He looked at her, thinking he'd misheard. Her eyes narrowed and her smile suddenly looked fiendish.

"You've been faltering for months," she said. "You stopped seeing Caila months ago. Did you ever think the two were connected?" She stood up and walked toward him. He was keenly aware of the way the skirt hugged her hips, of how shapely her legs were.

Brom suddenly felt his mouth go dry. Was she using magic on him?

"I'm here to help," she said, stopping half a foot from him, looking up at him.

"What are you doing?" he asked breathlessly.

She reached out, put light fingers on his chest, and a crackle of lightning went through his whole body. "You're the Anima," she murmured. "It's your job to bring wisdom, to unveil secrets we can't get from books. And you're not doing your job."

"Vale—"

"You're holding back."

"I'm not holding back."

"The Quad doesn't need you to follow the rules, Brom. It needs you to break them. It needs you to be fearless and step beyond the lines others draw. You think Royal or Oriana are going to break the rules?"

"What are you saying?"

She chuckled. "I really thought you were better at this. You keep asking 'what are you saying' and 'what are you doing'. Do I need to be more obvious?"

Brom swallowed.

She came closer, her hands on his chest. "I've wanted you since the first moment I saw you," she murmured. "But I held back for...a number of reasons. That was a mistake."

"We're in a Quad," he said, his mouth suddenly dry. He could barely speak. It felt like he was on a floor that kept tilting one way and then another. First, she'd attacked him for his failures, then suddenly she was so close he could smell her hair. By the gods, he wanted to pull her compact little body to him, run his hand over the curve of her hip until it passed the edge of the skirt, then run it back up, underneath...

She pulled him into a kiss. Her lips were soft and warm. Her tongue touched his, and he almost lost control. With every ounce of his willpower, he forced himself to pull away. She let him go, but not far. Their faces hovered an inch away from each other, and she looked at him with a smoldering gaze.

Lightning crackled through him.

"It's against the rules," he whispered. "We could lose the Quad. They'll expel us. Oriana would—"

"I know," she said. "But that's what we missed, you and I. We *need* to break the rules. It lights you up. I can feel it."

The lightning crackling frantically between them. It was like they both suddenly had twenty Soulblocks.

"What about the Quad?" he gasped.

"It's what's best for the Quad."

"The rules..."

"Let Oriana and Royal have the rules. We'll take this." She pulled him to the floor.

"Gods," he murmured.

"They can stay out of it, too."

He kissed her, and this time he plunged his fingers into her hair, let his hand slide over her curves, under the skirt. She moaned into his ear and wrapped herself around him.

The lightning raced through both of them, and they lost themselves to it.

4

BROM

Brom stood in the quiet practice room after midnight, kept awake by a strange foreboding. Of course, he wasn't supposed to be here after curfew, but he didn't care. The window on the west wall had a loose latch—because Brom had loosened it months ago—and he broke into the practice room whenever he wanted. These days, he felt more and more inclined to break the rules. Vale had been right, and Brom's education had vaulted forward the moment he'd begun racing along the edge of his life, poised to fall at any moment.

The room was dark, but he didn't need light anymore. Not here. He knew the practice room like he knew his own body. He knew the world like he knew his own body. The months had flown by, and his second year at the academy was almost over. He'd regained all of his earlier breakthroughs and surged past them, into new territory.

He raised his sword and faced the Gauntlet, the elaborate combination of mechanisms that would chew, beat, slice, or poison anyone who dared to step inside. Blades whirled, gears ground, and poison flung—either on the tip of a dart or rigged to drop from a reservoir overhead—trying to bring down any student who braved the machine. To traverse from the east side to the west side required preternatural reflexes and acrobatics.

Or the skills of an Anima.

Brom had recently tapped into the Soul of the World. This new magic allowed him to feel his environment and the patterns of nature so intimately it bordered on precognition.

He readied himself to step in, but his troubled thoughts harried him and he stepped back. Best not tempt the Gauntlet without full focus. He took a deep breath.

His thoughts from the past several months washed over him.

On the outside, everything seemed natural, fluid. Quad Brilliant's list of accomplishments continued to grow, and this time he was a part of it. He was holding up his end. The bond between them was stronger than ever, so why this uneasiness, like he was missing something?

At first, he'd thought it was because the exams for their second-year writs of passage were coming; they were only a month away. But that couldn't be it. None of them were afraid of passing this time. The writs of passage were a formality.

Of course, he had wondered if this foreboding stemmed from his and Vale's secret love affair. It was like an axe about to fall, every day, but each time he thought of her, the foreboding vanished. Like she was the cure, not the cause. Vale had been right about Brom's magical progress. He needed to feel on the edge. He needed to break the rules. From the moment they took up with one another, the wall between him and his magic had shattered.

He'd considered Quad Brilliant itself as the reason for this foreboding. Had they blossomed too quickly, succeeded too thoroughly? Were they poised to fall?

And what was the alternative? To intentionally slow their progress? Royal, Oriana, and Vale would never agree to hold back. And neither would Brom.

So what was it? He'd tried to dismiss it again and again as ghosts in his head. Doubts and worries, but maybe it wasn't simply in his head. He was an Anima now, connected to a greater sense of the lands, able to see the nature of people and the lands themselves. What if he was beginning to tap into something even greater? What if this foreboding was his power taking him farther? What if he was sensing something coming from a distant future?

He stood there in the dark and silence for long minutes, chasing it down, trying to find its source, but he couldn't. Nothing fit, and his fears grew. An unknown threat was far more dangerous than a known threat...

Enough, he thought angrily. He chopped his hand down through the empty air.

Whatever this foreboding was, he wasn't going to pierce its secrets tonight. If his intuition was trying to talk to him, it would have to speak louder.

He was going to run the Gauntlet. And who knew? Perhaps going through this exercise, sinking deep into the Soul of the World, would trigger something, reveal something that was missing.

He let his thoughts go and opened his first Soulblock.

Lightning crackled, striking inside his body. He channeled the magic, reached out with his senses, and became a part of everything around him.

The Soul of the World was different from seeing the soul of an individual. Instead of showing a person's desires and their intended direction, it showed the way the wind would blow, the exact path a leaf would randomly drift to the ground.

Brom could feel the intention of the elements, and as long as the lightning crackled through him, it lent him a kind of precognition. He couldn't predict what would happen to him tomorrow or five years from now, but he could sense what was going to happen in the next second.

The Gauntlet was expressly designed to test this skill. It created a random pattern with its deadly components, and an Anima should be able to dance through it by trusting in his magic. The Soul of the World would tell Brom when to duck, when to leap, when to block with his sword.

He walked calmly into the Gauntlet. He kept his eyes open but half-lidded. Seeing wasn't nearly as important as feeling.

The metal and wood of the Gauntlet—the very air itself—warned Brom of its attacks a second before they struck. He moved, spun, ducked, jumped, dove. Steel-tipped clubs whispered past his head, darts flew by him, missing by inches. He was faintly aware of deflecting a blade with his sword like he would have been aware of his mother calling him for dinner—distant but important. The magic crackled through him, tendrils of lightning connecting him to the dangers like they were parts of his own body.

Then, so quickly, it was over. He stood, breathing hard and sweating, on the other side of the Gauntlet. The wheels and gears of the machine whirred as they re-set, spinning into their caches, waiting for the next challenger, then they went silent. Brom seemed to float in the darkness.

As he came back to his normal awareness, the foreboding seeped into him again. He had hoped to flee it or plunge into some new understanding of it, but it settled on him again like a thick cloak.

No, he wasn't just jumping at shadows. The foreboding was real. Something was coming. Something horrible. He just didn't know from which direction. He blinked, and the drain of having used almost an entire Soulblock pulled heavily at him.

Then, suddenly, the lightning within him surged, crackling to life again.

"Heavy heart. Heavy fears," Vale said from behind him.

Brom spun.

She sat in the wide windowsill where he'd entered and, though the sill was only four feet across, she lounged on it like a couch. Only someone as small as Vale could "lounge" on that shelf of marble.

"Are you using magic on me, Motus?" he asked. His fatigue vanished as her nearness invigorated him. It was like that with all of his Quad mates now.

Being with just one Quad mate didn't double his Soulblocks, like being with all three of them did, but it was like a deep breath of fresh air and a splash of cold water on the face.

"I had half of a Soulblock lingering about," she said. "I didn't feel like waking up soul-sick, so I thought I'd find you."

"Soul-sick" was the word they used for the hangover of an unused Soulblock. If a student opened a Soulblock but didn't use it all, the lightning wreaked havoc inside the body. Sometimes there was vomiting.

"Royal says beer quells soul-sick," he said.

"I went to your room," she said. "When I didn't find you, I thought I'd have to search every woman's bed in the academy."

"Can I watch?" he joked.

"Would you like that?"

"I'm glad you came here instead," he said. "You give me this...tingle inside."

"Is it like lightning?" she asked wryly.

She dropped from the window and sauntered to him. He suspected she had never sauntered in her life before bonding with the Quad. But the powers of a Motus brought a heightened presence and a magical glamour that played on others' emotions. When she used her magic, she could make a person enthralled with her. Once she'd discovered this, the sauntering had come naturally.

She used her magic on Brom now. He could feel it. His heart beat faster. Her tumbling hair bounced, begging to be touched. Her eyes glimmered in the dark. He became aware of how her clothes stretched tightly over her curves.

"I know of another way to quell soul-sick," she murmured, wrapping her arms around his waist. She smelled like rain and Lavulin flowers. He leaned down and kissed her.

"That's better than beer," he murmured.

"Come on." She led him toward the empty bench where the Invisible Ones sat during the day.

He tugged her back toward him, and she curled up in his arm like they were dancing.

"I have a better idea," he said.

"Better?"

"On how to use up that Soulblock. I want to try something."

"Oh really?" She ran a finger up his belly, chest, neck, and flicked it off the tip of his chin. "You sure?"

"You're going to like it."

"I bet I will." She was always game for something new.

He stole a moment to simply drink in the sight of her. She'd blossomed from a spiteful little rat into a breathtaking legend. They'd all changed, but her transformation was astonishing. She kept turning like a diamond in the sun, new facets flashing into view every week, surprising them all. She was sexy, competent, brilliant. He found it impossible to get enough of her. Those glimmering, mischievous eyes, that cocky stance and her smile. Oh, that smile. It was a sultry invitation and a challenge at the same time. It pulled him to her like the sea pulled a river.

Oh, she was still dangerous. It lanced out every now and then. But she also had more depth than any of them could have guessed. She was loving and surprisingly gentle. She was frightened and courageous. She was daring and reckless. Whatever she did, she plunged in headfirst and her emotions vacillated wildly. There was no halfway with Vale. She was either all in or all out. When she'd decided to trust her Quad, her commitment had become absolute. She bound them together with a passion.

With Royal, she'd started acting like a little sister. She would stand close to him most days, no matter what they were doing, taking an unconscious comfort from being near the big man. And Royal had responded in kind. He liked feeling like he was protecting her. She would fling "large" jokes at him. He would fling "tiny" jokes back at her, which usually ended with her punching him in the arm. One day, the big man had spontaneously tossed her into the air and caught her like a little girl while she whooped. Vale had laughed until he set her down on the ground. Then she'd sneered and drawn her dagger, put it against his belly and said in a scathing tone, "Try that again and I'll spill your guts, ox."

Brom and Oriana had frozen in shock. She'd been like the old Vale, the Vale who'd stabbed Royal on that first day.

Then Vale had deftly spun the dagger and sheathed it.

"How was that?" She'd grinned. "Did you believe me?"

"Gods!" Brom had exclaimed.

"Brilliant," Oriana had said, amused. Royal and Brom had started laughing.

Like with Royal, Vale had also made a bridge to Oriana through the princess's expertise: academics. To everyone's surprise, Vale had an excellent mind for book learning. She had put her newfound knowledge of how to read to powerful use and devoured book after book. She became Oriana's academic assistant, following her to the library and digging through old texts on behalf of the Quad. Vale wasn't as talented at research as Oriana, but she easily surpassed Royal and Brom.

It was Vale's passion, Brom had decided, that made her so successful at everything she did. Her fire drove her past fatigue, past the point where most would quit. And her time on the streets of Torlioch, struggling to stay alive, had given her a relentless tenacity.

And with Brom... Well, she'd been his lover.

She had orchestrated that fateful day in the practice room, he was sure. But after his initial shock, he'd happily tumbled down her well and hadn't come up for air since. Gods, had it only been five months? It seemed like they had always been together.

It was dangerous, what they were doing. They both knew it. They'd seen the price for failing to keep their secret. At the beginning of the year, a couple in a new first-year Quad—Quad River—had been discovered having sex. The entire Quad had been expelled, their magic stripped away. They'd been sent home in disgrace as the Forgotten, damned to be *normals* for the rest of their lives.

Brom had been stunned at the harshness of the sentence. After connecting with Caila in his first year, Brom had met quite a few other students who had broken the rule of "fraternizing," as they called it. None of them had been punished. He began to suspect that what Caila and he had done was merely frowned upon. Sex between two students from different years and different Quads was discouraged, but the masters didn't seem to spend any time looking for it, nor meting out punishment.

But inside a Quad, the punishment was swift and irrevocable.

"Are you soul-seeking?" Vale asked, rubbing his arm affectionately and bringing him back from his reverie.

Brom blinked, realizing he'd simply been staring at her. He did that sometimes, often when he was looking into someone's soul. The others had become accustomed to his moments of "soul-seeking," as Oriana called it.

"Just thinking," he said.

"About me?" She winked.

"I was, actually."

She turned her head to the side, clasped her hands in front of herself and batted her eyelashes in mock coquettishness. "I bet you say that to all the girls."

"Never."

"You have a reputation."

"Me? Gossip."

"Is it?"

"Tell me you're not jealous."

"Jealous?" She was suddenly holding her dagger—he hadn't even seen her draw it—and turned it so the blade glimmered in the moonlight shining through the window. "When I'm feeling jealous, you'll know."

He laughed, though he wasn't sure it was a joke. She was still that feral urchin somewhere deep down. Even reading her soul didn't help him to fully understand her. It showed who she was and what direction she might go, but what did that matter when Vale was so unpredictable that even she didn't know what she might do from moment to moment?

Whether she was a hateful calf-stabber or everyone's favorite Quad mate, she was never dull.

"You were saying you had another way of using up the rest of my Soulblock," she reminded him.

"I want to test something. The Soul of the World. I want to try giving it to you."

Her eyes went wide. "That's fourth-year magic," she said, excited. "Can you really do it?" The internal and external applications of a given path were the easiest to master, usually. Most students learned to master these in their first three years. But transferring a connection to the Soul of the World from an Anima to someone else was part of the constructive aspect of the Anima, far more complex and far more difficult. Most Anima students studied the constructive and destructive aspects in their fourth year. And some never accomplished this particular spell at all.

"I have an idea," he said.

"Brilliant." Vale mimicked Oriana's over-articulated speech.

"Let's go."

"We're going somewhere?"

"By the river."

She sprinted to the window and leapt, catching the sill with her fingers and pulling her lithe, compact body up. She winked, swung her legs out the window, and dropped from view.

By the gods, that woman!

He followed her with a grin, and she led him across the moonlit Quadron Garden to the river. Only Fendra was out tonight, a quarter moon of silver-blue light that made it seem like the goddess was winking at them. The light lent a cool, silvery cast to the grass and the trees. The fresh smell of wet earth grew stronger and the rush of moving water grew louder as they neared the river. They slid down the bank into the little cove beneath the willow tree where Brom and Oriana had broken the first barrier of the Quad.

"Let's run," he said, and they jogged north along the river. Vale had a short stride, but she was fast. For several minutes, they just ran, leaping fallen trees and ducking branches, skirting the rushing water and running up and down banks when the shore shrank. Then, Brom opened his second Soulblock.

The magic crackled through him, and he reached into the Soul of the World. He felt the rushing of the river like it ran through his own chest. He felt the limbs of the trees like they were his own arms, the sand like it was his own feet. Unconsciously, he ran faster. He didn't close his eyes, but he stopped using them. Obstacles ceased to exist because they were all a part of him now.

He felt Vale behind him, struggling to keep up. She was smaller, lither, and she had far more practice dodging and ducking, but her instincts couldn't match his any longer. Her feet thumped hard on sand and fallen trunks as she labored to see her way. Branches cracked as she burst through them.

Slowly, Brom began his experiment. He twisted the lightning of the magic into a thin thread, then pushed it out of his back. He imagined it trailing behind him like a shimmering string in the wind. His concentration burned, but he held tight. Painstakingly, he let the thread out until it tickled Vale's forehead. Once it touched her, the bond between them sparked. Just as he felt the river, the trees, and the ground, he felt Vale's surprise.

He widened the bond, turning the thread into a thick crackling rope of lightning, and sent the Soul of the World through it. He connected their bodies, let his senses become her senses, let the things that he felt become the things she felt.

She drew a swift breath as it rushed into her. But in moments, her labored breathing eased. The thumping of her feet quieted. The cracking of branches ceased. With Brom's senses, she stopped fighting the terrain and began moving with it.

Together, they sprinted through the night like wolves.

"Try it with your eyes closed," Brom barely whispered, but he knew she would hear him. She obeyed immediately.

"Gods, Brom," she said.

They ran blind, racing along the river. The passage of time twisted, and it seemed only seconds before they jogged to a stop before the white wall of the academy. The river pushed into fierce rapids through a perfectly circular hole, covered with a portcullis.

Brom felt the steel of the barrier, the wild rush of the water. He could feel a space at the very bottom of the river, a break in the iron grate where a person could slip through. He could have dived into the water and found that space, swam under the wall, and Vale could have followed him. A part of him wanted to leave the academy, swim through that hole and simply keep running, but the foreboding within him surged, warning him not to go any further.

He was so deep in the Soul of the World that the foreboding jolted him. He thought he saw green flame where the rapids churned beneath the wall, but then it was gone.

"Wait," he murmured as Vale drew up alongside him. She was lost in the sensation too.

"What is it?" she asked.

"The green flame," he said.

"What green flame?"

She hadn't seen it. There was something here. Something...magical.

Brom let his awareness expand outward, becoming one with the wall, stretching to find that magical thing...

The green flame flickered again, and this time he was part of it. This was a spell that had been left behind, something worked on the wall itself, but he couldn't tell exactly what. A protection, some kind of barrier, perhaps to keep invaders out? Or was this the spell that safeguarded the students' Soulblocks? Kept them from crumbling until they became Quadrons and were allowed to leave?

The fuel from his second Soulblock ebbed. He was running out of magic. But he was afraid if he stopped now, he'd never know what this spell was.

He hesitated. The instructors required that students not open their third Soulblock until their fourth and final year at the academy. It was simply too easy for the uninitiated to hurt themselves. With every Soulblock drained of magic, a student moved closer to draining his entire soul. Using the first Soulblock was invigorating and tiring, like playing hard for a few hours on Quadron Garden. It usually took an hour of rest before the magic of that Soulblock refilled. Using the second Soulblock left a student feeling like they'd worked a fifteen-hour day in a mine. It took a good night's rest to recover and refill the second Soulblock. Using the third, the instructors said, could put a novice in bed for a week, make them susceptible to sickness, possibly even give them a chronic problem, depending on how they had used the Soulblock.

But the most dangerous aspect was that using Soulblocks was addictive. Many who opened the third felt an almost irresistible compulsion to keep going and open the fourth.

And opening the fourth Soulblock was certain death.

But Brom had to know about this spell. His foreboding was connected to it....

He opened his third Soulblock and gasped.

The magic crackled into him, so intensely it was like the lightning had turned into a thundering river. His awareness shot straight up like a catapult stone, high into the air. Fendra blazed like a sickle of silver-blue fire. If he'd had a mouth to gasp with, he would have gasped, but he'd risen out of his body. He had connected to the spell in the wall, and now he realized it wasn't just in the wall but over the entire academy, like a dome. His awareness spread across it like he himself was the magical protection.

High above, Brom saw the academy like he was looking at a map. He saw Westfall Dormitory for first-, second-, and third-year students, and the smaller houses for fourth-years. He saw the building with the practice rooms for third- and fourth-years, Quadron Garden, the river, the white stables, the guard towers at the front gate, the three towers on the northeast, southeast, and northwest and, of course, the Tower of the Four at the southwestern corner, looming over everything.

He felt drunk, wanting to laugh at the thunderstorm of magic inside him. Suddenly, he could see the souls of each student in the school like little different-colored candles burning far below, flame after flame after flame in the many dorm rooms. He also saw flame after flame of the instructors in their individual mansions on campus. He looked at himself, at his own floating soul, a translucent charcoal-colored replica of his own body.

Charcoal black. That was the color of an Anima. He laughed finally, overwhelmed by the scope of this new power. He almost looked away again, then something caught his eye.

Little wisps of green smoke trailed from the tips of his fingers. They leaked out, floating upward and joining with the dome of the spell over the school, becoming part of it. Brom looked closer and realized that it wasn't just his fingers leaking. The entire charcoal projection of his body was doing the same: the backs of his forearms, his thighs, his calves, his feet. And the more he looked at it, the brighter the green became.

The dome, this spell...it's pulling something out of me, he thought.

It was so minute it was almost impossible to see, even as deep as he was into the Soul of the World.

He tore his gaze away, looking back at the academy sprawled beneath him.

Each soul below was just a flicker of color, but he could see the same tiny green streams going up from them, high up, into the arch of the green-flaming dome. He looked back at Vale, and that green smoke was being pulled from her body as well.

He blinked and looked at the tower of The Four. It burned like a giant, sickly green torch.

That's where it was all coming from. That was the source of the spell. Brom had never seen that light burning at the top of the Tower of the Four before, and it was horrible. He tried to tear his attention away, but he couldn't. Panicked, he tried again and still he couldn't. He could only stare at that churning, flickering bonfire of green.

His instincts screamed at him to flee, and he knew that if he looked too long he'd go insane. This magic was awful, some horrifying act that he didn't understand.

What are they doing? he thought. *What are they doing!*

This was the source of his growing foreboding. It was as though the more facile he became with his magic, the more he became gradually aware of this thing, this green fire. It was pulling something from every master and every student in the academy. What was it pulling? Magic? Life?

Glistening green eyes formed in the midst of the tower's flame, angry eyes, and their gaze flicked left and right, searching.

It's looking for me, he suddenly realized. *I've seen this horrible thing, and the eyes... They've sensed me somehow.*

The disembodied eyes searched the campus, their gaze sweeping toward him. He froze, preparing for a godly wrath to fall on him...

...but the gaze swept past and continued on as though it hadn't seen him.

Why? Why would it overlook him...?

I don't have time to wonder, he thought. *I have to get away from here, have to get Vale away from here. Right now.*

He jerked, trying to leave, but still he couldn't tear his gaze away from the burning green light over the tower. Was it a trap? Did the green fire hold any student who might see it, keep them transfixed until they could be found?

A jolt ran through him, and his vision wobbled.

The vengeful gaze reached the far side of the campus, then started back toward him, more slowly and cautiously this time, like a person who'd dropped something and, after a quick glance at the ground, finally got down on hands and knees to look in earnest. The gaze came inexorably closer.

Brom...

The jolt ran through him again, and his view of the entire campus wobbled.

"Brom!" Vale barked, slapping his face.

Brom slammed back in his body.

He gasped. He was beside the rushing river and he suddenly realized Vale had been calling his name repeatedly and slapping him. His cheeks stung, and her eyes were wild. Their connection to the Soul of the World faltered, about to dissipate. Hot fear washed over him. No! He couldn't let that happen!

He suspected the only reason the terrible eyes hadn't found him was because he was so deep in the Soul of the World that he had blended with nature. If he let go of that connection, he might become as apparent as a stick bobbing to the surface of a lake.

He redoubled his focus, pulling more magic from his third Soulblock, and he held onto his connection.

"Don't talk," he whispered, grabbing her hand. "We're in terrible danger. Stay connected to me. Don't drop that connection. Follow me close." He plunged into the undergrowth near the river, hopping and skipping and dodging, dancing with his connection to the Soul of the World, and Vale followed. He felt the power of his third Soulblock dwindling. He was reaching its limit but he had to push through. He couldn't let the connection drop until they were safe.

He couldn't see the disembodied, vengeful eyes anymore, but he didn't look for them either. Somehow, he knew looking for them would only help them find him faster. He pushed forward, waiting for those eyes to appear in front of them, to burn him up in a foul green flame.

Then, suddenly, they were at the weeping willow, right across from Westfall Dormitory.

He led Vale up and over Quadron Garden. Only when they had reached the dormitory, walked swiftly through its quiet halls, entered his room, and shut the door did he drop his connection to the Soul of the World.

He fell onto the bed, staring up at the ceiling and breathing hard. He'd burned the entirety of his third Soulblock, right down to the top of his fourth, and that seductive fourth longed to be used. It trembled, wanting to break open and give him the lightning he needed.

He mightily resisted the urge and barely stopped himself.

Exhaustion settled over him like a blanket made of midnight. Questions bounced in his mind. How had he flown up over the entire campus? He had never heard of anything like that, had never even read about anything like that.

And the green, vengeful eyes... The eyes! Would the eyes be able to track them even here? Vale... He had to protect Vale.

"You...have to go. Don't...stay here." If they tracked him, maybe they'd think it was only him. Maybe they wouldn't think to look for Vale if she wasn't here.

"What did you do?" she demanded, angry and worried, leaning over the bed. "Back at the wall, you were soul-seeking deeper than I've ever seen. I couldn't wake you. You started twitching, and your emotions went ice blue with terror. And now you're fucking weeping green goo!"

Brom could barely raise his arm, but he wiped his hand across his eyes. His fingers came away with streaks of iridescent green slime the same color as the flame. His chest hurt, and his heart beat so slowly it felt like it was pumping mud.

"I couldn't...let them...find us." Gods, it was hard to talk! It was like his head was a hundred pounds and his lips were made of lead.

"Let who find us?" she pressed.

The blanket of darkness moved up his body toward his head like oozing oil and pressed down on him. His eyelids grew heavy.

Vale leaned over him. "Gods damn it, Brom. Tell me what happened!"

But her voice was far away and getting farther. The midnight blanket pushed him into the bed, as if he were descending slowly into a grave lined with his own sheets.

"Brom?" Vale warbled. Her voice couldn't quite get over the edges of that sheet-covered hole, couldn't quite get down to him without becoming twisted.

"Kelto's beard," she warbled, the exclamation drawing out slowly. Her voice grew less distinct. He couldn't understand the words. She gripped his shoulders and shook him, but he barely felt it.

"Brom!"

The midnight blanket oozed over his head, and everything went dark.

5
ORIANA

Oriana was sound asleep.

Suddenly, fear and anger slammed into her. Her pleasant dream about riding horses across the Sediron Valley with Ayvra suddenly became a nightmare. Ayvra became Vale—sweaty and muddy—dark hair tangled, screaming at Oriana.

She gasped and sat up, silk sheets flying. Her heart thundered. Those weren't *her* emotions. Vale had slammed her with a heart-spike, a form of Motus attack. Oriana's nerves jangled like she'd drunk a cup of terror.

"Get up," Vale whispered through the door.

"Kelto's fist," Oriana cursed, trying to find her equilibrium and stand up. After a wobbling moment, she mastered herself and strode barefoot across the floor. She undid the latch, and Vale burst through. She grabbed Oriana, turned, and pulled as if to haul her into the hallway in her nightgown.

Oriana twisted her wrist, breaking Vale's grip. "Compose yourself," she said.

Vale was as wild-eyed and wild-haired as she'd been in Oriana's short nightmare. She smelled of river water and a hint of the Lavulin perfume Oriana had given her. Her boots were spattered with mud.

Oriana quickly put the pieces together.

Brom's and Vale's love affair had finally blown apart. Of course, Oriana knew that Brom and Vale had taken up with one another this past month, and it had finally ended in tragedy.

An inter-Quad love affair was idiocy on every level. First and foremost, they could all be expelled. But even without the immediate threat of expulsion, an inter-Quad romance would eventually split the Quad into pieces. If Vale and Brom had ever once thought about rules and why they were created, they'd see that. If things went sour between the two—and they would—it would split the Quad right down the middle. Vale was volatile. Brom had a wandering eye. It was a disaster waiting to happen.

In fact, Oriana would bet ten gold pieces that Vale was here because one of the masters had caught them. Or because she'd stabbed Brom for infidelity. One of the two.

Oh, she'd longed to call them out, to expose their secret to Royal and demand they put an end to it. She'd thought it through several different ways, but there was no satisfactory outcome. Every option split the Quad. If Royal knew, he'd never forgive them. If Oriana commanded them to stop, they'd rebel. Brom and Vale both hated authority, and the only reason the Quad had bonded in the first place was because they saw Oriana as a peer, not a princess. If she took up the mantle of princess again—something all of her Quad mates expected her to do—*she* would become the focus of their rebellion.

She had worked too hard—and Quad Brilliant was succeeding too brilliantly—to throw it away. Kelto alone would have to sort this mess. Oriana's part was to play the supportive Quad mate. It was why she'd lent Vale the Lavulin perfume in the first place, even though she'd known where it would be used.

So she hadn't warned them, hadn't discouraged them or even told them that she knew. Oriana had clenched her teeth and said nothing, simply watching the quiet disaster build.

And now the moment she'd expected had finally come.

"Let me guess," Oriana said. "You were cavorting with Brom by the river and you were caught by one of the masters."

Vale's eyebrows shot up. Due to the invasive nature of the Mentis path of magic, Vale would instantly assume Oriana had read her mind. But she hadn't and wouldn't. She took their collective oath—not to use magic on each other except with permission—very seriously.

Vale turned red and opened her mouth to speak, but Oriana cut her off.

"I didn't read your mind," she said. "The story is spattered on your boots, dabbed on your neck, and written on your face. And yes. I've known about you and Brom for some time."

Vale's mouth hung open for a moment, then clacked shut, and she narrowed her eyes. She waved it away. "I don't care. This isn't about that."

"It isn't," Oriana said, unconvinced.

"It isn't *all* about that," Vale amended.

"Then speak plainly."

"Come with me. Now."

"I'm in my nightgown—"

"I think Brom unlocked his fourth Soulblock. He's hurt. He might be dying."

"What?" A spike of fear shot through Oriana. "Why?"

"Come on!" She pulled Oriana into the hallway, and this time Oriana didn't resist. The Westfall Dormitory was a three-story building with dorm rooms all around a grand foyer in the center. The first floor was the entrance and the practice rooms. Levels two and three were housing for first-year and second-year students.

Oriana said, "Let's get Royal—"

"We don't need him," Vale said. "And he's probably not going to like what we were doing anyway."

"Vale..."

"You know how he is about rules! We broke rules tonight. Royal won't want any part of that." Her hand gripped Oriana's wrist even harder.

Oriana once again twisted her wrist and broke the grip. She opened her first Soulblock. Magic crackled into her, swirling like a storm in a bottle. With her mind, she reached across the expanse of the grand foyer between their walkway and Royal's. Her magic went into his room and planted a loud thought in his head. It was the equivalent of banging a hammer on a cooking pot.

"Get up, Royal!" she shouted into his dreams, much like Vale had shouted into hers.

There was a muffled cry and a thud, as if someone had fallen off their bed. The seventh door from the end on the second level shot open, and Royal emerged with a sheet tied around his naked waist. He rubbed a fist in his eyes and blinked up at them.

Vale shot a venomous look at Oriana.

"We are Quad mates," Oriana said calmly.

Royal seemed about to shout at them, but thankfully he wasn't as dumb as his hulking appearance made him sometimes seem. He noticed they were running somewhere. Seeing Oriana in her nightgown, he must have absorbed the urgency.

"It's Brom," she sent to him.

That seemed enough information for Royal. Brom was the most likely to get into trouble. He had a knack for it. Like Oriana, Royal had probably anticipated the need to rescue Brom for months now. With a fierce yank, Royal secured the bed sheet around his muscular waist. Oriana gave a wry smile and kept running. While Royal was stringent about some rules, he had no modesty when it came to nudity. Most Impetus would probably run naked through the halls all day if it were allowed. Perhaps constant immersion in their own physicality made them this way.

Or perhaps they were all vain. Most Impetus were physically beautiful. Maybe the beautiful simply felt the need to cavort about in the nude.

The big man covered the distance to the stairway in a few strides, then leapt the entire flight in a single bound. He reached Brom's door before Vale and Oriana.

Together, the three entered Brom's room and shut the door. Vale and Oriana were breathing hard after the short run, though Royal showed no indication of exertion whatsoever.

Brom lay on the bed like a corpse.

"Fendra!" Royal whispered.

Oriana narrowed her eyes and concentrated. She unlocked the information in her mind relating to soul-shock, the deadly state that preceded the draining of a student's fourth Soulblock.

The internal aspect of a Mentis enabled Oriana to create organized repositories of information inside her own mind and quickly access anything she'd ever read or heard as though she had just read or heard it. It was like having an entire library in her head, complete with a librarian who could move at lightning speed. The symptoms of soul-shock flicked through her mind.

Slow breathing. Deathly pallor. Half-lidded, unblinking eyes. No movement, as though his body had forgotten how.

All of these described Brom's current state.

Kelto's teeth, he wouldn't really have been so stupid as to open his fourth Soulblock, would he? He was irreverent, certainly. He despised rules and hated authority. But he didn't have a death wish. Surely he knew that the rule about the fourth Soulblock wasn't optional. It was about life and death.

"Did he open his fourth Soulblock?" Vale asked.

"What?" Royal blurted, incredulous.

"I don't know," Oriana said, ignoring Royal's outburst. "Calm down. Just...let me think a moment."

There was no sure cure for a person who had drained their fourth Soulblock. Their entire Soulblock structure simply crumbled and they died. There were no accounts of someone opening their fourth Soulblock and surviving.

But there were a few rare accounts of soul-shock happening to a highly talented student who had opened their third Soulblock for the first time. For such a student, the rush of magic was so powerful that the soul-sickness was devastating.

"Well, what does it say?" Vale asked, annoyed. She knew exactly what Oriana was doing.

"Quiet." She continued to review her memories. Apparently, in the instance of such a student, Quad mates could pump him full of their own magic to offset the devastation. And the sooner the better. Every minute a student lay in soul-shock, the harder the recovery would be.

Dammit. Oriana was no physician. What if there was something else, some other risk she hadn't heard of? She flicked ahead of the text in her repository, all the way to the warning at the end.

There it was. Overloading someone with magic came with its own dangers. There was another reason a student could have these same symptoms.

A powerful Motus heart-spike could cause exactly the same symptoms as soul-shock. If given an overload of anger or spite, a student could fall into this same still, unseeing state. Such an attack filled the body with so much unused magic that they jumped past the typical soul-sickness to a comatose state. In that case, pumping them full of magic could kill them.

"What did he do?" Oriana asked.

"We were running," Vale said immediately. "By the river. He wanted to test the constructive aspect of the Anima, tapping into the Soul of the World and giving it to me."

"Giving it to you?" Royal repeated, like he hadn't quite heard her right. "That's fourth-year magic."

"He can do it," Vale said. "But then, something happened."

"Were you attacked?" Oriana asked.

"I don't know."

"Vale, were you *attacked*?" Oriana insisted, annoyed.

After a moment, she nodded. "I think so. He was scared. He said someone was trying to get to us. To...to find us, he said. He seemed to think we'd escaped them, but...I don't know."

"Did you escape them or not?" Royal demanded.

"How the fuck should I know? He barely spoke to me, sprinted like a frightened deer, then fell over and started bleeding green from his eyes!"

Oriana and Royal leaned over Brom at the same time. There was definitely something green crusting around his eyelids. Oriana spent a critical moment searching frantically in her repository, but there was nothing about crying green slime. She thought about searching other places that might mention it, but they didn't have the time. If this was soul-shock, he could slip into a coma if they didn't do something right now.

Oriana took a deep, calming breath. Her father's voice awoke in her mind.

A normal person can spend their entire lives second-guessing themselves. A ruler cannot.

"It's soul-shock," she said. "Let us hope it is only because he opened his third Soulblock and not his fourth."

"Opening the third Soulblock can do this?" Royal asked, surprised.

"It's rare," she said. "But exceedingly talented students are sometimes overwhelmed by the power of their third Soulblock. We already know Brom is exceptionally talented, so let us hope. Give him one of your Soulblocks. Each of you," she said, hoping to Kelto she was right. "Do it now."

Royal, Vale, and Oriana clasped hands. A storm of magic crackled inside each of them. Power roared out, and they poured it into Brom.

Oriana clenched her teeth, waiting for the keening wail that would indicate Brom's overload and death, but it didn't happen.

Instead, he sat up so forcefully that he actually vaulted into the air. Royal reached out, his arm a blur, and caught Brom around the waist before he crashed through the window.

Brom wheezed like he'd been punched in the stomach. Royal held him up for a moment, then set him on the floor. Brom's eyes were wide and wild.

"What did you do?" Brom gasped.

Vale breathed a sigh of relief.

"What did *we* do?" Royal growled. "What did *you* do?"

"We unfucked your soul-shock," Vale explained. "Now tell us why we had to."

"Good..." Brom murmured, nodding slowly at first, then faster. "Yes, that's good."

He had nearly plunged himself into a coma, but he was obviously still thinking about whatever had caused it. Oriana considered reading his mind without his permission, but she waited. The emergency was over. Her pact with her Quad mates was more important than her curiosity. For now.

Brom began shaking his head. "No. I mean bad," he seemed to change his mind. "Okay, you need to go to bed. Right now."

Vale swung at Brom. She meant to punch him in the face, but

Royal caught her fist. Brom flinched.

Royal laughed. Physical confrontation wasn't the same to Impetus as it was to everyone else. Punches were play. Royal didn't fear a fight.

But Vale wasn't amused. She ripped her fist out of Royal's hand and glared at Brom. "I'm not going anywhere until you tell me what happened."

"Brom, I'd like to read your mind to get the story," Oriana said.

"Brom, I'd like to kick you in your gods-damned penis!" Vale said.

"I'm sorry," Brom said firmly, holding his hands up. "But I don't want to tell you."

"You don't *what*?" Vale's voice rose several octaves.

"We stumbled across something tonight. And we're not out of danger yet." He turned to Vale. "The thing that was looking for me is probably still looking. If it finds me, I want it to find *just* me. Right now, that means you need to go back to your rooms and lie down like you're sleeping."

"Who is looking for you?" Vale demanded.

"I'll tell you. I promise I will. Oriana, you can read my mind tomorrow, but not tonight."

"Why?"

"Because if they send a Mentis to read *your* minds, I don't want you to know anything."

"This is bullshit," Vale snarled.

"Please," Brom urged. "Go now."

"Come on." Royal put a hand on Vale. She dodged underneath it, but he put it back faster than she could escape. She bared her teeth at him, and for a moment Oriana thought Vale would attack. But she relented. Even Vale knew it was futile to fight an Impetu full of magic.

"I'm going to slice your nuts off," Vale hissed and stormed out the door.

Brom's gaze followed her with such a dreamy infatuation that Oriana rolled her eyes.

"Sleep, Brom. You have much to tell us tomorrow," she said, and followed the other two out.

"In the morning," he said. "I promise."

"As you say." Oriana closed the door and went back to her room.

6

ROYAL

Royal waited at the rail, his belly tight with worry, watching Vale and Oriana walk to their side of the dormitory, their feet slapping quietly on the marble floor. He thought about what he must do.

Vale and Brom, and ironically the princess of Keltovar of all people, had made Royal's dreams come true, but now those dreams were broken.

Since he could remember, Royal had pictured the day when his people would draw strength from him. That was the purpose of his life, and the purpose of any community—to draw strength from each other. Especially for those like Royal, who had great strength. It was his job to use that strength in service to others. When Royal had come to the academy, he'd loved the idea of the four paths to magic. The structure of a Quad made perfect sense. Finding his power through connecting with three other worthy souls was as natural to him as the sun rising.

Yet in his dreams, he had imagined his Quad mates differently. He'd seen them strong of heart, true to purpose, and dedicated to the same cause. He had not envisioned an urchin whose desires shifted moment to moment, an irreverent builder's boy who despised all rules simply because they were rules, and the princess of his sworn enemies.

Royal loved his wooded homeland, and he thought about Fendir every day. Fendirans understood the power of tradition and ritual. They were passionate—renowned for poetry and art, and for the fearlessness of their warrior druids. The immortal legend of the rogue Bojalio, a folk hero in both kingdoms, had been penned by a Fendiran bard named Vauquelin. The masterpiece painting *The Delicate Grape* was wrought by Laudine, a Fendiran sculptor who, according to legend, only painted once—that one piece—and it was a masterpiece.

A young Fendiran might leap from a waterfall as part of his declaration of love, or spontaneously give all the gold in their pouch to a beggar child. A typical Fendiran acted much more like Brom than Royal—lusty and bright-eyed. Royal was not like that. In fact, his father had mused aloud at the dinner table several times, asking Royal if he was frightened of women, or perhaps he preferred the company of men.

But the truth was: Royal was already in love. With Fendir. His sole purpose was to preserve her, to protect her, and he simply didn't have time to indulge in other pursuits. The war over the Hallowed Woods threatened Fendir and all she held holy, and Royal had sworn to protect her.

Fendir herself was fragile and beautiful. Fendirans weren't methodical like the Keltovari. They didn't think years in advance, didn't have a taste for building empires. Given time, Keltovar would grind Fendir beneath the hooves of its oppressive culture if they weren't stopped.

Oh, for now the Keltovari claimed to only want the Hallowed Woods. But before that, it had been the land north of the Hallowed Woods. If Fendir retreated again, if they let the Keltovari have that holy place, they would soon want more. The Keltovari wouldn't be satisfied until the two kingdoms became one kingdom.

Royal had traveled to the academy with a singular purpose: to become an Impetu and turn the tide of the war. He'd been ready to show every master, even The Four themselves, that he was born to be a Quadron.

After the crushingly disappointing first year when Royal had despaired that his dreams were dead, his Quad had rallied, finally coming together. They had each looked deeper, seen the worthiness in each other, and worked together like Fendirans.

His three Quad mates, as flawed as he had initially seen them, had become vital to him, like three beating hearts that pumped his own blood. The future Queen of Keltovar had made Royal's dreams come true—the thought still stunned him. He was on his way to becoming a Quadron, perhaps one of the most powerful Impetus ever.

But tonight, he had the cold feeling that he'd made a fool's bargain.

In Royal's experience, human flaws only expanded over time, but his joyous achievement as an Impetu had blinded him to what was happening here. He hadn't seen the flaws of his Quad mates growing steadily larger, cracking the foundation they'd built. Quad Brilliant had achieved remarkable success...

But they hadn't passed the Test of Separation yet. They were still only students, only able to wield magic within the walls of the academy. Until they all took the Test and were able to leave the academy with their full powers, they must follow the rules.

It was now painfully obvious that Vale and Brom were never going to respect the rules of the academy. Their rebelliousness was as much a part of them as Royal's tattoos. Of course, he had noticed them breaking rules for months now in small, sneaky ways. Despite what most people thought—at least those who saw him from a distance—Royal wasn't stupid. He'd stood by because Vale and Brom were his Quad mates. He had allowed for their differences because he wanted to remain open-minded.

But their transgressions made Royal feel like someone was scraping his teeth with a knife.

Oriana never made Royal feel this way, and that irony was not lost on him. Vale and Brom caused him daily frustration while Oriana remained sane and dedicated to their collective purpose. By Fendra, how could it be possible that Royal had the most in common with Oriana? It was as though everything had turned upside down.

Against his will, Royal found himself admiring her. Oriana was a champion of order. She was predictable and straightforward. Whether a school or a kingdom, she believed civilization needed a framework of rules. The princess was smart, capable, and level-headed—all qualities that made a good leader. To his surprise, he even quietly found himself adopting her habits in an effort to improve his own leadership. He and Oriana were far more aligned than he wanted to admit. Ironically, he felt...calm around her. Serene and secure.

Brom could make Royal smile with his humor and quick wit, and Vale was like an endearing little sister. But Brom would leap off a cliff with that same smile. When he made those leaps, he didn't consider those attached to him, those who would go over the cliff with him.

And Vale...while he now enjoyed her company, it was impossible to forget how vicious she had once been. That malevolent little urchin was still inside her, and Royal often wondered when it would spring forth from the dark places of her heart. She sneaked out of her room at night, surely going places she should not, doing things she should not.

Brom and Vale had encouraged each other to break the rules. And now they'd gone too far. They'd flaunted the rules, and by the sound of it they'd nearly been caught. Now the masters were looking for Brom. He'd jumped off the cliff and had taken the rest of them with him.

The rules of the academy demanded that Royal go to one of the masters and tell them about this midnight excursion. The rules required him to throw Brom and Vale upon the mercy of those who stewarded the academy. It might even be good for Brom—teach him to respect the rules. It might keep him from hurting himself or anyone else in the future.

And yet...

These were his Quad mates. His natural duty as an Impetu was to protect them. They were his friends. They were dear to him.

He let out a sigh and watched until both Vale and Oriana had safely returned to their rooms and closed their doors. He stood vigil, keeping an eye on each of his Quad mates' doors from across the foyer, making sure no threat visited any of them as they drifted off to sleep. He contemplated what he would do if an academy master came here in the night to threaten one of his Quad mates?

I will fight them, the thought came swiftly, without hesitation, surprising Royal.

He clenched his jaw. Yes. Of course he would. That's all he *could* do.

Fendra damn him, he would fight the masters if he needed to. He would fight The Four themselves to protect his Quad. If someone was coming for them, Royal would stand as the wall between his friends and danger.

I am a fool, he thought.

He was tired, so he used the remaining magic crackling in his chest. He pushed it into a thin trickle of energy, used it to bolster his vigilance, to last him the night.

He stayed, arms folded and elbows on the rail, until first light speared through the tall window at the northern end of the grand foyer. At that point, he drew a deep breath, went into his room, and dressed for the day.

They all went to classes without speaking, and after lunch, Royal went to the practice room. Oriana was already there. As always, she was replete in a tailored and extravagantly embroidered gown. This one was white, of course, but with accents of red, perhaps an indication of her mood, and the collar covered her neck all the way to her chin. Clothes arrived for Oriana every month or so, and this dress was new.

Royal nodded at her, and she nodded back. He wanted to talk to her, to commiserate about the lawlessness of their Quad mates, but there wasn't time.

In moments, the Invisible Ones came in, the faceless people who had been paid to subject themselves to the mental and emotional manipulations of the Mentis and Motus of Quad Brilliant.

Vale entered next, giving a winsome smile to Royal as she crossed the room and jumped up onto her favorite windowsill. She dangled her legs like a mischievous child, despite the fact that she'd been ready to claw Brom's face off last night. She seemed completely unperturbed by what had happened, but Royal knew that could be a lie. Vale's emotions ranged all over. No one knew how she would react to any given situation.

Brom came last, which was no surprise. He was rarely on time to anything, as his mind was often roaming far afield. Oriana called it soul-seeking, and Royal wondered what it must be like to be able to see into the soul of another. Perhaps he, too, would be constantly distracted if he had such a power.

"I have something new to show you," Brom said dramatically, like he was putting on a play. "Let's take a walk by the river."

It was an obvious feint to get away from the Invisible Ones, who were the most innocuous people imaginable, but only a fool would think the Invisible Ones wouldn't report back to the masters about what was said in this room.

Nobody questioned. They followed Brom across Quadron Garden toward a giant willow tree by the river. When they reached it, Vale and Oriana picked their way down the slope like they'd been here before. The bank was only about as tall as Royal, so he jumped to the bottom, loving the impact of moist earth on his feet and the brief burn in his muscles. Vale clambered up onto a low, horizontal tree branch and began swinging her legs again.

"Okay," Brom said. "We need to talk."

"A fucking understatement," Vale said. Her jovial mask vanished.

"Quite," Oriana said with a small smile.

Royal sighed at Vale's profanity. Why did she feel the need to be vulgar? He also didn't understand why Oriana encouraged it by smiling. Oriana herself never swore, of course, but she always smiled when Vale did. Somehow Vale's profanity was novel to the princess. Royal could only guess at the reason. Perhaps she hadn't heard profanity growing up in the Keltovari palace.

"What happened?" Royal asked, trying to steer the conversation toward the real issue.

"I took Vale out to experiment with a new aspect of Anima I'd discovered," Brom said. "I wanted to connect her to the Soul of the World."

"Vale mentioned. That was ambitious." Oriana raised a thin silver eyebrow, which meant she was impressed. "She said you succeeded."

"Oh, it worked," Vale confirmed. "I ran like a wolf, faster than I'd ever gone before. It was like I couldn't do anything wrong, couldn't take a wrong step. It was an amazing feeling. It made me want to be Brom."

"And you ran into a master?" Royal tried not to let his annoyance show in his voice. If Brom had pulled Vale into the Soul of the World with him, he could convey it to Royal and Oriana as well. The thought was staggering. An Impetu with an Anima's precognitive ability would be unstoppable in a war. It was powerful magic, advanced even for a fourth-year student.

And Brom had accomplished it as a second-year.

But then he'd abused his position as a student of this academy and subsequently his power. He and Vale could have done the same work in the practice room, or on Quadron Garden, and they would have been applauded by the masters for their talent. But no. They'd had to sneak out after curfew and run across campus.

"When we reached the wall, I stumbled across a spell," he said. "A spell created by The Four, I think. The power comes from their tower. And they...sensed me. At least, that's what I think happened—"

"The Four!" Royal blurted. Hot anger flooded into him. "You were caught by The Four?" He looked at Oriana, and her face was tight. Her small smile at Vale's profanity had vanished.

"Not caught," Brom said. "They sensed me detecting it. They looked for me but they couldn't find me. So I grabbed Vale and ran."

"Well, of course they found you. They know it's you!" Royal slammed a frustrated fist against the trunk of the willow tree. He hadn't opened a Soulblock today, so the flesh scraped from his hand didn't start healing right away. He let the pain fuel his anger.

"I don't think so," Brom said.

"Of course they do!" he said. "They're *The Four*. They're..." He fought to find the right words. "They're a kingdom unto themselves." The Four had stewarded the two kingdoms for a century. They were demigods.

"Royal is right," Oriana said. "If The Four were looking for you, they found you. It is more plausible to think they simply haven't made you aware of it yet."

Brom hesitated, glanced at Vale. She was pensive now. Brom set his jaw, then met Oriana's gaze. "I don't think so."

"I think Brom's right." Vale spoke up. "Whoever was looking for him tried, but they failed."

"How do you know?" Royal demanded.

"Because I'm a Motus, Humongous," she said, using the sarcastic name she often called him. "I felt rage. I felt frustration. I didn't feel the spike of satisfaction that comes with success. Whoever was looking for us wanted to find us, but they couldn't."

"You can't possibly think you escaped The Four." Royal threw his hands in the air. It implied The Four were fallible, that they could be hoodwinked by this little rule-breaker. That was impossible. "They have to know what you did," he insisted. "For Fendra's sake, we're students! Oriana, support me here."

But Oriana remained silent, one long finger pressed against her lips, a gesture that meant she was lost in the labyrinth of her mind.

"Oriana," Royal prompted.

"I've been to the wall several times," she said softly. "I've never detected a spell, but it makes sense for there to be one. There could be half a dozen reasons for it, but the most likely is to bolster our fragile Soulblocks so that we might work magic in this place."

Brom shook his head. "No. This spell wasn't friendly. It was...sucking green fire from everyone in the school. And I went there... I think I was meant to find it."

"How were you meant to find it?" Oriana asked.

"My intuition led me there. I'm almost certain of it now."

"Your intuition?"

"A foreboding has been growing in my soul for a while now. I'm convinced it led me to the wall where I could discover the spell. That green fire is the reason for my unease."

"That green fire could be the bolstering of The Four," Oriana said.

Brom shook his head. "No. I don't think it's designed to help anyone. It's not a good thing."

"You think The Four are trying to hurt us?" Royal asked. He shook his head violently. "That's ridiculous. You're wrong."

"I bet even the masters aren't aware of this spell," Brom said. "It was sucking green fire from them too."

"It's not sucking anything," Royal growled. "If it's doing anything, it's helping us, like Oriana said."

"It made my stomach turn."

"Well then let's listen to your stomach over The Four," Royal hissed.

"I don't like the idea of anything being sucked out of me without me knowing about it," Vale said.

"That's not what's happening!" Royal ground his teeth. "If The Four wanted to hurt the Quad, they'd just hurt us. They could have used their magic to conquer Keltovar and Fendir if they wanted, but they haven't. They could have kept the secret of magic to themselves, letting young people drain their souls and die. If not for The Four, there wouldn't be Quadrons. We are indebted to them. We would have no magic if not for them."

"This magic isn't theirs," Vale said darkly. "It's ours."

"You know what I'm saying," Royal said. "This academy. The masters. Where would you be if you hadn't been invited here?"

Vale narrowed her eyes.

"Royal, I'm not making this up," Brom interrupted. "I didn't go looking to unveil The Four. I was just practicing my connection to the Soul of the World. And I'm telling you what I saw. A giant green flame over their tower, connected to this insidious spell, connected to me. To you. To all of us."

"And if you'd been practicing in the practice room where you should have been, you could have asked one of the masters to explain it to you," Royal said. "That's what we should do now. Tell the masters and ask them what it is."

"No," Vale said immediately.

"What if you're wrong about The Four?" Brom asked.

"Fendra, I'm not wrong! If The Four created this spell, it's the highest level of magic. You just don't understand what you saw," Royal argued.

"You're right. I don't know what it was," Brom said. "But I know what it felt like. It was the opposite of breathing or...or of kissing someone, the opposite of all things beautiful and natural. It was horrible. It wasn't made to benefit anyone. I'd stake my life on it."

"You've staked all of our lives on it," Royal growled.

"Don't be dramatic," Oriana finally said. "I hardly think The Four would kill a student."

"Except every year at the Test of Separation," Vale said.

"That's not The Four," Royal said darkly.

"Then who is it?" Vale demanded.

"It's the Test of Separation," Royal said. "It is the most deadly test in the two kingdoms for a reason. Only the strongest and most dedicated can become Quadrons." He chopped his hand through the air, cutting off her intended retort. "It has always been that way. It always will."

"What if it doesn't have to be?" she asked.

"No. We're not having this conversation again." Royal took a deep breath and said, "The Four have secrets. They have their reasons and that's good enough for me. We cannot conceive of what they know and the responsibilities they have. And you want to accuse them of malevolence and slap them in the face. Well, you don't know what you're talking about. And none of this would have happened if you had just followed the rules."

"The green flames would still be there if we hadn't followed the rules," Brom said.

"You think you've discovered something," Royal said. "But you're jumping at shadows. All you've done is seen something you don't understand, then made a wild accusation and threatened our chances of becoming Quadrons. Quad mates don't do that."

"Actually that's exactly what an Anima does," Vale said. "He's supposed to look deeper. He's supposed to push boundaries, to seek wisdom."

Royal glared up at her in her tree.

"We're supposed to *push* each other." She glared back. "We're supposed to force each other to grow. Brom is doing more for us than anyone."

"Antagonizing The Four isn't an act of wisdom," Oriana said. "It's the act of a belligerent child."

"Thank you!" Royal blasted.

Brom looked at them with such rebelliousness that Royal thought he'd storm away. He stayed that way for a long moment, and all they could hear was the rushing of the river.

"Maybe you're right," Brom finally forced out through stiff lips. His defiance softened, and for a moment, Royal thought he looked sad. Brom looked down for a long moment, and then he said, "You're right. I don't know exactly what I saw. I certainly didn't understand it. I only know how I felt."

"What?" Vale said. She stared down at Brom from her tree branch in disbelief. She seemed about to say something, then closed her mouth. She pushed that smug, assured smile back onto her face, but Royal could see it was forced.

"I think," Oriana said solemnly, using what Royal had come to think of as her queen's voice, "that Brom has overstepped his bounds. He achieved a great accomplishment, but he did it at great danger to all of us. And Brom, Vale..." She fixed them each with a hard stare in turn. "If you continue to flaunt the rules of the academy, they *will* expel you. And none of us become Quadrons. What you did, even accidentally, threatened us all."

Brom looked thoughtful. Vale looked outraged. She perched on the edge of her branch like an angry cat, like she was going to leap down and scratch them.

Brom looked increasingly more guilty and self-aware, thank Fendra. Perhaps he was finally realizing what he'd almost brought down upon them all.

"I'm sorry," he said softly. "That wasn't my intention."

"I'm sure it wasn't," Oriana said. "It sounds like you stepped into this unknowingly, but it doesn't change the fact that you stepped into it. I think we should try to stop that from happening again. I propose that we make a pact."

"You sound like one of the masters." Vale rolled her eyes.

"Perhaps one of us should."

"I'm not taking orders from you, princess," Vale said scathingly.

"You don't take orders from anybody," Royal cut in.

"You're fucking right I don't." She jumped down from the branch and pointed up at Royal's face. "I'm not bowing to these gods-be-damned masters. What did they ever do for me?"

Royal clenched his fists. Oriana's countenance went ice cold, like she'd been that entire first year.

"They let you train here," Brom interrupted softly.

"What?" Vale turned her burning gaze on him.

"They let you train. That's what they did for you," he said, his eyes sad.

"The masters haven't done shit," Vale said. "The only reason I know anything is because of Oriana and you and Royal. I sharpened my skills against *you*. I pored over books in the library on my *own*. I put the time in to be a Motus!"

"Yes. You did the work. But you never could have if you weren't here," Brom said. "Whether you like the masters or not, whether you want to hear it or not, you need this place. The masters and The Four are part of that. We have to respect them. Without this school, we fail. It's over."

"You're siding with *them*?" Vale said, aghast.

Brom frowned. "There is no *them*, Vale. There's *us*. We're Quad Brilliant. We're in this together, live or die. Our first year should have taught us that."

Vale opened her mouth, but she shut it again, crossed her arms, and leaned back against the trunk of the willow tree.

"Fine. What's your pact?" She flung the words at Oriana. "As if I didn't know," she murmured.

"I submit that we follow the rules," Oriana said. "*All* of the rules."

"What a surprise."

"I agree with Oriana," Royal said.

"Another shock," Vale murmured, and Royal frowned at her.

Brom looked at the ground, thoughtful, his brow furrowed. "I think..." He hesitated. "I think they're right." He looked up, found Vale's angry gaze. "Please, Vale. Once we graduate, we can explore these mysteries to our heart's content. Once we're *Quadrons*. Then everything will be different. We can do what we want."

Vale didn't say anything.

"Then we are agreed?" Royal asked.

"I agree," Oriana said formally.

"I agree," Brom said.

Vale pushed away from the trunk. "You're idiots. The masters, The Four...they don't give a shit about you. Whatever Brom stumbled across, whatever nasty thing they're doing to us, you're just going to let them continue to do it because you're too scared to find out more."

Royal opened his mouth to speak when Vale took the words way from him.

"But I *do* care about all of you," she said, looking up into Royal's eyes. He felt her genuine affection. Her gaze shifted, came to rest on Oriana. "We're Quad mates. So I'm with you. If this is our path, I'll walk it."

"Thank you," Royal and Oriana said together.

"But it's us against them." She shook her head. "If you don't see that, you're blind. They wanted our Quad to fail from the moment we arrived." She turned and vanished through the veil of willow fronds.

7
BROM

The next day, they attended their classes—the first on advanced Soulblock division, and the second on the external aspects of the magic paths. It was all knowledge they already knew, due to Oriana's and Vale's diligent off-hours research, but Brom listened anyway. There were a couple of things about advanced Soulblock division theory he hadn't known. He watched Oriana's face during the lesson, her finger on her chin as she recorded the information in the library of her mind.

That afternoon, when Brom came to the practice room, Vale was already there, which he had expected. He thought she might flaunt the new pact from the start, just once, just to show she didn't need to listen to Oriana. But, true to her word, she was where she was supposed to be at this hour, in the practice room with the rest of them. They stayed and worked on their skills in silence until the prescribed time was finished, and they all went to the Floating Hall for the evening meal. They sat with over a hundred other academy students at the long marble tables and ate their goat stew in silence.

After, Brom went into his room with a mounting thrill of excitement, shut the door, and carefully locked it.

He turned to find Vale sitting on his bed.

"You're a bit of a squirrel when it comes to climbing, aren't you?" he said.

"How did you like my performance?"

"Convincing," he said.

She smiled wide. "I didn't think for a second you agreed with them, but they did."

She was gleeful, but Brom felt a little sick. He didn't want to lie to Oriana and Royal. There just wasn't any other way around it. They would never convince Royal to question The Four. And it was almost as unlikely they'd convince Oriana.

But after what Brom had seen, there wasn't any other choice. Something horrible was happening at the Champion's Academy, and he couldn't ignore it.

"So what's *our* pact?" she asked.

"We don't get caught. We get caught and we lose everything."

Her smug expression faded, and she nodded solemnly. She knew what he meant. They wouldn't just get reprimanded or punished by the masters; they would lose the Quad. In a way, that was worse than expulsion.

"We owe it to our Quad mates to unmask this danger," Brom said. "We can't just stand by and let...whatever is happening just happen. But they'll never see it that way."

Vale nodded.

"Over the next couple of days," he continued, "we do nothing except study how to fool a Mentis. Oriana will know what we're doing the moment she looks into our heads if we don't find out how to stop her. And if we tell her never to look inside our heads, she'll be immediately suspicious. So...you're our researcher. Find out what we need to know, then we practice until we're ready. Then, and only then, I'll tell you my plan."

"Okay," she said, and then the excitement and mischief vanished from her face.

"What is it?" he asked

"Your emotions were all over me that night," she said. Her

liquid brown eyes were huge. "By the wall. I've never seen you so scared."

"I thought they'd kill us. They would have, if they caught us. I'm sure of that. I'm still reeling."

"You're sure it was The Four?"

"If The Four were standing right next to me, I wouldn't know it," Brom said. "Nobody has ever seen them except the Quadrons who graduate. But I'm sure. That spell... Well, Royal was right about one thing. I couldn't comprehend it. I still can't conceive of how a Quadron could do that. It was made by someone who is so far beyond what we're doing. It was The Four."

"Okay."

He pressed his lips into a determined line. "But they didn't kill us, and that was their mistake. Now we're going to piece together this mystery. The Champions Academy isn't what they say it is, and we're going to find out the truth."

"You're damned right," she said, and she kissed him.

8

BROM

It turned out that an unsuspecting Mentis wasn't nearly as difficult to fool as Brom had thought. Apparently, reading surface thoughts was relatively easy for a Mentis, but it took far more effort to delve into a person's memories. Memories were not thoughts, according to the tome Vale had unearthed, unless a person was actively thinking about them while they were being read by the Mentis. So unless Vale and Brom thought about their plan during their practices with the Quad, Oriana wouldn't pick up on it unless she did a deep memory dive.

Which meant all Vale and Brom had to do was be diligent about their thoughts during practice.

In an effort to allay the suspicion of the Quad mates, both Brom and Vale chose to mellow their rebellious natures. Brom stopped taking midnight runs by the river. He practiced in the practice room. He went to all his classes. He didn't draw any undue attention to himself. Royal and Oriana watched with vigilant gazes, always alert for infractions now.

And Quad mates aside, The Four might still be searching for

Brom. Even now, they could be watching all of the students, looking for the culprit who had seen their green fire spell.

So Brom adhered to the rules. Mostly.

One rule he couldn't stop breaking was loving Vale. During the day, she scoured the library for references to The Four, and Brom strove to break Anima boundaries, relaying new revelations about connecting to the Soul of the World.

At night, they made love and matched notes.

"There are no records of Quadrons before The Four," Vale said, lounging on the bed with her back against the wall. She draped her naked leg across his while he read a passage from one of the books she'd taken from the library.

"We knew that," Brom said.

"There had to be Quadrons before The Four," she said.

"The Four invented the term," he said. "No Quadrons before The Four."

"Don't be a dung head," she said. "Call them whatever you want. I'm saying there was magic before The Four, so there had to be magic users."

"The stories say The Four were the first to make Soulblocks. If there were others who tried, they died," he said. "They drained their soul because they didn't know how to divide it."

"I don't think so."

"It was a hundred years ago, Vale."

"So?"

"So people didn't know how to work magic yet."

"Have you ever actually seen a non-initiate drain their soul?"

"It's grisly."

"You've never seen it," she said.

"I have heard the stories."

"Stories," she emphasized.

He finally put his book down on his lap. He wasn't going to be able to retain anything he read with her hammering on him. "There are numerous accounts in these very books." He tapped the book. "You're saying soul-drain isn't a real thing?"

"Oh, it's real. But maybe it doesn't happen every time."

"You really don't trust anything."

"I don't."

"It's in the books!"

"The Four could be telling us lies," she said.

"These books weren't written by The Four," he said.

"Who cares who wrote them? The Four control the academy. No one even questions how they put the school together. Why?"

"Because they're The Four," he murmured.

"Because they're The Four," she repeated. "That's as far as people think. They're demigods. They're protectors. The entirety of the two kingdoms relies on The Four. Everyone believes this, like Royal, but nobody can answer why. It's simply unquestioned that they're working for our benefit."

Even though Brom thought The Four might be darker than they'd originally thought, he hadn't stopped to consider that everything—the entire academy and everything in it—might also be the enemy. Including the library. The foreboding wriggled in his belly.

"They've had a hundred years to remove whatever books they don't want others to see," Brom said.

"Yes," she said. She scooted behind him, wrapping her legs around him. She put her chin on his shoulder, pulled a book from her stack and placed it on top of the one he was reading. The book was bound in thick, warped hide, and it still had goat fur clinging to it in spots. "But even The Four are human. I found this," she said, flipping the book open to a marked page.

He pulled at a tuft of fur. "You found a book made of an animal?"

"It's old."

"And maybe still alive?"

"I took it from the masters' collection."

He looked at her sharply over his shoulder. "Vale!"

She kissed him on the nose. "Read."

"I thought we weren't breaking any rules right now."

"Says the man with his Quad mate's legs wrapped around his waist. Read."

He perused the page, blinked, then quickly reread it. It showed a roster of graduating Quads from almost a hundred years ago.

Two of them graduated as entire Quads.

He looked back over his shoulder. "Entire Quads *have* passed the Test of Separation," he whispered, stunned.

"Interesting, yes?" she asked. "But apparently only at the beginning of the school."

"What... What does that mean?" He leaned back against her, thoughtful. She was warm and soft.

Students were told that full Quads *could* pass the Test of Separation together, but that none ever had. According to this passage, that was a lie.

"Why wouldn't they tell us about this?" Brom asked.

"Why indeed?" she echoed.

She brought another book forward and laid it over the top of the first two, then flipped it open to a marked page. It appeared to be a daily tally of goods by the academy's quartermaster, which listed the number of sheep in the school's new flock, the poundage of vegetables taken in with the harvest. Carrots, cabbage, potatoes, and leeks. It also recounted recent news from nearby villages. The last entry had one of Vale's bookmarks stuck between the pages. It told of the death of a Quadron.

"He's from one of the full Quads that graduated from the brand new school," she said.

"How do you know?"

"Same year. Same Quad name." She laid another book atop the stack on his knees. It was getting heavy. Brom read where she had marked. It was the following year. It also talked about herds and harvests, and it noted the death of a Quadron from a town to the north.

"Let me guess..." he said.

"Another dead. And from the other full Quad that had graduated."

Brom felt cold.

"They killed them," she said. "They went after them *after* they passed the Test of Separation. And they killed them."

They. The Four.

"Why?" he breathed.

"Maybe they were naughty students," she said sarcastically.

She placed another book on his lap, flipped it open. "Here's another." She put another on his lap, open to another page that talked of harvests and deaths. "And another."

He couldn't sit still anymore. He pushed the books onto the bed and stood up.

"Gods Vale..." he said. "You're saying..."

"That The Four are fucking murderers," she said. "They don't want a full Quad loose in the two kingdoms. The Test of Separation is a slaughterhouse, a way for them to make sure no full Quad gets free of the school. I don't think it's because a Quad isn't strong enough to pass. I think it's because they fucking kill them."

"Why..." he trailed off, and his imagination went wild. "Why even create the school in the first place? If they wanted all the students dead, why even train them how to create Soulblocks? Let them open their souls, drain themselves, and die."

"That's why I think soul-drain doesn't happen in every novice magic wielder. Maybe a hundred years ago, some people were succeeding. I don't know. But whatever the reason, I'm sure now that it's about power. The Collector didn't want Quad Brilliant to bond. You know he didn't. And now we're their worst nightmare. They'll have to kill at least one of us—maybe more, like Quad Moonlight—in the Test of Separation. They need to break our bond because it makes us ten times as strong together as we are alone. Gods, it's even in the name! The Test of Separation. They're mocking us."

"The Test is designed to kill us..." he murmured.

"At least one of us, to break the Quad. A Quad is a threat to their power, and they prune us before we leave the school. You see how strong we are now. That's just one year of practice. How strong are we going to be in two years? Maybe as strong as The Four themselves."

He struggled to choose one of his many questions, but they just spun around in his head.

"Their green flame spell is about control."

"The whole school is about control. They've got us trapped inside this little sheep's pen," she continued, "to do with as they want." She waved a hand. "And who knows what that gods-be-damned spell you discovered is, who knows what they've been doing to us from the moment we set foot inside these walls. Which brings me back to my point: I think there were other users in the two kingdoms before The Four, ones who figured out how to divide their Soulblocks without this place. And what's more..." She paused for effect. "I bet there are Quads who've formed outside the academy even now. And those Quads would be a threat to The Four."

A chill ran up his back. "Gods," he breathed.

"All this time, I wondered why The Collector would bother to come to Torlioch and get me. I could never quite swallow that it was compassion. Why would they care about me? Why send a Quadron to test me, then The Collector to bring me here? But if I'm right about all this, it all makes sense. They need to make sure we come here, everyone who has magic. To them, we're a big problem," she said. "And they created the Champion's Academy to solve it."

"The academy is a trap."

"Question is, what do we do?" she asked. "Run?"

He glanced at her. She sat cross-legged on the bed now. The woman was as naked as the day she was born, which usually made a person look vulnerable, but she looked deadly. The rage in her eyes reminded him of that first day she'd stabbed Royal. She didn't look like she wanted to run.

Brom's foreboding permeated him. Vale was right. This school was an alluring, deadly trap meant to draw in callow youths. He'd never imagined the entire Champion's Academy could be a spider's web to catch magic users. Brom thought maybe The Four were up to something, but he hadn't believed they were intentionally trying to destroy him. But Vale was saying Brom was a sheep, brought here to be shorn or slaughtered, then pushed back into the lands once he'd been rendered harmless.

"They're siphoning magic," he said, suddenly guessing what the spell must be.

"What?"

"The spell. The green wisps were being pulled out of everyone, all the time. I bet they're taking magic from us. Just a little bit, every time we open a Soulblock. Or maybe even when we don't. It's so little we'd never notice, but multiply that times three hundred students and staff and it's...huge."

"And how would we ever know the difference?" Vale murmured. "We've never known anything different."

"They're parasites," he murmured.

She brought her knees up to her chest and hugged them. Brom shivered, feeling like every inch of his skin was being sucked by tiny invisible leeches. His heart beat faster.

"We can't... We can't stay here," he whispered.

"So we run," she said.

But running only meant that he and Vale would be hunted down and killed, like the Quadrons in the old entries she'd found. And once they left the school, they'd be as helpless as babes, with no magic and no Quad.

"No," he said.

"No?"

If they stayed at the academy and stayed hidden, they could learn more, expand their magic, become more powerful. It was the only way they could fight The Four. They needed to know more.

"We stay," he said. "Out of sight. We have to find a way to fight them." Fight The Four. The idea was ludicrous. A thrill of fear went through him, but Vale grinned and jumped off the bed. She stood on her tiptoes and kissed him.

"Gods, you're delicious," she said. "We stay. We fight."

"We're going to get destroyed," he said.

"But let's spit in their faces first."

"By the gods, we have a lot of work to do."

"Yeah," she said. "This is going to be fun."

"Fun? You're insane," he said.

"I *so* am."

9
BROM

Brom clung to the shadows as The Collector strode past him, black robes rustling. The setting sun made the alcove a pool of inky blackness, and Brom kept silent.

He could now see the flaming green bonfire above the tower of The Four every time he connected to the Soul of the World. The Soul seemed to want him to fly up, out of his body, and become part of the green fire spell again, but he resisted. The eyes had never reappeared to look for him, and Brom suspected it was because he hadn't touched that vile spell again.

The first breath of winter had come to the Champion's Academy a month ago, and it brought long days of falling snow. As the semester had worn on, snow drifts as deep as Brom's knees had swept over Quadron Garden, making it look like a sea of white, with frozen waves cresting but never falling. Straight trenches cut across the pristine, sparkling waves where academy staff had shoveled the cobblestone walkways. The Collector's boots made slight thumps as he walked the path. Two students hurried past the master, and Brom felt the touch of the master's magic on them, reading them, seeing their souls. Neither student looked at the cloaked and cowled master, but he knew everything about them. The Collector was the academy's Anima master, and he could see through both students like they were panes of glass.

But he didn't see Brom.

Brom had plunged so deep into the Soul of the World that he couldn't be seen by magic. His body could still be seen by anyone who could pierce the shadows in the alcove, but not with magic. To the questing mind of a Mentis, there would only be a thoughtless stone wall. To a Motus, just a wisp of winter wind. To an Anima, only the soul of the shadows would be apparent.

This was the last piece. This was why The Four hadn't been able to detect him that night at the wall, and this would be his and Vale's key to get into the tower of The Four.

Unwittingly, Brom had fallen deep into the Soul of the World that night at the wall. He had become one with the lands, and The Four hadn't had any physical eyes to locate his body, so his soul had been invisible to them.

With this same method, he'd been able to hide himself from Royal the other day, testing the Impetu's magically enhanced senses. The big man had never known Brom was trailing him. Next, he'd tried following Oriana on the way to the bath house.

She'd never caught a wisp of his thoughts.

Finally, he had experimented with Vale. It had been just as easy as the others. Impetu, Mentis, Motus. He'd almost considered the matter closed, that his ability to hide from magic was complete.

Then he'd spotted Caila and followed her. And she'd caught him. Surprised, he'd made small talk. He hadn't told her specifically what he'd been doing, just that he was practicing magic. She'd congratulated him on the success of Quad Brilliant, said that it was good to see him, and they'd talked for a while before she went about her day.

Brom had redoubled his efforts and tried trailing her the next day. That time, he'd managed to pursue her without detection.

He'd thought hiding himself from an Anima would be the easiest of all the paths. He knew the nature of Anima magic better than any of the others, after all, but it turned out that hiding from an Anima had been the most difficult by far. Perhaps an Anima looked deeper into a person. Perhaps it was harder to hide a soul than thoughts or emotions, but whatever the case, Brom stayed wary and he practiced. After trying to hide from students, he'd moved on to more difficult quarry: the masters.

At night, he'd placed himself in hidden alcoves near masters of the other paths, and he'd fooled them all. Master Saewyne. Master Tohn Gelu. Even the suspicious Master Jhaleen. They'd all walked past Brom without knowing he was lurking nearby.

Tonight, it was time to test himself against The Collector. And the master was actively using his Soulblock, reaching out and touching students. To fool him while he was actively using magic was a true test.

But he hadn't seen Brom.

Of course The Collector didn't know he was part of Brom's practice any more than the other masters had known, but he'd served his purpose.

The Collector rounded the corner of the library and vanished from view. Giddy thrills rippled up Brom's spine, and he almost laughed. Finally, after weeks, they were ready.

He thought of Vale and his thrill expanded. Vale...

Their secret project had turned into a secret society of two, a pair of lovers without boundaries. They worked on understanding The Four. They exercised together, running through the campus until they were sweaty, smiling and laughing. They delved into the secrets of the library, learning about the academy's history, and they practiced their magic over and over.

He loved her sharp mind and how she always seemed excited to see him. He loved her fierce focus, her mischievousness, and the playful swing of her hips when she knew he was watching. Gods, he loved the very sound of her name: Vale...

He had never trusted anyone like he trusted her. She was dedicated to him and to their mission. She pushed him, challenged his thinking, made him better. She waited on his vision, hungry to follow. Her confidence in him filled his soul. Everything was possible when Vale was around. She was the wind and he was the ship.

Oriana and Royal knew nothing about any of it, of course, which was a source of unease for Brom. What he and Vale were doing was vitally important, but his guilt grew in the back of his mind like a fungus. If Oriana and Royal ever found out, he feared it would pull the Quad apart. They were making fools of Royal and Oriana, and that couldn't end well unless it ended in exactly the right way.

However, though Oriana and Royal remained in blissful ignorance, the Quad had flourished more than ever. These secret activities burned brightly inside of Vale, and she shared that fire—if not the reason for it—with all of them, bolstering their optimism and driving them. For Royal, she still played the vulnerable and teasing little sister, and he glowed with protective instinct. No doubt he imagined his demand to follow the rules had created this next golden era of Quad Brilliant.

For Oriana, Vale continued to play the invaluable research assistant as the princess hungrily devoured tome after tome in the library, expanding the Quad's collective education daily. Her eyes glinted with pride whenever she and Vale returned from the library with new information. And when they applied that knowledge in the practice room, Oriana looked on in approval like her leadership had created this next golden era of Quad Brilliant.

But while Brom felt guilty, Vale seemed to thrive on the deception. She saw that it was working, and that was all that mattered to her. She was comfortable with lies and manipulation. Vale seemed to have the ability to be comfortable with whatever was needed.

When Brom was sure The Collector was gone, he drew a deep breath of the frigid air. It was pure. Clean. He wanted to be pure and clean again. He didn't want his soul cluttered with deception anymore. The sooner he and Vale found the needed proof that The Four were preying on the students, the sooner they could reveal almost all of their secrets to Royal and Oriana. What they currently had wasn't enough. A few passages in an ancient text and Vale's speculation simply wasn't going to sway Oriana. And Royal wouldn't see The Four as foes until stark evidence was shoved under his nose.

Gaining that evidence was going to be dangerous because there was only one way to do it. He and Vale were going to have to visit the tower of The Four and find the proof.

He felt a thrill at the thought, at the challenge. Who knew what else they'd see behind that wall that circled the tower? What wonders might be revealed?

The sun, nearly vanished, bled orange along a split in the clouds. At last, Brom emerged from the shadows, turned, and hiked up the path to Quadron Garden like he was any other student. He stepped high through the snow toward Westfall Dormitory, cutting through the drifts, uncaring of who saw him now.

He entered the marble building, shook off his cloak, and stamped his boots before heading to his room. Other students packed the hall, sitting and reading or talking with each other. Brom kept his head down and walked through them, though almost all gazes turned toward him.

Quad Brilliant had surpassed every other second-year Quad long ago. They'd been approved to work on third-year magic and, secretly, Vale and Brom were working on aspects of fourth-year magic. No second-year Quads challenged their dominance now. Brom had turned aside half a dozen requests for tutoring just this semester. He was sure Vale, Oriana, and Royal had received similar requests.

He climbed the steps and, once he was out of sight of the crowd below, began to grin again. Vale, having taken her studies as far as they could go, had been patiently waiting for him to master the Soul of the World. And he'd just performed his final test. She'd be excited to get started, and Brom felt a giddy optimism. Between her experience as a thief and his magic, The Four would never see them coming.

He entered his room, his eyes went wide, and he quickly shut the door behind himself.

Vale sat on his bed, wearing one of his own tunics and nothing else. One shoulder peeked out through the wide neck, and the bottom of the tunic rode high up her bronze legs to mid-thigh. Her dark wavy hair framed her mischievous face, and her eyes glinted.

Her actual clothes were neatly folded at the foot of his bed.

"There are students in the hall," he whispered urgently, hands on the door as though someone was going to try to shove it open. "Right outside on the balcony. Someone could have seen you."

She crinkled her nose. "Exciting, isn't it? I *was* naked for a while, but I've been waiting for an hour. I got cold."

"Gods..." he breathed, letting go of the door. He almost said *I love you*, but he held the words back. "You are...radiant."

His overlarge tunic created a loose, plunging neckline on her, revealing the shadowed curve of her small breasts. Her smooth thigh and hip were on full display through the slit in the side, and he couldn't look away. Desire and excitement rushed through him. He wanted to tell her about his success with The Collector, but he also wanted to pounce on her.

"We are taking tonight off," she announced. "You've been bound up trying to master the Soul of the World for weeks. Weeks!" She rose to hands and knees and stretched like a cat. "You soul-mongers have this need to feel...fluid," she purred. "Well, I'm here to help. We are going to relax you."

Languidly, she put one foot on the floor, and then the other, then moved to him. He felt the warmth of her small body as she pressed against him, felt the liveliness of her soul through his magic. She ran a finger up his chest, his neck, then flicked it off the end of his chin playfully. She always did that before they made love, like it was some kind of signature. She might as well have pointed at the bed and said, "Lie down."

It made him smile. She slid her arms around his neck and pulled his head down. Her lips were hot against his ear. "Get these clothes off." She tugged at his tunic.

Brom plunged his fingers into her wild hair and pushed it back from her face while she worked at his belt. He let the Soul of the World flow into her, and she sighed as she felt it.

"I can't fight you," he murmured.

"You really can't." She pushed him onto the bed, and he surrendered.

And she was right. By the time they had finished, he was relaxed. Day had turned to night. Kelto had risen. That thin crescent of indigo sent glimmers across the snow-covered trees outside. She snuggled into him, her leg across his, her head in the crook of his shoulder. She brushed her fingers across the stubble on his chin, back and forth, making a rhythmic scratching noise.

"This must be what happiness feels like," she murmured.

"Happiness feels like a stubbly cheek?"

She stuck a knuckle into his ribs, tickling him. "You know what I mean," she said.

He chuckled, flinching away from her for a moment, then settling easily back into her arms.

"When I was young," she said, "I thought I knew what people meant when they said they were happy. I thought it meant having a full belly. I thought it meant those moments when I wasn't afraid. But that's not happiness. Real happiness is..." she said, "it's this. It's nice."

"I love you," he said softly, stroking her hair.

Her hand stopped moving against his cheek. Her neck became an iron bar against his shoulder, and her thigh tensed where it touched him, like she was about to jump up.

"Oh," she said after a long silence. *Oh* was such a small word—barely even a word at all—but it said volumes.

He craned his neck to look at her. "I didn't mean to spook you. I've just... I've been feeling it for a while. I thought I should say it out loud."

She laughed, and that wasn't what he'd expected. She tried to make the laugh relaxed and easy, but it sounded forced. Her whole body was knotted up like a rope.

"I didn't think that you..." she began but trailed off. "Perhaps that was naive of me," she said, more to herself than to him.

"Naive?" he asked.

"I mean, to think that you didn't believe in love."

"What do you mean?"

"Love is not.... I mean, it's not real," she said matter-of-factly. "I thought you knew that."

"It's not *real*?" He wondered if he'd heard her correctly.

"Love isn't actually a thing," she said. "It's not real."

Was she joking? He wanted to sit up so he could see her face, but he calmed himself and remained lying down. His connection to the Soul of the World vanished as his Soulblock emptied. His lassitude went with it.

"It's a conjuring," she continued. "A...phantom. People make it up to give themselves purpose. It's not real, not for people like us anyway. I would have... If I'd thought this would be a problem, we could have talked about it before. I just never thought I'd catch you talking about love. You of all people."

He frowned. "Me of all people?"

"You already have purpose. You have more purpose than anyone I've ever met. That's why I..." She trailed off, as though suddenly deciding she didn't want to say what she'd been about to say.

"Why you what?" he pressed.

"That's why this works." She propped herself on an elbow to face him, and she pointed at his chest then at hers. She smiled. "Gods, Brom, you actually look wounded." She gave a little chuckle. "It's priceless. Come now. Tell me I didn't hurt your feelings."

"I'm just...surprised. You don't believe love is real?"

"Surely you must know that you don't *love* me," she said.

"I do love you."

"Like you loved all those other women?" she asked wryly, raising an eyebrow.

For a second, he couldn't speak. "You think I don't love you because I've had other lovers?"

"I think you dally where it pleases you. And that's okay with me. That's why I knew I wouldn't have any problems with... Well, with this kind of thing. This doe-eyed imagining of love."

"It's because of those other women that I know exactly what this is," Brom said.

"What this is," she said in a monotone, looking steadily into his eyes.

"Yes."

She waved that away. "Love. No love. Let's talk about what we know is real, Brom. Becoming a Quadron. That's real. That's what matters. That's why we're here. It's our purpose. We don't need to fabricate one. Let the deluded have their fantasies. We're working together to become Quadrons. Some of the work..." She opened both arms, presenting her bare breasts to him. "Just happens to be fun."

He tried to wrap his mind around what she was saying. "You think love is a weakness."

"I think love is a fantasy."

"Except it's what *makes* us human."

"Now you sound like a Fendiran poet," she said.

He pushed down his growing disappointment. "You can't claim that you've never loved anyone."

Vale's expression went eerily blank. Usually, she had a face full of expression, whether it was rage or joy or sadness or something else. This time, it was as though all her emotion had vanished, almost as though she didn't know which emotion to show him, and he had the creeping feeling he was seeing her real face for the first time.

She looked past him, like she was staring at something far away.

"I loved my mother..." she said in a monotone, then she blinked and focused on him again, and the Vale he knew suddenly reappeared. Her dark eyes sparkled, and a rueful smile curled the side of her lip. "Or at least I thought I did at the time. But I know better now. What I actually felt was reassurance. Having a mother meant I was safe. Or I thought it did, because I loved her and she loved me. So things were going to work out. Except that was a lie. I wasn't safe. She couldn't protect me from the world any more than I could protect myself."

"A lie?"

"Come on, Brom. We lie to ourselves all the time to feel safe. We fabricate what we need to feel to continue forward." She slapped his thigh playfully.

He frowned, trying to understand what she was saying, and trying not to be afraid that he had misjudged her so badly. How could she not believe in love?

"I'll tell you what is real, though," she said. "That night, when my mother was dying in that alley, a dozen people one wall away just let her. They drank and laughed while she coughed out her last breath. That's real. I couldn't make them help her any more than I could help her myself. I didn't have the power. Love didn't save my mother. It couldn't. But the power of a Quadron could have. So love... Not real." She chuckled. "But power? Yes. The powerful seem pretty safe to me."

"Vale... I'm sorry." Brom's heart hurt. He knew she'd had a tough time growing up on the streets of Torlioch, but she'd never told him that story before. "I'm so sorry..."

She waved it away like it was nothing. "It was a good lesson. It made me stronger. And strength is a kind of power."

"But... Don't you see that love is what *gives* us strength?" he asked softly. "Love drives everything we do. We'll go to further lengths to protect what we love than we will to protect ourselves. We will sacrifice for it, whether we love a person or even an ideal. Just look at Royal and his love of Fendir. Look at Oriana and her passion for her people."

Vale laughed. He couldn't tell if she was actually as breezy as she seemed, or if she was acting. "That's the worst example of all. Royal and Oriana prove *my* point. Not yours. They see only what they want to see. It's all made up in their heads. You're the one who showed me that. It's the reason we can't tell them what we're doing. They want to see the Champion's Academy as a safe little cradle in which to learn magic and The Four as smiling grandparents." She shook her head. "Illusions. Inside their heads. The only thing that's real is having the power to do what you want. Or to stop others from doing what *they* want to *you*. Ask The Four about that."

"So this thing between us.... You and me, it's for power?" he asked, sick to his stomach.

"Gods, Brom! Don't look so serious. Remember why you're really here. I've seen the passion inside you, focused on becoming a Quadron. I am, too. There is nothing I wouldn't do to get there. Nothing. We are going to break into the tower of the gods-be-damned Four. Are we doing it for love? No. We're doing it for power. To gain knowledge, to be free, to use our magic without manacles. To do what we choose to do and not what four ancient Quadrons tell us to do."

A cold realization crept up Brom's spine, and everything about Vale suddenly made chilling sense. She'd described their relationship as "working together." That's how she saw it. To her, he was just like Oriana and Royal. This... This person she was with him, this secret and sexy lover, was a construct for his benefit.

All this time he'd felt sorry for Royal and Oriana because they didn't know the real Vale, not like he did, but she had put on a face for him just like she'd done for them.

How could Brom have been so profoundly blind? How could he have thought she was playing parts for them but saving her real self for him? She'd even told him what she was doing that first night in the practice room.

I'm here to help...

She'd said it right before she'd kissed him. She'd become the forbidden vixen to entice him, inspire him, push him forward again.

To make the Quad more powerful.

He saw it all in a flash. She'd worked her way into all of their hearts, being exactly what they craved, being a mirror that showed the self they desperately wanted to be. She made Royal feel like a protector, Oriana like a leader, and Brom like a rebel with access to her secret heart...

"Brom?" she said softly.

He forced a laugh, but it was painful, like fingernails raking his throat. He wanted to say something, but he couldn't push the words out.

She bit her lip, seemingly caught in indecision about whether to lean over and kiss him or to leave. After an excruciating moment while Brom kept a frozen smile on his face, she slid her legs off the bed and stood up.

"I'm going to go," she said, picking up her leggings from the pile at the foot of the bed. She put them on, then pulled her tunic over her head and belted it. She studiously ignored him while she dressed, donned her boots and laced them up. She flung her red cloak over her shoulders, fastened the clasp, and only then did she look at him. She cocked her head, regarding him like she might a troublesome stream she didn't know how to cross. She seemed to want to say something, but instead, she let out a little breath.

"Good night, Brom. I will see you tomorrow." She emphasized the word *tomorrow* like she was a master reassuring a failing student. She went to the window and opened it. Cold wind swirled in, crisp and wintry. She climbed onto the sill, crouched lightly on her toes, and paused.

He felt he needed to say something. He felt he could make her fall back into his arms with just a word, but he didn't know what that word was.

"Vale—"

"Don't do it," she cut him off, swiveling on her toes to face him, so compact and agile. Her cloak fluttered out behind her.

"Vale, don't go—"

"Don't let it make you smaller," she interrupted him again, as though she knew what he was trying to say, and she wanted to stop him. "I couldn't stand it if someone like you made yourself smaller because of love. Please, Brom. You already have purpose. You have the best and brightest purpose I've ever seen. You don't need love."

She swiveled and vanished into the night.

10
BROM

Brom sat in silence. The open window let the winter breeze into the room, and it swept the warmth of their intimacy into the snowy night. He sat there until his skin felt cold, until he felt like his heart was breaking.

He got up, got dressed, and scaled down the drainpipe outside his dorm window. He ran across the windswept drifts of Quadron Garden toward the willow tree by the river. He reached it, panting white clouds, and slid down the bank into the hollow protected by the drooping, frost-covered fronds. The half-frozen river gurgled against sheets of ice, and his thoughts ravaged him.

She used me, he thought. *She's using me still.*

How could he not have seen she'd been playing a part for him? And now that he did see it, why did it hurt so much? His need for her lodged in his throat like a bone.

She was right, after all. They'd come here to be Quadrons. All of them. That shared goal remained the heart of Quad Brilliant's bond. They could all pretend they were friends, but they weren't. They were partners. Each of them was a means to an end for the other three. A way to become Quadrons.

If he thought about it, really thought about it, had he actually believed Vale wanted to fall in love with him, or with anyone?

No.

She had lived her whole life in hunger and desperation. She had walked hand-in-hand with death every day, with no power and no prospects. Then she'd come here, had the chance to make every one of her dreams come true. When she became a Quadron, it wouldn't be for her like it would be for Brom. She wouldn't just return to sleepy little Kyn, triumphant, ready impress her parents and her friends. No, Vale would become something utterly different than what she'd been. She would never have to beg for anything. She would never go hungry. She'd never be at the mercy of anyone ever again.

Vale had been honest with him tonight, maybe for the first time. She'd dashed cold water in his face, yes, but maybe he'd needed that. He was letting their affair cloud his thinking, letting his passion for Vale overcome his reason for being here.

He thought of that moment—gods, it seemed a lifetime ago—when Roland had rejected him from the village guard, all because he'd put his tryst with Myan over his dedication to the guard. It had all been over in an instant.

Not this time.

He drew a deep breath. Pure. Clean. Cold.

Brom was here to become a Quadron. Not to fall in love. If he'd wanted to fall in love, he could have stayed in Kyn with Myan.

He blinked and looked around at this little sheltered area by the river, surrounded by the willow branches. This was where he and Oriana had bonded, where they'd broken the first barrier of the Quad together. Now, each of his Quad mates was giving everything they had, to the furthest reach of their ability, to elevate the Quad.

Was Brom?

His bruised heart saw Vale as a manipulator, but he realized she'd only proven she was more dedicated to becoming a Quadron than he was. She'd served the purpose of the Motus, bringing their passions to a boil by doing whatever she had to do, by being whomever she had to be. She had fit every role without a thought of the cost to herself, all to drive the Quad forward.

And she would never give up on them. Of that, he was sure. In fact, Brom had no doubt that despite what had happened in his room tonight, despite his pain at her rejection and his shocked response, she would return to his bed in an instant if he asked her. She'd probably do it without being asked if she felt her presence would make him stronger, happier, more able to elevate the Quad.

He had to think like Vale. He had to play his part.

A Motus's job was to bring passion. A Mentis's job was to bring knowledge. An Impetu's job was to protect. And as Vale had said months ago, it was the purpose of the Anima to pierce illusions, to put words to the unnameable, to bring wisdom.

His Quad mates had all done their parts. They'd all seen clearly from the beginning.

But what wisdom had Brom brought to the Quad?

Certainly, he'd talked with Vale about secrets and dangers. He'd shared his foreboding about the green fire spell. But instead of spending every ounce of time and energy delving deeper into those mysteries, what had he done? He'd lain in Vale's arms. He'd basked in the pleasure of her gift to him.

A notion formed in his mind, crystalizing like the icy sheets over the river, and as it formed, it twisted into a pointy, desperate need. He knew what he had to do. He knew exactly how to bring wisdom to the group. He was going to invade the tower of The Four.

And he was going to do it alone.

11

BROM

Brom still had two Soulblocks left. That was enough. It *had* to be enough.

He opened his second Soulblock, established a light connection with the Soul of the World, and began jogging along the river. It led across the campus to the southwest corner where the enormous tower oversaw the entire academy. It suddenly struck Brom as an eerie anomaly that the monstrously tall tower of The Four didn't seem to dominate the Champion's Academy day-to-day. Somehow, he had barely thought of it until the night he'd seen the green flame and the vengeful eyes. But now, as he turned his focus on the tower while the Soul of the World flowed through him, that green flame raged, and the tower seemed to fill the entire sky.

He stopped, panting, and peeked out between the thick bushes along the bank. Though even an owl would have had difficulty seeing Brom right now, stuffed in the snowy bushes underneath a nearly moonless sky, with the Soul of the World flowing through him, he felt as if he was being watched.

The short jog had heated him up nicely, but lying in the snow erased that in moments. Still, though he was aware of the cold, it wasn't painful. His soul lived in the snow, the trees, the wind, the sky, and he was coming home.

Before him, a decorative hedge ran from the edge of the river to the tower's wall. He left his concealment and ran low near the hedge, letting it shield him. He ran fast, his steps high, and made it to the tower's wall with a few dozen elegant leaps like a bounding deer.

The tower rose higher and higher into the sky like it was growing. It seemed to go on forever. How could Brom never have realized just how big the thing was? Standing here, looking up at it, he felt dizzy, like there was some magic concealing its grandeur until a person stood right next to it. If Brom wasn't so deep inside the Soul of the World, he would probably have run in terror.

Being connected not only meant he was part of everything, including the tower, but it lent him confidence. He was sure he was exactly where he ought to be. That magical edifice thrummed through him. The magic here was staggering, and he felt it trying to frighten him, but Brom wasn't frightened. He only noted the dazzling magic. Instead of fear, it filled him with an uncontainable excitement.

The wall that surrounded the tower was about as tall as Royal, ostensibly to keep people out, but Brom didn't think for a second the wall was the real protection.

Two ordinary-looking guards stood at the gate far to Brom's left. They were wrapped in full cloaks, their cowls drawn. Each held a spiked halberd in a single gloved hand, and their free hands remained tucked beneath the warmth of their cloaks. It would be impossible, even connected to the Soul of the World, for Brom to get through that small gate without fighting the guards.

And he had no intention of fighting anyone. He had no intention of going through that gate. He was going over the wall because he knew its secrets. Brom *was* the wall.

He charged through the snow, knees pumping high, and leapt onto the wall. There was a missing brick there, creating a perfect foothold, and the toe of his boot found it as though it were part of his own body. He grasped the sharp edge of the wall and vaulted over. Snow came with him, clearing a spot along the top, but it fell softly, making no sound.

He paused inside the thin courtyard between the wall and the tower itself. Inside the curve of the wall, he could see the gate to his left and the silhouettes of the guards. One of them shifted, transferring his halberd from one hand to the other. Their backs were turned to him, and neither had seen nor heard Brom's leap.

He almost ran across the brief courtyard to one of the tall archways leading into the tower, but he hesitated. The foreboding in his gut clenched and bid him stay still.

Taking that risky moment, exposed and in the open, Brom leaned his back against the wall and let out a slow breath. He concentrated on the lightning crackle within him and imagined crackling threads of magic springing from his fingertips, his toes, his shoulders and chest and head. These threads quested out in front of him, seeking anything made of magic.

He began to see shapes in the air. They started as colors. Smoky gray and powder blue. But as Brom's heart slowed, he saw more. The colors coalesced, transforming into smoky apparitions.

An amorphous gray spiderweb hovered right in front of him, barely a foot away. It surrounded the entire base of the tower, stretched along the wall, and only at the gate did a hole widen for passage through. If he'd charged across the short courtyard, he would have run right into that web.

And just beyond the spiderweb was a double-headed axe of misty blue. It was as tall as a house, just as ephemeral as the spider web and just as magical. The haft was suspended a foot above the ground between two archways.

A drift of snow piled against the tower moved in the slight breeze created by the axe's descent, and Brom suddenly realized that the axe, though it looked like an apparition, was as solid as steel. The axe-head chopped in front of one archway and stopped a hair's breadth from the ground. It rose up, swinging to the other side, and chopped down in front of the other archway like a pendulum, the haft turning on some invisible fulcrum.

That massive blue axe head could easily chop any unwary person in two if they tried to get through one of those archways.

He squinted and looked down the flat side of the tower. Slowly, a half dozen other giant axes resolved in his vision. Every pair of archways had its own deadly axe pendulum. Chop...chop...chop...chop... They all continued ceaselessly, chopping down suddenly, stopping just before they hit the ground, then rising again.

The two guards at the gate were nothing but a feint. These sophisticated spells were the real protection. They would all undoubtedly summon The Four if they didn't kill the intruder outright.

And nobody can see them but me, he thought. *These spells, this tower, they are all part of my body now. One doesn't fear one's own body. One uses it.*

A giddy confidence flowed through him. He felt invincible.

He inched forward, through the gaps in the spiderweb, careful not to touch any of the glistening gray threads. Once he was through, he moved toward the swaying axe. He stood before it until he was sure of its timing, then he ran past, through the right-hand archway.

He half-expected to feel a tingle, some indication that he'd been caught, but there was nothing but the floor beneath his feet, the air rushing into his lungs, the hard walls on either side of him. Inside, the walls were black stone, glistening like they were wet, and Brom saw another spell down the hall ahead of him.

A misty white grate blocked the hallway, iron bands crisscrossing like a loose basket weave, leaving diamond-shaped holes that could barely pass a fist. There was no way to duck under, climb above, or sneak through.

But there was a misty white door in the center.

He approached it cautiously. The door was three feet wide and seven feet tall with no handle or lever, just a giant key sticking out of a lock in the door's center. The head of the key was a life-sized skeletal hand, fingers fanned out a handshake.

He studied it, thinking for a moment. A key in the lock, ready to turn. So obvious that it made him suspicious.

Unless, of course, the creators of the spell were the only ones who could see it. If The Four thought their spells were invisible to everyone but them, the door could indeed be that simple, an easy way to pass in and out of the tower without hindering themselves.

He reached out to touch the handle.

The deep foreboding clenched in his belly, and he stopped with his hand inches from the bony fingers.

He studied the grate again, looking for some hidden handle, some unseen hole. But there was nothing.

Still, there had to be a way for The Four to pass. Could they just walk through it, unaffected? Were they simply immune to their own spells?

No. That couldn't be true. Why make a door at all, then? The key was meant to be used.

He looked back the way he had come. The head of the blue axe chopped down in front of the archway, nearly striking the ground, then rose and vanished from view. Three seconds later, it chopped down again like clockwork.

The axe was a light, sky blue. The web was gray. And this grate, misty white...

The colors represented the four paths of magic! Blue for Impetu. The gray of the spider web, a faded black. That was an Anima spell. And this misty grate, faded white, had to be Mentis.

He yanked his hand back like the key was a snake. Touching it would have been disastrous. A spell created by a Mentis would have to do with the mind, not the body.

He composed himself, tried not to think of how close he'd come to tripping the trap. He reached out with his mind like he was sending a thought to Oriana.

"Open," he thought.

The skeletal hand bent, grasped itself, and turned. The gate swung open noiselessly. It happened so fast that it stunned Brom, but he was jolted to attention when the gate slowly began to close. He jumped through, careful not to touch any part of the construct—not the key, the door, or the grate itself.

The door swung shut, silent as mist, and the key turned vertical again. The bony hand unfurled, fingers splayed open.

I'm in, Brom thought as he turned around. *Gods, I'm in the Tower of the Four.*

He moved forward cautiously. The black hallway opened into a foyer with an enormous red-bordered mirror attached to the wall over a long red marble table, exquisitely carved. The mirror was as tall and wide as the archway Brom had entered, and he wanted to look at his reflection. He walked toward it—

The foreboding in his belly clenched so hard it felt like he'd been poisoned.

Brom gasped, doubled over and fell to his knees. He raised his head, still badly wanting to take one more step and see his reflection. He knelt that way for a long, torturous minute, fighting the pain in his belly.

He needed to see the mirror! He knew the moment he looked in it, he'd see what he most wanted to know. About himself. About Vale. About The Four. The mirror held vast secrets. He could feel it like he felt his own heart beating—

It's the fourth trap, Brom thought, his own voice breaking through the desperate need. It seemed as though he'd been trying to tell himself that for a long time, but his desires had overwhelmed his rational mind.

He blinked, stared hard at the mirror's border and at the edge of his shoulder in the reflection. A pink haze appeared, barely perceptible, over the mirror. Magic.

Brom backed away, and with every step the compulsion to look into the mirror diminished.

Gods... That had been close.

A black marble stairway spiraled upward to his left, opposite the mirror. The steps were at least twenty feet wide, and they swept elegantly in a curve, rising to reach the next landing. There. Up there. He had to get away from that mirror before he was tempted to look again.

The enormous spiral staircase twisted around and around into a seemingly infinite darkness above, hitting landing after landing, but always continuing upward into the dark. At each landing, it changed color. Black to blue. Blue to white. White to red. Red to black. Over and over.

Brom stared, caught between the need to get away from the insidious mirror and his slack-jawed awe at the tower. The four paths of magic dealt with altering the emotions, the body, the mind, or the spirit of a person. Nothing Brom or his Quad mates had done so far could create something concrete, something separate from another person. The magic of building this tower, those ephemeral traps, all the other miraculous things on the academy campus like the little automatons in the library, the Floating Room... This was magic so far beyond Brom's comprehension that his heart beat faster. This was the magic of The Four.

What am I doing here? he suddenly thought. *It was insanity to think I could come here without being caught.*

He felt like he'd suddenly tumbled off a cliff into a freefall. He looked back at the white grate down the hallway and felt he should sprint from this place in terror and never come back.

But he couldn't see the white grate anymore. Beyond that, there was no axe swaying into view over the archways at the end of the hall. All he could see was the indigo moonlight on the snow beyond the archway.

He couldn't see the spells anymore... Gods, he'd slipped out of the Soul of the World. His heart thundered in his chest. Terror gripped him, and he froze like a rabbit, hoping not to be noticed.

Gods...gods... gods...

He tried to reach into the Soul of the World again, but it was like trying to exhale after having the wind knocked out of him. There was no air left. He couldn't... He couldn't reach it!

His magic was gone. He no longer part of the tower, that he belonged here, that his body was part of its body. He couldn't feel where to step and when. He didn't know what to do next. There was no...

A vision of Oriana came to him. Oriana, who always looked past her emotions to see what was needed. Oriana, who never panicked.

Compose yourself. He could almost hear her voice in his head.

He clamped down hard on his panic.

I've run out of my second Soulblock, he thought. *That's what this is. That's why the Soul of the World is gone.*

He looked back at the vanished grate. He'd known he was going to have to access his third Soulblock in this mission, but he didn't think he'd use up his second so quickly. The compulsion to look into the mirror trap had been so strong he'd barely broken it. He wondered if it had drained his magic like a siphon.

In fact, now that he thought of it, the mirror might have those answers. It obviously contained a great many secrets. If he looked into it, he could understand what was happening here.

He turned to look into the mirror.

Brom shut his eyes.

No!

It didn't matter why his second Soulblock was gone. He needed magic. That was the only answer. The mirror couldn't tell him anything more than that. He had to open his third Soulblock. But he'd only use it to get back out of the tower. He'd learned a great deal. The tricks and traps were simple to evade now that he knew them. He could go back to his room and try again when he was fully rested, when he had all of his Soulblocks.

He opened his third Soulblock and drew a sudden, swift breath. The magic crackled through him, jolting his jittery limbs, filling them with power.

His heart calmed. His thoughts calmed. The misty white grate shone down the hallway, no longer misty. It looked like it was made of glowing ivory. The swaying head of the giant axe came into view, bright blue steel chopping down, then rising. Chopping into view, rising. He could even see the spiderweb beyond them, black as midnight against the snowy wall.

He didn't look at the mirror, but he was sure the frame would be glowing dark crimson.

He took a deep breath. This was much better. His panic had vanished and it suddenly felt childish. He chided himself for his fearful thoughts, especially about his plan to leave as quickly as he could. That was utterly foolish.

Leave? He wasn't leaving. He'd successfully passed each of the traps of The Four. He was on the edge of victory. He wasn't about to run home with his tail tucked between his legs.

He was going to find out more about this tower than its defenses. He was going to find out why the green fire spell surrounded the school. That was why he was here, after all.

Just as he was about to set foot on the staircase, he heard a voice.

Like the darkness itself, he melted into the shadows against the wide black marble bannister.

The voice spoke again, deep and rumbling. It had come from the first landing above, just far enough away that he couldn't make out the words.

Thinking of the Gauntlet in the practice room, Brom crept quietly up the stairs, keeping low behind the wide obsidian rail. He'd just have to make sure he weaved his way through this new gauntlet without a mistake. He was careful not to look to his right and accidentally view himself in the mirror on the way up. He kept his focus forward, one step at a time. Soon, he saw a doorway to a blue room. The floor of the second story was made of thickly-veined blue marble, just as the floor of the first story had been made of black marble.

As he crept nearer, the rumbling voice became clear enough to understand. "...should simply get rid of the entire class." The man's voice sounded like rocks being crushed together.

"Can you think of anything more stupid that that?" came another man's voice, as different from the first voice as two voices could be. This new voice was smooth honey poured into the ear. His words were clearly antagonistic, but they sounded warm, like he was telling an old friend an inside joke.

The gravelly voice growled.

The room was just above Brom's line of sight, right across from the staircase. He could see the blue ceiling, and with two more steps, he'd be able to see the room through the doorway...

...and if anyone was looking out, they'd be able to see him.

But no foreboding clenched his gut. He stepped confidently up the staircase to the landing. He saw into the room, but he couldn't see the people who spoke. He felt an excitement about entering, so he padded quickly forward, went through the doorway and ducked behind a blue marble bar just inside the room.

The voices continued their discussion uninterrupted.

"Is it possible for the two of you to have a logical discussion without resorting to these petty squabbles?" a new voice said. It was high pitched and cultured, speaking with clearly enunciated words, much like Oriana did, but this was a man's voice and definitely older.

Gods! No one had seen Brom enter the room. He'd just run into the room and hid, and no one had seen him.

He crouched under the bar, completely concealed from the rest of the room, and he assessed his surroundings. In front of him was the blue marble wall. To his left, the underside of the bar stretched on for twenty feet, the entire length of the room. Directly behind him and to his right was the backside of the bar. He pressed himself against those two cool walls.

Just to his left, there was a hole in the bar, as though something, a spout or a pipe, was meant to have been there, but it either hadn't been installed or had been removed. Brom put his eye up to the hole, and saw the rest of the room.

There, standing no more than ten paces from him, were The Four.

12
BROM

The legendary Four.... Olivaard, Arsinoe, Wulfric, and Linza stood right there in front of him!

Arsinoe, their Motus, was dressed in a stylish red courtier's doublet and tight-fitting breeches. He lounged on a red velvet divan, which looked like it had been made expressly to display him. Somehow, this ancient man looked to be in his early twenties, with dark auburn hair that tumbled carelessly to his shoulders. Two days' worth of stubble made his handsome face rugged and irresistible. At just a glance, Brom felt like he would never be this man's equal in anything.

Arsinoe was relaxed and he smiled lazily, as though everything was easy for him. His face indicated that he'd be happy to show you exactly what you needed to know to conquer your petty challenges, if you liked. But his emerald gaze was as sharp as a blade, cruel and narrow. The man wasn't looking toward Brom's peephole, gods be thanked, but that green gaze stabbed at Brom's confidence, deflating him, owning him. Brom's muscles twitched with the urge to leap from concealment and kneel in obeisance, but he stopped himself.

Olivaard, their Mentis, had to be seven feet tall at least, taller even than Royal, but the man was as thin as a willow switch. Snowy white robes draped his body from his high, stiff collar all the way to the floor. His face was inhumanly stretched, oval eyes taller than they were wide, his head long and thin as though it had been squeezed in a vise. His ears were as large as a hand, the lobes dangling almost to his chin. His eyes glistened, wholly green, with no pupils or irises. Both his and Arsinoe's eyes were the same green color as the flame Brom had seen at the top of this tower that fateful night. The same green color as the ooze that had leaked from Brom's eyes. Olivaard's nightmare face was pinched into a haughty expression that made Brom feel there were only a finite number of ideas, and this man had thought of them all.

The thickly-muscled Wulfric was, surprisingly, Brom's height, but he was literally as wide as he was tall, a boulder of a man. Everything about him was grotesquely muscular. Armor encased the Impetu's body from his hoof-like feet—as wide as dinner plates—to the square helmet on his neck-less head. The armor had been molded to his body like a second skin, showing the swells and divots in his exaggerated physique, and the metal seemed to move when the man shifted. In places, the armor shimmered like it had been polished, but tendrils of corrosion and rust crept from the crevices between his muscles, from the shadows beneath his arms, chin, knees, chest, and groin. Patches of sallow fungus grew near the corrosion, sometimes reaching far enough to cover the shiny spots. Things moved in the shadows of those cracks, as though bugs scuttled just beneath Wulfric's armor.

Their Anima Linza, wrapped in midnight robes, stood in front of a tall arched window with a stained-glass border. The light of the room dimmed around her as if it were falling down a dark well. Outside, the softly falling snow had turned into a blizzard, framing her in flurrying white, a forbidding figure that sucked in all hope. Brom panicked.

His connection to the Soul of the World suddenly wavered, and it seemed a pathetic shield against this woman. It was impossible to hide from Linza. Any second now, she would turn and sense him, look through the marble of the bar and straight into Brom's soul...

He wrenched his gaze away from the hole, stifling his gasp. He expected the Four to go suddenly silent and discover him, then stride to the bar and yank him into view. But they didn't. They were engaged in their conversation. Brom drew a quiet breath and sank back into the Soul of the World. Its calming influence washed over him, and when his heart settled, he turned his eye back to the hole. This time, he didn't look directly at Linza.

"Wulfric has a point, I am loathe to say," Arsinoe said. "While killing all second-years is idiotic, we should decide who's going to make it through, and who is not. And sooner rather than later."

"We have not yet sorted out the fourths," Olivaard said with his over-articulated words.

"Dear Ollie, the fourth-years are pedestrian. They contain no..." Arsinoe paused for dramatic effect. "Brilliance." He winked at Wulfric, who didn't acknowledge him. "Let them run the normal course of the academy. It's the second-years destroying the order of things."

"It *is* a different kind of year," Olivaard acknowledged.

"A unique year, you mean," Arsinoe said. "When have we ever seen this?"

Linza sauntered closer with the quiet physical grace of a mountain cat. Brom suddenly realized the Anima had shifted her position so that The Four stood in an exact square. Impetu across from Anima, Mentis across from Motus, equally spaced apart. Each was of such vastly different size and shape that, at a glance, Brom didn't notice their near-symmetry before. But now the pattern leapt out at him. He wondered if being equally spaced apart increased a Quad's power. Physical proximity had increased the magic of Quad Brilliant, but they'd never experimented with patterns. Brom resolved to test this when he got out of here.

"You're talking about Quad Brilliant," Linza said in a crone's voice, seemingly plucking the words from Brom's mind. His blood chilled.

"Yes." Olivaard nodded sagely, his long earlobes wobbling.

They were all silent for a moment.

"They have elevated nearly half the Quads in their class simply by their example," Arsinoe said.

"It is...interesting," Linza creaked in her ancient voice. "They outperform the third-years, even the fourths, in some cases."

"Not all the fourths," Olivaard said.

"Please. The fourths seem like dullards by comparison," Arsinoe chided.

"Kill them," Wulfric said darkly. "Make it look like an accident."

Arsinoe rolled his eyes. "Could you please offer a different suggestion for once?"

Wulfric put a threatening hand on his sword.

Arsinoe ignored the gesture, turned a lazy gaze to Olivaard. "Tell me, does Quad Brilliant remind you of anyone?"

"Us, a hundred years ago," Wulfric said, though the question hadn't been directed at him. "And we hated each other back then."

"Back *then*?" Arsinoe said, amused.

"It almost kept us from bonding, but it made us strong in the end," Olivaard said thoughtfully, tapping his too-long chin with his too-long finger. "It's doing the same for them."

"It wasn't supposed to," Linza creaked. "The Collector assured us they would never bond."

"By all means, let's set our course by what little Damon says," Arsinoe drawled.

"It's dangerous to let them live," Wulfric said.

"Exciting, rather," Olivaard said. "We built this school to leash power. Imagine what we could do with theirs..."

"We built this school to *stop* that kind of power," Arsinoe corrected.

"Kill them," Wulfric said.

"Gods, shut up." Arsinoe sighed.

"They are not so very grown up yet," Olivaard said.

"Kill—"

"Wulfric, stop," Olivaard interrupted, exasperated. "We can't kill the princess. You know that, so stop saying it. She's the next in line for the Keltovari throne, and she'll be queen in a matter of years. Having a slave queen is too perfect an opportunity."

"Kill the others." Wulfric persisted. "Let Arsinoe play with the urchin until she bursts. Let Linza suck their oversized Impetu dry. One night, and the Quad will be done. We will spread some story that the urchin and that giant Fendiran broke the inter-Quad relationship rule, fucked, and fled to Fendir rather than face punishment. The Fendiran's family will look for him for a year, then forget him. And no one will look for the girl."

"And their Anima, Brom?" Linza asked.

A wave of chills rolled through Brom as she said his name.

"I'll take him to the top of a tree and drop him," Wulfric said. "Young Animas are accident-prone, always pushing their boundaries because of their false confidence."

"*False* confidence?" Linza asked.

Wulfric waved her comment away with one of his thick, steel-covered hands, and his gesture flung a bug across the room. It hit the floor and scuttled away.

"Or we could use them," Olivaard said.

Wulfric let out a frustrated breath.

"Come now. Their power would make them strong slaves," Olivaard said. "If we graduated them, we could use them. We'll take a personal hand in the Test. Make sure it happens exactly the way we need."

"Or we could just kill them and be done with it!" Wulfric thundered, practically yelling.

But Olivaard was obviously past listening to Wulfric. "Royal is exceedingly talented," he mused. "Think of what we could do with him in Fendir, against the Sacintos. Imagine Royal scouring his homeland and purging the outlanders. He would be a holy terror. He already wants to expunge the Keltovari from Fendir. We would simply...adjust his focus." Olivaard pursed his lips. "No. They must be allowed to take the Test of Separation." He flexed his fingers. "I want my hooks in them."

"Yes," Linza creaked.

"You play with fire," Wulfric said.

"Are you afraid of fire?" Arsinoe chuckled.

Wulfric drew his sword this time, so quickly Brom barely saw him move. Suddenly a six-foot blade pointed at Arsinoe. But Arsinoe didn't seem to care. He lazily plucked a grape from the platter on the table, popped it in his mouth.

Around his chewing, he said, "Please. We all know you're not going to use it, so put it away."

"One day..." Wulfric growled, "you'll be wrong about that." He sheathed his blade.

"It's decided. We keep the princess and the Impetu," Arsinoe said.

Wulfric shook his head, metal scraping on metal. "We kill the urchin and the Anima boy in the Test."

Fear thrilled through Brom. Vale was right. This entire academy was a trap. The Test of Separation wasn't a test at all. It was a way for The Four to cull the Quads, to rip them down, make sure no one ever challenged the supremacy of The Four. The Four didn't want to *train* Quadrons, they wanted to enslave them or destroy them.

"One loss breaks the Quad as easily as two," Linza creaked.

"Yes," Olivaard said. "Failing both is wasteful."

Brom began to shake. Even deep within the Soul of the World, he had difficulty finding his calm. Brom, his friends, the rest of the attendees at the academy, they weren't students. They were livestock.

The betrayal slithered like worms into Brom's veins. He could barely hold still. His anger and fear threatened to pull him out of the Soul of the World. He thought of Oriana, and he hastily banished his emotions, forced himself to look through the hole again.

"I want the urchin," Arsinoe said, a sly smile on his face.

"We know you do," Linza creaked, as though this had been discussed before.

"You're not a Motus, you don't know," Arsinoe said, nearly whining. "I see her when I sleep. I see her when I wake, that cute, defiant little face contorted in ecstasy. You can't know how it...fills me. I hear her screams of pleasure transforming into screams of pain, and I..." He trailed off, shivered. He plucked another grape and popped it in his mouth. "She will make a most vigorous meal."

Hot anger spilled inside Brom, and he wanted to leap from behind the bar and strangle the vile man. He suddenly hated

Arsinoe more than he'd hated anyone in his life.

"As you wish." Olivaard waved his hand like he didn't care. "Brom passes. Vale fails."

"Now that Arsinoe has relived his fantasy, might we turn our attention to the problem we came to address?" Linza creaked. "Quad Brilliant is a mere annoyance. The Sacintos are a real threat. They may have spears leveled at our hearts."

"They're going to regret it," Wulfric growled.

"Stop posturing." Arsinoe rolled his eyes. "You were less than worthless when they broke into the academy. You ran headlong into the night, stomped about the river for a while, and came back with mud on your hooves. Besides that, what did you find?"

Metal squeaked as Wulfric clenched his fist.

"We were all caught unaware," Olivaard said. "We cannot afford to be so ignorant again. The Sacintos are stronger with the Soul of the World than we previously guessed. They poked at our tower and slipped away like a breeze..." He gave a terse shake to his head. "This cannot be allowed. If it were known that these branch-heads could invade the academy with impunity..."

"I have scoured the lands around the academy," Linza said.

"As have I," Wulfric rumbled. "There isn't a trace, not for miles. Obviously they sent someone stronger than we supposed to avenge their Quadrons."

"They don't have Quadrons," Arsinoe drawled. "They have witch women and legend-keepers."

"Maybe we simply haven't seen their Quadrons," Wulfric said.

"It is the same thing," Olivaard said. "They can use magic. They've mastered Soulblock division. Therefore, they are dangerous. And if the Keltovari and Fendirans discover that they can divide their own Soulblocks without our help, we lose control."

Brom reeled with that news. So it was true. Soulblocks could be created outside the academy. He desperately wanted to know how to accomplish that. If he could understand how to make Soulblocks strong enough so that they didn't crumble upon leaving the academy, Quad Brilliant could flee these walls with their power intact.

"If the branch-heads have figured out how to divide

Soulblocks," Arsinoe said, "perhaps they have figured out how to stay so deep in the Soul of the World that we can't see them except with our own eyes."

"Speculation is pointless." Olivaard waved a long-fingered hand, annoyed. "We need certainty."

"They touched the spell by the wall," Linza said. "That is where I found the greatest concentration of residual magic."

Arsinoe picked up an apple from the table and tossed it into the air, caught it. "We've heard all this before."

At the mention of the spell and the wall, Brom twitched. They thought the Sacintos, that foreign, odd-looking race of people who had been filtering into Fendir from across the sea, were somehow Quadrons, that they'd breached the school and escaped.

But it hadn't been a Sacinto. Linza was talking about Brom and Vale, she just didn't know it. She was talking about the night Brom had shot into the sky with the Soul of the World.

It suddenly became clear why The Four hadn't searched the dormitories after his and Vale's narrow escape. These monsters had thought the threat had come from outside the school, not inside. They hadn't guessed it was a student.

In five scant minutes, Brom had learned more about The Four than all the masters or students for a hundred years. The Champion's Academy was a trap. The Test of Separation, an intentional slaughter. Soulblocks *could* be created outside these walls. And these monsters intended to devour Vale during the Test, then enslave the rest of Quad Brilliant.

I have to get out of here now, he thought. He had thoroughly accomplished his mission, and every second he stayed was more dangerous than the last.

His confidence began to drain away. Fear turned to a cold sweat on his forehead, under his armpits. His palms turned clammy.

He realized with a spike of horror that his third Soulblock was running out. He was slipping out of the Soul of the World.

Sweating, Brom looked longingly at the sliver of the doorway beyond the edge of the bar, and he quailed. He didn't even know how he'd made it *into* the room without being seen. That had been some miracle of timing generated by the Soul of the World. How was he going to get out again?

The Soul of the World softly slipped away. He felt like a cork, submerged beneath the water, suddenly bobbing to the surface, exposed. The last of his third Soulblock crackled through him and vanished.

The conversation in the room suddenly stopped as Linza hissed.

"Someone is here," she creaked.

13

BROM

"What?" Wulfric roared. "Inside the tower?"

"I don't know," Linza said, her ancient voice tight with concentration.

Metal rang on metal as Wulfric drew his sword. A low rumble escaped him as his heavy hooves charged to the doorway, Brom's only escape.

Brom's fear paralyzed him. Olivaard could find people by searching for their minds. Linza would be able to see his soul like a burning flame, just as Brom himself had seen the fires of people's souls when he'd flown up over the academy. She should be able to see him right now.

He was as good as dead. If he ran, Wulfric would catch him. If he stayed, the others would. There was nothing he could do...

Except...

He could open his fourth Soulblock.

It was certain death, but it would give him magic enough to sink back into the Soul of the World and feel what he must do next. It might even give him a chance to escape. And if he could escape, he could deliver this critical information to his friends before he died.

If Brom died after passing on his information, his friends had a chance. If Brom died in this tower, everything he'd discovered was for nothing. It would die with him, and his Quad mates would continue on in ignorance. They'd be lambs with their necks exposed to a knife.

That boiled all his choices down to one. He couldn't leave his Quad mates exposed, not when he could help them.

He took a deep breath, and then he opened his fourth Soulblock.

The magic burst within him, an unbelievable lightning storm. It was like opening his first three Soulblocks all at once. His entire body crackled with raw power, and he sank back into the Soul of the World like he was plunging to the bottom of the sea.

Suddenly, he didn't need to look through the hole in the bar to see The Four. He was a part of every rot-filled, decaying part of them. He knew exactly where they were and where they were going.

He also knew what to do now. The Soul of the World showed him every course of action that would bring him to safety.

There were two doorways in the room. The one through which Brom had entered, and one on the other side of the room on the same wall. Arsinoe and Linza had gathered at the far doorway, and Olivaard had joined Wulfric at the closer one.

Flipping his cowl up to hide his face, Brom stood and sprinted alongside the bar, running as fast as he could in the opposite direction.

The Four spun at once, like they were all parts of the same creature, but they seemed sluggish to Brom's hyper-active senses. They all saw him just as he threw his hands up over his head and leapt at the window at the end of the bar.

It shattered.

Brom's body became a tool of the Soul of the World. He didn't think; he listened to what *must* be done. He reached out and snatched the curling drapes that had blown out with him. It arrested his momentum just enough to bring him back toward the wall. He landed on his toes on a decorative ledge of snowy stone, a body length below the row of second-story windows. He pushed off, flipped in midair, and landed in the snow just in front of the spiderweb in the narrow courtyard, which was no longer gray in Brom's enhanced vision, but solid black. Snow whipped hard in the howling wind, blinding him. The blizzard was so absolute that his physical eyes couldn't see the guards at the wall's gate anymore, nor even the window from which he'd just jumped.

But he could feel the guards. He could feel The Four at the window behind the swirling snow, and he felt Wulfric leap after him, roaring. The man's giant hooves blew the snow apart in a white cloud and cracked the cobblestones right behind Brom.

Cold, glowing green eyes flared inside that square helmet as Wulfric glared at Brom. The giant blue axes swung left and right behind him.

Brom turned and leapt at the black spiderweb.

Wulfric leapt after him. Time seemed to slow, and Brom twisted, pulling his arms in to his chest as he corkscrewed between the strands of the web, touching none of them. Wulfric's hand swiped through the air where Brom's ankle had just been.

Brom landed in a heap in the snow, right where he'd come over the wall in the first place.

Wulfric slammed into the magic web and screamed. His steely, muscular arms curled up, and his back arched like he'd been struck by a lightning bolt. The spiderweb wrapped around him, grabbing hold of him, then pulled his limbs into tortured positions as it expanded again. Wulfric drew a ragged breath and screamed again.

Brom didn't take time to watch the spectacle. The other three might not be able to jump from that window, but they'd be after him like an arrow. He ran at the wall, found a small chink in the bricks with his toe and propelled himself high enough that he could grab the top and throw himself over. He sprinted into the blizzard, unable to see more than a few feet in front of him, but he could feel. He ran alongside the hedge, using it to guide him back to the river.

He reached the rushing water, breathing hard. Wulfric's screams had ceased, and Brom knew the chase had begun again. He didn't know how much time he had before his fourth Soulblock was done and, shortly thereafter, he would die.

He felt a sudden stab in his mind, like a giant scorpion's tail. Brom stumbled, going down to one knee, and he clapped his hands to his ears.

I have you, little Sacinto, came Olivaard's high-pitched voice in Brom's mind. *Ah, you've opened your final Soulblock. Clever. But your sacrifice will amount to nothing. You'll never reach your fellows, and we know how to keep you alive. Yes... We'll keep you alive for as long as we require.*

Brom ignored the arrogant voice. The Soul of the World knew what to do, and he listened to it. As the scorpion's stinger seemed to turn into a hand, grasping, trying to get a hold on his mind, to find more thoughts to plunder, Brom staggered to his feet, stumbled down the snowy, muddy slope, and dove into the icy river.

Olivaard's voice vanished, and Brom's thoughts cleared. He flowed with the icy water, which practically paralyzed his body. He let it in, let it rush over him and its essence rush through him. He also felt the snow, whipping down the narrow trench of the river. He felt the trees overhead. He let them all flow through his body like he flowed down the river.

He felt the stab come again, hitting next to him, as though desperately searching, as though Olivaard was flailing, trying to strike at him in the dark.

Brom rushed downstream with the current. When he felt the fronds of the willow tree—his and Oriana's willow tree—brush over his face, he reached up and grasped them with stiff fingers. His entire body filled with pain as he pulled himself up, out of the water. Hand over hand, muscles stiffening, he climbed up the fronds into the high branches of the tree, then he lay there. His body was freezing to death, but he forced himself to hold still.

Brom slipped into a death-like state as he waited high in the tree. He felt other stabs at the water below, at the bank on either side, but none hit him, and none were as close as the first. He let the cold seep into him, stayed safe within the howling wind and snow.

Mud squished and branches cracked as Wulfric arrived, racing like a bull alongside the river. Wulfric slipped and slammed into the trunk of the willow tree, shaking it. He cursed, and Brom swayed with the tree, as did the other limbs. Snow showered down onto Wulfric. Spitting epithets, he scrambled to his feet and raced past, continuing up the river at tremendous speed. He never looked up, never knew that Brom was perched barely five feet over his head.

Then the deadly Impetu was gone. Soon, even the crashing noises of his passing faded. Only the howling wind and whipping snow remained, coming down so thickly that the limbs that had been shaken free of snow were already beginning to turn white again.

Brom slipped down the tree and landed on the slope. His arms and legs were numb, but he sluggishly clawed his way up the incline and lumbered into the storm. Anyone else would have been lost by now, turned around, and possibly would never have found their way back to the dormitory. It was impossible to see anything, and once Brom left the river, he couldn't have told which direction it was by sight alone. But he was still connected to the frozen earth, the swirling snow. He could feel Westfall Dormitory directly ahead of him, and he went unerringly to it.

He slipped inside, a half-frozen walking corpse. He stumped across the grand foyer and up the steps, one painful leg at a time. He made his way down the walkway until he stopped in front of Oriana's door.

He knocked, three heavy thuds.

Powerful magic from his fourth Soulblock coursed through him, and he knew it was the only reason he could still stand upright, probably the only reason he had not yet died of exposure.

Oriana opened the door, blinking the sleep from her eyes. She wore a light blue silk nightgown, barefoot, and her toenails were painted the same color as her eyes.

Those indigo eyes went wide, and she gasped. "Brom!" She put an arm around him, and he slumped into her.

"Kelto, you're a block of ice!" She led him inside and kicked the door shut with her heel. "What did you do? We agreed you'd stop this nonsense—"

"You have to leave." He grasped her arms with what strength he had left. "You, Royal, Vale. Flee tonight. Don't wait. Use the cover of the storm. It's a trap. All of it. Everything is a trap."

"What are you talking about?"

"Read my mind," he said. "Do it. Find out everything I learned. Do it."

She nodded tersely. Through their bond, he felt her open her first Soulblock, felt the magic crackle into her, and he felt her enter his mind. Contrary to the feeling of Olivaard's scorpion stab, Oriana's mind felt like a warm, gentle hand. Brom opened himself to her, let her see it all: his invasion of the tower, the conversation between The Four, and all the horrifying secrets they had revealed. It took only seconds.

"Kelto's beard!" she said softly. It was the only time Brom had ever seen Oriana aghast.

"It's a lie..." he said. "The academy. The whole thing. The Four..." He slumped to his knees, finally allowing his body to fail.

"Brom!" She jolted with realization. "You opened your fourth Soulblock," she hissed incredulously. "Brom, no!"

"It was...the only way," he said.

"You little idiot!" she whispered harshly.

"Go," he said. "They'll...they'll kill you."

"Brom," she said in her stern, princess voice. "Stay awake."

He slumped over backward, and she struggled with him, falling over him as she laid him down on the floor.

It isn't so bad, dying, he thought. He was so cold he couldn't feel anything at all. He wondered if there would be pain when his soul bled out into the lands.

But he'd succeeded. He'd gotten back to his Quad. He'd told Oriana. Told her everything. His friends might live. They'd have a chance to escape this trap, a chance he'd given them, and that was enough.

That was enough...

"Brom!" Oriana's voice was desperate, and he couldn't tell if she'd spoken inside his head, or if her voice was simply getting warmer. Oriana was so pretty... She always knew what to do... Brom fell in love with her just a little bit then.

"Brom!"

Thinking about love made him think about Vale. Perhaps

this...at the end...would let her know how he felt. Love *was* real...

"Tell Vale..." He tried to force his numb lips to speak, but it was so hard. He tried again. "Tell Vale that..." But the rest didn't come out. Or maybe he'd spoken what he'd wanted to say already, but just couldn't hear it all. The words didn't matter. Vale would know how he felt, and he'd done his job. He'd brought wisdom to his Quad. What mattered was that his Quad had a chance. They'd run. They'd be safe.

The room went black, and even Oriana's urgent voice faded away, hissing at him to stay awake.

Part III

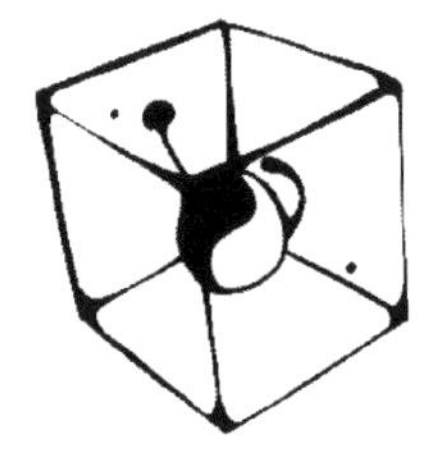

The Test

1

ORIANA

Oriana had heard the varied legends of what happened to Quadrons who used their final Soulblock. They fell to a pile of dust. They became demons who hid in forest shadows or underneath the bed. They screamed in a high-pitched voice, never stopping until they suffocated. Horrific stories, all. Whether the specifics were true or not, Oriana didn't know.

What she did know—what everyone in the academy knew—was that draining your fourth Soulblock was certain death. The books in the academy library agreed that the fourth Soulblock was the most powerful of all, that it filled the user with unimaginable magic as well as a sense of invulnerability, right up to the point that the fool dropped dead—the soul drained away, the body shriveled, the skin as pale as snow.

Brom was already deathly pale.

She laid him down and shot her thoughts into the sleeping minds of Royal and Vale.

"Wake up! Brom is dying. Come to my room immediately," she thought

to them, then added, *"and quietly."*

Mere moments passed before Royal opened her door without knocking. The giant man hadn't made a sound. He'd obviously opened his first Soulblock and was using his Impetu magic. His face was alive with a protector's instinct. His gaze flicked about the room for enemies, and he stepped inside, ready to use his body as a shield.

"Where?" he thought to her. *"Are we being attacked?"*

"Not directly. Not yet," she replied.

Vale came next, her frantic pattering feet audible a few seconds before she arrived. The moment she entered the room, Oriana felt the crackling rush of her own Soulblocks doubling, giving her far more magic than before in addition to a seductive feeling of invincibility.

Vale's gaze shot to Brom on the floor. Her face remained expressionless, which Oriana thought was decidedly odd. Either Vale had expected this, or she was intentionally keeping her true feelings off her face.

Since they'd broken through their individual barriers and bonded as a Quad, Vale's face had worn as many expressions as a rainbow had colors. It was always one thing or another—joy, excitement, interest, sadness, frustration... But Oriana couldn't remember the last time she'd seen Vale impassive.

"What happened?" Vale asked in a monotone.

The non-expression, the monotone... Together they sent up a flag of warning to Oriana. Whatever had happened to Brom tonight, Vale was a part of it somehow. They'd broken the rules together. Again.

It frustrated her. All this time, she thought they'd all been operating smoothly and honestly.

Fine, she thought. *If they're going to break rules, so will I.*

Angrily, Oriana reached into Vale's mind without her permission.

Wiggling Will, he drunk the draught.
And spun his dagger by the haft.
The giggling maidens showed delight.

And spun his dagger through the night.

Wiggling Will, he drunk the draught.
And spun his dagger by the haft.
The giggling maidens showed delight.
And spun his dagger through the night.

Oriana narrowed her eyes. Vale was repeating a drinking song in her mind, over and over. It was a crude but effective method of temporarily blocking a Mentis. Oriana could dig deeper, of course, but that would take time, concentration, and more magic. She couldn't afford to spare any of those, but she didn't need to. Vale had told Oriana everything she needed to know by throwing up that makeshift mental wall. The little urchin wanted her thoughts hidden. She was guilty. Whatever had happened to Brom, Vale knew about it.

"Oriana," Vale repeated. "What happened?"

"You tell me," Oriana said.

Royal picked up on Oriana's frosty tone, and turned to Vale.

"What happened?" Royal growled.

"I don't know," Vale said, again in that monotone.

"I think you do," Oriana said.

The little woman's eyes flashed angrily, the first emotion she'd shown since stepping into the room.

"Are you going to let him die to keep a secret from us?" Oriana pressed.

"What secret?" Royal asked. He glanced back and forth between the two of them.

"Brom opened his fourth Soulblock," Oriana said. "He's dying."

"What?" Royal roared. He flinched, jumped to the door, closed it softly, then lowered his voice. "What?" he whispered.

"He snuck into the tower of The Four," Oriana said. "They chased him."

"The *Four* chased him?" Royal blurted, incredulous.

"No..." Vale whispered, and genuine surprise broke her impassive mask. She sank to her knees next to Brom. "No,

Brom..."

Royal shook his head. "If The Four chased him, they'd have caught him."

Oriana gestured to Brom's unconscious body as if to say: here's the proof. But even she had her doubts, and she'd plucked the story from his own mind. "He opened his fourth Soulblock to escape them."

Tears stood in Vale's eyes as she bent over Brom, clutching his shoulders. "You idiot," she whispered.

"Why did he go there?" Oriana asked.

"We were going to do it together," Vale suddenly said.

"Vale!" Royal blasted, looked guilty again, and lowered his voice a second time. "You planned to break into the tower of The Four? The Four!"

Oriana had known Vale and Brom were capable of deceit, but that they'd successfully kept this from her worried her on multiple levels. Honesty obviously wasn't important to Brom or Vale, even with their Quad. Second—and more important—they'd actually been able to keep a secret of this magnitude from Oriana. She had read their minds on multiple occasions over the past weeks, in some cases quite thoroughly. She should have been able to pick up something of their secrets unless they'd worked hard—very hard—to deceive her. They had to have planned it.

"You were keeping secrets from us," Oriana whispered. Even now she didn't want to believe it. "From your Quad."

"The Four were keeping secrets from *all* of us," Vale said, "And you two refused to look at it, what else could we do?"

"*Not* break the rules," Royal growled, obviously frustrated. His big fists were clenched. "*Not* do what you were doing! Of course The Four have secrets. They're *The Four*!"

"There are deadly things happening here on this cursed campus. Brom tried to tell you. You ignored him. Just because you're determined to be blind doesn't mean I am," Vale said.

"I'm not determined to be blind. I'm determined to have honor," Royal said.

"Fuck your honor! I'm talking about truth."

Royal shook his head. "I thought you were growing, Vale. I

thought you were learning what it means to be part of a team, part of a family—"

"She's right," Oriana said softly. She hated that she had to take Vale's side. She wanted to agree with Royal. Order was paramount. She wanted to believe in the rules. She didn't want to believe this horrible truth that Brom had unearthed. She didn't want to think the academy was a pen for slaves. This was supposed to be a place where people came to find their power, not lose it. But just because she didn't want to see this horrible truth didn't make it go away.

Both Royal and Vale watched her.

"Brom and Vale were right. The Four aren't what they seem," Oriana said. "They plan to... They're going to put hooks in us, some kind of magical control. They do it to all Quadrons who pass the Test. And those who don't pass..." She let that hang. They all knew what happened to those who didn't pass. Or they thought they did. "They don't just die. They...are used. And then they die. And Vale..." Oriana remembered Brom's thoughts about Arsinoe, about what he wanted to do to Vale.

"What about me?" Vale asked.

"They chose you. You're the one who will fail the Test. They already know what will happen. And they have something...horrible planned for you."

"Why?" Vale said, frustrated, angry. "Why me?"

"Apparently Arsinoe...their Motus—"

"I know who Arsinoe is," Vale said gravely.

"He has...taken a fancy to you."

"What are you talking about?" Royal asked.

"The Test of Separation isn't a test," Oriana said. "This academy is...it's like a pen for cattle. It's where they brand us, castrate us, then send us back into the two kingdoms. If we survive that long, that is."

"I was right..." Vale whispered.

"What do you mean you were right?" Royal growled. He was a step behind in piecing this together, and his frustration was obviously mounting. Oriana knew Royal could only be pushed so far before he resorted to violence. Raging into the corridor. Looking for the fight. He was an Impetu and a Fendiran both, after all.

And she couldn't let this disaster spread any further than this room. If Brom had actually stung The Four tonight and escaped, it would be exceedingly dangerous for Quad Brilliant to draw attention to themselves. The last thing they needed was the student in the dorm next to Oriana's waking and overhearing this conversation, then passing it on to a master.

"Brom revealed to me what he has seen and heard. I will relay it to you," Oriana said in both of their minds.

She opened her mind to Royal and Vale and delivered every bit of information she'd gleaned from Brom's story, quick as a flash of light. It wasn't much, and it came scattered, with parts missing. But two things were clear: the academy was a trap, The Four were monsters.

Royal's jaw dropped. Vale bared her teeth, furious.

For Oriana's part, she felt ashamed. She should have seen this. No Quads ever graduated whole. How had she not thought of that as insidious? It was so obvious that Oriana suddenly wondered if their minds had been altered when they'd come into the academy.

Was this inclination to ignore the obvious part of Brom's green fire spell?

"That's what Brom learned," Oriana said. "Leastwise, that's what he was able to tell me before he fell unconscious. But we don't have time to be horrified or outraged, to think about how we're being prepped like livestock. He is dying, and we must make a decision."

"I can't believe it..." Royal spoke softly to himself. He seemed to reel from the information. He'd put one hand on the wall, and his gaze was far away.

"What decision?" Vale asked Oriana.

"To try to save him or not," Oriana said.

"Save him?" Royal asked, snapping his focus back to the conversation. "Is that even possible?"

"Perhaps, but..." Oriana trailed off.

"But what?" Vale said.

"We could die with him."

"We do it," Royal said without hesitation. Oriana gave him a little half smile. Despite the fact that he was a Fendiran, Royal made it very hard to dislike him. His unthinking bravery and total dedication to the Quad inspired her.

"It will require all three of us," Oriana said. "If we do not succeed, we die. Even if we do succeed, we may die trying."

"I'll do it," Royal said immediately.

Vale went silent. She glanced at Brom, who was now as white as the snow outside. Finally, she narrowed her eyes at Oriana. "You can't come back from opening the final Soulblock. You open it, you die. No one has ever survived, not in the entire history of magic."

"There are two stories," Oriana countered. "Two attempts to save someone like this that almost succeeded."

"*Almost?*" Vale said.

"I've been researching Soulshock since we thought Brom had done it after his first discovery. There may be a way. We have to give him our Soulblocks. We have to fill him up and...repair his fourth Soulblock. Close it again."

"The fourth Soulblock can't be closed. The first three only close themselves because they're regenerated from the fourth," Vale said. "They all come from the fourth. It's why the fourth doesn't regenerate."

After a moment, Oriana nodded. "I know. But there has to be a way. Some way."

"That's your plan?" Vale asked. "By Kelto, you want to try this, and you don't know how to do it?"

"Nobody knows how to do anything until someone does it first," Oriana said.

Vale bit her lip, looked back at Brom.

"If we don't," Oriana said, "then we have to run."

"Run?" Royal said. "Why?"

"Brom escaped The Four," she said. "But Olivaard knew he'd opened his fourth Soulblock. Once Brom shows up dead tomorrow, sucked dry from a drained fourth, they're going to know who invaded their tower. And then they're going to kill all of us."

Royal seemed like he wanted to be angry. His face reddened, but then a reluctant smile curved his lips. He shook his head. "He jumped from the cliff with us attached to him," he said. "But by Fendra... It's the bravest thing I've ever even heard of." He looked down at Brom with admiration.

"They were going to kill us anyway," Vale said. "Well, they were going to kill me. You two were just going to be slaves. *That's* all."

"So our choices are," Royal mused, and he seemed to have his anger under control now. "We run. Or we try something—as second-year students—that's never been achieved by a Quadron before, not even by The Four themselves. And then if by some miracle we succeed, we still have to flee."

"If we can repair the damage, we may not need to flee," Oriana said.

"Why not?"

"Because then we won't have a corpse to explain," Oriana said.

"And you think The Four won't find us because there isn't a corpse?" Royal asked. "They're The Four."

Vale, hands on Brom's chest, stared at him without seeing anything, as if deep in thought.

"Vale?" Oriana said.

"We have to try," Vale whispered. "Either we all escape this, or none of us do. It's the way it's supposed to be."

Royal nodded. "That, I agree with."

"Then let's be quick," Oriana said. "Royal, put him on the bed, pull it away from the wall." Royal lifted Brom gently and put him on the bed like he was a child, then picked the entire bed up, Brom and all, and moved it to the center of the room.

"Vale, here. Royal, on that side." Oriana indicated that they kneel on either side of Brom and put their hands on his chest. She knelt at Brom's head, put her fingertips on his temples. Royal crossed to Brom's other side, knelt, and put his hands next to Vale's.

"Royal, you've already opened your first Soulblock. So have I. Vale?"

"No."

"Okay, so... We could open one Soulblock at a time and feed them into him," she said, "like we did when he drained his third Soulblock. But I don't think we should."

"You want to open them all at the same time," Vale guessed.

"Being together, we all have twice as many Soulblocks to work with. Now is the time to use them. Open your first five, right down to the top of the sixth, then stop. Save your sixth, seventh and eighth or we could all be bedridden for a week. That would be almost as suspicious as a corpse. I've never opened more than one Soulblock at a time, but what I've read says it varies from student to student. For some, it is exhausting. For some, it is euphoric and addictive. You begin to feel omnipotent, and will keep opening them. So you must set your intention strongly to stop after the fifth. Just stop. No matter what your mind or heart or body wants to do. Stop."

"And if we need more than the first five Soulblocks?" Royal asked.

"We will cross that bridge if we come to it," Oriana said. "I will let you know."

"Okay," Royal said gruffly.

Oriana closed her eyes and composed her mind. She felt the others doing the same. Thoughts silenced. Just as she was about ready to give the signal, Vale spoke.

"Oriana, what happened to the others, the ones who tried this before?"

Oriana hesitated, then said, "They died. They couldn't stop opening their Soulblocks. The euphoria took them and they forgot themselves. They burned through their magic like a bonfire and ended up an empty husk, just like the person they were trying to help. So," she emphasized. "Stop with five. I'll tell you if we need more. The key will be in repairing Brom's fourth. If we can't do that, it won't matter. We could pour a thousand souls into him and still fail."

"Why do you think we'll succeed where the others failed?" Vale asked. It was the first time Oriana had seen her timid.

"Because we are Brilliant," Oriana stated.

"We are Brilliant," Royal echoed.

A genuine smile spread across Vale's face. "Yes," she whispered. "Brilliant."

They closed their eyes again and unleashed their Soulblocks.

2

BROM

Brom felt his Quad mates inside his body. He felt them coming to his rescue in a cacophony of sensation. But this time, he perceived their souls differently than he ever had before. There was no lightning. There were no colored flames, not red or white or blue.

Instead, Oriana's soul tasted like sugar and steel. He felt Vale's soul like oiled skin sliding against him. Royal's soul blared like trumpets in a canyon. They surrounded him, and they brought memories.

He should be dead. He'd drained his fourth Soulblock, but they were coming to rescue him.

This had to be some kind of dream, something happening inside his mind. It certainly wasn't Oriana's dorm room, which was the last thing he'd seen before he passed out.

His dream self floated halfway down the depths of a canyon filled with blaring trumpets, sugar and steel, and sensuous oil. His Quad mates' nonsensical presences twisted together. Taste, feel, and sound transformed into a raging river of magic, a torrent that poured over the tall cliffs and into the canyon.

Magic sluiced down. Magic fell from a stormy sky overhead and rushed as rivers over the edges into the canyon. Suddenly, Brom swam desperately in the rush, a drowning man barely keeping his head above water. He thought the torrent would fill the canyon in an instant, bringing him up to level ground above, but no matter how much magic rushed into the canyon, it only filled it halfway, draining away as quickly as it came.

Swimming desperately within that ocean, Brom twisted about, realizing the canyon could not hold the magic because it was rife with cracks and splits.

Fear and uncertainty tightened around him. That was wrong. He couldn't articulate his foreboding at first because of the strange sights, sounds, and sensations, but this was going to end in disaster. His Quad mates were pouring their magic into this canyon...

...and it was going to drain away anyway.

This was his fourth Soulblock. This...canyon was how he perceived it. They were trying to save him by filling up his drained Soulblock, but it couldn't last. It was temporary, and at the bottom of this attempt was death for all of them.

As long as he floated on this ocean, he would live. He could think. And perhaps he could work magic as well.

He concentrated and tried to affect the ocean of magic, to reach out and connect himself to the Soul of the World outside this dream.

It obeyed instantly. Roiling water grew into a pillar, then into a tentacle, and then into a thin rope that reached into the sky.

Go, he thought. *Reach past the dream. Connect me to the Soul.*

Assurance flowed into him. Certainty.

He was still trapped within this deadly canyon, but he could somehow feel the dorm room in which his body lay. He could sense his three friends surrounding him, pouring their wills and their magic into him, trying to make him live.

The Soul of the World opened its wisdom, and Brom knew two things at once: First, he could wake on the power they were giving him, but only to die again in moments. Second, those beautiful fools had thrown their lot in with him, and now they'd drain themselves dry if he didn't mend this Soulblock.

Was that even possible? He'd never even heard of a Quadron doing that.

He studied the cracks in the canyon wall. If he woke, he was dead. The work, if it could be done, had to be done here in this dream. He had to close those cracks. He had to stay inside his fourth Soulblock and somehow heal the damage.

He stopped swimming and began to sink, but did not panic. He let the ocean of magic soak into him, and he envisioned himself standing on the edge of the canyon.

He opened his eyes, and there he stood at the edge, looking down at the cascading rain pouring into the canyon, at the dozen rivers rushing over the edge, making the churning ocean that was slowly draining away.

He closed his eyes again and saw himself floating, flying out over the raging magic and descending partway down one of the walls.

He opened his eyes to find he'd done exactly that. He hovered before one of the giant cracks visible above the ocean. It was as wide as Brom's own body, and he set to fixing it.

Close, he commanded.

The rock ground together, becoming smaller and smaller, but torrents of magic still flowed through it until it slammed shut. Brom flew to the next crack, set his will to it, and slowly forced it closed. He went to the next, but even as he did, magic coursed through the innumerable other cracks, lowering the ocean faster than it could be filled. He didn't know how long his Quad mates could keep up this flow of magic, but it couldn't possibly be for long.

He turned around and around. There were hundreds of enormous cracks in this canyon, and those were only the ones he could see. He wasn't going to be fast enough.

Something nudged him, like someone was poking him with a finger. He turned, and saw nothing but the storm and the ocean, the cracks in the walls.

Suddenly, the sweet metallic taste of sugar and steel filled his mouth.

"Brom..."

"Oriana!"

"There you are," she said in relief.

She materialized from white mist next to him, the sheets of magic rain falling through her like she was a ghost. She wore a high-necked, floor-length white dress studded with indigo jewels on the collar and cuffs of the sleeves.

"We are giving you the magic from our Soulblocks, but it will not last."

"I know! I'm trying to mend the cracks," he said. "But I...I can't do it fast enough."

"I have an idea."

Brom laughed ruefully. "Is this like the stupid idea that made you try to save a dead man?"

"We can discuss the concept of stupidity later," she snapped.

His guilt rushed through him. She was right. He'd put all of his Quad mates at risk. If they couldn't fix this, he would be responsible for their deaths. Did he think they *wouldn't* try to save him?

"Tell me," he said, subdued.

"You control this avatar of yourself, just as I control mine. You control your body, too, everything about it, including your Soulblock. You are picturing this Soulblock as a vast canyon. Make it smaller. Make it manageable. Make yourself the large one, the powerful one, the one who commands how things must be."

"Are you sure?" he asked.

"Of course not," she snapped. *"Do you have a another idea?"*

"No," he said sheepishly. No one had ever repaired a fourth Soulblock. But he couldn't look at it like that. He had to shift his perspective, use his imagination. He had to see it as possible, not impossible.

"I'm going to make it a box," he said. "A proper wooden box."

"Make it steel," she said. *"Make it smooth. No cracks."*

"Help me." He held out his hand.

"I am here." Her fingers clasped his. Steel and sugar filled his nostrils.

The roaring river continued to spill over the sides of the canyon. Rain plunged down from the sky.

Brom tried to push the canyon down, to compress it. It rumbled, but shrank only a little. Boulders and shards of rock fell into the churning water. It seemed like he was trying to push a mountain with his bare hands. He gasped.

"Your belief in it makes it strong," Oriana said. *"Take that belief away. Remove it from your thinking. Then remake it."*

He took a deep breath. He cleared his mind of roaring rivers, deep canyons. He removed everything, forcing his mind to be a blank slate.

"Yes..." Oriana whispered.

He opened his eyes, and the canyon was gone. Instead, he stood on a white floor that stretched away on all sides, flat as far as he could see. Overhead was a blue sky that faded to dark blue at the horizon.

Before him stood a perfect glass box, just a head taller than he was. It was flawless and clear, with no cracks, but the entire top was open. On the far side, he saw Royal as a blue mist, hands extended, his face contorted in intense concentration. Blue light flowed from his hands, arcing up and down into the glass box to the sound of trumpets. To his right, a misty red Vale raised her arms, lips pressed together tightly. Red oil shot from her palms like water from a fountain, joining Royal's blue light, twisting together and filling the box.

The proportions of everything—the magic, the Soulblock—were the same, but it was manageable now. This container, unlike the canyon, could hold the magic. Everything they were putting into it was staying.

"We aren't finished," Oriana said, standing on the opposite side of the glass box from Vale. A river of liquid steel and white sugar poured from her outstretched palms. She nodded at the open top. *"Finish it."*

Brom floated up over his pristine, glass Soulblock. It wasn't steel, as he had imagined, but at least it wasn't cracked. It seemed sensible that this box would have a top, perhaps something that had been opened, but could still close. He shut his eyes and imagined it so.

At first, he couldn't. It was as though his very body resisted him. His mind kept sliding off to think of something else. Escaping The Four. The frigid water of the stream. Vale kissing him for the first time. His mother and father fighting...

"Brom. Hurry," Oriana's voice came to him. *"Royal has fallen."*

Brom forced his wandering, slippery mind back, made it focus. A great keening sound began, far away, and seemed to be coming closer. It was like air being forced through a crack in a drafty house.

Do it, Brom thought. *Make it! Make a lid!*

Suddenly, something ripped. Deep inside, it felt like a muscle coming away from bone.

He screamed at the pain, but suddenly he could envision the lid.

He gasped and opened his eyes.

A lid of glass poised upright over the box, so perfectly clear that it could have always been there, and he simply hadn't noticed it.

Close, he commanded, and the lid slowly descended, cutting off the flows of red and white. Finally, it clicked shut, filled with blue, red and white colors, swirling and twisting together, but never blending.

The misty blue Royal, now unconscious and prone on the floor, dissolved. The misty red Vale, on her knees but still pushing red oily magic from her fingertips, finally stopped. She, too, vanished.

Oriana, stooped in exhaustion, turned to look at him. A triumphant smile flickered across her lips. She gave a little shake to her head, like she couldn't believe he'd done it, then she vanished too.

"It is done..." Her voice faded away.

Brom gasped and fell to his knees. The edges of the blue horizon blurred, and he began to float upward. He continued rising into that blue sky, floating toward consciousness. The blue surrounded him.

He drew a breath and opened his eyes.

3
BROM

Brom drew a sharp breath. His eyes fluttered open, and he saw Oriana's room. He lay on her soft feather bed, pulled into the center of the room.

The tapestry of a red dragon stared fiercely at him from across the room, its furious face lit with the fire about to come out of its mouth. To his left was a painting of the Hallowed Woods, with the scaly bark of the Lyantrees rendered in meticulous detail, stretching into the misty distance, purple and silver leaves glimmering.

He felt bruised all over, like his Quad mates had taken turns beating him with a cudgel. Nausea bubbled in his stomach, and he felt drained of all strength.

Royal lay on the floor to his left, unconscious. Vale knelt at his right, her head against his chest and her fists twisted into the white sheets beneath him.

"He is back," Oriana said in exhaustion from behind him, letting out a soft breath. She knelt behind the head of the bed, lightly touching Brom's temples with her fingers.

Vale raised her head. "Well, *that's* something no one has ever done before." She grinned wearily.

"Royal?" Brom said, looking at the big man, felled like a tree. "Is he okay?"

"He will live," Oriana said. "The man unleashed four Soulblocks at once, then stopped immediately. I think he has never opened two Soulblocks at once before, let alone four. I suspect the shock felled him. But he is Impetu. He will recover."

"Gods..." Brom gritted his teeth. He struggled to sit up. The room tilted unexpectedly, and he almost threw up.

He settled back down on the bed, clenching his teeth and forcing himself not to vomit. Oriana slid her hands underneath his head again and slowly, gently helped him sit up. He let out a shuddering breath. "I feel awful."

"You're the healthiest dead man I've ever seen," Vale said wryly.

What his Quad mates had done was miraculous. He was going to live. Gods... He was—

Cold fear slithered through him. His narrow escape from the tower. His flight into the snowstorm. He'd threatened The Four. They would come for him. They'd come for his Quad.

The Four would still be looking. They wouldn't just stop, not for a threat inside their own tower. They would overturn every stone to catch him, and this time they would search inside the school too.

"You should have run..." he said.

"You should have told us what you were attempting," Oriana replied. "We cannot work as a Quad if you keep secrets."

Royal stirred. With a grunt, he sat up like some mythical bear, growling as he shook his head to clear it. The big man regained his senses, blinked, then focused on Brom.

"He's alive," Royal rumbled, and a fatigued smile spread across his handsome face.

"No, Oriana, you don't understand," Brom said. "How long until morning?" He had no idea how much time had passed, and every second counted. "The Four are looking for me right now. Gods damn me, I told you to run!"

"The gods may damn you after I am finished," Oriana said

coldly. "Right now, we have decisions to make. And this time..." She gave a meaningful look at him and then at Vale. "We're going to do it together."

"Listen to me," Brom protested. "Olivaard was inside my mind. He probably knows who I am—"

"If Olivaard knew who you were," Oriana cut him off, "The Four would already be here. No. They're searching for you in that blizzard." She gestured at the window. "And your advice is to run *into* the blizzard?"

Brom blinked, and he saw how ridiculous that must seem. But if they stayed here, they were simply waiting for the inevitable.

"We stay calm," Oriana said firmly. "We use our heads. And if we do flee, we do it according to a plan."

"We can't stay here," Brom said. "Staying here means death. Or slavery."

"I want to know what happened, from Brom's lips," Royal rumbled. "Suddenly, I have come to a slaughterhouse, not an academy. Suddenly, I am a criminal instead of a student. I want to know why."

"Tell us what happened, Brom," Oriana said. "The scatter of your thoughts and memories hardly makes a full picture."

Brom gave Vale a quick glance. She shrugged. She was undoubtedly curious about the parts she didn't know.

So he told them everything. Well, almost everything. He didn't mention his love affair with Vale. He described the approach to the tower, spying on The Four, and their entire nefarious conversation as best as he could recall it.

He told them about the Sacinto, and how The Four feared the branch-heads, that the foreigners were more magical than anyone had guessed. He described how he and Vale had secretly researched The Four because of their suspicions.

He ended with the news that The Four had decided Oriana, Royal, and Brom were to pass the Test of Separation, and that Vale was to fail and become...a meal for Arsinoe. Brom shuddered, thinking of the lascivious look in the fiend's eyes.

Royal wrinkled his nose. Vale looked impassive.

"They devour those who fail," Brom said. "I think they drain them, kind of the opposite of what you just did for me. The Four don't repair Soulblocks. They eat them."

"I still don't understand how you escaped them," Royal said. "The Four are...well, they're omnipotent."

"Obviously they are not," Oriana said.

"I was lucky," Brom said honestly, thinking about his narrow escape: the luck of the blizzard hiding him, of Wulfric passing beneath his branch without noticing him. If Brom had shifted even a little, Wulfric would have glanced up. "I surprised them. And I was quick enough, fortunate enough, to get away before they brought their full power to bear."

Vale snorted.

They all looked at her. Oriana raised a quizzical eyebrow.

"He's not lucky," Vale said.

"What do you mean?" Oriana said.

"I mean he didn't escape because he's lucky. He escaped because he's ridiculously powerful." She looked from one to the other, then she rolled her eyes as though she was explaining to children. "Brom is so strong with Anima magic that he pulled me into the Soul of the World, so powerful he uncovered something The Four have successfully hidden for a century. Kelto, he slipped into the Soul of the World so deeply he was invisible to magic." She paused, waiting for a reaction. "*Invisible,*" she emphasized. "Fully graduated Quadrons can't do that. I've never even read about anyone who could do that. The Soul of the World dances with him in a way it's never danced with anyone."

"Hmmm," Oriana said, thoughtful. Whenever she contemplated something, she looked icy and regal, like she was overseeing a distant battlefield.

Brom cleared his throat. "The Four could burst in here at any moment. Oriana says it's stupid to run into the blizzard. But I say now is the time to escape. It may be our only chance."

"We're not going to escape," Oriana said.

Vale looked at her. Royal crossed his muscled arms and nodded emphatically.

"I came here to become a Quadron," Oriana said. "I'm not leaving until I become a Quadron."

"But the Test of Separation is a sham!" Brom said. "You're not going to become a Quadron, you're going to become a slave." He couldn't get Arsinoe's vile expression out of his mind, like he wanted to pluck Vale's limbs off one at a time while she thrashed and screamed.

"The knowledge is here. The power is here. I'm not leaving until I have it," Oriana said.

"Neither am I," Vale agreed.

Royal smiled in satisfaction. He *wanted* a fight. Whether it was against the Test of Separation or The Four themselves. Fighting was what made sense to him.

Brom quailed. His daring invasion of the tower, his harrowing escape—it was all for nothing if his Quad mates didn't run. He'd wanted to make them safe, but instead they were going to spit into the teeth of The Four and get themselves killed.

"We find a way around the Test," Vale said, her brown eyes flashing. "Knowing what we know, we can use our time here differently. We can all four continue what Brom and I were studying. We have two years to come up with something."

"Yes," Royal rumbled.

"Two years?" Brom said. "We don't even have two weeks. They're going to find me, and when they do, they'll devour you, one way or another."

"I have an idea," Oriana said quietly.

"I'll leave." Brom said. "I'll go tonight. I'll lead them away. The three of you deny you knew anything about this."

"Chivalrous," Vale said with a warm smile. "But stupid."

"Olivaard would read our minds," Royal said. "They could find out what we know regardless."

"Which is why we *all* have to run!" Brom insisted.

"Run away from those who have betrayed us? Who hold hundreds of students in thrall?" Royal growled. "I think not."

Brom threw his hands up in the air. "We can't beat them!"

"You did," Vale said softly.

That stole Brom's wind so suddenly and completely that he couldn't think of what to say. Vale had talked convincingly about not loving him, but her eyes glowed with admiration and a fierce pride. His heart ached. "All I did was run away," he said.

"Successfully."

"I have an idea," Oriana said quietly, and this time, everyone looked at her.

"We fight them," Royal said.

Vale rolled her eyes. "Maybe we should just ignore the men for a moment. What do you have, Oriana?"

"They are looking for someone," Oriana said. "But they think it is a Sacinto."

"That's what they said before they saw Brom. But they can't think that now," Vale said. "They chased him. They mind-probed him. Kelto's beard, they *saw* him. He jumped out their window."

"I think they still believe he is a Sacinto," Oriana said.

"Why?" Royal asked.

"Because they aren't here," she said.

"Sacinto have branches growing out of their heads!" Vale said. "You don't need a good long look to realize someone doesn't have branches growing out of their head."

"Not all Sacinto branches are long," Oriana countered. "Brom was wearing a cowl, and there was a blizzard. I will bet my life they don't know it's him. I don't think they suspect a student could invade their tower. *We* can scarcely believe he did it."

"No," Brom said. "Olivaard knows everything about me and everything about you. He mind-probed me."

"That is why I think I'm right," Oriana said.

Royal gave a frustrated sigh. "*That's* why you're right? That doesn't make any sense."

"To you," Oriana said. "But you are not a Mentis. Listen. Assuming that Olivaard obeys the same rules of magic that I do, it is unlikely he knows everything about Brom." She turned to Brom. "What you described is called a mind-stab. It is meant to break mental defenses and seize top-level thoughts. It is not meant to grasp details, deeper memories. That takes more far more effort. Being inside a person's mind is like seeing words floating on a river. Primary, immediate thoughts rise to the top; they are the easiest to read. In your case, this would have been fear of The Four, terror at having opened your fourth Soulblock, and hope for escape. Those were the big thoughts in your mind at that moment. Olivaard commented on your fourth Soulblock. But he called you *little Sacinto.*"

"He did," Brom said, stunned. He'd thought it was an insult; he hadn't thought for a second that Olivaard believed Brom himself was a Sacinto. "He said that."

Oriana nodded. "Your lesser concerns at that panicked moment would have been far more difficult for Olivaard to detect, like the fact that you were cold, or that you must soon decide where to go next. That kind of thing. And your memories—your sense of identity, your own name, your thoughts about all of us—were far deeper and much less important to you at that instant he mind-stabbed you. It would have taken time and effort to read them. He had neither."

"What is your point?" Vale asked.

"I cannot see the face of someone I mind-read," Oriana said. "I can almost never pick up their name unless they tell me directly. How often do you think of your own name? My point is: it is quite possible The Four still think they are chasing a Sacinto."

"Unbelievable..." Royal said, though he was obviously thinking it might be believable.

"It doesn't matter," Brom said. "They're going to search the school. Whether they think it was me or not, they'll scour the campus."

"I agree," Oriana said. "So we must hide."

Vale sighed, as though she'd been waiting for a great reveal and was disappointed. "Hide?"

"Olivaard isn't going to come at us with a mind stab this time," Brom said. "They'll line us up and dig as deep as they want."

"And they'll have all of the Mentis masters working for them, too," Oriana said. "Yes. They'll find what's in our head. We can't stop them from looking, so we must forget what we know."

"Forget?" Royal asked.

"Brom's visit to the tower, The Four, and the insidious nature of the Test," she said. "Everything."

Royal's brow furrowed, and Vale's eyes narrowed dangerously.

"You're talking about mind control," Brom said. "Memory

erasure."

"That's fourth-year magic," Royal said.

"She can do it," Vale said at the same time Oriana said, "I can do it."

Oriana looked sidelong at Vale. "How did you know?"

"Because I'm not an idiot. I saw the books you were reading, the spells inside. It's not a far jump to assume you were trying to master them."

"Since when?" Brom asked.

"For the last two months," Oriana said.

"And how did you practice that, I'd like to know," Royal said, a flush of anger on his cheeks.

That brought a whole new slate of questions. Had Oriana used mind control on them? Would Brom have noticed if she had? He thought back over the last several months, trying to decide if he'd ever done something out of character and passed it off as a quirk to be ignored. He couldn't think of anything. But if she really could do mind control, she could have made him forget whatever she wanted. Frantically, he began to search for any conspicuous blank spots in his memory—

"I have not used it on any of you." Oriana interrupted his thoughts. "As you know, I have never even read your minds without your consent. Every time I've read your mind, I've told you, and you've agreed to let me. We worked too hard to break the boundaries between us. To keep secrets." She gave a pointed look at Brom and Vale. "And I, at least, wish for this Quad to thrive."

Vale held Oriana's gaze with a wry smile. "You think just because Brom and I hid a few things from you, I'm going to let you jump into my head and rearrange me?"

"If you trust me," Oriana said.

"I don't like this idea," Royal said.

"No sane person likes the idea of being mind-controlled," Oriana said. "But our options are few, and this may be the best of them."

They fell quiet, and Brom felt each of his heartbeats like the ticking of a clock. Every second was another opportunity for The Four to burst through that door.

"I say we do it," Vale said, suddenly flipping sides, as she often did. "How does it work? If you wipe our memories, how does this plan succeed? You'll still know what we know. Once they snap the lock on your mind, they'll have it all anyway."

"No," she said. "I will...manipulate my own mind as well."

"That must be handy," Vale said. "Being able to erase whatever you don't like about your life."

Oriana fixed Vale with a stare. "I have never taken anything vital from my own mind, only a few things in practice, and I have always restored them. There are dangers to manipulation, especially of one's own self. Our experiences make us who we are. Quadrons who erase too much of their own memories...it doesn't end well."

"So we could lose ourselves?" Royal asked.

"It is possible, but it is certainly no more dangerous than attempting to restore a fourth Soulblock," she said, arching an eyebrow.

"This is insanity," Brom said. "We should simply run. Give up being this slave of a Quadron they have planned for us. Give up on this entire school!"

"No," Royal said firmly. "We are already victims of some kind of green flame spell. I am not running from these monsters. We make things right, or we die trying."

"I'm not leaving, either," Vale said.

"The Four are *deadly* to us!" Brom blurted. He felt like he was trying to convince children not to dive beneath the ice of a frozen lake. "There is no happy ending if we stay under their thumbs. Forgetting what we know makes The Four *more* dangerous, not less. In the long run, they'll pick us apart like carrion birds."

"We will not forget forever," Oriana said. "I will...hide it. Then restore it."

"How?" Brom asked.

"What do you mean, hide it?" Vale said.

"Memories inside a person are like..." Oriana paused, as though struggling to find the right words. "They're like...trinkets, let's say. Inside many different boxes. A thousand boxes stacked a hundred high. I will...take the memories of Brom's adventures and discoveries. I'll take them out of you and put them in a hidden box in my own mind."

"And a Mentis wouldn't be able to find that box?" Brom asked.

"No," Oriana said, too quickly. At his look, she pursed her lips. After a moment, she said, "There is a chance. There is always a chance. But the Mentis would be forced to search every single one of my memories. It would take days, even weeks, and they'd have to know exactly what they were looking for. With just a cursory look, a Mentis would never find the box. And they would never look that deep, most notably because they would never suspect a second-year student capable of such a spell."

"They might suspect Quad Brilliant," Vale said. "The Four said we were messing with the system because we've accomplished so much."

"How do we get our memories back after?" Royal asked, waving away Vale's warning.

"A tripwire," Oriana said.

"What is that?" Royal asked.

"It's like an animal trap." Vale spoke before Oriana could. "A wire that triggers the trap. Likewise, a wire that triggers a spell."

Brom had read about tripwires, but only a little. They were magical mechanisms, set to lie in wait until a condition was met. Once the condition was met, the waiting spell activated. The spells he'd encountered in the tower of The Four were all tripwires.

"So when something specific happens," Brom said. "That trips the tripwire, and the box opens. And you'll get your memories back?"

"Yes," Oriana said.

"And you give us our memories back," Royal said.

She nodded. "It will happen all at once, for all of us, if we are in close proximity. If we're far apart, then the memories will return once I am near you."

"What is the tripwire going to be?" Vale asked.

Oriana held her hands out, palms up. "We would have to agree on that."

"I don't like the idea of forgetting what I know about The Four," Brom said. "It would be like turning my back to them and pretending I don't know they're evil. Except without the pretending."

"That's what makes it a brilliant plan," Vale said. "Not only are we too young to pull it off, but we'd be foolhardy to try. That's what they'll think. I like it."

Royal looked like he'd eaten a piece of rotting fish and was trying to choke it down.

Oriana spread her long-fingered hands across her lap like she was spreading cards on a table, and she drew a steady breath.

"At any rate, that is my idea," she said softly. She looked like she hadn't made up her mind about whether it was a *good* idea or not.

Brom hated the notion of losing his hard-won knowledge, even for a short time, but...Vale had a point. Oriana's plan was so bold it was insane, and that made it hard to predict. Even for The Four. Was running really a better idea?

"We can't make the tripwire be something that happens too soon," Vale said slowly. "It would have to be a month away at least, past the end of the school year."

"Why?" Royal asked.

"If we regain our memories too soon," Vale said, "they might still be searching. We can't know how long they'll take to get around to looking at the students, or how long it will take them to look at all of the students' memories."

"So you really want to do this?" Brom asked her.

"I want to stick the dagger in these fucks," she snarled, once again the feral urchin. "They lured me here, trapped me here, and from the sounds of it, they never intended to let me leave. Yeah, I want to hurt them. And we can't do that if we run away. Like Oriana, I came here to become a Quadron, even if it kills me. And in this moment—only this one—we have the advantage of surprise. I don't think we should waste it, no matter the risk."

Royal's chest puffed up at her fervent declaration, and any doubt in his face vanished. "Yes," he said with conviction. "We fight."

"Not the 1st day of Summermarch," Oriana said quietly. "The last day of Summerdawn. Year's end testing."

Vale snapped her fingers and pointed at Oriana approvingly.

"Yes. Perfect. When they give us the writ of passage. That is our trigger."

"That's more than a month away," Royal agreed. "If they don't find their culprit by then, they'll stop looking."

"It is a good tripwire," Oriana said. "Certain. Soon. And the year-end ceremony is something we have done before, so I'll be able to imbed it accurately in my mind." She nodded. "Except we don't know which master will be giving us the writ of passage."

"So make it anyone," Vale said. "Who cares who it is? Simply make it that if any one of us is given a writ of passage by anyone else, it trips the wire for you," Vale said.

Oriana looked thoughtful for a moment, then she nodded. "Yes. I can do that."

Brom felt a deep foreboding, but he didn't have a better plan. He suddenly realized that once Oriana began poking around in his head, she would discover that he and Vale were lovers. It would be another surprise in a night of surprises, but he gauged that Oriana must take that in stride, in the face of their larger problems. The secrets were mounting, and if the Quad got free of this immediate threat, they were going to deal with a lot. But if they didn't move fast, none of the rest of it was going to matter.

"What will you take?" Brom asked. "I want to know exactly. What are you going to remove?"

Oriana nodded as though she had expected the question. "As little as possible. For Royal and myself, I will remove tonight's activities from the moment Brom showed up at my door. Luckily, in our case, we didn't know what you were planning or what you were doing. So it will be fairly simple. Removing an anomaly during the night when we should have been asleep anyway will make easy sense to our minds. Vale will be trickier. I must remove tonight's activities, but in addition I must take away the plans you two made to storm the tower. I may need to go back weeks for that, but it must be done. I don't want the two of you getting it in your heads to try again before we've recovered our memories."

"And for me?" Brom asked.

"You will be the most difficult. I must remove your visit to the tower and all of your preparation for it. I must also remove that night when you ran the river with Vale, when you discovered the green fire spell at the wall."

"That far back?"

"The memories are all built upon one another." She pursed her lips and glanced downward, in thought. Her delicate brows wrinkled slightly. "Imagine your mind like a pile of rocks, each rock a memory that creates your current state of mind. I must carefully remove all the relevant rocks, otherwise your mind will go searching for them. But I cannot remove too many or your mind will tumble in upon itself. In short, I must be precise. The fewer gaps I leave, the less your mind will fight, trying to recover what was lost. The most difficult will be removing the inciting moment."

"What is an inciting moment?" Brom asked.

"The one that pushed you to do something so ridiculously dangerous as invade the tower of The Four. For this, I'll need Vale's help."

"Why?" Vale asked.

"Because this is Brom," Oriana said. "And his inciting moment will have been spurred by some great emotion. While I remove the memory, I'll need you to remove the passion surrounding it. If the emotion is still there it would act like a..." She paused, searching for the right words. "...like a tremor beneath the pile of rocks. If the emotion remained, Brom would know that he wanted desperately to do something, but he won't be able to remember what it is."

Vale nodded. "I see."

Brom's heart began to race. The idea that Oriana would be plucking out pieces of him was terrifying. He swallowed it down.

"I don't like it," he said reluctantly. "But I trust you."

"Then we are decided," Oriana said, as though they were simply agreeing on what to have for dinner. She looked at each of them expectantly.

"Yes," Brom said. Vale nodded, and Royal said, "I'm in."

A shiver ran through Brom, and a ring of golden light rippled out from the four of them. It hit the walls, and the room seemed to expand, then shuddered back to its normal size.

Then the golden light vanished.

They all looked around, eyes wide. Brom tensed, pushing up on his hands as if he expected The Four to crash through the wall. But nothing happened.

"What was that?" Vale whispered, tense and breathless. She crouched like she was ready to spring for the window.

"I don't know," Oriana said. Her eyes narrowed to slits, and she flicked a quick gaze all about the room.

"Was it some kind of spell?" Royal asked. "Was it The Four?"

Oriana hesitated, then slowly shook her head. "I don't know." She looked ill, which is how she always looked when she didn't know something.

They stood there, tense, waiting for an attack. When it didn't come, they waited some more. Eventually, Oriana cleared her throat.

"Let's finish this quickly," she said. "We will start with Brom. Then Vale, then Royal. Then myself." She knelt at the head of the bed. "Vale, if you would move closer." She knelt next to Brom, just to Oriana's right. "I will guide you, and I'll let you know when to help. Please don't do anything more than what I ask."

"Just don't make us all forget that we like each other, okay?" Vale joked. "That was a lot of work the first time around."

"Is that possible?" Royal asked, concerned. "Could we forget our bond?"

"I was joking," Vale said.

Oriana didn't answer the question, which made Brom even more nervous.

"Lie down, Brom," she said. He hesitated, and she said softly, "It will be all right. Trust me."

Brom lay down, his chest heavy. The bed seemed to sway. His body reminded him that he'd been an inch from death minutes ago, and he wanted to vomit again. Instead, he put his head between her hands and waited.

Royal came closer, looming over the three of them.

Vale stroked Brom's hair, and it calmed him. He wanted to tell her that he loved her. Even more than that, he wanted her to smile and tell him that she loved him too. Instead, she winked. "Sweet dreams," she whispered.

"After we get our second-year writs of passage, we'll talk about next steps," Oriana said. "Until then, we are just students again. We're just Quad Brilliant."

She gently pressed two fingers to each of Brom's temples and closed her eyes.

"Be right, Oriana," Brom whispered. "Gods, please be right about this."

She took a deep breath and gave no indication that she had heard him.

White light flared, and the room faded away.

4

OLIVAARD

Thump. Thump. Thump.

The sound of a human head smacking into wood filled the study. Olivaard listened to the satisfying rhythm of it, and it calmed his nerves. The thumping seemed louder than it actually was due to the sullen silence in the room.

Wulfric sat on the couch before the fire, one foot resting on the chest of one of the dismembered gate guards. The corpse's pieces were strewn beneath him, some wedged between the couch and the low table. Wulfric cleaned his dripping blade with a piece of the guard's own tunic, using long, deliberate strokes as he watched the crimson stain spread into the blue and white insignia. Wulfric had been so infuriated after losing the Sacinto in the blizzard that he'd almost lopped off Arsinoe's head when the Motus had made a poorly-timed joke.

Thump. Thump. Thump.

Linza stood perfectly still by the window, much where she had been when the Sacinto spy had burst from concealment and thrown itself out the window at the end of the bar. The only way to know she was upset was by the dimness of the room. Twelve lanterns burned brightly in the parlor, but it was as dark as if those torches were guttering candles. When Linza was upset, she sucked all available light toward herself.

Olivaard contemplated the covered window through which the brazen spy had escaped.

Thump. Thump. Thump.

The curtains over the villain's escape had been turned to stone, perfectly covering the broken window and keeping the slowly-dying blizzard outside. The four of them had done that in a fit of pique when they'd returned. In addition, they had put violent spells at every window and door in this room. Even a servant within the tower would die a horrible death if they dared disturb The Four tonight.

Thump. Thump. Thump.

"Where is Arsinoe?" Olivaard asked, peeved.

"Venting his frustrations, like you," Linza creaked in her ancient voice.

Olivaard glanced over at the second gate guard, who gripped the edges of the bloody wooden pillar by the door and slammed his forehead against it. Initially, the thumps had been good, solid sounds, and the guard had screamed in horror at each vigorous blow. Olivaard had made him cease his caterwauling, though. Now the thumps were distinctly wet, and he thought he'd heard a cracking noise on the last one. It wouldn't be long.

"On whom?" Olivaard asked.

"He mentioned something about the new baker," Linza said. "*Cute* was his exact word."

Olivaard sighed. The new baker was talented at his craft. Arsinoe could at least have had the courtesy to choose someone incompetent. But then, courtesy was not Arsinoe's style unless courtesy could provide him with something he wanted.

Using his powerful mind, Olivaard pushed out a message to Arsinoe.

"Get in here now. Playtime is over."

Arsinoe gave a mental grunt, but Olivaard cut the connection before he could hear anything else. The pleasures of the flesh repulsed him, and he had no desire, even accidentally, to overhear any of Arsinoe's current thoughts.

Thump. Thump. Crack. Thump... The guard's skull caved in, and his body twitched. He head butted the column one last feeble time, then he slid to the ground and didn't move again.

"Now what?" Wulfric growled, as though he had been waiting until the guard was dead to ask his question. He gave one last swipe to his now-clean blade and sheathed it. He tossed the rag on top of the corpse pieces below him.

"Those requiring punishment have been punished," Olivaard said. "Except the Sacinto."

"I could not see them," Linza said, referring to the Sacintos as they referred to themselves—in the plural. Each individual Sacinto was both male and female. "Even searching for their soul, I could not find them."

"I did," Olivaard said, "but it was sheer luck. And I could not grab hold of its mind." Olivaard, on other hand, thought of the damned Sacintos as animals, not people. "Somehow, it wrenched its mind away from me, and when I looked again, it was gone."

"This Sacinto is deep in the Soul of the World," Linza said.

"Obviously."

"Explanation?"

"A guess only," Olivaard said. "They are closer to nature. They are part tree, after all."

Arsinoe appeared in the doorway. His face looked as though someone had hacked off his jaw, leaving only a gaping hole below his nose. It made his neck look grotesquely long. He held his jaw in his hand. There was no blood, of course. It wasn't the first time Arsinoe had removed one of his body parts to....do what he did.

Breathing hard through the hole in his face, Arsinoe leaned casually against the doorjamb and put his jaw back into place. The flesh melted together like candle wax, and then he moved his jaw around in a neat circle.

"What," Olivaard asked impatiently, "are you doing?"

"Something new," Arsinoe said, catching his breath as though he'd run from the top of the tower. "Novelty stirs the blood. You ought to try it. "

Olivaard checked the urge to mind-stab the man. Really. Working with Arsinoe was like working with one of the sweaty students that crawled all over the academy. Rutting little rats.

"May I presume there will be no more pastries in the tower?" Olivaard asked.

"I was angry." Arsinoe shrugged. "Obviously I wasn't the only one." He regarded the blood-splattered pillar.

"Tonight, we are failures," Olivaard said. "How long has it been since we could say that?"

Wulfric growled.

"The spell at the wall was untouched," Linza said. "Somehow they moved past it."

Olivaard shook his head. "Undoing a spell of that magnitude requires more than a rapport with the Soul of the World. Perhaps they are using a magic we have not yet encountered."

Arsinoe scoffed. "What are the odds of that?"

"The Sacinto are a mystery," Olivaard said icily, hating his own words. "Apparently."

Arsinoe suddenly pursed his lips and brought his hand up to his newly-intact jaw. For a moment, Olivaard thought he might remove it again. Instead, he just stroked his chin.

"Has anyone considered that it might be a student?" Arsinoe asked.

Olivaard glared at Arsinoe and frowned. The man simply could not take anything seriously. He sometimes wished Arsinoe would shut his mouth and save the rest of them from his idiocy.

Wulfric spat into the blood at his feet. "The Quadrons who graduate from the academy cannot escape our notice by using the Soul of the World. How could a student do it?"

"What about Quad Brilliant?" Arsinoe replied.

"Fuck Quad Brilliant!" Wulfric boomed. "They're students! They're dogs who've been taught to walk on their hind legs. They're nothing! We have run to fat, fearing inconsequential students while Sacintos scuttle about our tower like roaches. Our focus should be on finding these Sacintos, destroying them, and getting back to our real task: the One Beneath. We've spent altogether too much time talking about the gods-be-damned students in Quad Brilliant. Squash them and be done with it!"

"And destroy the reputation of the school," Arsinoe said. "Brilliant." He chuckled at his own pedestrian wit.

"The school serves our needs. Not the other way around." Wulfric stood up, growling.

"Wulfric has a point," Olivaard said. "A student could not accomplish this thing, and we have spent far too much time talking about it."

"Graduate them now," Linza said suddenly, and the rest of them fell silent. "Be done with it now."

"What?" Olivaard asked, incredulous.

"Use their prowess against them," Linza creaked. "Use the Test to put them in their place. Shower them with accolades and say they are prodigies. Trumpet it from the walls of the academy that Quad Brilliant has learned so much so fast that they have leapt over two grades. Then put them through the Test of Separation. The Quad will be broken, and those who remain will have our hooks in them. Collar them and fling them into the two kingdoms. Then we can think on them no more."

"We have never graduated second-years before," Olivaard said thoughtfully, pulling on one of his dangling earlobes.

"Fine," Wulfric said. "Send a primer tomorrow. That's as far as they'll get. Send the best of the fourth-years. Let Quad Phoenix beat them into meat. Perhaps then you'll all see them as the children they are, and I can stop hearing about Quad Brilliant."

"I like this plan." Arsinoe clapped his hands together delightedly. "Let Quad Phoenix kill Quad Brilliant. All save the Motus. I'd still like to play with her after."

Olivaard rolled his eyes.

Wulfric sighed, clearly exasperated. "Now can we stop talking about gods-be-damned students and get back to the real problem?"

"Very well," Olivaard said. "The primer will be Quad Phoenix."

"Excellent idea. That way we won't even need to send Brilliant to the Test," Linza said, satisfied.

"Wait," Arsinoe said. "What of the princess? After your passionate defense of her usefulness, we'll kill her, too?"

"A point," Olivaard said. "Yes, the princess lives. We send her back to her father, saying we stepped in and broke the rules to protect her because of his importance to us."

"Such a diplomat," Linza said.

"Can we get back to the Sacintos now?" Wulfric demanded.

"Thank you for being so patient," Arsinoe said with dripping sarcasm. "May I pose a question?"

Wulfric growled.

"If this Sacinto so easily avoided our spell at the wall because they never touched it, shouldn't we continue to consider that they might somehow be hidden inside the school, even if it's not a student?"

Wulfric seethed and Olivaard marshaled his inner strength not to lash out at Arsinoe.

"They would have had to bury themselves in the dirt to avoid detection. Who wouldn't notice a Sacinto walking around the campus?" Olivaard asked.

Arsinoe shrugged. "I'm simply saying it may be possible. Doesn't it seem more plausible that the Sacinto is somehow hiding inside the academy than that they are so powerful they can break through our defensive spell without harm and without seeming to touch it?"

"No," Wulfric growled.

"Then maybe it is one of the masters," Arsinoe said. "Or, I maintain it could potentially be—"

"If you say it is one of the students, I'm going to chop your head off," Wulfric warned.

"I think Arsinoe has a point," Linza said.

All gazes swiveled toward her.

"Knowing we are the most powerful Quadrons in the two kingdoms might have made us overconfident. It is the very definition of arrogance to assume we are right without knowing for certain."

"What do you propose?" Olivaard said, surprised that Linza was defending Arsinoe.

"Read them," she said.

"Two hundred and forty students?" Wulfric asked incredulously. "Ridiculous!"

"That would take days," Olivaard said.

"This is exactly the kind of distraction that is hindering us," Wulfric said.

"It is the only way to be certain," Linza creaked. "And I think it is worth being certain."

"I agree." Arsinoe nodded emphatically.

Wulfric drew his sword and pointed it at Arsinoe. "You put this in her head," he growled.

Arsinoe put his hands up helplessly.

"He put nothing into my head, Wulfric," Linza said. "You talk about our laziness, and yet you don't wish to spend the time we would need to be sure that Arsinoe is wrong."

With a howl of rage, Wulfric turned and chopped his bench in half. Splintered chunks of wood flew in every direction.

Olivaard thought about it a moment. There was absolutely no way a student could have evaded them, but he liked the cleanliness of Linza's idea, as tedious as it would be.

"I agree with Linza," Olivaard said. "We will start a mind probe first thing tomorrow. We will call it a mandatory Mentis exercise for all students, to determine their readiness."

Wulfric's enraged breaths whooshed inside his square helmet. "Do what you fucking want. I'm going to look for that gods-be-damned Sacinto." He stormed out of the room, his hooves thooming loudly.

"I'll inform Quad Phoenix," Arsinoe said gaily.

"Gods no," Olivaard said, shaking his head. "You inform The Collector. He will orchestrate the primer. Tell him Quad Phoenix is to be ruthless, sparing only the princess."

"Olivaard, please..." Arsinoe said reprovingly.

Olivaard sighed, then said, "Fine. The Motus girl as well. Make sure The Collector knows this is Phoenix's primer too. Tell them only one of the two Quads will advance to the Test of Separation. The other will be expelled. If they still live."

"I want to watch." Arsinoe pouted. "To make sure my prize is only sufficiently injured, not gutted."

Olivaard ignored Arsinoe and turned to Linza. "Make the preparations for the mind probes."

She nodded her head and left the room as silent as a breeze.

5
BROM

Brom woke up, and he felt like he'd forgotten something. Morning light trickled into his dorm room through the split in the heavy black drapes. He sat up and gasped at the pain, then lay back down. Gods, it felt like he'd rolled down a hill and hit every rock along the way. His entire body was tender. His head felt like it had a metal band bound around it, squeezing. His stomach roiled, and his arms and legs were feeble.

What happened to me?

Had he spent his third Soulblock again? It was like that time by the river with Vale. That time that she and he...

...had run by the river. He remembered the rush of the water, the smell of wet earth, Fendra in the sky, blazing silver blue. He remembered connecting to the Soul of the World, bringing Vale along with him. And he and Vale had run next to each other until they...

Until they what? He couldn't remember. Had they just run along the river?

Clenching his teeth, he pushed himself to a sitting position.

Gods, he hurt...

He focused, then reached inside himself, gingerly checking his Soulblocks. A filling Soulblock always felt like a glass box with mist slowly thickening inside until it became like a lightning storm, crackling within. Brom's second Soulblock was in that process, actually on the verge of being full. So he'd used his first and second. Then why did he feel so awful? His third Soulblock was full. He should just feel tired.

He paused, assessing.

Perceiving and dividing one's Soulblocks was the first and most important lesson he'd learned at the academy. Brom had spent a great deal of time looking at his Soulblocks in the beginning, and then every time he'd used his magic since. Ever before, the storm inside each Soulblock had been a thick charcoal mist, with lightning lancing between. His second Soulblock looked exactly this way.

But his third and fourth Soulblocks did not. They were filled with swirling red, blue, and white mists, with lightning forking through.

A chill went up his back. His third and fourth Soulblocks had been altered. But...by whom?

He looked around his room, at the banner of the Champion's Academy coat of arms on the far wall. It bore a shield with four colors of the paths of magic and their four icons: a red dragon, a white owl, a blue bear, and a black moth in front of Fendra's moon. That banner was in every student's room, a standard decoration unless the student was wealthy enough to replace it with decorations of their own, like the wall hangings in Oriana's room.

Brom's Soulblocks had been invaded and altered by a Motus, an Impetu, and a Mentis.

He tried to push down his fear, but it was obvious his Quad mates had done something to him, and the fact that he felt foggy, felt like he was forgetting something, strongly suggested he'd been mind-controlled.

But mind control was a fourth-year spell. Oriana couldn't have done it. She simply didn't have the ability...

...unless she did. Quad Brilliant had broken boundaries this past year. They were the talk of the school, like no other second-years had ever been. And Brom had performed a fourth year spell, connecting Vale to the Soul of the World. Why couldn't Oriana...?

Stop it, he thought firmly. *Just because it fits doesn't mean it's true.*

He stood up, clenching his teeth against the wave of nausea and the ache of sore muscles.

The sunlight beckoned to him, and he staggered to the window, thrust open the heavy drapes. He gave a sigh of satisfaction. The morning sun danced across drifts of snow, and it felt amazing, as though the sun alone helped replenish whatever his body had lost. He closed his eyes and basked in it, then blinked and looked down at the snow. Gods, it had piled up, at least a couple of feet over paths that had been shoveled yesterday. Brom remembered the paths cutting through the drifts, but he didn't remember last night's storm. Gods, it must have been a blizzard.

He suddenly realized he couldn't remember anything of last night after Vale had...after he'd declared his love for her. She'd told him she didn't believe in love and then she'd slipped out the window. It hadn't been snowing that hard then. The blizzard must have come after.

And what had Brom done? Had he simply lain back down and slept? He didn't remember that, didn't remember even closing the window.

That chill of fear returned.

My mind has been altered, he thought, now certain. *Oriana has plucked memories from my mind.*

He walked to his wardrobe and saw one set of clothes on the chair next to the hot chimney that ran through his room. The chimney brought warmth from the fires of the furnace in the catacombs beneath Westfall Dormitory. He touched the tunic, and it was cold and wet all the way through.

So either he'd jumped into a barrel of water after Vale left, then crawled into bed...or he'd been out in that storm but couldn't remember a thing about it.

He needed answers. He pulled his spare tunic and breeches from the wardrobe and grabbed his boots from where they lay next to the chimney. They, too, were wet through and through. He put everything on, shivering at the chill on his feet.

By the time he left his room, he felt more normal. It was morning. He was going to class and he was ravenous for breakfast. He emerged onto the walkway amidst the twenty or so other second-year students on this level. He saw Royal several doors down, and the big man looked just like Brom felt. Tired. Ill. Brom thought about going to talk to Royal about his strange morning, but one of the foreign colors in Brom's Soulblock was blue. That meant whatever had happened to Brom, Royal had been a part of it.

Instead, Brom decided to go straight to breakfast, to pretend it was just like any other morning. He shuffled along with the other students, down the stairwells to the Floating Room where all the meals were served.

The Floating Room was to the south, and it was a marvel that had long since become commonplace. The long room rotated slowly on a magical axis, and every wall was a floor, with tables, benches, and food. Each floor had its own gravity, and each was a different color: red, blue, white, and black to represent each magical path. A dining Anima could look up and see the tops of all the heads of the students on the path of Impetu, look to the right and see those who followed the path of Mentis, to the left and see those of Motus sitting sideways, devouring their soup. It was expected that Quad mates ate outside their Quad, sitting instead with others of their chosen path.

When Brom had first entered the Floating Room, he'd been agog at how powerful The Four must be to create a room that not only defied gravity, but slowly turned about. Most new students vomited the first several times they ate in the Floating Room.

Now it was simply a place to eat, and Brom was lost in other thoughts that were much more troubling. He stood at the edge until his floor rotated around, then he strode into the hall with a dozen other Animas from various years.

The moment he gathered his food and sat down, he tore into the bread, shoving down mouthful after mouthful, and the morning's vegetable stew tasted better than anything he'd ever tasted before. Almost immediately, he felt his body strengthening. Vigor returned to his limbs, and his mind began to think more clearly. The feeling of a constricting steel band around his head eased.

Brom looked at the faces of the students around him, most of them bent on breakfast. A few watched him, but that was nothing new. He, Vale, Oriana, and Royal had become famous lately, not only among their class, but even among the third- and fourth-years. He glanced to the right at the tops of the heads of the Mentis students, the white floor a wall to him, cluttered with tables and students and meals that defied gravity. Could someone over there have used their magic on him?

He finished two bowls of soup and three small loaves of bread. His belly was fit to burst, and yet he still felt like he could eat more. That was how it felt when a student was soul-sick—like you could never eat enough.

Once he was finished, he left the Floating Room and went straight to his classes. He tried to focus as the masters and instructors droned on, but his mind wandered, and he kept looking inside himself at those bizarre and suspicious third and fourth Soulblocks.

Finally, lunch came, and he quickly gorged himself again, feeling stronger, then went to the practice room.

Oriana was already there, standing by the Invisible Ones, and she watched him as he entered. It looked like she had been about to practice her Mentis abilities, but she paused, then gave him a soft smile.

He tried to analyze that smile for artifice, but it looked genuine. Was she capable of simply stealing memories from his head and then smiling at him like that?

The answer was: of course she was. She had been trained from birth to hold her emotions in check. For Oriana, everything was second to her duty, to her purpose of ruling Keltovar after her parents were gone. He had come to think of her as a friend, but...was that naive?

Royal came in next, looking troubled but also heartier after half a day and two meals. He walked over to the corner of the room that was as far from the Invisible Ones as it was possible to get, and then he seemed to study the wall. Obviously, he wanted to talk to his Quad mates out of earshot of the Invisible Ones. Royal wasn't a subtle man.

Suddenly, Royal's voice was in Brom's head, and he caught the tail end of what must have been a telepathic conversation with Oriana.

"...strangest feeling when I woke up."

"Brom can hear you now," Oriana spoke inside Brom's head.

"Then we need to talk," Royal said.

Brom moved toward Royal, happy to get away from the silent Invisible Ones. Though the Invisible Ones were instrumental in students increasing their skill, they had always made Brom uneasy. These silent men and women accepted money in return for having someone manipulate their minds, emotions, souls, and bodies. It seemed like a horrible job.

And, of course, the Invisible Ones made him uneasy in another way, too. They could be spies for the masters, neatly positioned in every practice room in the academy.

Vale entered the practice room last. Her gaze flicked from the Invisible Ones to her Quad mates and then all about the room, as though she was looking for someone else. Her face had that stony look that Brom had realized, just last night, might be her real face. Last night...when he'd declared his love for her and she'd painfully told him, in no uncertain terms, that she didn't believe in love.

That much, at least, he remembered. So why couldn't he remember...other things?

"Are we talking in each others' heads?" Vale asked as Oriana projected her thoughts to Brom and Royal.

"Good morning, Vale," Royal said politely.

"So we're being sneaky," she said.

"I thought suggesting a nice little stroll through six-foot high snow drifts might seem suspicious," Oriana said.

"Why would someone be suspicious of us?" Vale asked, and the question fell with the weight of a broadsword.

"I don't know," Oriana said.

"Ah," Vale said. *"So you just woke up this morning and felt the need for secrecy?"* Brom could hear her anger. *"Just wanted to give that extra little attention to detail, did you?"*

Oriana's eyes narrowed. *"What are you saying?"*

"I'm saying somebody's mucked in my head, Princess, and by Kelto it better not have been you." She squeezed the hilt of her dagger.

"It wasn't," Oriana said.

"Easy, Vale," Royal said, and he reached out a gentle hand toward her. She spun, and this time her dagger came out, pointed at him.

"Don't touch me," she said aloud.

This was all wrong. Brom suddenly felt like they were right back at their initial meeting in the Collector's room, reverting to their personalities before their bond.

"Let's all calm down," Brom said. *"I have...missing pieces from my memory as well."*

"I awoke while my second Soulblock was still filling," Royal said. *"Only after lunch did my first finally fill. Obviously, I used them last night. But I don't recall how."*

"So you're missing memories, too." Vale thought to Royal.

Royal thought on that, confused. *"No, I... No. That's just it. I'm not. I went to sleep as normal. I woke up as normal, except I was exhausted, and I'd used two of my Soulblocks."*

"I, too, was missing my first two Soulblocks," Oriana said. *"Like Royal, I don't know how I spent them. I clearly remember going to bed last night. I remember falling asleep. That is all."* But even as she said it, she got the same thoughtful, confused look on her face as Royal.

"I lost memories from last night," Brom said, realizing he had to lie to them, or they'd know that he and Vale had been lovers for weeks now. *"I was down by the river, watching the snow fall. I guess I must have come back to my room, but I don't remember."*

Vale glared at Oriana. *"Did you do this?"*

"Mind control you? Steal your memories?" Oriana's voice was curt and derisive. *"I have never once used my powers on you without your consent."*

"Because you wouldn't do that." Vale sneered.

"That's right."

"Even if you accidentally found out something you didn't like? Something you thought we ought to be punished for?"

"And exactly what should I punish you for?" Oriana asked.

"Nothing!" Vale's voice sounded like a shout in their minds. *"It's not your place to punish anyone!"*

Royal looked befuddled. *"What do you mean, find out something she didn't like? Find out what?"*

"Like something private. Like something that's none of her fucking business!"

"Vale!" Brom said.

"I don't like people messing with my head," she shouted so loudly in their minds that everyone winced. *"Stay out unless I invite you!"*

"I did," Oriana said.

"I don't believe you."

"I cannot control what you believe," Oriana said.

"That's exactly *what you can control,"* Vale replied.

"If I mind controlled you, I would make you less of a raving lunatic." Oriana's indigo eyes flashed angrily.

Vale lunged at Oriana, but Brom put a hand on Vale's chest and stepped between them. Her dagger whipped around and stopped an inch from his throat.

"Stop it!" he said aloud.

Her snarl pulled back, exposing white teeth.

"Clearly something happened to us," he said.

"Clearly one of us has a guilty conscience," Oriana said.

"Fuck you!" Vale said.

"Hey!" Brom shouted over them both.

"We should work together to find out what this is, not fight!" he said through the mental link. He put a finger on the tip of Vale's blade, gently pushed it away. *"What if this is an attack from some rival Quad? Or if this is some test by one of the masters? What if we are being assaulted, and whoever it is hopes we'll blame each other?"*

Vale glared at Oriana for a long moment, then sheathed her dagger and turned away.

"It can't be a Quad from our class. Mind control is a fourth-year spell," Royal said.

Vale swiveled back, her eyes mean slits. *"Oriana knows it,"* she said. *"I've seen the books you're studying. Strange how I noticed you reading those passages, then suddenly I wake up and I'm missing memories."*

Oriana looked surprised.

"Is that true?" Brom asked. *"Have you already learned mind control?"*

Oriana hesitated, then nodded. *"But I've not used it yet, and I would never use it on any of you. I—"*

The double doors opened, and The Collector stepped into the room, shrouded in his black robes. Only his pointed beard and mouth were visible beneath his black cowl. Behind him, spread out in a half-circle, were four others: two males and two females. Each wore the color of their path. Blue, white, red, and black.

The larger female wore blue. Brom had seen her on Quadron Garden before, had noted her because of her unusual size. She stood over six feet tall, and her blue robe did nothing to hide her bulging muscles.

The second woman, slightly shorter than Oriana, had her hands tucked into the opposite sleeves of her form-fitting black robes. She was the only one with her cowl all the way down, shadowing her face like The Collector.

One of the men wore red robes. He leaned slightly forward, fists clenched and eyes brimming with ferocity.

The other man was thin and stood spear-straight at the back of the group, his fingertips steepled together in front of his face. He wore a Mentis's white robe with the cowl drawn back, and gave a cool glance to each of Brom's Quad mates.

Vale turned her smoldering gaze to the newcomers. *"What's this, then?"* she said using Oriana's mind link.

"That's Quad Phoenix," Brom said.

"Fourth-years," Royal said. *"I heard they're expecting to be called for their Test of Separation any day now."*

The Collector stepped to the left of the door, held his hands up.

"Quad Brilliant," he proclaimed. "Your impressive progress draws the gaze of The Four. You have outstripped your second-year classmates. You have outstripped the third-years as well. You should be applauded for your efforts and your talent. The Four have sent me to determine if you are, indeed, ready."

"Ready for what?" Royal growled.

"This is your primer," The Collector said, waving a hand at the Quad that had come with him.

Vale gasped.

The primer was a challenge leveled at advanced fourth-year Quads, and only those invited to take the Test of Separation. On a few rare occasions, it had been leveled at incredibly talented third years. Brom had never heard of the Test of Separation being given to second-years.

Success in the primer meant immediate advancement to the Test of Separation.

Failure meant possible expulsion, injury, or death.

"We are not fully rested," Oriana said. "Come again tomorrow, and you shall find us prepared for the challenge," she commanded in her princess voice.

The Collector chuckled. "Destiny does not call on you at the moment of your choosing, Princess. I will find you equal to the challenge now, or not at all," he said.

"We are second-years!" Brom protested.

"You are Brilliant," The Collector said softly. "And everyone knows it. Show me just how brilliant, or prove you are imposters." He turned to the fourth-year Quad. "Kill them."

"What?" Royal roared

Vale crouched, her dagger back in hand. Oriana took three cool steps to the wall, and her voice filled each of their minds.

"This is real. We fight," she said. *"We put our bickering aside and we show them what we are."*

Brom felt like his head had been shaken. His disorientation from believing someone had controlled and altered his mind was suddenly intensified with the news that The Four were sending them to the Test of Separation.

He should have been happy, should have felt some kind of elation that The Four, the benevolent keepers of the academy, felt that much confidence in Quad Brilliant.

But his stomach was in knots.

He felt Royal's Soulblock open first, and the big man released a floodgate of confidence into Quad Brilliant. All of Brom's Soulblocks doubled, and he opened his first as well, letting the magic explode into him. He reached into the souls of his opponents, reached out for the Soul of the World all around him. And he laughed aloud.

Let Quad Phoenix come.

Royal roared, picked up the steel block with the ring, and hurled it at the charging Impetu woman. She bashed it aside with a gauntleted hand. Brom heard her forearm crack, but she did not break stride.

"No!" Oriana said. *"Don't fight your counterparts. Remember the immunities!"*

Two weeks ago, Oriana had shown them an obscure text unearthed in the library. It theorized that each path of magic had natural immunities to a specific other path. It said that an Impetu should be able to throw off the mind control of a Mentis by sinking into pure physicality, essentially reverting to an instinctual, animal state, leaving higher mental functions behind and leaving the Mentis nothing to work with. A Mentis could shield herself from the emotional twisting of a Motus by retreating into pure intellect, cutting herself off from human emotions completely. A Motus could glut the soul-sucking drain of an Anima with rage while keeping her soul undamaged. And an Anima could bring down an Impetu by mapping their soul, seeing every weakness, and staying one step ahead of them.

But they were only theories, and Oriana had found no other texts to support them. So far as they knew, no Quad had ever attempted this, let alone succeeded. It was common wisdom that, in a primer, Quad mates fought their counterparts.

"Remember that—" Oriana was suddenly cut off, and Brom's Quad mates were no longer connected mind-to-mind. Oriana staggered back, hand to her head, obviously under attack by the opposing Mentis.

"You heard her!" Royal roared, spinning around the strike of the opposing Impetu with a speed and grace that belied his size. He charged past her, bearing down on Quad Phoenix's Mentis. The thin man's eyes flew open, and he fell back. Oriana gasped her relief as the attack on her faltered.

If Oriana was right, this strategy could only work if they attacked quickly, before the opposing Quad knew what they were up to. Vale scurried forward near the wall to get to the Anima.

The female Impetu hissed at Royal's escape and incautiously

turned her back to Brom. He snatched a sword from the practice rack, dove forward, came to his knees right behind her, and swung. But she was an Impetu. She felt him coming and leapt straight up. His blade whistled beneath her feet.

Brom looked into her soul, looking for her weaknesses. Despite her hulking stature, she was behind the rest of her Quad in her progress. Her confidence was brittle, and she saw all of her fellow Quad mates as having crossed more thresholds than she had. She worried that they looked down on her, that they saw her as the weak link in their chain. She worried she would be the one to die in the Test of Separation.

Brom rolled through his strike as she jumped over him. He had no wish to engage her physically. Not yet. If he cut her, she would heal, just as she had already healed her broken forearm. She'd simply growl though the pain and come up swinging. No. Brom had to play to her weakness.

Humiliation.

He had to take her vulnerability and display it to her Quad mates. If she felt they were judging her, that she was failing them, she would falter. She would make mistakes, leave an opening for him to exploit. Then he would strike.

He rolled to his feet and stood up in front of her.

Astonished, the Impetu hesitated, then brought a crushing, gauntleted hand down at him. But he saw it coming a split second before she struck, and he stepped to the side. She roared, swinging sideways. The Soul of the World flowed through him, and he saw that thunderous strike coming, too. He ducked gracefully beneath it.

She wailed, brought both fists down at him, but he sidestepped, this time only barely avoiding her. Gods, she was fast! One small misstep and he was a dead man.

Staying connected to the Soul of the World, he pushed his magic back into her. Her frustration was mounting, growing quickly into anguish. She swung again, low at his knees. He hopped over the swing, danced around the next strike that was so swift and so powerful she fell to her knees, cracking the stone with her steel gauntlets. He slid behind her, imagining this as another test like the

Gauntlet, and he let the Soul of the World guide him.

Before she could lift her head, he slammed the pommel of the dagger into the base of her skull. It was a mighty blow that would have killed anyone else, but she just staggered drunkenly, blinking and spinning about to find him.

Of course, Brom hadn't intended to put her down with the strike, only to humiliate her. She'd been driven to her knees by a scrawny Anima, right in front of her Quad mates.

And it worked.

The thickly-muscled woman flicked a guilty glance at her Quad mates. Her exposed vulnerability seemed to drive her mad with rage. With a scream, she lunged at him.

But Brom had already seen how she'd react, and pure confidence coursed through him. He danced backward like he'd choreographed the moves, and threw the lever on the Gauntlet, activating it.

The machine started up, blades whirling, stones rising and falling, thumping as they hit the ground. To Brom, it was painfully obvious what he was about to do, but this Impetu didn't see it. She was actually keening with rage. He dove into the Gauntlet, and she charged after him like a bear. She was so fast that her first grab nearly had him, her fingers brushing his ankle.

That was the only chance she got.

Brom closed his eyes and relied entirely on the Soul of the World. He leapt, spun, danced and dashed. Blades whipped over his head. Poison darts zipped past him. Crushing weights launched sideways or from above. Oak cudgels swung left and right. Buckets of poison rained from above, but he saw them a second before they came. And he avoided them all.

Behind him, he was vaguely aware of the Impetu's grunts, growls, then howls of frustration and pain.

When he emerged from the far end of the Gauntlet, he turned. The Impetu lay in the middle of the apparatus, half-buried under one of the stone weights, unconscious. Bright wounds slowly closed on her arms and legs where she had been wickedly slashed. A dozen darts stuck out of her back, and she lay in a bubbling pool of poison. She twitched twice, then lay still.

Breathing hard, Brom came out of his trance, blinked, and looked around the practice room.

The enemy Mentis lay crumpled underneath Royal's hulking form, dropped after one punch.

Their Anima was on her back, Vale kneeling on the woman's chest and punching her bloody face over and over, dagger still in hand but not used. The woman's head groggily wobbled with each strike, and she was barely able to bring her arms up, ineffectually attempting to fend off the blows.

The enemy Motus scooted backward on his butt, one leg scrabbling for purchase while he dragged his injured leg, which had an arrow sticking out of it. He hit the wall with his back and clutched the wounded leg with both hands. Across the room, Oriana held one of the practice bows. Smoothly, she nocked another arrow and leveled it at the Motus. He held his bloody hands up in surrender.

"No, please!" he said. "I yield."

Vale continued punching her foe.

"Vale!" Brom yelled, and she hesitated, bloody fist raised in the air for another strike. With a hiss of disgust, she stood up and stepped back. Then she snarled and lunged forward, stabbing the Anima in the thigh with the dagger. The woman wailed and passed out.

"Vale!" Brom barked again.

"I left her alive," she growled, wiping her dagger on her enemy's black cloak. She crept back, watching all of them like she had that first day they'd met. Distrust. Veiled malevolence.

The battle was over, and they were the overwhelming victors.

"Gods," Brom said, realizing how swiftly they'd just put down the finest Quad in the school.

The Collector, who hadn't moved from his position next to the door, was also clearly stunned. His cowl had crept back to his forehead, and they could see his entire face now. After a moment, he wiped his shocked expression away and narrowed his eyes, regarding them all with a glittering black gaze.

His jaw worked. He should have congratulated them, should have told them that they had overcome the final hurdle before their

Test of Separation. He didn't.

"You will report to the Testing Dome tomorrow at noon," he snapped. "There, you will take the Test of Separation."

A harpoon of fear stabbed into Brom's guts, a sense of doom so profound he wrapped his arms around his belly. "Test of Separation..." he gasped.

The Collector opened his mouth, as though he was about to say something more, then he snapped it shut and exited the room.

Royal, having obviously descended into his animalistic nature to avoid the Mentis, stood hunched over like some beast. He growled, and then, with effort, pushed himself to stand upright. "They..." he rasped, then cleared his throat. "They can't be serious."

"They are serious," Oriana said in a monotone, looking more cold and distant than ever.

No, Brom thought. *It's all wrong. This is all wrong.*

"We can't take the Test," Brom protested. "We're not ready. We're just second-years."

"We are Brilliant," Vale whispered, a maniacal smile on her face, and then she started laughing.

6

BROM

They didn't practice any more that day. The Invisible Ones, undoubtedly by some mental command, stood up and began carrying each of the injured—or possibly dead—out of the room.

Brom was sick to his stomach both by the carnage and by the horrible foreboding in his gut. Each of his Quad mates, though, seemed lost in their own thoughts. A deep distrust had fallen between them in the quiet.

"I think that's enough practice for the day," Vale said, walking toward the door. There was no saunter there, nothing playful. She'd said she had one goal here at the Champion's Academy: to become a Quadron. She hadn't come to make friends. She hadn't come to fall in love. She'd bonded with the Quad because it was required. And now she had what she wanted—a chance at the Test. She glanced at Royal and Brom and saved a final glare for Oriana before leaving the practice room.

Looking half-scared and half-stunned, Royal regarded his remaining Quad mates. "I...must be alone right now. I will see you tomorrow morning." And he, too, left.

Oriana turned to Brom. He considered reading her soul, delving into her to see if he might find some truth to Vale's words, but for the first time Oriana's emotions were written on her face. She looked wounded, frustrated. She had spent so much effort trying to bring this Quad together—they all had—that it must be killing her to watch it crumble right at the end, right when they'd nearly reached their goal.

Of course, maybe this was the way it was supposed to be. Maybe a Quad could only be united this far, and no farther. One of them, at least, was likely to die tomorrow. No Quad had ever graduated together. Once they'd been invited to take the Test, it was every Quad mate for themselves.

Brom had been sure Quad Brilliant would be the first to succeed together, to pass as a full Quad. But he couldn't feel that certainty anymore. How could they stand together in the Test if they couldn't come together now?

"Tomorrow it ends," Oriana murmured. "Two years ahead of schedule. We should be exultant." Her voice was anything but exultant.

"We can't take that Test," he said.

"We are ready. The primer is meant to indicate our readiness." She waved a hand at the blood flecks on the floor where Quad Phoenix's Anima had been before the Invisible Ones took her away. "They came for us. We destroyed them."

"There is something terribly wrong about this," he insisted, but he didn't know why. "Don't you sense it?"

"What is wrong?" Oriana asked, again waving a hand at the empty room. "How else might they judge that it is our time? We worked hard, Brom. This is our reward, to graduate so early."

Her words twisted in his gut. It was as though she was speaking an elegant lie, and he'd caught her. But he didn't know what the lie was. He didn't understand why his body rebelled against what was happening here. Oriana was right. This was the official way Quads were tested, and they had passed. No, they had *dominated.*

He hesitated, trying to come up with the answer, but he couldn't. He was so certain, but he had no proof.

"I'm...the Anima," he said. "It's my job to bring wisdom. And this..." He trailed off.

"Yes?"

"This is..."

"What is this?" She measured the words, seeming to grow impatient.

"I...don't know."

"Are you frightened?" she asked bluntly.

"Of course I am!" he blurted. "We should all be frightened. But that's not why I think this is going to be a disaster. Ask yourself, why would The Four test second-years? Why?"

"Because we are exceptional," she said coldly. "It is a fact."

He opened his mouth to speak, and he expected that some convincing bit of proof would come tumbling off his tongue. "Yes, but..." He faltered. He could think of no reason that could dispute her, only a sick feeling in his stomach.

"This is the reason we came," she said. "The reason we made our sacrifices." Her indigo eyes glinted angrily. Perhaps she was thinking about everything she, personally, had given up to bond with Quad Brilliant. "Feel blessed, Brom. You worked hard. I worked hard. We all did. And we are ready two full years early. Go rest. We will meet in the morning beforehand." She walked to the door.

Finally, he said the only thing he could think of, the thing he knew was on everyone's mind that no one would say.

"It doesn't bother you that one of us is going to die tomorrow?"

Oriana froze, her graceful footsteps ceasing, and she held very still. Finally, she half-turned, speaking to him over her shoulder. "It bothers me that you seem to have lost your spine," she said. "Weren't you the one who said we could be the first Quad to graduate together?"

"Not like this," he replied. "Not with Vale waving her dagger and Royal crawling inside his own head. Not with you calling me a coward."

Annoyance flashed across her face and spots of rouge colored her pale cheeks. "Now is the time to rise, Brom. We have been challenged. We stand. There is no other option. Would you have us run away after we have fought so hard to get here? Take the path of the Forgotten?" She practically spat the last word.

"Tomorrow, one of us is going to *die*," he repeated breathlessly.

Her lovely profile was outlined by the light of the grand foyer. "Yes," she said. "And I told you to prepare your mind for that. I told you last year. Apparently you did not listen."

"Oriana—"

"Listen now, Brom son of Brochan. Prepare yourself now. If one of us is to die, make sure that the dead one isn't you. I will do the same." She swept out of the room with a flare of her dress.

Dazed, he stood in the practice room for a long time, his gaze unfocused.

Finally, he left and made his way back to his dorm room. He'd only used his first Soulblock in the fight against Quad Phoenix, but he felt completely exhausted. He lay down on his bed, knowing he was missing something vitally important.

I could stop this, he thought. *I should be able to stop this.*

He felt the answer niggling at the back of his mind, loitering in the depths of his heart, but he couldn't see it, couldn't find it.

He lay down on his bed, and exhaustion swept over him. The afternoon sun slanted in through his window and made his eyelids heavy. Troubled, he sought the answer to this riddle for a brief, wandering moment, and then he fell asleep.

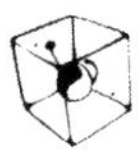

He jerked awake early the next morning, fully dressed in his clothes from yesterday. The sky had only just begun to lighten outside. He shook his head, groggy. His rest had been so profound he hadn't dreamt.

His Soulblocks were fully restored. He felt better than yesterday morning, but the moment he woke, his gut began to twist with that same foreboding. He felt a need to run out and stop his Quad mates from taking the Test, but he didn't know why.

He got up and put on his other set of clothes, which were now dry. He pulled on his boots, breeches, and tunic, all black for the path of Anima with the silver piping that designated him as a second-year student. He included a dagger to wear at his belt. First-years weren't technically allowed weapons—though Vale had flaunted that rule—but second-years were allowed daggers for eating and other tasks.

Of course, it was well-known that weapons weren't allowed in the Test of Separation, but he was going to wear it anyway. Deep down, he felt that somehow he was being cheated by this school, by its masters. He didn't know why, but if he didn't trust his own intuition, then he was no Anima at all.

He spent the next hour until the sunrise working at his right boot, hollowing out a straight hole through the sole and inserting a thin metal spike. It had leather wrapped on one side, a makeshift handle.

After, he sat on his bed trying to settle his mind, trying to chase down that feeling of having forgotten something, that he'd overlooked something critical. He went over Oriana's spiteful words from the practice room, trying to find a flaw in her logic, but there simply wasn't any.

He tried another tack and searched his emotions. Was Oriana right? Was he simply scared to take the Test? Was he a coward?

The sun filtered between his black curtains, and he watched the dust sparkle in the air. By this time tomorrow, it would be over. Either he would be a Quadron...

Or he would be dead.

Both prospects left him feeling ill, which made no sense at all. Becoming a Quadron was his deepest desire. It was his singular goal in coming here. But to have it at the expense of one of his Quad mates, to have everything they'd endured, the unlikely bonds they'd formed with one another sacrificed...

Which was more precious? His connections to his friends, or becoming a Quadron? Oriana knew her answer. So did Vale and even Royal. But Brom didn't. The idea of backstabbing his friends, of allowing one of them to die so he could grasp at power... He'd known that was the price before he'd ever entered the academy, so why did he balk now? Did he not *want* to become a Quadron anymore? What was wrong with him?

He left his room confused and came out onto the balcony overlooking the grand foyer. He was tempted to rush straight to the practice room, but he hesitated, then went to the Floating Room instead. As he waited for the rotation, he noticed a few of the other Animas looking at him.

They've heard, he thought. *They know we're testing today.*

The Anima floor slowly aligned with the platform, and a dozen Animas, including Brom, stepped into the room. He went to the far side, to the wheel of gravity-defying shelves, each stacked with every kind of food that could be imagined. He chose a bland porridge, strawberries, and a glass of milk, then took it all back to one of the tables. Conversations hushed when he walked by, and then picked up again when he sat down. He didn't have to read their souls to know they were talking about Quad Brilliant.

He wolfed down the porridge and left the room with all eyes on him. He went through the halls toward the practice room, wondering what he would find, if anything, when he arrived. Oriana had said they should meet up before the Test today, but she hadn't said to meet in the practice room.

Along the way, he saw The Collector leading a line of third-years, a dozen of them, all from different paths. They went through the front doors and outside. It struck him as odd, and then he remembered a snippet of conversation from the Floating Room. Someone had mentioned that all third- and fourth-years were participating in a Mentis exercise being conducted by the masters. He'd never seen that kind of procession leaving the dormitory before, nor heard of any exercise that would take students from their meals.

Then he saw Vale loitering outside the practice room and he forgot about The Collector. She looked like she had been waiting for Brom. The grand foyer, which led to each of the practice rooms as well as the stairways to the dormitories, was bright with light slanting in from the giant stained-glass window at the front of the building.

Vale had managed to stand in the only shadow along the wall, cast by an overhead beam. She raised one finger to her lips and beckoned him with her other hand. He came closer, his heart beating faster. Her wild brown hair tumbled to her shoulders as though she'd just finished running here. Her lips looked wet, eager, and her brown eyes smoldered with desire.

She gave him the sexy smile she'd used on him time and again. He knew she was just playing a part, that this was one of the many disguises she put on, that what they'd had together had nothing to do with love. At least not for her. He knew all this, but he still wanted to wrap her up in his arms and kiss her.

He came close, practically vibrating with need.

"They're both inside," she said softly. "They don't know I'm here yet. I waited for you."

He nodded, tried to find his tongue, tried to find something to say.

"The Collector is taking a line of third-years somewhere," he said, and it sounded like he was awkwardly trying to talk about anything except how much he wanted her. "Something about Mentis magic," he finished lamely.

She gave a sad smile, as though she could see right through him.

"I don't want to talk about The Collector," she murmured.

"I know." He sighed.

"I want to talk to you." She glanced at the floor, seemingly shy, then drew a quiet breath and glanced back up at him. "This may be our last moment alone, you know."

He hesitated, then nodded.

"I really thought you'd visit me last night," she whispered, putting a hand on his chest. "I would have visited you, but...I wasn't sure if you wanted me."

He swallowed, tried to hold onto something of himself, some certainty that would give him strength, something besides his aching desire. He cleared his throat. "I didn't think it mattered to you."

Her earnestness dissolved into hurt. "I said I don't believe in love, Brom," she said softly. "I didn't say I don't believe in you."

"I don't even know what that means. I would die for you, Vale. But you...."

"I have to believe in love for you to matter to me?" she asked. "Gods, Brom. You matter more than anything in my life."

"Almost anything..."

"Don't," she said, and she held up a finger, her eyes glistening. "Don't make that comparison. We all came here to become Quadrons. You did, too."

He shook his head slowly. "It's all wrong, Vale. We shouldn't be taking this Test. I feel it in my gut. Tell me you feel it too. Tell me your stomach isn't churning at the idea of taking the Test today."

"It's not. I don't feel anything of the kind," she said. "We're finally here! We did it! How can you not be excited?"

"Because one of us is going to die."

She swallowed, hesitated. "Let's just make sure it isn't either of us. You make it through the Test, okay?"

"I want you so much," he whispered. "Maybe we could just—"

She touched his chin with her fingers. "I... I feel like I hurt you, Brom," she whispered. "And I didn't mean to. I wanted to be honest with you. This thing between us... It's important to me. So important. And if you want to call it love, then call it love. I don't care. Just make it through the Test today, okay? Just meet me on the other side."

"Vale..."

She leaned in, and it was like she was suddenly the ground and he was a stone falling toward her. He grasped her, and their mouths met desperately. Her fingers slid into his hair, making fists, and he lifted her up in a crushing embrace. She wrapped her legs around him as he pushed her into the wall, kissing her, kissing her, kissing her...

Finally, they stopped, their foreheads together, panting. She slid her cheek along his and held him tightly with arms and legs.

"I love you, Vale," he murmured.

"You meet me at the other side, do you hear?" Her voice was thick with emotion. "You do what you have to do, and you meet me after."

He didn't want to let her go, but she held on only for another moment, then finally released him, putting her feet softly on the ground. Tears stood in her eyes. "Today, more than any other day in our lives, let's be our best," she said. "This thing between us, whatever you want to call it, we're going to use it to be the best we can be."

He nodded.

Her gaze flicked past him. She quickly brushed away her tears, and a wry smile spread across her face. She cleared her throat and tipped her chin over his shoulder. Brom turned.

Behind them, a few dozen students had clustered in the grand foyer, mouths open, watching them.

Fear spiked through him. They'd seen the kiss. They'd tell the masters—

Vale's calm hand on his cheek brought him back to face her.

"Doesn't matter," she said. "Not anymore. We've been called by The Four. We're not students, and rules are for students. In a few hours, we take the Test. Let the sheep bleat and cry about the rules. We're going to make history."

He raised a gentle hand to her cheek, mirroring her gesture. "After the Test, we're going to talk, you and me," he said. "And I'm going to convince you that love exists."

"Promise?" she asked.

"I promise."

7
BROM

The Dome was the building where all Tests of Separation were held. It was enormous—fully ten stories tall and three times that wide. It shone white in the sunlight and looked like a half-sphere of snow placed atop a flat, square, one-story building. It had four archways along the front, and wide, shallow steps leading up to them.

They all stopped at the base of the steps, the banks of snow high on either side of them, the cobblestone pathway meticulously shoveled.

"There are sixteen," Oriana said.

Brom looked at her.

"Steps," she said. "There are sixteen steps."

Brom waited for her to explain why that mattered. She didn't, her haughty mask back in place, and he suddenly realized she'd simply spoken because she was nervous, cataloguing something aloud for no reason.

Royal cleared his throat but didn't say anything.

Vale, beyond Royal, looked down the line of them. "This is

where we go our own way," she said. "After the Test, we're not Quad Brilliant anymore. We're Quadrons in our own right."

Because the Quad will be broken, Brom thought. *Because one of us isn't coming out of there.* He put a hand to his stomach as if that could quell his misgivings. He wanted to vomit.

"But we are a Quad until then," Oriana said.

Brom reached out and took Oriana's hand. Her long fingers curled around his. They were cool, but they gripped his tightly. Royal's beefy hand suddenly closed over Brom's on the other side, engulfing it, and Brom glanced over at him. His gaze was fixed on that enormous dome, and he looked sad. After a moment's hesitation, Vale latched on to two of Royal's giant fingers with her small hand.

"We should go in," Royal said. "They're watching us."

They started up the steps together. Beyond the arches was a foyer not unlike the grand foyer in Westfall Dormitory. It had a lower ceiling, but similar arches down the hall on either side. Everything was made of marble.

Directly ahead of them was an arch with two guards, one on either side. The woman, tall and rangy, wore tight chainmail under a blue surcoat emblazoned with the coat of arms of The Four: a red dragon, white owl, blue bear, and black moth. She had the look of someone who could move very fast if she wanted to. Her deep-set hawk's eyes watched them carefully, starting with Vale, then moving to Royal, Brom and Oriana, then starting again with Vale and proceeding down the line once more.

The second guard wore snowy-white robes with the same coat of arms on the front, bordered in black. This man had light brown eyes and a round head with a thatch of black hair plastered to his scalp that did nothing to break its perfect roundness. Both guards had the same arrogant mien as the masters, but Brom hadn't seen either of them in any classes.

"Mentis and Impetu," Oriana suddenly said inside their heads, again stating the obvious.

At first, Brom was surprised Oriana would have opened one of her Soulblocks before the Test began, then he revised his thinking. This could *be* the beginning of the Test. Hastily, he opened his own first Soulblock.

The magic crackled into him, lighting up his extremities. His doubled Soulblocks seemed like an endless stack; it made him feel invincible. Reflexively, he connected to the Soul of the World.

"Mentis and Impetu?" Vale responded sarcastically. *"Do you really think so?"*

"Don't spend time bantering, Vale. Focus," Royal thought to them.

"Don't spend time telling me what to do, Royal. Focus," Vale shot back. Brom tried not to smile, but it crept onto his lips anyway. Gods, that woman.

Brom's intuition suddenly nudged him, and he looked up at the Mentis guard, who had narrowed his eyes. Brom braced for the attack, but even though he knew it was coming, he could do nothing to stop it.

An invisible blow struck him, like someone had boxed his ears. He gasped. Beside him, Oriana lowered her head, clenching her teeth. Aside from a slight tightening around his eyes, Royal didn't move. Vale hissed and crouched, drawing a hidden dagger and hurling it at the Mentis, fast as a striking snake. It flipped end-over-end, flying true—

The Impetu's long arm flashed out, a blur, and she snatched the dagger from the air. She flipped it her hand, spun it around her wrist, then set it gracefully on the small table in front of her.

"YOU WILL NOT SPEAK MIND-TO-MIND," the Mentis guard shouted in their heads so loud it hurt. Vale hissed again.

"And you will bring no weapons into the Test," the Impetu guard said out loud. "You will bring no jewels, baubles, possessions of any kind save the clothes you wear."

Royal, Vale, and Brom wore the uniforms that had been provided them. Oriana, though, wore a shimmering white dress with an exquisitely embroidered white owl on the front, wings spreading over her chest. It was high-necked, like almost all of Oriana's dresses, but this one had no jeweled adornments. Instead, silver thread bordered the hem, cuffs, and collar, and she'd tied a silver sash around her waist.

The Impetu beckoned them forward. "Your Motus and your Mentis will come to this side of the table."

"Your Impetu and Anima to this side," said the Mentis guard, aloud this time instead of in their minds. He pointed at the spot of floor next to him.

"This isn't the beginning of the Test?" Brom asked, cautiously moving forward.

The round-headed Mentis gave a derisive snort, then pointed again to the floor beside him. Royal went to stand where indicated.

"Remove your boots," the Mentis commanded, and Royal complied. The guard searched inside the first giant boot, felt quickly around the outside, then inside, then set it down, then repeated with the second boot. Once he was done with that, he patted Royal all over, even under his armpits and around his groin.

Brom glanced over to see the Impetu giving Oriana the same treatment. Her face had frozen into a sneer, but she gave no word of complaint as the Impetu ran her hands all over her body. Then it was Vale's turn. Her naked hatred would have made Brom step back, but the Impetu took her life into her own hands and searched Vale, finding another hidden dagger, which she put on the table with the first.

It took a little bit longer for the Mentis to search Royal's giant body, but he finally finished and turned to Brom.

To mask his thoughts and any chance they'd find the hidden spike in his boot, Brom began actively thinking about the Mentis guard's robe.

Gods, look at that white robe. So very white. Like freshly fallen snow, that robe. What a fastidious person this Mentis must be to have robes so very white. And that coat of arms. He well represents The Four with that. Could anyone do better, I wonder?

The Mentis methodically searched the inside and outside of Brom's boots, then moved on to Brom himself, stopping first to remove the dagger at Brom's belt and set it on the table.

I daresay my own mother, a seamstress of great skill, couldn't have embroidered something so keen for her only son, whom she adores. I wonder how often he washes that robe. Or does he perhaps wick away the dirt and grime with magic of some kind?

Brom continued to make loud mental observations the entire time the round-headed Mentis searched him. Finally, it was over, and the Mentis had thankfully overlooked the spike hidden in the sole of Brom's boot.

"Go in," the Mentis said as soon as Brom had his boots back on.

The guards each took hold of one of the double doors and pulled them open.

"What's in there?" Brom joked with the guards, but neither said anything nor looked at him.

"Victory," Royal rumbled.

"Pie," Vale replied irreverently.

Brom chuckled as they proceeded under the glares of the guards. Quad Brilliant entered The Dome.

8

BROM

They entered a cube of a room, twenty-five feet wide and twenty-five feet tall. Brom felt a tingle as he passed through the archway, similar to the tingle he'd felt when he'd first arrived at the academy two years ago. In the middle of the room stood four tall mirrors at right angles, facing outward in a perfect square, each parallel with its opposite wall.

On the opposite side of the room, two other guards—also a white-robed Mentis and an armored Impetu with a blue surcoat—stood in front of open doors. They looked identical to the two that had just ushered them into the room.

Brom felt a strange vertigo. Again, his gut clenched, warning him.

He spun. He could see sunlight and trees beyond the arch on the other side of the room beyond the two guards, just as he could see sunlight and trees through the door they'd entered, and the two guards they'd just left. That meant they were seeing all the way to the other side of the Dome and out onto the campus. But that was impossible. This room was only twenty-five feet long, and the

Dome itself had to be more than three hundred feet across.

He turned, looked at the guards. With sour faces, they took hold of the doors and began to pull them shut. Brom whipped his head about, and the guards on the far side of the room were doing exactly the same thing.

"They're the same guards!" Brom exclaimed.

"What?" Vale, looking disconcerted, glanced back and forth between the guards. Sure enough, each pair was moving in perfect synchronicity, mirror images.

The doors thoomed shut, and the guards were gone.

"This room is too small." Oriana spoke Brom's exact thoughts aloud.

Royal scanned all about, uncomfortable, flexing his fists over and over.

"This place makes my skin crawl," Vale growled.

"I suspect that is its purpose," Oriana said. "Keep your emotions in check—"

"Stop telling me to put my emotions away, Princess," Vale said.

Oriana continued her scan of the room, but she seemed to decide, as Brom already had, that the only items of note were the four mirrors in the center.

Brom walked forward carefully, hands out, half expecting to collide with a giant mirror bisecting the room. That would explain why it seemed like there was an identical doorway on the far side. But there was nothing. What they'd seen was somehow real. Brom suddenly shared Vale's apprehension. Their Test had begun.

He turned his attention to the four mirrors in the center. At first glance, he'd thought they were identical, but they weren't. They were all the same shape and size, but each sat in a different border: red, blue, white, and black.

"We're supposed to look into those?" Brom murmured, hesitating to come closer.

Vale approached the white-bordered mirror and looked inside. She shivered and backed away.

"What?" Oriana asked.

"There's no reflection," Vale said.

"It's not a mirror?" Brom asked.

She shook her head. "No, it's a mirror. I could see the room behind me, but my own reflection wasn't there."

"And mine is not here," Royal said, standing before the red-bordered mirror.

"Try your own color," Brom said.

Royal walked to the blue-bordered mirror. "Nothing," he said.

"This is the separation," Oriana said softly, and Brom knew she was right. "It won't begin until we are all staring at ourselves in our own mirrors. Until we are divided according to our paths."

"Did we really think we were going to go through this together?" Vale asked nervously. "It *is* called the Test of Separation."

Brom's foreboding twisted in his stomach, harder this time.

Only his trust in The Four kept him from running from this room. They were the only ones who could call for a Test of Separation for second-years. And if they thought Quad Brilliant was ready, he had to believe they were. He had to trust that. He *had* to.

Didn't he?

"Does anyone else feel like they just want to stop now and flee the academy?" he asked.

Royal raised his chin, which was what he did when he was scared but refused to admit it. Oriana ignored Brom's statement altogether. Which was what *she* did when she was scared but refused admit it.

"Take the path of the Forgotten?" Royal asked disdainfully.

"I'm not about to give up my chance at being a Quadron," Vale said.

"There are fourth-years who cannot face the Test of Separation," Brom said. "We're second-years. Why is no one even questioning that? We were supposed to have two more years to prepare. What if The Collector is behind this? What if he never wanted us to succeed and this is his last attempt to make sure we don't?"

Nobody answered. Oriana and Royal looked into their mirrors, didn't even glance at Brom.

"Enough," Vale said. "We're already here. We've already

started. Stand in front of your mirror, Brom." She walked to hers.

Brom's mirror was on the far side, obscured by Oriana's, and his revulsion was so strong he didn't want to move, didn't even want to glimpse it.

"Did it occur to you that you're already failing?" Vale asked. "That your indecision, your fear, is part of the Test? Stand in front of the gods-be-damned mirror, Brom!"

"Courage, man," Royal said.

"When there is but one path, that is the path you take," Oriana said. "This is what we came for."

Despite his misgivings, Brom knew Oriana was right. There really was no other choice. Could he simply leave his Quad mates here, unable to continue the Test because he refused to? To steal away their hopes at becoming Quadrons because he was afraid? Their faces were against the wall, and they either had to break through or fail. There *was* no other path. No other path that Brom would ever live down, at least. They weren't going to walk away from the Test, and he wasn't going to abandon his Quad.

Finally, his right foot moved, and then his left, and he started walking. He passed Vale and stepped up to his mirror. As Vale had said, he could see the reflection of the room behind him, the eerie copy of the double doors they'd entered, but his own reflection was absent.

"I still don't see anything," Royal rumbled.

"Nor do I," Oriana confirmed.

Vale flicked a glance at Brom, probably to ensure he was actually looking, then gazed back into her own mirror, frustrated. "What does that mean?" she asked. "Did we wait too long?"

Brom's foreboding had begun to leak away, as though its warning was no longer relevant, as though whatever he was supposed to have learned, he'd missed it.

He harnessed the magic that crackled within him and sank deeper into the Soul of the World. He became one with the mirrors, the room. Each one of his Quad mates became living parts of his own body, his head, his heart, his arms.

"It's blank. Is it still blank for youuuuu..." Royal said, but his last word stretched out, like a lowing cow falling down a well.

A flicker of green flame appeared inside Brom's mirror. He gasped, and that, too, stretched out like Royal's word, as though time had slowed and he was drawing in that short, sharp breath forever.

In the span of that minutes-long gasp, the curl of flame formed into an ethereal hand, smoke twirling out behind it. The flame turned into a forearm, then upper arm, shoulder, head, and body.

A sea-green figure formed inside the mirror, and in the span of that breathless gasp, those greenish fingers, limned in flame, took hold of Brom's tunic just below his neck.

Time returned to normal. Brom's gasp sounded loud. Royal roared. A surprised, breathy huff came from Oriana, and Vale hissed.

The hand yanked Brom into the mirror.

9

BROM

Brom tripped over the edge of the mirror as he went through, and a loud metallic *clang* sounded. He tumbled to the grass, looking about for some giant steel gong.

He drew in a swift breath. He wasn't at the academy anymore. And it wasn't daytime anymore.

He stood up in the cemetery at Kyn. Fendra, full and round, shone her silver-blue light down on everything. Behind her, just a slim crescent, Kelto hung in the sky, a slash of faded purple. For a moment, Brom couldn't think. The twisted willow tree was there, right where it should be, its roots bulging against the white fence that ran around the entire cemetery, sketching a perfect square. Every detail was so perfect, from the hills in the distance to the dirt path beyond the gate, to the rise in the road that obscured the rest of the town.

This was his home. This was where he'd kissed Myan a lifetime ago, before he came to the academy.

The flaming green figure that had dragged him here stood calmly, arms crossed, where the mirror portal had once been. There was no portal now. The figure's features were lost in the green flames that surrounded it.

"What is this?" Brom demanded.

The flames rising from the figure went out, becoming wisps of smoke trailing up from the figure's shoulders and head. It gained definition. Its chest resolved, a dark green tunic forming. Green breeches formed on its legs. Its bare arms resolved into sea-green-colored skin. As Brom watched, the figure's face formed, and it smiled with shiny green teeth. The nose and the mouth became apparent, and the all-green eyes glowed.

The man looked just like Brom.

"Do you feel me, Brom?" the green creature asked, and its voice was ancient like an old woman's, too creaky and too high-pitched to be coming out of Brom's face.

Brom's throat went dry, and his palms were suddenly clammy. He'd heard that voice somewhere before.

"Did you feel me coming?" the creature repeated. "You should. I'm you. In the Test of Separation, you face yourself. The only enemy that really matters...is yourself."

"You're not me," he said.

"I'm what you might be, Brom. Powerful. A Quadron. If you defeat me, I'm what you could become. But you won't. Because you're a liar and a rule-breaker. We've known this from the very beginning with you. And here, the only person you can cheat is yourself, the only rules you can break are your own. And when you do, you won't just lose a spot with the Kyn guardsmen. You'll die."

The creature moved so fast it might have been an Impetu. Brom barely threw up an arm before it slammed its fist into his cheek. Stars exploded in his vision, and he went down, almost hitting a headstone.

"If that was your best..." His adversary chuckled. "This isn't going to take long."

Brom got to his hands and knees as the creature kicked him in the ribs so hard he couldn't breathe. He hit the headstone he'd narrowly missed before and crumpled at its base, nearly losing consciousness.

The creature leapt on top of him, surreal in shades of green. It snarled down at him, wearing Brom's own face, and struck him again and again.

He tried to roll out of its grasp, but it latched onto him and dragged him back, slamming him against the headstone. Another fist to the left side of Brom's face. Another fist to the right.

It was just too fast, too vicious. He couldn't move quickly enough to block the blows, couldn't get his bearings enough to get away. His Test was going to be over before it had even begun. Brom was going to die...

In the depths of his belly, that familiar foreboding twisted, warning him.

Yes, he thought desperately. *I'm getting beaten to death. I don't need an Anima's intuition to tell me that.*

It felt like there was a knot of roots in his belly, tugging on him, tugging him downward, insistent. Distantly, he felt his head slamming to the side again, and again, and he went limp, let the creature hit him. He ignored the pain and followed the compulsion, dove deep into his own soul.

That foreboding, whatever it was trying to tell him, might be his last chance.

As he looked into his own soul, like he had looked into countless others, he began to hear whispers—his adversary's whispers, sly and hidden before now, twisting like smoke inside him. This thing was using magic, sending insidious words into the deepest parts of him.

You can't fight me, the whispers curled around his heart. *I'm too fast, too vicious. You can't move quickly enough to block my blows. You'll never get your bearings enough to get away. Your Test is over before it has even begun. You're going to die...*

The creature had used Anima magic to suck Brom's hope away. This was the destructive aspect of the Anima! Fourth-year magic, something Brom knew about but hadn't practiced yet.

Just as the constructive path of Anima could extend the supreme confidence and the knowing of the Soul of the World to another Quad mate, the destructive path enabled an Anima to sap a person's clarity, to steal their confidence, to render them impotent.

Brom opened his second Soulblock, releasing a storm of

crackling magic into himself, and he put it all into plunging himself into the Soul of the World.

His awareness suddenly extended to the headstone behind him, the grass beneath him, the air around him, and his adversary before him. He became the blue-silver light from Fendra, the barest sheen of purple light from Kelto. He became the still air over the graveyard. He became his adversary's own fists, flecked with Brom's blood, driving down at him like hammer blows.

Yes, he thought. *I feel you now. I feel everything. Yes, you* are *me, but not like you think.*

He could see the ephemeral, magical tendrils of green connecting the creature to himself as those fists came down again and again. A half dozen more blows, and the creature would kill him, but Brom had what he needed now. He could see the blows coming before they fell. He could see them... And if he could see them...

With all of his strength, Brom threw his head sideways. In the same instant, he caught the doppelganger's incoming blow by the wrist. He didn't try to stop it, but pulled it past his bloodied head, yanking the creature forward and slamming its face into the headstone with terrible force. Teeth cracked. Blood flecked the stone. The creature's head wobbled. Brom grabbed it and slammed it down again. His adversary collapsed.

With a shout, Brom shoved himself upright. His nose felt like it was the size of a potato, and his ears rang. Blood ran into his slowly swelling right eye so much that he couldn't see out of it.

But this time he didn't forget his magic. He didn't need to see with his eyes if the Soul of the World was whispering to him. He let his fears swirl away like leaves on a river, and he listened...

His adversary, though hurt and momentarily stunned, had already staggered to its feet, but it didn't charge this time. Its two front teeth were cracked in half, and its nose broken. There was a deep gash on its forehead, and blood ran into its left eye, an eerie mirror-image to Brom's own injury.

Brom felt the intuitive nudge in his belly the moment before the creature attacked. It feinted left, then came right, lashing out with a foot. It wanted to trip him, wanted him on the ground again, wanted to leap atop him.

Brom hopped over the strike, feeling looser, less frightened.

The dance began. The creature lashed out with an elbow, and Brom leaned back, timing it perfectly and putting himself half-an-inch out of reach. He struck back, tried to knee the thing in the belly. But it was already twisting, grabbing for Brom's hair.

He wrapped his arm around the creature's arm in a corkscrew motion, trapping its hand against his chest and locking its elbow joint. Brom dropped to his knees, twisting the arm viciously.

But the thing jumped up, unwinding the joint lock by flipping over Brom's shoulder. On the way over, it kneed Brom in the head. Stars burst in his vision, and he staggered back.

His adversary was also using the Soul of the World, sensing what Brom was going to do before he did it.

Another fist lashed out, and Brom blocked it, but didn't see the second fist. It hammered into the other side of Brom's face, and he collapsed, his right leg twisted under him.

Fear crept back in, a sure sign that his magic was faltering. He had to stay connected, had to anticipate the next strike, but his thoughts were so scrambled he didn't know which way was up.

"I thought you were stronger than this," his adversary creaked in that old woman's voice. "But I was wrong. That will make twice this year I was wrong. You're just a rule-breaker who cuts corners, puts on a good show." It smiled, its green teeth so close to his face he could smell the decay on its breath. "Well, you won't cheat your way out of this. One loss breaks the Quad as easily as two."

One loss breaks the Quad as easily as two...

A chime sounded inside his mind at those words. He'd heard them before. They rippled through his soul, and Brom's foreboding—so bound up and knotted until now—unwound, sending tendrils of wisdom into him. There were no memories, no thoughts, just...a knowing.

The Test of Separation was a lie.

That shocking realization crackled through him. He didn't know how he knew it, but he was certain.

This wasn't a test of magical skills. It was a coming-of-age threshold he had to break through. It was designed to break a

Quad, to inhibit the power of any Quadron who emerged from the academy, to enslave them. It didn't matter if one of a given Quad died, or if all of them died, just so long as there weren't four at the end to lend power to each other.

A full Quad of magic users could be powerful, as powerful as The Four themselves, and The Four wanted to make sure their power was never threatened.

The sudden knowing sickened Brom. The academy was a lure, and young people with magical talent buzzed to it like flies. Once they were caught, they were destroyed, through death or enslavement.

Brom floated in his connection to the Soul of the World like he was submerged beneath a lake. Never before had he been this deep, in a place where vague intuition transformed into profound assurance.

Then suddenly, it was as though someone grabbed his ankle and yanked him downward. He plunged deeper into the depths of the Soul. His consciousness went so far down he hadn't even realized such a place had existed.

He didn't just feel everything around him now, didn't just make the lands a part of him, couldn't just anticipate what would happen a second from now, but instead he saw the grand view. He saw...the future. Instead of merely being a part of everything, he now saw its purpose, its origin, and its destiny.

The mirror was a portal made by The Four. This cemetery wasn't an illusion created by the test makers; Brom actually stood in Kyn at some future or past time, perhaps the coming night, perhaps a night from a dozen years ago.

And he suddenly realized there were greater threats to the two kingdoms than the war of the Hallowed Woods, greater threats to him than the struggles of this slaughterhouse academy.

The lands were under attack. There was a secret invasion by creatures from another land, some land below them. Some place...that Brom didn't understand. Another world. These invaders had already breached the barrier between their land and Brom's many times, and they longed to invade the two kingdoms through portals just like this one.

And Brom saw that his green adversary wasn't a replica of himself at all. It was one of The Four in disguise.

Brom's new eyes stripped away her disguise. He saw her wrinkled lips and bony chin beneath her black cowl. He saw her midnight robes. The green-skinned image of his adversary hovered like a mirage over her real form.

She raised her fist.

"Linza," he gasped. The word came Brom's mouth unbidden, as though it had been waiting behind his teeth, unfettered by the blank spots in his memory. It was as though that knowing, that recognition, had been placed there by the Soul of the World herself, waiting for this moment to emerge. Brom grappled with the name in his mind, trying to follow some string that would unlock his missing memories. There was something personal here, something vast between Linza and himself, but though he had perfect certainty of who and what she was, he had no details at all.

The old woman's fist froze, hovering in mid-air.

"What did you say?" she creaked.

"You're Linza. You're the Anima of The Four."

His newfound wisdom changed the nature of the Test. He wasn't fighting to become a Quadron. There was no prize here. He was fighting to escape the jaws of a trap closing down on him and his friends. He had to get away from this place, back to the academy. He had to warn his Quad.

"Remarkable..." Linza creaked. "How did you see that?"

Using her magic, she tried to fill him with despair again. He felt the attack coming, knew exactly what she was trying to do, but he was submerged in the Soul of the World, and the attack had no effect. Her despair came down like rain on top of that lake, unable to reach him because he was so far beneath the surface. Instead, it thrummed on the top, but he only felt the ripples of her vile intent, not the soul-crushing despair.

"Clever, Rule-breaker," she creaked. "Perhaps I'll keep you after all. The hooks burn at first, but the pain goes away quickly enough. You'll soon come to like them. In fact, you'll come to love them..." Green flames appeared, dancing over her bony fingers.

Brom groped with his hands along the grass, seeking something, anything that he might hit her with, dislodge her so he could get up. But his right leg was twisted under him, and he had no leverage to push her off. His knee was torqued so awkwardly that his right foot lay next to his chest.

She knelt on his thigh, and he cried out. Fierce agony shot up his knee.

"Tell me how you knew my name, and you'll pass the Test," she said. "You'll go on to fortune and adventure, just like you wanted."

His hand scrabbled frantically with his right boot, trying to shove it down, shove it free, to ease the pressure on his knee.

The ball of roots in his gut tightened, and he suddenly remembered the hidden metal spike in the sole of his boot.

Linza lifted Brom's head by the hair and put his bloody face next to her own. She brought her yellow teeth so close to Brom's ear that he could smell that decay on her breath, like a mouse had died in her mouth. "Tell me what I want to know, and you live. Don't, and you die. That is my rule, and there's no breaking it."

"Watch me," he growled through clenched teeth.

Brom swung his left fist at her head. With a laugh, she blocked it...

...and she didn't see the spike coming up from the other side. He drove it into her chest with the Soul of the World guiding his hand. The steel went in just under the ribcage, straight into her heart.

She screamed and her eyes went wide as her hands clasped his fist. She tried yank it out, but he fought her with all his might. She tried to scramble away, to free herself, to pull herself off the deadly spike, but he clung to her and shoved it deeper still. She twisted, wailing, and he felt her magic falter. The rain of despair slackened.

He imagined doing to her what she'd tried to do to him. He imagined her soul being sucked from her body, flowing into the sharpened steel spike, and creating a vacuum of despair inside her. He imagined that spike drawing the very life from her.

With a creaky wail, Linza gave a last feeble shove with her legs. He let her, driving awkwardly with one foot as he pushed himself after her. They flopped to the ground, this time with her beneath him, and he jammed the spike the rest of the way, his fist pressing against her bony ribs.

She twitched one last time, then let out a long, thin breath. Her cowl fell back, exposing her bald head, which looked like a skull with skin. Her death grimace was horrible. Brom pushed himself off, rolling his aching, battered body away from her.

He levered himself to his feet using a headstone and gingerly tested his right leg. After a few hesitant steps, he found it would bear his weight. Linza stared sightlessly upward, the spike sticking out of her chest.

She didn't breathe. She didn't move.

He forced himself to approach her again, and he prodded her with his toe. It jostled her body but she didn't revive. She was dead. It was over.

To his right, a light appeared, tall and square. It resolved into a portal the exact same size as the mirror, and beyond it was the mirror room where he'd started. He could see the marble walls and the double doors.

He charged through. A loud *clang* sounded as he crossed the threshold, and the portal vanished behind him.

10

BROM

Brom fell flat onto the marble floor and groaned. His face was hammered meat. His head felt soft, his teeth loose. His bones ached. His breath fogged the polished marble, and all he wanted to do was lie down and pass out.

The Four were evil!

And he'd just killed one of them.

It just wasn't possible. It didn't even seem real.

He levered himself onto one elbow, looked at the four mirrors. He couldn't spend any time on his dizzying victory or what it meant that The Four weren't the benevolent overseers he'd thought they were. The last of his second Soulblock still crackled through his body, but it was almost done. Sinking that deep into the Soul of the World had been costly, and this fight wasn't over. He had to get his Quad mates out of those mirrors.

With a grunt, he took a deep breath, pushed himself up from the ground, and opened his third Soulblock.

The magic charged into him like a lightning storm. His senses became hyper-alert, and he joined with everything in the room, the solid walls and floors, the portals disguised as mirrors.

A loud *clang* sounded, and Oriana stumbled out of her own portal. The silver sash she'd tied around her waist had come free and fluttered down behind her, wreathed in green fire. She turned, not seeing Brom, and stared back at the mirror. Then she stopped moving altogether.

"Oriana." He went to her. She was transfixed, her mouth open in horror as she stared back into the mirror. Her silver-and-gold hair was flung in disarray across her face, as though she'd been in a hurricane, and charcoal burn marks striped her temples from eye to hairline.

He hesitated to touch her. Though she'd come out of the portal just as he had, her Test would have been different—a battle of the mind. If he interrupted her, he might do her more harm than good.

But time was short...

His gut twisted, and his gaze fell on the fluttering silver sash Oriana had dropped. It lay across the threshold of the portal, half inside the testing room and half beyond, which was a nightmarish land of dark cliffs and purple lightning.

This was no quaint and grassy graveyard from Brom's hometown. It was a wet, black granite cliff overlooking a dark green lake. Purple lightning forked back and forth across low-hanging black clouds. Brom didn't see a figure in that landscape but he had a feeling someone was there. He peered hard, but while he was connected to the portal itself through the Soul of the World, he couldn't feel anything beyond it. Several times he thought he saw something move, but it could have been just leaves on the wind.

In Brom's Test, the portal hadn't reopened until he'd defeated his adversary. So Oriana had passed. Why, then, was it trying to draw her back?

He stood in front of her, grabbed her by both shoulders and shook her. "Oriana!"

She sucked in a breath but still gazed past him at the mirror as if that was all she could see.

He glanced back at the portal. The silver sash lying across the threshold suddenly flickered with green fire. At the same instant,

Oriana twitched and her mouth trembled. Her already-wide eyes widened more, and she stepped into him, trying to move toward the portal.

Brom released her and lunged away. He snatched up the sash and yanked it all the way into the room. There was a flash of green fire, and the portal winked out. The dark land vanished. The mirror returned to its previous state, reflecting everything in the room except Brom and Oriana.

Oriana gasped, and her mouth snapped shut with a click of teeth. She shook her windblown head and blinked, finally seeing him.

"Brom," she whispered. A wave of expressions crossed her face. Horror. Pain. Worry.

"Are you okay?" Brom asked.

Oriana pulled her typical impassive mask into place. "I am well," she said, though she didn't look at all well. She had always been pale-skinned, but she looked as white as snow now, with haunted dark rings under her eyes. There were bright red marks on her wrists and neck. "I believe...I passed."

Her self-possession reasserted itself. She glanced down at him. "I see that you did too. Are you in pain?"

"Quite a bit, actually—"

The room rocked with an explosion, and both Oriana and Brom cringed. He threw his hands up to protect his tender head and almost stumbled when his ravaged knee flared in pain. Royal hit the far wall like he'd been shot from a catapult. The big man was covered with bloody lash marks. His own fists were also bloody, and small curls of green smoke rose from blackened scorch marks on his body. He lay completely limp on the floor near the wall. Only his prodigious arm muscles twitched, as though they wanted to keep fighting.

Brom ran to his Quad mate, wondering if Royal was dead. He knelt next to the big man and could immediately see that, while injured, he was still alive. His great chest rose and fell.

Brom turned to find Oriana studying the blue-framed mirror, but whatever land Royal had been to, it was gone now.

"He's alive," Brom said. He was about to say that they needed to hurry—they needed to get as far away from here as possible, as soon as possible. But he hesitated.

Linza had talked about putting "hooks" into him rather than killing him. If Oriana had passed her test... If she'd left her mirror alive, did that mean the hooks of The Four were already in her?

"You were the first," she said distractedly, like she often did when she was working things out in her head. "You emerged before me."

"By a few seconds only."

"After my victory, just as I was passing through the mirror, my...foe tried to haul me back," she said. "I had won, but it was as though the Test had started over again. I think when you emerged, my Test began again." She looked over at Royal. "I wonder if his did, too."

He stood up. "We have to get to Vale. They're going to kill her. They can't have all four of us living."

"Who can't?"

He staggered past Oriana, toward Vale's mirror. "The Four."

"What?"

"It's a trap. This isn't a test. It's meant to kill us, at least one of us."

"But...I passed," she murmured.

"Nobody passes." He ran to Vale's mirror. She stood in a dark glade of Lyantrees, surrounded by a cone of green fire that came down from somewhere above the purple-silver Lyantree canopy. She looked as though she'd been running toward the portal when the fire hit her.

She'd gone to her knees and it seemed she couldn't move. There was no adversary, no other creature within that glade except Vale and that flaming cone. She screamed continuously, her back arching, her face turned toward the top of her fiery prison. Red sparks rose from her body, sucked up the length of the cone like smoke up a chimney.

It was her soul. He could feel those little sparks of flame—her beautiful soul—being pulled out of her. The green fire was draining her life, pulling the magic from her Soulblocks, draining them so she couldn't use them. It would take them all and leave her a dead husk.

Brom took a step toward the mirror.

Oriana grabbed his arm. "Don't," she warned.

One word. So simple, yet it fractured the Quad forever.

"We can't save her," she said. "I'm out of Soulblocks. And you don't have the strength."

"We have to try."

"If we do, we will only succeed in dying with her," she said. "Vale wouldn't throw her chance away if your positions were reversed. You know she wouldn't."

"She would," he said, but he wasn't sure about that.

"Only three ever pass," Oriana said.

"It doesn't matter. I can't just leave her."

Tears welled in Oriana's eyes, but her expression remained stony. "You've won, Brom. Take your victory. You're going to become a Quadron." Oriana had obviously calculated the odds of success and she'd made her decision. Royal was down, Oriana was drained, and Brom was on his last Soulblock. "She is simply... She is the fourth."

"I can't."

"Don't be a fool," she said.

He yanked his arm free of her grip.

"I was always the fool," he said, and he launched himself at the mirror.

"Brom!" Oriana screamed.

The portal clanged.

He landed just outside the cone of green fire in the Hallowed Woods. If there was a chance to save Vale, if it was at all possible, he would find a way. He focused the storm of magic inside himself and sank deep into the Soul of the World.

And he suddenly knew what to do.

He ran at the green fire. It was like hitting a stretched animal skin. It didn't want to let him in. It hungered for Vale, but he pushed his hand through and touched her arm. The green fire surged within the cone, turning vicious. A hundred green needles stabbed into his arm. He almost yanked it back out but he gritted his teeth and grasped Vale's wrist.

He jammed his leg through the fiery cone, scrabbling for leverage, and he spun, hauling Vale out of the fire and throwing her to the forest floor.

The cone grabbed hold of him with a dozen invisible hands. The green flames roared higher, and the invisible hands yanked Brom inside.

He shouted. As he continued to spin, he felt like wolves were chewing at him, pulling out the coils of his intestines.

But the Soul of the World showed him the truth: the damage was an illusion. His body was unchanged. All the fire could do was deal pain and steal magic. It couldn't kill him, not until it drained him dry.

And he wasn't going to let that happen.

He used his momentum to continue spinning. With a mighty yell, he hit the far side and pushed his way out, tumbling to the ground. The cone tried to follow him, cover him again, but he anticipated the movement and rolled to the left. He came lithely to his feet and spun. The Soul of the World told him when to leap, to spin, to kick, so he did.

The green fire coalesced into a handsome man in a red doublet...

...just as Brom's foot smashed into his face. The man crashed to the ground, his jaw flying off his face. There was no blood. No gore. It simply...came off, as though the man were made of painted wood.

Brom landed, fists up. "Arsinoe," he growled. Brom didn't quite recognize the man, though he felt he should. Again, the name came from the Soul of the World, as though it had been shoved past Brom's mouth by some other force, as though the Soul of the World was speaking through him.

Arsinoe's jaw thumped to the leaf-strewn ground and rolled to a stop.

The portal clanged. He spared a quick glance over his shoulder and saw that Vale had escaped. Both she and Oriana stood safely on the other side of the portal. Thank the gods!

He moved to join them. Quad Brilliant would reunite, doubling their Soulblocks, and they could lean on each other to escape this infernal trap.

Brom sprinted past the handsome man—markedly less handsome without his jaw—toward the portal.

Two more clangs rang out as Brom leapt toward freedom—

A monstrously strong, metal-clad hand grabbed Brom's ankle, yanking him back just as his fingers touched the portal. Time slowed, and he saw Vale shouting denial.

"Help me!" Brom shouted, reaching out for her in that brief frozen second. "We can beat them. Together!" They wouldn't double their Soulblocks with just the three of them, but their magic would increase.

Vale hesitated.

The monstrously strong hand threw Brom to the ground like a doll.

His concentration shattered as he tumbled. The Soul of the World vanished. He came to his knees and looked up. Ahead of him, the portal glowed, and Vale stood frozen in indecision, eyes wide. Behind her, Oriana's indigo gaze burned into him. Tears now streaked down her cheeks.

I told you, she mouthed. *I warned you.*

"Then run!" he shouted.

"Brom!" Vale mouthed, stepping toward the portal.

But it vanished with a clang, and they were gone. Vale... Oriana... He was alone.

With a grunt, Brom stood up and faced his enemies.

11

BROM

Every nerve in Brom's body prickled, vigilant. He regained his connection, and the Soul of the World told him to wait, that the first move must be made by the enemy.

Arsinoe retrieved his jaw and put it back in his face, completing the illusion that he was human. He looked furious, like he wanted to leap on Brom and tear the face from his skull. From some deep compulsion Brom couldn't identify, just looking at Arsinoe made his blood boil.

The squat, ridiculously-muscled man in head-to-toe armor seemed like he wanted to crush Brom too, but both he and Arsinoe waited. A tall Mentis walked forward between the trees, and the other two seemed to be waiting for him. The Mentis had a grotesquely elongated face, huge ears, and eyes that looked like they were dripping down his face. He held his hand up, and the mere gesture seemed to hold the others at bay.

He looked like he might have once been five feet tall but had been stretched by a machine to a towering seven-foot height. Everything about him was longer and thinner than it should be, from his head to his hands to his dangling ear lobes. His eyes were sea green from lid to lid, without any pupils, any whites. The man's snowy white robes seemed to give off light in the dim forest, and he tapped his overly long fingertips against his palm in an understated clap.

"Brilliant," he said, like everything was falling into place exactly as he had envisioned. "Simply brilliant."

The foreboding in Brom's stomach twisted. But the Soul told him to stay, so Brom remained still.

"You have a knack for breaking the rules," the white-robed man said. "You've succeeded in making even Arsinoe jealous, and he is a legendary rule-breaker."

"I'm not jealous," Arsinoe growled. "I've just changed my mind about who I want to keep. I don't want the little bitch anymore. I want this one."

The white-robed man *tsk*'ed reprovingly. "Alas, I have an aversion to wasting talent. He would be an amazing addition to our flock."

"We have to kill him," the armored man said.

"My, my... You truly have done the miraculous today, young Brom. You have Arsinoe and Wulfric agreeing with each other," the white-robed man said. "Do you know who I am?"

"Olivaard," Brom said. Again, the name fell from his lips without him actually knowing it. He hoped his missing memories would soon return. He felt in his gut that he knew much more about these monsters than he had recalled so far. "You were all part of The Four," he said hoarsely.

Olivaard raised his eyebrows, amused. "Were?"

"You're one of The Three now," Brom growled. "Linza is dead. I killed her."

The little glade went silent at that.

"And I'm going to do the same to you," Brom promised. "Every single one of you."

Olivaard, stunned by the announcement, shot an uncertain look at his comrades. "You realize your bravado doesn't impress anyone."

"I wonder, how many Soulblocks do you feel inside you right

now?" Brom asked.

Olivaard's white eyebrows came together so fiercely it seemed there were a hundred wrinkles bunched up on his tall, inhuman forehead. Wulfric drew his sword. Arsinoe put his hands together in one giant fist, as though he was about to cast some kind of spell.

A loud clang sounded as another portal opened.

Linza emerged from a ring of black flames, her black robes covering every bit of her except her thin hands and bony chin.

Brom's confidence sagged like a sail that had lost its wind.

She walked silently to stand next to Olivaard.

"Linza," Olivaard said, "I confess to being relieved. The boy gave us a fright. He almost had me convinced. He said he killed you—"

"He shoved a fucking spike through my heart." She turned her cowled head toward Brom. "But he'll pay for it, as will the incompetents who let him into the testing room."

"How...are you still alive?" Brom asked.

"Because I'm Linza, you little bastard," she said. "And you're just a plague rat."

Arsinoe grinned, licking his lips.

"The Soul of the World chooses her champion," Linza rasped. "And if you're the Champion of the Soul, you don't live—or die—like anyone else."

Brom heard his own breaths, coming faster. He couldn't seem to get enough air. The Soul of the World wouldn't let her die? What did that mean?

Did it mean the rest of them couldn't die, either?

This is suicide. It's just me. Against The Four. I don't have a chance.

Brom had been ready to face three of them, win or lose, to dance with the Soul and fight to his last breath, but now...

He glanced over his shoulder, longing to see the portal that would take him back to the academy, back to his Quad, back to his friends.

But there was only dark, scaly Lyantrees all around, and The Four lined up in front of him.

His chest seemed to open like a chasm, filling with despair...

He suddenly realized he had slipped out of the Soul of the

World, that Linza's confidence-cutting magic was viciously at work already. It was the same thing she'd done to him during his Test.

"Nice...try..." he growled, and he pushed himself down into the Soul of the World, plunging beneath the surface of that lake. He left Linza's nasty magic behind like raindrops on the surface. Either he was going to die or he was going to take them all down.

Linza hissed her frustration.

The Four charged.

Wulfric struck first, but Brom had learned a valuable lesson during his battle with Quad Phoenix. Oriana's dusty, little-known theory had been true. An Impetu's natural weakness was an Anima.

He spun, ducking Wulfric's sword by a hair's breadth. He bent so low that his hand dragged the ground, and he grabbed a thick broken branch that seemed to have been dropped there just for him. It was as sharp as a dagger on one side. Brom snapped upright beneath Wulfric's arm and stabbed the stick into the gap under the armpit.

A half-dozen bugs showered onto Brom's hand, and Wulfric stumbled past him at blinding speed, crashing into the trunk of a Lyantree so hard, his helmet caved in. Blood gushed from the mouth slit.

Brom didn't stop to assess Wulfric's damage. The Soul of the World told him to keep moving, never stop moving. He heard music in the trees, coming up from the ground, thrumming from The Four themselves, and he had to dance or die.

"You came to kill me," Brom said. "But I'm going to kill you. Every last one of you. You'll never enslave another student."

"How does he know this?" Olivaard demanded.

Linza came for Brom next with a sucking hollow of despair, and then Arsinoe—a heart-spike of fear. They were raging beasts that wanted to eat him alive, but all they could do was splash the top of the lake.

Brom felt like he wasn't even in his body. The core of him, his very consciousness, *was* the Soul of the World, and everything else—including his real body—were extremities meant to be used. He wasn't his own body any more than he was the grassy ground, the scaly trees, the horrible Four. Their attacks hit Brom's body, but they couldn't reach Brom.

Linza cried out in rage. She leapt at him with bony hands like claws, dancing with the Soul herself, trying to anticipate his movements, but it felt as though Brom watched everything from above, from ten seconds in the future, seeing how the entire dance would go.

Linza's precognition would have kept her a second—even two—ahead of a normal person, but Brom saw more. Linza was suddenly predictable. They all were.

He jumped over her first strike and kneed her in the head. As her head snapped to the side, making her second strike a limp swing of her arm, he rolled over her shoulders and landed right in front of Arsinoe.

The Motus's eyes went wide, realizing too late that his attacks had failed. Brom spun and flung out his heel, pounding into Arsinoe's head. The man's jaw flew off again, and his head cracked in half. Again, there was no blood, just flying wooden doll parts.

Brom didn't let up, and unlike Linza and Wulfric, he felt compelled to put Arsinoe down for good. He didn't know why. No memories came to his aid, but he knew he hated this man more than he hated anything else.

Brom landed in a crouch, spun, and kicked out Arsinoe's knee. The knee folded in half, coming apart as easily as the jaw. A keen wail went up from Arsinoe's jawless face as Brom spun forward, lashing out with fists and feet.

Another kick, two punches, and a jump-kick with both feet to the chest, and Brom literally took the man apart. The disassembled body parts fell across the grassy ground, quivering.

Breathing hard, Brom got to his feet, ready to face Linza and Olivaard. Only a scant few seconds had passed. Wulfric, beyond them, was shaking his head as he pushed himself up on all fours.

"And now it's your turn," Brom growled.

Olivaard, shocked, actually looked poised to run. Linza's mouth hung open.

Brom's third Soulblock ran out.

The music faded. His consciousness popped to the top of the lake. Terror, despair, and reality hit him all at once.

"Gods!" he gasped, and he stumbled backward.

"He's out!" Olivaard crowed.

A spike of pure pain drove into Brom's head, and he crashed to his knees, grasping his ears with his hands.

Linza leapt forward, her claws driving into his neck, slicing through muscle and driving his face into the turf. Brom grunted through clenched teeth. She yanked upward, lifting him off the ground with inhuman strength.

Brom tried not to shout, tried to keep the pain inside, but a gasp escaped his lips.

"Have you ever seen the like?" Olivaard said in awe as Linza slammed Brom into a Lyantree. Wulfric regained his feet, spinning, searching and finally spotting Brom. His crunched helmet made his head look lopsided. He roared and charged.

The fourth Soulblock... Brom had to open his fourth Soulblock. It would cost him his life, but if he could destroy these monsters, it would be worth it. He could save all the other students in the academy. He could save his Quad mates. He could save Vale.

He had to try.

Clenching his fists, he opened his last Soulblock. Magic roared into him, so much that he could barely contain it, magic that even The Four couldn't understand because only the dead knew what it was like to open their fourth Soulblock.

Brom plunged back into the Soul of the World and he saw the future. The images came fast and furious, and he could barely sort them. He stopped, stunned, as they flowed into him.

Arsinoe wouldn't get up for long minutes. Linza would try using her green fire to suck away his magic. Olivaard would hesitate. Despite his fear, his greed overpowered him. He wanted to enslave Brom, not kill him. And Wulfric—

Brom's gut twisted, and he started into motion.

Wulfric's charge had reached Brom while he had hesitated under the deluge of sudden knowing. Brom twisted desperately, but there just wasn't time.

Wulfric drove his sword through Brom's chest. White-hot pain shot through his body, through the lightning storm of magic within him. Suddenly, he couldn't think.

"Wulfric!" Olivaard shouted. "No!"

He heard music, and it seemed to tell him everything was going to be all right. The Soul of the World assured him there was a way through.

He just had to keep moving.

Linza dropped Brom, and he slid down the length of Wulfric's blade to the hilt, coming to rest against the thick man's giant fist.

Brom twitched, trying to free himself, but the strength in his arms had vanished. The most he could do was grapple with the blade, cutting his hands.

Wulfric kicked Brom off the end of his blade. The blade ripped through Brom as he fell off it, and he gaped. He thumped to the ground like a turtle on its back. He tried to get up, but his limbs wouldn't work.

It is okay, the Soul of the World whispered. *It will be okay.*

But Brom's magic leaked out of his body with his life. The lightning storm in his chest quelled, and the assurance of the Soul of the World went with it.

"Nnnn..." he grunted. Blood bubbled out of his mouth. "Nnnooo."

"Dammit!" Olivaard growled. "Did you see what he did? Did you see him spin past Linza? Did you see him destroy Arsinoe?"

"He needs to die!" Wulfric shouted. Blood stained the front of his square helmet and dripped from the neck onto his breastplate.

"Idiot! You're so thick you don't see. No one can sink that deep into the Soul of the World. Not even Linza. He is the one. The one who invaded our Tower!"

Brom's body grew colder. His body was dying, and the Soul had no more suggestions for him. It had gone quiet. All roads had come together into one, and it was a dead end.

Olivaard's elongated face leaned close to Brom as he gasped for breath.

"How did you keep yourself hidden from us?" Olivaard demanded. "How did you do it?"

"He won't tell you," Linza rasped angrily.

Brom coughed, and blood flowed down his chin. Gods! He was dying. He was dying!

This was the vaunted overconfidence of the Anima. He'd truly thought he could fight The Four all at once, all by himself, and win.

"Yes he will..." Olivaard said. Linza and Wulfric gathered behind the tall Mentis, looking down. "Tell me. How did you do it?" he encouraged.

"Fffff..." Brom began. Mentis leaned closer, his tall form practically bent in half.

"Fuck you," Brom spat blood on the side of the man's elongated face, all over those ridiculous earlobes.

Olivaard rose to his full height, seeming not to care about the streaks of blood across his face. Instead, he looked victorious. "Ah..." he said. "You don't know."

"What do you mean he doesn't know?" Linza creaked in her old voice.

"He doesn't remember how he knows us. He doesn't remember how he kept himself hidden from us."

"Kelto's teeth, Olivaard," Wulfric growled. "Speak plainly!"

"His memories were stolen by a Mentis. Most likely the princess. She's mastered mind control." He pursed his lips, marveling. "Truly impressive. I daresay we didn't pay enough attention to Quad Brilliant. Oriana is nearly as talented as this one."

"What?"

"Who would suspect a second-year to have such talent?" Olivaard continued. "She made her Quad mates immune to our surface mind probes. They would have slipped by us."

Brom tried to get up and barely twitched. It couldn't end this way. It couldn't! Oriana, Vale, and Royal were vulnerable. They were lambs living with wolves. He had to warn them.

"Ah," Olivaard said. "He is only now thinking about the consequences of his actions. Rejoice, Brom." He wiped the spit and blood from his face with the sleeve of his robe. "Revel in your little victory; it is the only one you shall have. The rest belongs to us. As do your Quad mates."

"No..." Brom rasped.

"Oh, yes."

Brom tried to grab hold of Olivaard's tunic, but his hand only twitched.

His fourth and final Soulblock leaked out, going nowhere, and the dim forest became dimmer. He felt cold, so cold. He heard the music of the Soul of the World, but he couldn't do anything with it. He simply didn't have the strength to dance any longer.

Olivaard leaned over him, so close. Brom wanted to spit on him again, but he simply didn't have the strength. "We shall visit such horrors upon your Quad mates as you can scarcely imagine," he whispered. "Again and again. And after...I'll wipe their minds and send them into the two kingdoms as ordinary Quadrons." He glanced at the pieces of Arsinoe lying quivering on the grass. "Of course, Arsinoe... Well. I think he deserves a little something for what you put him through. He is going to feast on that feisty little Motus of yours. I think it will be all I can do to restrain him, to stop him from devouring her entirely."

"D-Don't...touch...her," Brom said, and the forest grew darker.

"Oh, he will touch her. He will take everything. Every. Bit. You've made that a certainty," he hissed.

Brom clenched his teeth, but soon he didn't even have the strength for that.

The dark forest faded to black, and Olivaard's evil smile was the last thing he saw.

12

BROM

The funeral procession left the Dome on the western side of the academy, beginning the march that would lead them along the wide main path all the way to the gate. The cart went first, with The Collector himself walking on the left side, as grim as The Ragged Man in his black robes. Behind him came Master Saewyne, Master Jhaleen, and Master Tohn Gelu. Black, red, blue, and white robes flapped in the breeze.

It had been one short day since Brom's death. Physically, Royal had recovered, but the specter of his failure lingered.

He should be happy. He had succeeded. Fendir would have its Quadron. Moreover, Quad Brilliant had made history. They were the only second-year Quad to take the Test of Separation, and they had succeeded marvelously. They'd done as well as any fourth-year Quad ever to take the Test.

And they'd lost Brom.

Royal had prepared himself for the death of a Quad mate; they all had. But he had secretly hoped Quad Brilliant would break that barrier as they'd broken so many others, that they would succeed where all others had failed. He'd hoped they would become the first full Quad to graduate since The Four.

But in the end, Brom had paid the price for their successes. Royal, Oriana, and Vale would be full Quadrons in less than an hour.

And Royal hated himself.

The cart which carried the coffin trundled on. Oriana, Royal, and Vale walked along the right side, opposite the masters. Magic coursed through Royal, and his senses took in everything with supernatural acuity. He heard and smelled the crowd of students lining every foot of the path between here and the gate. The blue of the sky was so rich he could almost taste it. A flock of seagulls gave their plaintive cries as they flew over the Dome.

Oriana walked in front of him in a white dress with silver embroidery at the cuffs, hem, and neck. Her silver-gold hair had been twisted up into an artful mass on the top of her head with one spiraling lock trailing down her back to her slender waist. She wore her crown today, and it shone in the sunlight, a work of art comprised of beautifully interwoven bands of gold set with a large indigo stone at her forehead.

Vale came next. She didn't have fancy clothes, just the uniform provided by the academy for a Motus—a dusky red tunic and breeches with silver piping. She cried freely as she walked, her gaze on her burgundy boots. Her little fists were clenched, and she did not look at any of the other students.

Royal came last.

This ceremony had been performed hundreds of times with hundreds of students. It was nothing new. A ritual. And all it meant to those students standing on the roadside, watching Royal carry his friend to the gate, was fear. Royal remembered that fear, remembered watching the nearly-destroyed Quad Moonlight only a year ago, reminding him that one day he might face this consequence.

They marched the length of the academy, and Royal felt the minute grooves in the cart's wood grain as he touched it. He felt every wisp of breeze across his scrubbed and clean-shaven face. He heard every sob from Vale like it was his sob. He watched every sway in Oriana's hips, every step like it was his step.

Brom had been the best of them, the most talented. It was a mystery to Royal how Brom could have failed while the rest of them had passed. He would have bet on Brom to be the first to emerge.

Royal had fought a greenish replica of himself during his Test, and in the final exchange of blows, he'd barely won. He vaguely remembered turning toward the portal, seeing it open. Then he remembered green fire, an explosion... Then...nothing.

He had been unconscious for the last part, and the haunted look in both Oriana's and Vale's eyes indicated there was a story there, but they'd not told him yet. He'd desperately wanted to find out what they knew, but he hadn't had the chance. Since he'd awoken, there had been formalities for every moment between then and now. They had put Brom's body in a coffin. The wagon would take it to the gate, and then to Brom's parents in Kyn.

They reached the gate, and the wagon paused just before the great portcullis, the wagoner turning in his bench above two hitched horses, waiting. The Collector and the other masters peeled off to the left, standing to face the long assemblage behind him. Oriana went to the right and turned, her impassive expression fixed on the coffin.

The Collector nodded.

The wagoner turned forward, flicked his reins, and the horses began to move. Everything about this felt so horribly wrong, and Royal wanted to charge after the wagon and snatch the coffin back, tell them they couldn't have it. He would take Brom home himself. He would run all the way to Kyn to deliver the coffin, to deliver the news to his friend's parents.

But he couldn't. If he left the academy now, his Soulblocks would collapse, and he'd become a *normal.* His magic would be stripped from him because he hadn't completed the final ceremony where The Four themselves would give their blessing and strengthen his Soulblocks so he could use them outside these walls. Royal, Oriana, and Vale were actually going to meet The Four.

And that would be the official end of Quad Brilliant.

In a few short hours, Royal, Oriana, and Vale would be

Quadrons. They'd likely never see each other again, save at opposite ends of a battlefield. They would be more powerful than anyone else, save other Quadrons and The Four themselves.

Royal watched the wagon as it got smaller and smaller.

"This way," The Collector said, gesturing down the road. Royal paused one last, long moment, then turned and followed the line of masters. The students lining the road had already started back to the Dome and they slowly filed inside.

Royal, Oriana, and Vale followed the masters at the back of the procession until every single student in the academy had entered the Dome.

The Collector led them up the shallow steps and through one of the archways, a different one than they'd entered for their Test. He took them to a room with a round table and three chairs.

"Wait here," he said, then closed the door.

The room was circular, unlike their testing room, and everything within was made of white marble. The table, the walls, the floor and ceiling. Even the chairs were marble, and they looked like they had been carved directly from the floor, more sculpture than furniture. There were no adornments on the walls, no windows, and only one thick wooden door—the one through which they'd entered.

Oriana lowered herself onto one of the hard chairs, crossed her legs, and put her hands on her knees like she was posing for a portrait. Vale stood, distracted, behind a second marble chair, gripping its back with her small hands.

Royal looked from Oriana to Vale, then back. Neither of them would meet his gaze.

"What happened?" he finally asked.

Vale looked up with red-rimmed eyes. She began crying again and looked away.

"Brom died," Oriana said matter-of-factly.

"That part I know," Royal growled. "How?"

"Does it matter?" she asked.

"It matters to me."

"What was promised has been delivered. We came to the Champions Academy to be Quadrons. We did. They said one of us would die before it was over. One of us did." Her voice dropped to a near-silent whisper, and only because of his Impetu-enhanced ears did he hear her repeat, "What was promised has been delivered..."

"How did he die?" Royal repeated.

She shook her head.

"I want to know."

"Be glad, Royal. Cherish your ignorance. It is a gift."

Vale turned her back to the chair and slid down the length of it to the floor, vanishing from sight, and sobbed.

"Tell me," he insisted.

Oriana's gaze became unfocused, looking past him like she didn't see him, and her chin lifted. He clenched his fist. He'd never wanted to throttle Oriana more than he did at this moment. Arrogant Keltovari!

"HOW!" he yelled so loudly it hurt his own ears. Oriana actually startled. Vale leapt to her feet, her eyes wide and her tears forgotten.

Oriana glared at him, her eyes wild for the first time since he'd known her. Her silver eyebrows crouched angrily. And, by Fendra, he saw tears there.

"We betrayed him," she stated.

The rage drained from Royal, and he felt cold, like his blood was draining away too. His fists fell to his sides, nerveless. "You didn't..."

"We did," she said, "what was necessary. The Test became progressively harder for each of us when one succeeded. Brom was the first to emerge. He... It is possible he saved my life. I'd spent my Soulblocks. I'd escaped my mirror, but I was being drawn back in, and he stopped it. And you barely emerged with your life. Vale was the last. Once all three of us emerged, her Test became impossible. She was doomed."

Royal looked at Vale, and she looked back at him through welling tears. In her gaze, he saw regret and terrible sorrow. He saw self-loathing.

"He saved Vale," Royal whispered.

"He took her place, pushed her out of her Test," Oriana said.

"Her Test became his, and it killed him."

"It was going to be me," Vale whispered. "It was going to be me."

Confused, Royal said, "Then how did you betray him?"

"We didn't," Vale said. "There was nothing we could do for him."

"He wants to know the truth, then let him hear the truth," Oriana said, and her haughty sneer returned. "Royal wants to be a leader of the people. Let him bear the burden of knowledge."

"What are you talking about?" Royal said.

"We could have thrown our lot in with him, Fendiran," she said. "He asked us for help. He reached out to us. There was a brief moment we could have followed him through that portal."

"Why didn't you?" he growled.

"Because we would have died. We could choose to become Quadrons or die together with Brom. We chose to become Quadrons."

"What?" Royal roared.

"You bitch," Vale growled.

Oriana leveled her glare on Vale. "You could have stayed with him, Vale. You could have run back to him. You didn't. You didn't believe he was right, just as I didn't."

"What are you talking about?" Royal demanded.

She turned her gaze back to him. "Brom saw something. His Anima wisdom showed him something none of the rest of us could see. I think if we'd followed him into his Test, the three of us might have had some kind of chance. If Vale and I had stepped through that portal, Brom felt there was a chance we'd have all emerged alive."

"Why didn't you do it!" Royal roared.

Her indigo gaze pierced him like fishhooks. "Because there were two seconds to decide. Because it was impossible. From what I could see, we would only have died, but Brom..." She shook her head. "My Soulblocks were spent. Vale's were spent. We might have elevated his Soulblocks...a little," she said. "Who can say if it would have been enough? I calculated we could not give him enough to make a difference."

"You calculated?" Royal growled.

"You wanted the truth," Oriana said. "That is the truth. Now bear its bitter sting."

"You calculated!" he roared. He lunged at her so fast she barely had time to flinch. He clenched her neck in his hand and lifted her up, slammed her against the wall.

Her whole body tensed, but she didn't struggle.

"Royal!" Vale screamed. "Stop it!"

But this was his moment. He could kill her now. His people would applaud him. One quick twist and the heir to the Keltovari throne would die. She'd never have time to mind stab him before he snapped her neck.

He should do it for all the crimes her people had committed against Fendir, but most of all he should kill her for her betrayal of Brom. *She had calculated his death!*

She twisted her head to the side so she could breathe. "Kill me," she rasped. "Do it. But know that you damned Brom every bit as much as I. I simply have the courage...to face it."

"*I* damned him?" he roared incredulously. "I was unconscious!"

"Exactly," she choked.

The fire left Royal's breast. He held onto her a moment longer, but there was suddenly no strength in his arm. He dropped her, and she collapsed to the floor, coughing vigorously. He backed away.

"You..." she coughed. "If we'd had you, I would have taken that risk. Our chances would have doubled. *That* I would have tried."

"Liar!"

"No." She slapped a hand against the ground and pushed herself to her knees. Her shimmering white dress was scuffed, wrinkled. She rose on shaky legs. "I spent one precious moment hoping you'd rise in time. I even looked for you, but you were unconscious. And that was the end of it."

"Because you calculated..." He spat.

"Someone had to," she said.

"I hate you..." he whispered. "I hate you and everything you stand for."

"Well," she said icily, "I shall endeavor to live with the disappointment." She rubbed the angry red marks on her throat, left by his hand. "You got what you came for. We all did. In a few short moments, we'll be Quadrons. Take your prize and be grateful, Fendiran. Take your righteousness and return to Fendir. But stop pretending that Brom's life meant more to you than becoming a Quadron, because it didn't." She turned her fiery gaze on Vale. "And don't you pretend, either, urchin."

"If I had a knife—" Vale began.

"You'd fling your steel and your emotions around with reckless abandon," Oriana interrupted. "We know. But you wouldn't have traded places with Brom. I was there. You had a chance and you didn't. That is the truth. It's true for all of us and it always was."

"I hate you!" Vale screamed, clenching her little fists.

"And so here we are," Oriana said. "Precisely where we began. Let Quad Brilliant die here. It has served its purpose."

She paused a long moment, as though waiting for Royal or Vale to say anything else. When they didn't, her eyes narrowed to slits. "Now..." she said in her arrogant princess voice. "If either of you try to touch me again, I will burn your minds out."

Royal clenched his fists. He almost went for her but he held his rage in check long enough for his reason to save him. If he attacked her, he might have the chance to kill her, but this time she would be ready. She'd definitely kill him. And then he'd never be able to use his new powers to help his people.

"I will see you on the battlefield," he growled.

"No," she said through her teeth. "I have soldiers who do that sort of thing for me."

"I don't want to see either of you ever again," Vale swore. "The best of this fucking Quad was Brom."

"Indeed," Oriana agreed coldly, and then she ignored both of them and stared at the wall.

Vale looked as if she might leap on Oriana like a feral cat and finish the job Royal had started, but she stayed where she was, red in the face, fists clenched.

They'd all recovered enough to have at least some magic to use, and Oriana didn't make idle threats. That was the last time Royal or

Vale would ever put their hands on the Keltovari princess.

The door opened. As a group, they turned.

The Collector entered, sliding his hands into the dagged sleeves of his black robe. There was a smile on the mouth that peeked out from underneath his cowl as he surveyed the tense scene. He waited a long moment, watching them, as if he was too polite to interrupt.

"Well," he said, "if you aren't going to kill each other, then let us begin the ceremony. Shall we?" He gave the barest of nods toward the open door. "Today, your dreams come true."

Oriana strode out without a word. Vale gave one rough swipe across her tear-stained cheeks with her sleeve, then followed.

Royal wanted to destroy something. He wanted to hurt someone. He'd longed for this moment for as long as he could remember, but now that it was here, all he felt was frustration and anger. All he tasted was bitter bile.

He'd come here to be stronger, to gain power to protect his people, to start a new life where he could fight the Keltovari. But it all seemed hollow now.

Oriana's words burned inside him because she was right. And he hated it. Royal had failed. He was the Impetu. The protector. He was supposed to be the last man standing, not the first man down. If he'd been the protector he thought himself to be, he would have been on his feet at that final moment. He would have persevered until he could come to the aid of his Quad mates. And had he been there when Brom made his heroic choice, Royal would have stood with him. He'd have made the difference. He could have given Vale the spine she lacked. He could have given Oriana the correct numbers to complete her "calculations." He could have brought them all to Brom's aid, and they would have prevailed.

Or if they had died, at least they'd have died as Quad Brilliant.

"Come," The Collector said in a soft voice, breaking Royal's reverie. "It is time for you to receive what you deserve."

EPILOGUE
BROM
ONE YEAR LATER

The kiss was a dream. It had to be, because what it told him was a lie.

Vale's lips pressed against his lips. Then she moved further back, her cheek sliding against his, and she whispered in his ear.

"I love you..."

Except Vale had never told him that. She didn't believe in love.

Still, he drank in the sight of her: her liquid brown eyes, her tumbling hair, her mischievous smile. He wished it could be real. He wanted to stay in this moment forever, and he almost didn't care if it was a lie—

Vale's eyes widened and her hair pulled tight, yanking her head back. She flew away from Brom into the arms of a tall thin man in white robes. Olivaard!

The Mentis's elongated face looked like it had been melted down to his chest. He drew a knife and held it to Vale's throat.

"He is going to feast on that feisty little Motus of yours...."

"Vale!"

"You've made that a certainty."

Brom reached for her, but the dream popped like a soap bubble. Darkness rushed in, surrounding him so absolutely he thought he'd gone blind. His hands thumped against hard wood, bending at the wrists. His arms fell weakly to his sides, and he sucked in a cold, stale breath. The air smelled of wet earth.

Above him, there was a muffled digging sound.

scratch scrape, scratch scrape, scratch scrape

Disoriented, he felt around. His numb fingers groped in the blackness, hitting walls on all sides. Wood beneath him. Wood above. Wood below. Panic blossomed in his chest. Gods, he was in a coffin!

I failed the Test. I'm dead. I died at the hands of The Four, and now Vale is at their mercy. Brom's entire Quad was in danger.

Above him, the rhythmic digging continued.

scratch scrape, scratch scrape, scratch scrape

His awareness expanded excruciatingly. It was as though he were made of ice, and hot water had been poured over him. His mind twisted, cracked, and popped as memory after memory returned. His muscles seized. His bones seemed about to snap.

He moaned, clenching his fists in pain.

scratch scrape, scratch...

The rhythmic digging stopped. Whatever was up there had heard him moan.

The digging began faster, frantic, like a badger trying to reach its prey.

scrapescrapescrapescrape!

Brom's heart beat faster.

scrapescrapescrapescrape THUMP...

The noise boomed on the coffin lid. There was a pause, then claws tore into the wood, rending and cracking. A single claw broke through, creating a hole. Green fire lit the claw, and Brom saw the sea-green skin of the hand. Brom had only seen that color of skin once before—during his Test of Separation. This wasn't a friend coming to dig him out. It was Linza, the Anima of The Four, still wearing that horrible disguise.

He twisted away, and his elbow hit something hard and metal.

He groped with it and held it up against the penetrating light. It was a wide-bladed dagger with a wicked hook at the end, a knife-fighter's weapon. He touched the razor-sharp blade. This was his ceremonial weapon for the afterlife.

He grabbed the cold bone handle and yanked the sheath off. The green fire from the claw lit up the confining space. He *was* in a coffin. They had buried him.

The dead in the kingdom of Keltovar were given three things for their harrowing journey to the afterlife: a blanket to keep them warm, a pomegranate to consume—one seed for each day of the journey—and a weapon to fight the Ragged Man, the guardian of the wastelands, the last challenge that stood between a soul and Kelto's promised paradise. The Ragged Man was said to have no face and was wrapped head-to-toe in tattered, multi-colored rags, each torn from the clothing of his victims.

A wealthy man might be buried with the finest sword, the poor sometimes with no more than a sharpened stick. Brom's parents, gods bless them, had given him a fine weapon, had sharpened and oiled it.

Everyone knew about the Ragged Man, knew about the wastelands, but Brom wasn't dead. Not yet, anyway.

The frantic claw broke through again, making a second hole. Now a thumb and a finger thrust in. They were the same sea-green color, gnarled and incredibly strong-looking. They pinched the stubborn shard of wood and ripped it away.

Moonlight spilled into the coffin, silver-blue and ghostly. Fendra's moonlight. Now Brom could see everything—the withered knot of the pomegranate and the half-shredded blanket. The claw thrust back in to the elbow, slicing about, blind. Brom shrank away, just out of reach. His panicked mind screamed at him to stab the thing.

But he waited.

A frustrated growl came from above as the claw groped again. Linza grunted, breathing hard. She withdrew and began tearing at the lid, widening the hole, ripping great chunks away.

Heart hammering, muscles tense, Brom gripped the smooth bone hilt of the dagger.

This time a greenish, human-shaped head thrust through, looking, searching.

Now!

Brom stabbed the disguised Linza in the neck. She howled like a beast, vanishing back through the hole.

He hastily wiped the blood from his eyes. This wasn't finished. She was still alive. Or if he'd killed her, she could come back to life. She'd done it before. He'd seen it. And Brom was trapped in a coffin with nowhere to go. He had to get into the open air quickly.

With a roar, he pushed up through the jagged hole. Splintered wood tore at his tunic, stabbed into his back.

Hands scrabbling, legs pushing, he forced himself into the moonlit hole in the ground. The fresh air was a blessed wonder, smelling of warm night and summer leaves. He took great big gulps of it. A trail of black-looking blood zig-zagged up the dirt slope to the ground above. She had retreated.

Brom knew he couldn't fight down here on this low ground, trapped in a hole. He had to get up there—

Linza appeared at the lip of the hole, one slick claw pressed to her neck, except she looked nothing like Linza, nor like Brom. A dark stain ran down the front of her tunic. Every bit of her visible flesh—face, neck, forearms, and hands—was that sea-green color. Her face was maniacal, with a mouth that was too wide, and stretched eyes slanting upward, nearly touching in the middle and at the edge by her pointed ears. Her gritted teeth were long and pointed.

"Show yourself!" Brom growled, gripping the dagger. "Show the real you!"

This thing, whatever it was, looked like a monster impersonating a man, not Linza impersonating Brom. It was dressed like a normal person in a short-sleeved tunic with drawstring neck, breeches tucked into boots, and a brown workman's belt around its waist.

"This is the new face of your world," the creature said, impossibly forming words with a forked tongue the size of a snake, which licked out through that overly-wide mouth and past those pointed teeth.

With a yowl of hatred, the creature threw itself into the hole, claws first.

Instinctively, Brom reached for his magic, tried to open one of his Soulblocks....

But no lightning crackled through him. No Soulblock opened. In fact, his Soulblocks were just...gone. In their place was something hard and tiny, like the shriveled pit of a Fendiran peach, incapable of holding anything.

The creature slammed into him, slicing with its ragged fingernails and biting for Brom's neck. Brom shouted, half in pain, half in surprise at his startling realization: he had no magic.

He was a *normal.* He was just like everyone else now, and it paralyzed him for one breathless moment. Claws dug into his back. Teeth came ever closer to his neck.

And then he fought. He fought like a man who'd lost everything but his life. This dirty hole was the last patch of earth he'd ever see if he didn't win. And worse than his own death, The Four would torture his friends. Those monsters might have already done it while Brom lay here. How many hours had he lain in this grave? Had it been days?

He lashed out with his elbows. He stabbed and slashed with the knife, again and again. He shouted, his voice rising to a desperate shriek.

The claws weakened, then stopped. Brom's assailant fell to the broken lid of the coffin.

Gasping for breath, Brom blinked down at the maniacal creature who was dying of a dozen puncture wounds. Brom felt his own wounds—burning stripes across his arms and back—but he was still standing, and the creature was down.

"Damn..." the creature gasped, tongue slithering out, its words impossibly articulate through those wide lips and pointed teeth. "Damn it..."

And then the creature died. Its chest stopped rising as its last breath leaked out. Its eyes turned glassy.

Brom waited for the illusion to fade, for it to reveal Linza beneath the disguise. But nothing changed. The monster remained the monster.

But if it wasn't Linza…what was it? Why was this creature attacking him, and who had sent it?

Confused, in pain, scared, Brom wanted to run away from this blood-spattered hole, but he held himself still. He pushed down his terror and focused, moving slowly. Common motions brought calm, so he moved like this was a normal situation. He wiped his dagger on the dead creature's tunic, stuck it in his own belt, then he knelt and searched the thing's clothing for anything that might give him clues as to who, or what, it was.

The creature carried no money or food or documents. The only thing it possessed was a shiny tuning fork stuck in its thick belt. Brom took it.

He stared for a long time at that inhuman face with its needle teeth and elongated eyes, no less frightening in death than it had been in life.

He steeled himself, then knelt on the ground where the thing had ripped a hole into the coffin. He groped around, grabbed the sheath for his dagger and, attaching it to his belt, sheathing the dagger properly.

He scrambled out of the hole and looked around.

He was in the graveyard in his home village of Kyn. Tall and small headstones surrounded him. There was the twisted willow tree at the northeast corner, right next to the white-washed fence. This was the very place he'd faced Linza during the Test of Separation. But he'd bested her. He'd charged back through the portal, then jumped through Vale's portal to a completely different place—a Lyantree forest where he had fought The Four. Where he fought the gods-be-damned Four...

And they killed me, he thought. *I died, but now I'm alive again....*

How was that possible? He remembered dying, remembered the reassuring whispers of the Soul of the World as everything went black in that Lyantree forest.

A chill ran up his back. The Lyantrees... Is that why he was still alive?

Legends told that those who died near Lyantrees sometimes rose from their graves, roots wrapped around necks and arms, squeezing, moving the bodies like puppets. But the spooky bedtime stories of Lyancorpses all agreed that they didn't have the wits of a man. Lethargic and aimless, they wandered about, attacking whomever they found. They killed and killed until they were finally chopped into pieces.

Brom reflexively patted himself, seeking roots wrapped around his arms or ankles or waist, but there was nothing. He wasn't a Lyancorpse.

He stumbled away from the grave, memory after memory flashing through his mind: The Four fighting him. Brom fighting back, opening his fourth Soulblock, tearing Arsinoe apart, wounding Wulfric, even evading Linza. He remembered almost winning...until Wulfric stabbed him through the chest.

He felt his chest, but there was no wound, nothing save the slashes the green-skinned creature had given him.

It made no sense, but he was alive. And if he was alive, he had to save his friends. He remembered the vile promises of The Four. What they were going to do to Vale, to Oriana, to Royal...

I have to get to them, he thought. *I have to warn them.*

Brom staggered out of the graveyard. He circled the outskirts of the town and went to his house. For a moment, he just stared at the large stone cottage next to the Kyn River. The big water wheel turned lazily in the stream next to the maple tree Brom had climbed as a child. The wounds on his arms and back burned. He needed help first, before the long journey back to the Champions Academy. He needed food, medicine, bandages for his cuts.

He ran down the trail toward his house, stomped onto the porch, up to the door, and grabbed the handle...

And he stopped.

No. What was he thinking?

The desperate child within him wanted to burst inside his house and fall into his parents' arms, let them take care of him like they used to. But he wasn't a ten-year-old boy anymore, running to his mother because he'd skinned a knee. A monster had just dug him out of his own grave.

He pulled his hand back from the handle like it was hot, leaving a bloody smear. What if that monster wasn't the only one? What if there were more? He was part of a different world now, a student at the Champions Academy. He'd endured things *normals* couldn't even understand, let alone handle. That creature, that spawn of some Quadron's vile imagination, had come to destroy him. This wasn't a childhood injury or a fear of the dark. This was real, horrific magic. His parents couldn't protect him, not even for an instant, and if he opened that door, he was putting them at risk.

He retreated, stumbling backward off the porch just as he heard footsteps inside the house. Lamplight flickered to life in the windows, warming them with an orange glow.

Father opened the door and looked in shock at the droplets of blood on the porch. He hastily searched the dark with stern fear on his face. But Brom had already hidden himself behind the maple tree. Father quickly shut the door and threw the bolt. Brom swallowed in relief.

Quietly, he broke from the maple tree's shadow and jogged toward the road that ran close to the house. As he crested the hill at the edge of town, he turned and looked back at the little village of Kyn, nestled peacefully beneath the silver-blue moonlight of Fendra.

The last time Brom had left his hometown, he hadn't looked back. He had practically skipped away, with dreams of becoming a Quadron filling his head.

A part of him longed to reach back to that time, to tell his younger self just how precious those innocent moments were. To be able to dream and to believe those dreams would come true just as he'd imagined them. He wanted to tell his younger self to enjoy the carefree days of climbing trees and swimming in the river, of kissing Myan the miller's daughter in the graveyard and thinking there was nothing more horrible in the world than missing a chance to become a Kyn guardsman.

Now he lived in a world of powerful magic and horrible betrayal. Brom's life had become a nightmare, and he couldn't inflict that on the innocent villagers of Kyn.

No. There was only one place he belonged now: the Champions Academy. He had to reawaken his magic, to reunite with his Quad. The only question was, would he be in time?

Looking over his shoulder, Brom gave one last glance at his

childhood, then banished it. He turned and started up the dark road, just like he'd done a lifetime ago, back when he thought he was walking toward his dreams and not into a deadly trap.

I'm coming for you, he thought silently to The Four. *You're liars and murderers, and I'm going to bring you to justice or I'm going to die trying.*

Pawns of Magic

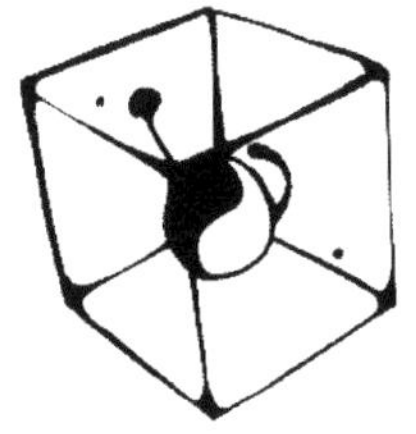

A Tower of the Four
Short Story

Tarvic was dead.

He seethed as he stood at the edge of the graveyard. It was all wrong. He'd had a life. He had been destined to be a hero, a magical Quadron who helped people. But now he was this.

His Quad, the three lifelong friends who'd helped him learn his magic even as he'd helped them learn theirs, stood behind him, and the forest draped them all in darkness. That was how they had to live now. They couldn't let the living see their hideous true forms, so they skulked at the edge of towns like this. If the living saw, they'd flee screaming. And then, inevitably, more living would return with torches, cudgels, swords and knives. And then Tarvic's Quad would have to run again.

The injustice of it seared through his soul like a white hot flame. There was one thing—only one—that drove him forward and made this half-existence tolerable: he would find a way out of this horrible fate. He was going to get his life back, become the hero he was meant to be.

That was all that mattered.

He didn't know why he was standing in front of a graveyard outside the village of Kyn. He didn't remember coming here. No doubt they'd been chased out of the last village because of his Quad mate Moll's insanity. Or because of Lira's.

His Quad mates were insane now. It shattered the mind, dying and returning as the undead. Tarvic feared that he, too, was insane and simply didn't know it. He…forgot things, like how he got here. He didn't even know how much time had passed since they'd died. He just remembered place after place, forest after forest, town after town. There was nowhere for the dead to go in a land of the living, so they just kept running. And they always would, forever….

He squeezed his eyes shut and banished the thought. The rage seared through him.

He glared back at his Quad mates. Their bodies were rotting, held upright and bound together by the magical roots of the

Lyantrees. His Quad was what the living called Lyancorpses, dead bodies brought back to life by the magic of the Hallowed Woods.

He had heard stories of Lyancorpses when he'd been alive. Everyone had. Lyancorpses were supposed to be mindless killers, with no memory of their previous lives.

But Tarvic and his Quad mates weren't mindless. Tarvic knew exactly who he'd been. So did his other Quad mates, except for maybe Lira. Lira's death had been the worst of all. Even Tarvic felt sorry for Lira.

And Lyancorpses had no inherent desire to kill; they were guided by the ghosts of the people they'd once been. Tarvic's ghost—and the ghosts of his Quad mates—hovered alongside their Lyancorpses, and their ghosts retained their memories.

The stories didn't mention the ghosts because the living couldn't see them. At the very first village north of the Hallowed Woods, Tarvic had tried talking to a group of villagers. He'd pleaded with them for help, but the villagers hadn't heard his ghost, hadn't seen it. Apparently all they could see was Tarvic's horrifying, rotting body entwined in roots, shuffling toward them, moaning.

I was going to be a hero, Tarvic thought. *I was going to save people.*

During their lives, Tarvic and his Quad mates had done the miraculous. They'd bonded and learned magic outside the famous Champions Academy. That was supposed to be impossible, but they'd done it.

They took from each other, gave to each other and each chose their path to magic: mental, emotional, physical or spiritual. Mentis, Motus, Impetu or Anima. Doing this outside the academy, they'd crossed a threshold no one else had, save The Four themselves. The Four, centuries-old demigods who had founded the Champions Academy.

The Four, who had discovered Tarvic's Quad and killed them, turned them into Lyancorpses.

The rage burned through Tarvic's ghostly body.

"Ooooh." Moll's ghostly form—as striking and voluptuous as she'd been in life—sauntered up to Tarvic, walking on air. "Is this a new town?"

Her Lyancorpse shuffled after her ghost in a horrible parody, hips swinging jerkily. A clump of greasy hair fell from her corpse's scalp, slapping onto the forest floor. Her white ribs were visible where a villager at the last town had stabbed her with a pitchfork, laying open her pallid flesh. Moll lost pieces wherever she went.

In life, she had been their Motus, a magic user capable of manipulating the emotions and desires of others, and she'd been a voracious flirt. Now, in death, she insisted on flirting with the living. That, of course, sent them screaming and running away. To them she was a nightmare, but she refused to see that. To Moll, she was just as desirable as she'd ever been. That was *her* insanity.

"I think I'll take a lover at this town," she whispered conspiratorially to Tarvic.

He clenched his teeth and tried to ignore her.

"I am oh-kay. I am aaaaaaallll-right," Lira sang in a bright voice. She smiled all the time now, as though being a Lyancorpse was a life of bliss. And every now and then she would sing about her happiness. It was always the same two sentences: *I am okay. I am all right.*

If Moll's mind was a broken branch, Lira's had snapped into a thousand little twigs. She acted truly happy when there was nothing to be happy about.

All that remained of Lira's corpse was her head. It was stuck on the top of a slender cluster of roots connecting it to mismatched root shoulders. Root arms twisted out from the shoulders, thick and powerful, though the left arm was longer than the right. The roots bound together in a thick chest, giving the barest indication of breasts, sloping down to a thin waist and wide hips. Three long and gnarled root legs sprouted from those hips, moving her like some unlikely three-legged animal.

Inexplicably, Lira's head wasn't rotting like Moll's or Tarvic's bodies. In the first week, her head had deteriorated just like everyone else's, but then she'd begun singing her silly phrase. That was when her decomposition stopped. In fact, her skin had become pink and flush with life. And Lira was also the only one who could actually speak through her corpse's mouth.

At first, Tarvic had been excited about that development. He could only get his corpse to moan. He'd wanted to use Lira to try to communicate with the living, get someone to help them, but unfortunately she wouldn't say anything except—

"I am oh-kay. I am aaaaaaallll-right," Lira sang again. Her ghostly head floated forward, white mist trailing away from her neck, until it hovered right next to her physical head. She was the only one of them who looked the same in her ghostly form as she did in her physical form.

"Where are the people?" Moll asked brightly.

"It's a graveyard," Tarvic said. "It's midnight. There are no people."

"Oh," Moll said, disappointed, then she turned her smoldering gaze on Tarvic. "Well, I suppose you and I could find a way to spend the time, handsome." She leaned close, her ghostly lips nuzzling his ghostly ear as her Lyancorpse leaned awkwardly into his.

He shrugged her off, and his Lyancorpse made a stiff and jerky swat at hers.

"Stop pretending," he said. "Stop living in a dream. We have a real problem, and we have to find a real way to solve it."

Moll's bedroom eyes flickered, like she was seeing a flash of sunlight through split curtains. She blinked, and then tears formed in her ghostly eyes, streaked down her cheeks. "I don't want to be dead, Tarvic," she said helplessly. "I… I want—"

"I know," he said. "We all do."

He loved her. He loved them all, but he could barely keep his own sanity; he didn't have enough strength to take care of her, too. If he indulged Moll even for a second, he'd lose himself. He was sure of it. She just had to hold herself together until he figured this out.

"I am oh-kay. I am aaaaaaallll-right," Lira said.

Roven, the fourth member of their Quad, emerged from the

shadows. "Someone is coming," she said. Her ghost form pointed at a lone figure entering the graveyard, running hunched over like he was afraid someone would see him.

Roven's small ghost drew up alongside Tarvic as they watched the man together. Her huge Lyancorpse shuffled forward as well, looming over Tarvic's. In life, Roven had been small and slight of build, but her Lyancorpse was taller and bulkier than Tarvic's. Her little body looked like it had been crucified on a human-shaped thatch of roots, covered with leaves and dirt. Her actual feet didn't touch the ground anymore, only the roots that had subsumed them. And while her body showed signs of decay, it wasn't nearly as far along as Tarvic's or Moll's.

But Roven's ghost form was much worse off than either Moll's or Tarvic's. She looked like she'd been cracked into shards like a shattered mirror, all of her pieces hovering close enough together that her face and body looked nearly the same as they had in life. Nearly.

Roven was Tarvic's only blessed respite from the insanity of his other Quad mates. He couldn't look to Moll or Lira for help, but Roven seemed to understand their plight. The only downside was that she seemed frightened all the time.

"Moll, take Lira further back into the woods so no one can hear her," Tarvic said.

"Did you ever think," Moll said in a sultry tone. "That maybe this newcomer would like a kiss—"

"Moll!" Tarvic whispered.

Moll looked downcast, then led Lira into the woods.

Tarvic turned back to look at the man who'd arrived. He moved with purpose through the headstones.

"His skin looks…green," Tarvic said. "Do you see that?"

"Yes," Roven said.

The man also had a strange mouth and eyes. They each looked…elongated.

The green-skinned man moved to a small headstone, dropped to his knees and clawed at the dirt with his bare hands.

"What is he doing?" Tarvic asked Roven.

She had been their Mentis—able to work magic of the mind—and she was the only one of them who'd retained a sliver of her magic in this undead form. Moll could no longer change people's emotions. Lira couldn't look into another's soul. And while Tarvic's corpse had the strength of a Lyancorpse, he couldn't use any of his physical Impetu magic. Roven's power was inconsistent—and it wasn't always accurate—but sometimes she could read minds.

"I'm…trying…" she whispered in a small voice. Roven had become timid since her death. Every time something startled her, a new crack appeared in her ghostly form. Tarvic worried that, at some point, this undead life would be too much for her, and her ghost form would shatter and blow away altogether.

Dirt flew as the green-skinned man dug like an animal, shoulders bunching, arms flinging earthy clumps.

Roven took a swift breath, and a crack split from her hairline all the way to the bridge of her nose.

"It's okay," Tarvic whispered quickly. He put ghostly hands on her ghostly cheeks. "You're okay."

Roven shook in fear. Another crack started at the edge of her left cheek, but Tarvic smoothed it with a finger, and the crack stopped. "I'll take care of you. I'll take care of us all. I promise."

"He's not human," she said.

Tarvic craned his neck to look back at the man, but he'd dug so deeply that the hole now obscured him. "Not human? What is he?"

"I don't know. Tarvic, I don't know!"

"It's okay," he soothed.

"We should go," she said. "We should leave."

But Tarvic wasn't going anywhere. He wasn't going to let Roven's fear infect him. He didn't know what was happening here, but he felt it was important.

"You go back and help Moll," Tarvic said. "I need to see what happens."

Roven shook her head. "N-No. I'm going to stay with you. I'm going to help." The new crack on her cheek closed, leaving whole ghostly flesh.

Tarvic smiled. That sounded like the Roven he'd known when they were alive.

Dirt continued to fly up and out of the hole. Suddenly, the digging paused, then began again frantically.

"He..." Roven said shakily. "He wants to kill whoever is in there. That's what he's thinking. That's all he's thinking."

"Someone is alive in the coffin?"

"There wasn't..." she stammered. "I mean... Yes. Someone is alive."

"They were buried alive?"

"Yes... No... I don't know, Tarvic."

"Did the person in that grave come back to life?" he demanded, and an idea began to form in his mind.

"It's hard to read him."

"Him?"

"Yes. I... I think he's a Quadron."

"A Quadron..." Tarvic murmured excitedly. "Come back from the dead."

Hope bloomed in his mind. Sweet, golden hope. If that grave contained a Quadron who had overcome death, it could be the answer. If one Quadron could do it, they all could. Unless...

"Is he a Lyancorpse?" Tarvic asked quickly. If the Quadron was just another Lyancorpse, he wouldn't be able to help them.

"I don't know, Tarvic," Roven said, her voice thin and strained. "I don't know. I hear...voices in his head. But they're not voices. Let's... Let's just leave."

"Roven..." He tried to push down his frustration. His Lyancorpse ground its teeth. "Tell me what you hear," he growled.

"It's like the hearts of two worlds beating, like...they're talking to each other, but I don't understand the language."

There was a sound of cracking wood. The inhuman creature had reached the coffin, was tearing his way inside.

The creature suddenly howled in pain, and he leapt back out of the hole, holding his neck. Blood trickled through his fingers. He turned, snarling, then leapt back into the hole with a vengeance. Shouting, growling and scuffling rose from the hole. Then…silence.

A new man emerged, and he didn't have green skin. He was a young man, maybe Tarvic's own age. He was smaller than Tarvic with short, wavy black hair. His workman's clothes were dirt-smeared and tattered. He hunched over, obviously pained by the wounds the creature had inflicted, but his intense gaze swept about the graveyard like he was looking for someone.

Tarvic put a hand on Roven's ghostly arm, and they both held completely still. The living couldn't see the ghosts, only the Lyancorpses. If they held still, their undead bodies would also remain still and might be mistaken for strange-looking trees.

The man didn't seem to see them and began jogging toward the white fence that surrounded the graveyard. He leapt it and ran up the road.

"He's going to town," Tarvic said. "We follow him."

"No. I don't want to…do this again," she said.

He ignored her and floated along, following the young man. Tarvic's Lyancorpse shambled along beside him. Thankfully, the forest bordered the road that the young man had chosen, providing some cover.

"Tarvic, please?" Roven's ghost and her Lyancorpse followed him.

"Quiet. This is important."

After several moments, Moll and Lira emerged from between the trees, their Lyancorpses shambling to catch up. None of the Quad could move too far away from the others without feeling it. They were bound together in this unholy death just as they'd been bound as a Quad in life.

"Oooh, are we going into town?" Moll asked.

"No," Tarvic said tersely.

"I am oh-kay. I am aaaaaaallll-right," Lira sang.

They all followed the young man, stopping when their quarry

reached a stone house by a river. The young man ran up to the door, raised his hand, but then stopped without knocking.

"He's so handsome," Moll purred.

"We should go," Roven said.

"Stay where you are," Tarvic snapped.

The young man jumped off the porch and fled behind a giant maple tree just as the door opened. An older man, who bore a strong resemblance to the young man, peered outside, then slammed the door and bolted it.

"It's his father," Roven said. "The man from the grave doesn't want any other monsters to come here, to hurt his family. That's why he didn't go inside. Please Tarvic, let's leave him alone. He seems…like a good man. We could just leave him alone."

"He's going to help us," Tarvic said.

The young Quadron silently left his hiding place and started back down the road, away from the village of Kyn. He stopped at the top of the hill and looked back over the valley wistfully, then continued on.

Tarvic's Quad followed. For the rest of the night and the entire next day, the young Quadron didn't rest, and they pursued him at a distance. Tarvic watched, waited for some sign that the young man did indeed have magic, but he exhibited nothing. Tarvic couldn't even tell which path the young man followed. Mentis? Motus? Impetu? Anima?

When Tarvic had been a Quadron himself, he couldn't go a day without using physical magic to run through the Hallowed Woods faster than a wolf, to jump to the top of a tree, higher than a dew cat. Using the magic had come as naturally as breathing.

"Are you sure he's a Quadron?" Tarvic asked Roven.

"I…think so," Roven said. "The voices were very loud and very strange at the grave. Except…"

"Except what?"

"It's… I can't hear anything now," Roven said.

He clenched his ghostly fist in frustration.

The young Quadron made a makeshift camp for the night. He

seemed intent on getting far away from Kyn. He hadn't stopped jogging or stopped to eat for a day. Now, obviously exhausted, the man put together a few sticks, started a small fire and curled up beside it to sleep.

Tarvic couldn't wait any longer. This man was hiding his magic, and Tarvic's Quad needed that magic. They needed to know how this man had returned himself to life.

He started into the little clearing, but Roven grabbed his ghostly hand.

"Tarvic, please," she pleaded, her frightened eyes wide.

"He is going to make us whole," he said. He was done indulging his Quad mates' insanity. The only thing that mattered was returning to the life they'd once had. He twisted his hand out of Roven's and continued into the clearing.

"I am oh-kay. I am aaaaaaallll-right," Lira sang from right beside Tarvic. He hadn't noticed her or her Lyancorpse approach, and her words pierced the silence of the glade.

The young man jolted upright.

Tarvic rushed toward the man before he could flee, and Tarvic's Lyancorpse lumbered after.

"Gods!" the young man exclaimed, scattering embers as he scrambled to his feet.

"Wait," Tarvic shouted, holding up his ghostly hands. His Lyancorpse mimicked the gesture and moaned.

"I am oh-kay. I am aaaaaaallll-right," Lira sang, and her Lyancorpse shambled forward awkwardly on its three legs, her head smiling atop the twisted nightmare.

Unbelievably, the young man hesitated. He breathed hard, his body tense, his gaze flicking from Lira's Lyancorpse to Tarvic's. But he didn't flee. He was not nearly as skittish as the other villagers Tarvic remembered meeting. Instead, he studied Tarvic and Lira with intense, dark eyes.

Then he looked past them and saw Roven and Moll in the trees.

"You're Lyancorpses," he said.

"I am oh-kay. I am aaaaaaallll-right," Lira sang.

The man let out a breath—it sounded like an exhausted laugh—and he stood up straighter. He still seemed wary but confident.

"How many of you are there?" he asked Lira.

"Four," Tarvic said reflexively. His Lyancorpse gave a low moan, and Tarvic gnashed his teeth, knowing that the man couldn't hear him.

Surprisingly, the man turned at Tarvic's words, peered in the direction of Tarvic's ghost.

"I am oh-kay. I am aaaaaaallll-right," Lira sang.

"Quiet, Lira," Tarvic snapped.

"Lira…" the man echoed, and he looked like he was straining to hear something distant.

"By Fendra, can you hear me?" Tarvic asked, floating closer. His Lyancorpse mirrored the movement, shambling up to the man.

The man tensed, ready to flee, but stayed where he was.

"I can hear you," the man said, squinting in concentration. Suddenly, his eyes went wide, and he jerked back.

Now he was looking directly at Tarvic's ghost, into Tarvic's eyes.

"Gods…" the man whispered. "You're ghosts."

His gaze flicked to Lira, then to Moll and Roven, focusing on their ghosts, not their Lyancorpses.

"You can see us?" Tarvic asked. This man had to be a Quadron. He could see and hear them when none other could. Tarvic had been right. This man would bring them back to life. This was destiny.

"You don't act much like Lyancorpses," the man said. "'See a person. Kill a person.' At least, that's what the stories say."

"No, we're… We need your help," Tarvic said.

"Of course you do." The man laughed and bowed his head. "I've never needed help more than I do at this moment. So of course you need mine." But he seemed to relax. "Gods…"

"Why aren't you afraid of us?" Tarvic asked.

The man gave a rueful laugh. "Well… You didn't try to kill me right away. That's always a good sign. And frankly, you're not the most bizarre thing I've ever seen." He paused. "Though you're a close second." He hesitated again, then indicated his small fire. "Please, sit. Or…whatever would be most comfortable for you."

The offer of hospitality momentarily rendered Tarvic speechless.

Moll broke the silence as her ghostly form sauntered forward, followed closely by her rotting body encased in roots.

"Thank you, kind sir. I shall sit right here next to you," she purred, settling her ghostly self beside the man and putting an arm around him. Her Lyancorpse came close, looming behind them.

"Moll!" Tarvic said. "Don't—"

"It's okay," the man said, holding up a hand. "Please sit. My name is Brom."

Glowering at Moll, Tarvic settled himself onto the ground across from the man who called himself Brom.

"I am oh-kay. I am aaaaaaallll-right," Lira sang, her ghostly head sinking to hover just to the left of the man. After a moment, Roven positioned herself to his right. Her timid gaze flicked back and forth between Brom and Tarvic.

"Lyancorpses…and ghosts…" Brom murmured. "And there are four of you." His eyes went wide. "Wait, you're a Quad!" he exclaimed, looking at each of them quickly as if their very appearances confirmed his guess.

How had this Brom pieced it together so quickly? Was he a Mentis? Stunned by the man's insight, Tarvic glanced at each of his companions to see if they found it equally unnerving.

Moll was gazing adoringly at Brom, stroking his brow with a ghostly finger. She didn't look at Tarvic. Roven watched Tarvic worriedly.

"I am oh-kay. I am aaaaaaallll-right," Lira sang.

"How did you know we're a Quad?" Tarvic asked Brom.

"You…move like a Quad. I mean, your ghost forms do. You move together; you respond to each other."

"You're right. These are my Quad mates. And I am Tarvic." He introduced Lira, Moll and Roven, all in turn. "We were killed by

The Four."

Brome snapped his fingers like he suddenly knew their story. "You gained your power outside the academy, didn't you? You put your Quad together on your own."

"Yes. How did you—"

"Because The Four couldn't have that," Brom said darkly, and he seemed just as angry as Tarvic felt.

"How did you know?" Tarvic asked.

"You aren't the only ones The Four have killed for learning magic without their…supervision."

"They found us," Tarvic said through clenched teeth. "They told us we weren't allowed to wield the power without their leave."

"And then they killed you," Brom whispered. He glanced at the dwindling fire. "Yeah. They killed me, too. Gods…"

"But you came back," Tarvic said. "You came back as yourself." He waved his ghostly hand at Brom's living, breathing body. "How did you do it?" Tarvic's rage flared at the injustice of his Quad's fate.

But this man had somehow escaped that same fate. And he was going to tell Tarvic how he'd done it.

"Ah. That's why you're here," Brom said. "You saw me come out of the grave."

"We need to know how you did it," Tarvic said. "How you conquered death."

Brom glanced at Moll's ministrations; her ghostly form continued to stroke his forehead. He glanced at the Lyancorpses all around him and licked his lips nervously. "You came here to get information from me," he said.

"Tell us," Tarvic said.

"I don't know what happened," Brom said.

"You know."

"I really don't."

"No," Tarvic growled. "You just don't want to tell us." In response to Tarvic's anger, his Lyancorpse shambled closer to Brom.

Brom tried to stand up, but Moll's Lyancorpse wrapped her roots around his shoulders, sat him back down. He tried to break free, but Moll was strong.

"Tarvic," Rowen said nervously. "No. Not again."

"I am oh-kay. I am aaaaaaallll-right," Lira sang frantically.

"Please, Tarvic," Rowen said. "Let's just go."

"I'm not going anywhere," Tarvic snarled. "This man can help us. And he will."

"Please!" Rowen begged.

"I really don't know how it happened," Brom said, and he seemed more stern than afraid. "I remember dying. Then I remember waking up in that coffin with that monster digging down to get me."

"Lies! You know, and you're going to tell us," Tarvic said. "Look at me. I was meant to be a hero. I was meant to save people. And look at me!"

"I want to help you," Brom said. "But I don't have what you need."

"No," Tarvic said. "You have the answer. And you're going to give it to us or we're going to take it from you."

"How?" Brom asked calmly. Moll's roots held him tight, but he wasn't struggling anymore.

"What do you mean?" Tarvic asked.

"How are you going to take it from me?"

"If you won't give it willingly, we're going to take it."

"By killing me?" Brom asked, his intense gaze holding Tarvic's. He didn't seem afraid.

"Please Tarvic," Roven pleaded. "Don't kill him."

"I'm not going to kill anyone," Tarvic said. "I don't do that… I'm not…like that."

"I am oh-kay. I am aaaaaaallll-right," Lira sang like a hasty prayer.

"Don't you see?" Tarvic shouted at them. "We can't just let him walk away when he has the answer."

"I don't have it," Brom said. "But maybe you do."

"What?" Tarvic spun to glare at the man.

"Look at Lira. She's only a head, and yet she seems more flush with life than any of you. Why?"

"Because she's insane!" Tarvic roared.

Brom glanced at Roven. "And her. Her Lyancorpse is more alive than yours. Did you ask yourself why? She's the only one trying to stop you from murder. Do you think that is a coincidence?"

"I don't murder people," Tarvic said, but his rage roared through him such that he could barely hear Brom's words.

"Twenty three people," Roven said in a high voice. "Twenty three, Tarvic." A crack started up the left side of her jaw. "Three at the last village alone."

"Tell us how to return to life!" Tarvic shouted at Brom. His Lyancorpse loomed over the man. Brom struggled, but Moll held him firmly in place. Tarvic raised his fist—a gnarled heavy ball of roots—and brought it down hard, intending to crush Brom's lying face—

The strike smashed into the raised arms of Roven's Lyancorpse. She'd thrown up her forearms in an X to stop the attack and interposed herself between Tarvic and Brom.

"What are you doing?" Tarvic said.

"Not again," Roven squeaked, and her cracked ghostly face was crying. Tears also leaked from her Lyancorpse's eyes. "This isn't you. Don't do this."

"I'm not going to kill him. Can't you see? I'm…." Tarvic hesitated. "I'm just… He needs to tell us. Don't you see?"

"He can't help us," Roven said. "I think…maybe we can't come back. Maybe this is all we have now."

"You don't know!" Tarvic tried to break free of her, but her roots had intertwined with his, holding him. "We are going to come back. He's going to show us how!"

"And what if this is the only life we have?" Roven asked. "Is this who you want to be? Do you want to be a murderer? The Tarvic I knew wanted to save people, not kill them."

"I *am* going to save people. Just as soon as I… Just as soon as we're alive again." He turned his ghostly form to Moll. "Moll, make the man tell us."

"Oh, he'll tell me," she purred. "He'll sing sweet music for me. He wants to." Her Lyancorpse roots slithered around Brom's neck.

"I am oh-kay. I am aaaaaaallll-right," Lira sang, crashing into Moll. Lira's roots interlaced with Moll's, twining around them everywhere they gripped Brom.

Brom shouted as Moll and Lira fought for control of his body.

"Stop it, Lira," Tarvic shouted. "Let her get the information we need."

Moll's ghostly face contorted in concentration as Lira forced her struggling roots apart. Finally, Moll's grip loosened enough, and Brom slipped out. He jumped away from them, huffing, watching them, eyes wide.

Tarvic lunged at him, but Roven shouted and held him tight. They went down in a tumble of roots, gripping and pulling.

"Go, Quadron," Roven said. "Run."

Brom hesitated, as though he would say more, as though he wanted to help them somehow. But he set his mouth in a line, turned and sprinted into the night.

"No," Moll wailed. "My love, come back."

"He's getting away!" Tarvic's Lyancorpse struggled, but Roven held him tight. Tarvic's ghost flew after Brom but pulled up short like he was on a leash. A ghost couldn't go very far from its Lyancorpse, and Roven made sure Tarvic's Lyancorpse stayed put.

"Roven *please*!" Tarvic said frantically. "He's our only hope."

"Shhhh," Roven said. "It's okay. Shhhh."

"My love!" Moll shouted after Brom.

"I am oh-kay. I am aaaaaaallll-right," Lira sang.

Tarvic thrashed and Moll wailed, but their Quad mates held them down.

The rage coursed through him until it ran its course, and then it was like he was waking from a dream. He couldn't quite remember how he'd come to this place or what had happened. How long had they been in this clearing? An hour? A day?

He remembered going to the village of Kyn. They had stopped at a graveyard and then….

Roven's Lyancorpse disentangled from his, freeing him. Why had she been holding him down?

"The villagers…" Tarvic said. "They chased us away again?"

Roven's frightened gaze turned down to her ghostly shoes, and she said nothing.

"I am oh-kay. I am aaaaaaallll-right," Lira's head sang, smiling, and her Lyancorpse released Moll's.

"Ooooh," Moll cooed, her ghostly form sidling up to Tarvic. "Are we close to a town? That could be fun. We deserve a little fun."

He ignored her. Moll insisted on flirting with the living, imagining that she hadn't changed in death. But her Lyancorpse terrified them. Inevitably, it led to them being run out of town. That's probably what had happened this time, too. Didn't she realize they were never going to find a way to become alive again if she kept doing that? Didn't any of them?

They had to find a way to go back to what they'd once been. Tarvic had wanted to be a hero, to save people. That was his destiny, and he planned to have it again.

But his Quad mates were all insane. They didn't understand. They didn't know what was really happening here, not like he did. The only one he could really talk to was Roven.

"Someone is coming," Roven said in her timid voice.

The little campsite had a smoldering fire and stood a small distance away from a road. Tarvic looked toward the road, and he could hear the patter of approaching feet. Someone was jogging quickly but trying to stay quiet.

Tarvic floated closer. His lumbering Lyancorpse followed. The newcomer came into view. He had green skin and a maniacal face that wasn't quite human. His wider-than-normal mouth hung open as he breathed.

A memory flickered in Tarvic's mind. He'd seen this creature before. *He's not human*, Roven had said.

"Do we know that creature?" he asked her.

"Let's go," Roven said. New cracks had appeared on her ghostly face. "We should just go."

"Roven, tell me." The rage inside him began to rise, flames and heat burning through him.

Tears stood in Roven's frightened eyes. "Let's just go," she whispered.

"What aren't you telling me? Why… Why can't I remember?"

"Because we are broken!" Roven screamed. "We are all horribly broken, and you keep killing!"

Tarvic jumped back from her in surprise, his ghostly form floating away. His Lyancorpse stumbled and almost fell over. He'd never heard Roven scream before.

"You're killing people, Tarvic," she said. "You're making up stories in your head, convincing yourself that some villager or another can bring you back to life. You and Moll pursue them. And when you catch them, no matter what they say, you… You kill them."

"No…" Tarvic whispered. "No, I'm not that… I was supposed to… I just want us to…"

"Let's just go," she pleaded.

More memories flickered in Tarvic's mind.

Roven is right, he thought.

A man had risen from a grave, and a green inhuman had attacked the man. A man whose name was…

Brom. The man in the grave was called Brom.

Tarvic glanced back at the smoldering fire, and now he remembered everything. Everything he had done. Everything he'd wanted to do. He remembered his rage, remembered the struggle.

"Gods, I tried to kill him. You stopped me."

Roven blinked, surprised. "You remember?"

"How long? How long have I been doing this?" Tarvic asked, aghast.

"It's been a year, Tarvic," Roven said. "But you've… You've

never remembered before. You always forget what you've done. And then…you do it all over again."

I always forget, he thought.

"Let's just go," Roven said.

"No," Tarvic said. He didn't become who he was by running away. He had to face this.

"Please," Roven pleaded.

Why do I forget? he thought.

"Oooooh," Moll purred, seeing the green creature padding toward them down the road. "He's handsome."

Because I don't want to be this, he thought. *That's why I forget. I'm like Moll and I don't want to be dead. I want to be what I once was. Just like Moll. And Moll is insane. And that means…I'm insane, too.*

His head hurt as he tried to hold onto his revelation. His Lyancorpse shuffled to the side as though it had lost its balance.

"I'm pretending…" he said aloud. "Just like Moll. We can't… We can't come back to life, can we?" He looked at Roven. "Not ever."

"I don't know, Tarvic," Roven said. "I don't think so."

The pain of that seared through him, and the rage flared again. He pushed it down, holding tight to his new realization.

"I can't be alive again," he said aloud, and saying it made the memories more solid. They transformed from wisps of uncertainty into reality.

"No," Roven said.

"I can't be alive again," he said once more, as though carving it in stone in his mind.

"Let's just go," Roven said.

"But maybe I can still do the right thing," Tarvic said. "Even if I'm dead."

"What?"

Tarvic floated forward, out of the concealment of the trees, and his Lyancorpse followed. The green-skinned man had almost reached them, and when Tarvic's Lyancorpse appeared, the creature pulled up short. His too-wide mouth snapped shut on pointed teeth, and his elongated eyes narrowed.

"What is this?" The creature bared its teeth and crouched as Tarvic's Lyancorpse blocked the road.

"You're chasing a man," Tarvic said. "A man named Brom. With the intention of killing him. Leave him alone or answer to me."

Tarvic's Lyancorpse moaned unintelligibly.

The green creature growled and tried to dart around Tarvic's Lyancorpse, but Lyancorpses were much faster than they seemed. Roots shot out and tripped the creature, and it tumbled to the dirt at Moll's feet.

Moll's Lyancorpse loomed over the creature. "He's positively gorgeous," she crooned. "I just want to eat him up."

The rage flared within Tarvic. This creature was bent on hurting Brom, and Brom had been kind to the Quad. He hadn't brought them back to life, true, but neither had Brom done anything wrong. He'd treated Tarvic and his Quad like people when others only saw monsters. Brom was a decent man. Roven had even said so when Brom had left his father at that stone house to keep him safe. Safe from creatures just like this.

That's what a hero would do.

"I can't be a decent man anymore," Tarvic said, more to himself than anyone else. "But maybe I can protect those who are." He glanced up at Roven. She looked thunderstruck, but she slowly nodded.

The green-skinned creature roared and leapt at Moll's Lyancorpse, tearing with his claws, trying to get past her. She wrapped him up in thick roots, hugging him.

"Ooooh, I just love him," Moll said.

"Don't kill him, Moll," Tarvic said.

"Oh, I wouldn't do that," she said, even as her roots slithered around his neck and began to constrict. The creature choked, struggling desperately.

"Moll!" Tarvic put all of his rage into his tone, and Moll's ghost jumped. Her Lyancorpse shuddered and stopped squeezing. "Don't kill him."

"Not even…a little bit?"

"Not even a little, but…" Tarvic thought a moment. "But hold him."

"I can keep him?"

"Yes, but don't kill him."

"Oooooh," Moll crooned. "Okay."

She released the creature, who coughed and fell to his knees. As he wheezed, recovering his breath, Moll's Lyancorpse arm split apart, sending tendrils of roots all around the man, forming a cage.

The green-skinned man's thin gaze darted from Tarvic to each of his Quad mates in turn as he realized he was trapped.

"No!" he growled. "Let me go. You must let me go!"

The golden hope Tarvic had briefly felt at the graveyard swelled within him again, but this time there was no desperation to it. It wasn't linked to Brom or what he might do for Tarvic. It was linked to what Tarvic might do for Brom. It felt…good. It felt pure.

"Tarvic," Roven said. "You're not going to kill him?"

"We are going to remember what we are," Tarvic said. "Even if we can't be what we were."

"Tarvic, your chest!" Roven exclaimed.

Tarvic looked at his ghostly self and saw nothing, then he saw Roven was pointing at his Lyancorpse.

He shifted his gaze…

…and stared in astonishment as a patch of skin on his chest went from gray to pink. The transformation wasn't large, barely the size of three fists, but the skin had become as healthy as when Tarvic was alive. A wound that had laid open the flesh near his sternum pulled together and healed.

"Ooooh," Moll said, staring transfixed at her new pet. "Pretty." She had brought the cage holding the green-skinned creature to her body. The cage rose up her side, borne by her slithering roots, until it settled atop her shoulder. Her left Lyancorpse arm was now missing, its roots comprising the cage, and her human arm wrapped around the outside of the cage, bound to it by the roots, like she was holding it up.

"Let me go!" the creature raged, shaking the bars. He clawed at them, bit them, but Moll shook herself violently like a wet dog. The creature tumbled about in the cage, then crouched, stunned and breathing hard.

Roven stared at the miraculous regeneration of Tarvic's skin. "You chose not to kill him," she said. "That's when your flesh healed. You did what you would have done if you were alive. You did what your living self would have done."

"Maybe Lira has been right all this time," Tarvic said. "Maybe she's been the only sane one. Maybe we just have to…be okay with who we are now. And do what we can do."

Roven smiled, and it was like the sun emerging from behind the clouds. It had been so long since he'd seen her smile, and her ghostly face seemed less cracked than it had before. "Oh Tarvic, could we?"

"If you help me remember. If you help me keep my anger from taking control."

She nodded. "I will. I promise."

He took her ghostly hands in his. Moll's ghost floated over and put her arms around both of their shoulders. Lira's ghostly head bobbed closer, hovering between Roven's and Tarvic's heads.

"We'll all help each other," Tarvic said. "From this moment forward, we're not monsters. We're heroes. And we act like it."

"Oooooh, I like it," Moll said.

"Yes, please," Roven said.

"We are oh-kay. We are aaaaaaallll-right," Lira sang, smiling.

Mailing List/Social Media

MAILING LIST

Don't miss out on the latest news and information about all of my books. Join my Readers Group

AMAZON AUTHOR PAGE

AUTHOR LETTER

The *Tower of the Four* began as something completely different than this episodic series you're holding now. It started off in Vale's hometown of Torlioch where Brom, a twenty something failure of the Champions Academy, languishes, drowning himself in ale because he's lost his magic. Royal and Oriana—former classmates and sworn enemies on the opposite ends of a decades-long war—find Brom there. They tell him that Vale, their fourth Quad mate and Brom's old girlfriend, has essentially transformed into Maleficent, killing innocents from a forest stronghold. They must convince him to help them reclaim her soul…or kill her. For the good of the two kingdoms, of course.

As I started writing this story, I kept thinking about how these four characters originally came together, and what had gone wrong to split them apart so long ago. As the story opened up, they downright hated one another. They had such diverse backgrounds and value systems, how could they possibly have bonded to come together as a Quad and learn magic in the first place?

I resolved to put in two chapters of Champions Academy flashback during their journey to Vale's stronghold.

When I reached that spot, two chapters became four. Four became eight, then twelve. Suddenly, I did a quick word count on my manuscript and realized that two-thirds of the story I'd written was this Champions Academy flashback.

Too much. Far too much, I told myself. *This is going to unbalance the story, throw the reader into the past for far too long.*

I looked for ways to cut it.

Just then, my intuition piped up. And let me tell you that this little voice has seen me through many an ambiguous stage in many a novel, and here it was again, trying to get my attention. It said, "Dude (my intuition says "dude" a lot), your story begins at the academy. I've been trying to tell you that for twelve chapters now. When you gonna listen?"

I sat back, stunned. Instead of searching for parts to cut, I flipped my perspective around. Did I have enough meat in the flashback to tell an entire story?

"Dude, I've been trying to tell you for twelve—"

"Okay, okay!"

So I dove into the backstory, following my intuition. Twelve chapters mushroomed to thirty-seven. How did Brom come to the academy? How did the Quad meet for the first time? What were their struggles? How did they overcome them? And on and on.

Tower of the Four Parts 1-3—collectively called *The Champions Academy*—was born.

In Episodes 4-6 we will explore what happens to Quad Brilliant a year after the academy, starting with Vale's journey directly after the academy.

Tower of the Four is close to my heart, and I hope you enjoyed it. Stay tuned, because the adventures of Brom, Royal, Oriana and Vale have only begun.

Also, if you want to keep up to date on everything *Tower of the Four*-ish, be sure to sign up for my Readers Group at toddfahnestock.com.

Thank you so much for reading,

-Todd

ALSO BY TODD FAHNESTOCK

Tower of the Four

Episode 1 – The Quad
Episode 2 – The Tower
Episode 3 – The Test
Episode 4 – The Nightmare
Episode 5 – The Resurrection
Episode 6 – The Reunion
The Champions Academy (Episodes 1-3 compilation)
The Dragon's War (Episodes 4-6 compilation)

Eldros Legacy (Legacy of Shadows)

Khyven the Unkillable
Lorelle of the Dark
Rhenn the Traveler
Slayter and the Dragon (Forthcoming)
Bane of Giants (Forthcoming)

Threadweavers

Wildmane
The GodSpill
Threads of Amarion
God of Dragons

The Whisper Prince

Fairmist
The Undying Man
The Slate Wizards

The Wishing World

The Wishing World
Loremaster
Spheres of Magic (Forthcoming)

Standalone Novels

Charlie Fiction
Summer of the Fetch

Memoirs

Ordinary Magic

Short Stories

Urchin: A Tower of the Four Short Story
Royal: A Tower of the Four Short Story
Princess: A Tower of the Four Short Story
Pawns of Magic: A Tower of the Four Short Story
Here There Be Giants: *Fate's Dagger*
Talons & Talismans 2: *The Darkest Door*
Parallel Worlds Anthology: *Threshold*
Fantastic Realms Anthology: *Ten for Every One*
Dragonlance: The Cataclysm – *Seekers*
Dragonlance: Heroes & Fools – *Songsayer*
Dragonlance: The History of Krynn – *The Letters of Trayn Minaas*

ABOUT THE AUTHOR

TODD FAHNESTOCK is a writer of fantasy for all ages and winner of the New York Public Library's Books for the Teen Age Award. *Threadweavers* and *The Whisper Prince Trilogy* are two of his bestselling epic fantasy series. He is a finalist in the Colorado Authors League Writing Awards for the past two years, for *Charlie Fiction* and *The Undying Man*. His passions are fantasy and his quirky, fun-loving family. When he's not writing, he teaches Taekwondo, swaps middle grade humor with his son, plays Ticket to Ride with his wife, scribes modern slang from his daughter and goes on morning runs with Galahad the Weimaraner. Visit Todd at www.toddfahnestock.com.

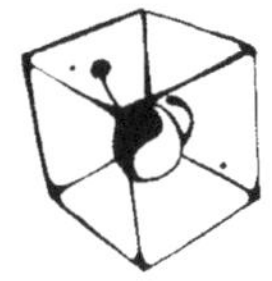